# THE ALASKA SANDERS AFFAIR

# THE ALASKA
# SANDERS AFFAIR

## JOËL DICKER

*Translated from the French by*
*Robert Bononno*

MACLEHOSE PRESS
QUERCUS · LONDON

First published in the French language as *L'Affaire Alaska Sanders*
by Éditions Rosie et Wolfe, Geneva, in 2022
First published in Great Britain in 2024 by

MacLehose Press
An imprint of Quercus Editions Ltd
Carmelite House
50 Victoria Embankment
London EC4Y 0DZ .
An Hachette UK company

A CIP catalogue record for this book is available from the British Library.

ISBN (HB) 978 1 52943 381 4
ISBN (TPB) 978 1 52943 382 1
ISBN (Ebook) 978 1 52943 383 8

10 9 8 7 6 5 4 3 2 1

Typeset by CC Book Production
Printed and bound in Great Britain by Clays Ltd, Elcograf S.p.A.

Papers used by Quercus are from well-managed forests and other responsible sources.

*For Marie-Claire Ardouin,*
*without whom nothing would have been possible*

# Contents

# The Day Before the Murder

*Friday, April 2, 1999*

The last person to see her alive was Lewis Jacob, the owner of a gas station on Route 21. It was seven thirty in the evening, when Jacob was getting ready to leave the small convenience store near the gas pumps. He was planning to take his wife out to dinner to celebrate their anniversary.

"You sure you don't mind closing up?" he asked the young woman behind the cash register.

"No problem, Mr. Jacob."

"Thanks, Alaska."

Jacob watched her for a moment as he was getting ready to leave. She was beautiful and kind and had been a ray of sunshine in his life. In the six months she had been working there, she had changed him.

"And you?" he asked. "You have plans for tonight?"

"I have a date," she said, smiling broadly.

"From the looks of things, it's more than just a *date*."

"A romantic dinner," she confided.

"Walter's a lucky guy," Jacob said. "So things are better between you two, then?"

Alaska shrugged. Jacob adjusted his tie while checking his reflection in the window.

"How do I look?" he asked.

"Perfect. Go on now, don't be late."

"Have a good weekend, Alaska. See you Monday."

"You too, Mr. Jacob, have a good weekend."

She smiled again. He would never forget that smile.

The following morning, at seven, Lewis Jacob returned to the gas station to open up. When he arrived, he locked the door to the store behind him so he could get ready to receive the first customers. Suddenly, he heard frantic knocking on the glass. He turned and saw a jogger, her face twisted with terror. She was screaming. He ran to open the door. The young woman threw herself at him, shouting, "Call the police! Call the police!"

That morning, the future of a small New Hampshire town was about to change.

# Prologue

## *Concerning the Events of 2010*

The years 2006 to 2010, in spite of the triumph and the glory, are burned into my memory as trying times. They were, unquestionably, a period of great upheaval.

So, before I embark on the story of Alaska Sanders, found dead on April 3, 1999, in Mount Pleasant, New Hampshire, and explain how, in the summer of 2010, I became involved in an eleven-year-old criminal investigation, I must briefly return to my personal life at the time, especially my burgeoning career as a writer.

This had taken off with a bang in 2006, when my first novel sold millions of copies. Barely twenty-six at the time, I became part of the very small club of rich and famous authors and was propelled to the summit of American letters.

But I was soon to discover that glory was not without its consequences. Those who have been following me since my early career know how the immense success of my first novel would destabilize me, leading to a breakdown and writer's block—the crisis of the blank page. Failure.

Then there was the Harry Quebert affair, which you have certainly heard about. On June 12, 2008, the body of Nola Kellergan, who had disappeared in 1975 at the age of fifteen, was exhumed from the garden of Harry Quebert, a titan of American letters. The case affected me deeply. Harry was my former college professor, but, most important, my closest friend at the time. I found it hard to accept his guilt. Alone against the world, I crisscrossed New Hampshire to conduct my own investigation. And although I was finally able to prove Harry innocent, the secrets I uncovered destroyed our friendship.

Based on that investigation, I wrote my second book: *The Truth About the Harry Quebert Affair,* which was published in the autumn of 2009 and whose runaway popularity firmly established me as a writer of national importance. It was the final confirmation my readers and critics had been waiting for, ever since my first novel, of my anointed status as a writer. No longer was I considered a one-hit wonder, a shooting star swallowed up by the night, a trail of burnt gunpowder. I was a writer recognized by the public and accepted by his fellow authors. This came as a tremendous relief. As if I had found myself after three years of wandering in the desert of fading success.

This explains why, during those final weeks of 2009, I was overcome by a feeling of serenity. That December 31, I celebrated the arrival of the new year in Times Square, surrounded by a joyous crowd. The last time I had done that was in 2006, after the appearance of my first book. That night, lost in the anonymous crowd, I felt at ease. My gaze met that of an unknown woman, to whom I was immediately drawn. She was drinking champagne. She offered me the bottle, smiling.

When I reflect on the events of the months that followed, I remember that scene and how it gave me the illusion of having finally found peace.

The events of 2010 would prove me wrong.

# The Day of the Murder

*April 3, 1999*

It was seven in the morning. She was running alone down Route 21, past verdant fields. Music played in her ears. Her pace was steady, fast, her breathing under control; in two weeks she would be at the starting line of the Boston marathon. She was ready.

It was a perfect day for a run. The rising sun shone over the fields of wildflowers, beyond which rose the expanse of the White Mountain National Forest.

She soon reached Lewis Jacob's gas station, exactly four miles from her home. She hadn't planned to go farther than this but decided to push herself a bit. Passing the station and continuing to the intersection at Grey Beach, she turned onto a dirt road. It led to a parking lot, and from there a footpath wound its way through the forest to the long, stony beach that ran along the shore of Lake Skotam. As she crossed the parking lot, she saw, without paying too much attention, a blue convertible with Massachusetts plates. She turned down the path and headed for the beach.

When she reached the edge of the tree line, she noticed, there near the shore, a silhouette that caused her to stop. It took her a few moments before she understood what was going on, and then she became petrified with fear. Luckily, he hadn't seen her. *Don't make a sound, don't show yourself. If he sees you, he'll be after you as well.* She hid behind a tree.

Adrenaline gave her the strength to quietly head back up the path, and when she felt she was out of danger, she ran as fast as she could—like she had never run before. She had left her phone at home, intentionally, and she was angry with herself now that she needed it.

She made it back to Route 21, hoping a car would pass. She felt alone in the world. Breaking into a sprint, she headed back to the gas station. Surely, she'd find help there. When she arrived, breathing hard, the door was closed. Seeing someone inside, she banged on the glass until it opened. She threw herself at him, yelling, "Call the police! Call the police!"

# Excerpt from the Police Report
## Interview with Peter Philipps

*[Peter Philipps had been with the Mount Pleasant police for fifteen years. He was the first officer to reach the scene. His report was recorded on April 3, 1999, in Mount Pleasant.]*

When I got the call from the operator about Grey Beach, I thought I had misunderstood. I asked her to repeat herself. At the time, I was near Stove Farm, which isn't far from Grey Beach.

*Did you go there directly?*
No, I stopped at the gas station on Route 21 first, where the witness had called for help. Considering the situation, I thought it was important to talk to her before doing anything else. I wanted to know what to expect at the beach. The witness in question was a terrified young woman. She described what she had seen. In fifteen years of police work, I'd never been faced with anything like this.

*And then?*
I went directly to the scene.

*Alone?*
I had no other choice. There wasn't a moment to lose. I had to find him before he escaped.

*What happened next?*

I drove like a madman from the gas station to the parking lot at Grey Beach. When I got there, I noticed a blue convertible with Massachusetts plates. I grabbed my pump-action and headed down the path to the lake.

*And . . . ?*

When I reached the beach, he was still there, going at that poor girl. I screamed at him, hoping he would stop. He just lifted his head and stared at me. Then he began to move slowly in my direction. I understood that it was going to be him or me. Fifteen years of service and I had never fired a shot. Until that morning.

# Part One

## *The Consequences of Success*

# 1

## After the Harry Quebert Affair

*Montreal, Quebec*
*April 5, 2010*

A springtime snowfall was settling on the cavernous warehouses along the St. Lawrence, where the film studios were located. For several months now, they had been shooting a film adaptation of my first novel, *G, Like Goldstein.*

Thanks to a quirk in scheduling, the start of filming happened to coincide with the publication of *The Truth About the Harry Quebert Affair.* Carried along by my triumph in the bookstores, the film had already garnered considerable attention, and the initial footage had caused a bit of a stir in Hollywood.

While the snow whirled in the cold wind outside, it felt like summer inside the studio. On the set of a busy street, almost shockingly realistic, the actors and extras, lit by powerful spots, looked as if they were caught in bright sunlight. It was one of my favorite scenes from the book. On the terrace of a coffee shop, looking out over a crowd of passersby, the two protagonists, Mark and Alicia, had found one another again after being separated for years. There was no need for words—a single glance was enough to make up for the time they had spent apart.

Seated behind the control screens, I followed the shot.

"Cut!" the director cried, breaking that quiet moment. "It's good." Next to him, the first assistant repeated his command on the radio: "It's good. Let's wrap it up."

The set erupted into a hive of activity. Technicians gathered their equipment, while the lead actors returned to their dressing rooms under the disappointed gaze of the extras, who would have enjoyed a brief exchange, a picture, or an autograph.

I wandered around the set. The street, the sidewalks, the lampposts, the store windows, it all looked real. I entered the coffee shop, filled with admiration for the attention to detail. I had the feeling I was walking around in my novel. I slid in behind the counter, laden with sandwiches and pastries—everything that might appear on screen had to look real.

My reverie was short-lived. A voice tore me from my thoughts.

"Are you serving, Goldman?" It was Roy Barnaski, the unpredictable CEO of Schmid & Hanson, my publisher. He had flown in from New York that very morning, without warning.

"Coffee, Roy?" I offered, grabbing an empty cup.

"I'd rather have one of those sandwiches—I'm dying of hunger."

I didn't know whether the food was edible but, without hesitating, I offered Roy a turkey and cheese.

"You know, Goldman," he said after biting greedily into the sandwich, "this film is going to be big! We're preparing a special edition of *G, Like Goldstein*; it'll be sensational!"

Those of you who have read *The Truth About the Harry Quebert Affair* will be familiar with my ambivalent relationship with Roy Barnaski. For the rest of you, all you need to know is that his affection for his authors was proportional to the money he made from them. Two years earlier, he had criticized me publicly because I hadn't delivered on time, but the record sales of *Harry Quebert* now gave me pride of place in his stable of cash cows.

"You should be floating on air, Goldman," he continued, not appearing to realize that he was annoying me. "The success of the book and now this film. Remember, two years ago, how I worked my ass off to get Cassandra Pollock to play the role of Alicia and you did nothing but complain about it—repeatedly? But it was worth the effort, wasn't it? Everyone agrees she's sensational!"

"I'm not about to forget, Roy. You convinced everyone she and I were having an affair."

"And here's the result! I always have a sixth sense for these things, Goldman. That's why I'm the boss! But I didn't come all the way up here just to shoot the breeze. There's something important we have to discuss, very important."

As soon as I had caught sight of him arriving on set that morning, I knew he hadn't come to Montreal just to say hello.

"So what's it about?"

"You're going to be very pleased with the news, Goldman. I wanted to tell you myself, in person."

Barnaski was trying to be tactful. It wasn't a good sign.

"Get to the point, Roy."

"We're about to sign a contract with MGM for a screen adaptation of *The Truth About the Harry Quebert Affair*. It's going to be huge! They want to sign a preliminary agreement as soon as possible."

"I don't think I want to turn it into a film," I replied dryly.

"Wait till you see the contract, Goldman. All you have to do is sign and you get two million dollars up front. Just scribble your name at the bottom of the page and boom! Two million right into your bank account. Not to mention the income from royalties and all the rest."

I had no desire to argue. "Talk to my agent or my lawyer," I said, to cut short the conversation, which greatly annoyed Barnaski.

"If I wanted advice from your shitty agent, Goldman, I wouldn't have come all the way up here."

"It couldn't have waited until I got back to New York?"

"Back to New York? You're worse than the wind, Goldman, you never stay put."

"Harry wouldn't want a film," I said, frowning.

"Harry?" Barnaski gasped. "Harry Quebert?"

"Yes, Harry Quebert! The discussion is over. I don't want a film, because I don't want to go back to that time. I want to forget about it. Turn the page."

"Will you look at this crybaby!" Barnaski snarled, unable to put up with being contradicted. "You offer him a spoonful of caviar and Baby Goldman makes a fuss and refuses to open his mouth."

I had heard enough. Barnaski regretted his outburst and tried to make up for it. In his gentlest voice, he said, "Let me explain my project, my dear Marcus. You'll see, you'll change your mind."

"I'm going to start by getting some fresh air."

"Let's have dinner together this evening. I've made a reservation at a restaurant in Old Montreal. Shall we say, eight o'clock?"

"I have a date tonight, Roy. We'll talk about it in New York."

I left him there, with his ersatz sandwich in his hand, and walked off the set, heading for the main entrance to the studio. There was a food stand just before the large swinging doors. Every day, after shooting was over, I would stop there for a coffee. It was always the same waitress. She offered me a paper cup filled with coffee before I said a single word. I smiled in thanks. She smiled back. People often smile at me. But I no longer know if they're smiling at me, the human being standing before them, or the writer whose books they've read. And just then, the young woman picked up a copy of my book from the counter.

"I finished it last night. What a book, I couldn't put it down! Would you mind signing it for me?"

"With pleasure. What's your name?"

"Deborah."

Deborah, of course. She had told me ten times already. I took a pen from my pocket and wrote, on the title page, the ritual sentence that I used for all my dedications:

> *For Deborah, who now knows the entire truth about the Harry Quebert affair.*
> *Marcus Goldman*

"Have a good day, Deborah," I said, returning her copy.

"Good day, Marcus. See you tomorrow!"

"I'm going back to New York for ten days."

"See you soon, then."

As I was about to leave, she asked, "Did you ever see him again?"

"Who?"

"Harry Quebert."

"No, I never heard from him again."

I passed through the doors of the studio and climbed into the waiting car. *Did you ever see Harry Quebert again?* Since the release of the book, people had been asking me that. And every time, I forced myself to reply, pretending the question didn't upset me. As if I didn't think about it every day. Where was Harry? And what had become of him?

After driving along the St. Lawrence, the car headed for downtown Montreal. I could already see the skyscrapers outlined before me. I loved that city. I felt good there. Maybe because someone was waiting for me there. Maybe because there was finally a woman in my life.

In Montreal I stayed at the Ritz-Carlton, always in the same suite on the top floor. I had just entered the hotel when the receptionist stopped me to tell me I was expected at the bar. I smiled. She had arrived.

I found her sitting at a quiet table next to the fireplace, sipping a Moscow mule, still wearing her pilot's uniform. When she saw me, her face lit up. She kissed me and I threw my arms around her. The more I saw of her, the more I liked her.

Raegan was thirty years old, like me. She was a pilot for Air Canada. We had been seeing one another for three months. When I was with her, my life felt bigger, more fulfilled. The feeling was even more intense because it had been so hard to meet someone I really liked.

My last serious relationship had been five years ago—with a girl by the name of Emma Mathews—and it lasted no more than a few months. When I finished writing *The Truth About the Harry Quebert Affair*, I had promised myself I would focus on my love life. So I had several affairs, but without much success. Maybe I had put too much pressure on myself. My dates felt more like job interviews: observing the woman who spoke to me, for no more than a few minutes, I would wonder whether she would make a good partner and a good mother for my children. And the next moment, my mother, rising up in my mind, would intrude upon our evening. She would grab an empty chair, sit down next to the unfortunate woman, and start pointing out her many defects. My mother—or, rather, her specter—became the umpire of our date. Using a hackneyed expression she was especially fond of, she'd whisper to me, "Markie, do you think she's the one?" As if we were going to be together for life, when we didn't even know whether we were going to make it through the evening. And since my mother saw a great future before me, she would add, "Really, Markie, do you see yourself in the White House, receiving the Medal of Freedom with this girl on your arm?" This last sentence was pronounced in a tone of disdain, urging me to reject the unfortunate candidate. And so I would. And in this way, my poor mother, without her knowing, merely prolonged my celibacy. Until, through her, as it happened, I met Raegan.

\*     \*     \*

*Three months earlier, December 31, 2009*
As I had done every New Year's Eve, I had traveled to Montclair, New Jersey, to visit my parents. As we were having coffee in the living room, my mother uttered the following idiotic question, one she asked periodically and which annoyed me greatly: "What do you want for the new year, dear? You already have everything."

"To get in touch with a friend I've lost," I replied angrily.

"Are they dead?" my mother asked, who had never understood the allusion.

"I'm talking about Harry. I'd like to see him again. Find out what's become of him."

"Oh, to hell with Harry Quebert! He's been nothing but trouble for you. Real friends don't cause problems."

"He's the reason I became a writer. I owe him everything."

"You don't owe anyone anything, except your mother, and you owe her your life! Markie, you don't need friends, you need a girlfriend. Why don't you have a girlfriend? Don't you want to give me grandchildren?"

"It's hard to meet people, Mother."

She forced herself to adopt a more understanding tone. "Markie dear, I don't think you're making much of an effort. You don't go out enough. I know you sometimes spend hours looking at a photo album of you and this Harry Quebert."

"How do you know?" I asked, surprised.

"Your cleaning lady told me."

"Since when do you talk to my cleaning lady?"

"Since you stopped telling me anything about yourself."

At that moment, my gaze fell upon a framed photograph. It pictured my uncle Saul, my aunt Anita, and my cousins Hillel and Woody, in Florida.

"You know, if your uncle Saul . . ." she murmured.

"Don't talk about that, Mother. Please!"

"I only want you to be happy, Markie. You have no reason not to be."

I had to get out of there. I stood up and grabbed my jacket.

"What are you doing tonight, Markie?" she asked.

"Going out with some friends," I lied, to reassure her.

I kissed her and my father, and left.

My mother was right. I did keep an album that I pored over whenever I was feeling nostalgic. When I got back to New York, that's exactly what I did. I poured myself a glass of Scotch and leafed through it. The last time I had seen Harry was exactly one year earlier, a December evening in 2008, when he had shown up at my place for a last get-together. Since then, there had been no sign of him. By trying to prove he was innocent of the murder he had been accused of and clear his name, I had lost him. I missed him terribly.

Obviously, I had tried to find him, but my efforts proved futile. I returned regularly to Somerset, New Hampshire, where he had lived for the previous thirty years. I had walked up and down the streets of that small town for hours on end. In all weather, at all times of day. To find him. Maybe to fix things. But Harry never showed up.

As I was absorbed in my album, recalling the memories of what we had been, the phone began to ring. For a second, I thought it was him. I ran to pick it up. It was my mother.

"Why did you answer, Markie?" she reprimanded me.

"Because the phone rang, Mother."

"Markie, it's New Year's Eve! You told me you were with friends. Don't tell me you're alone at home looking at those damn photos again! I'm going to ask your cleaning lady to burn them."

"I'm going to fire her, Mother. Because of you, a hard-working woman is going to lose her job. Are you satisfied?"

"Get out of the house, Markie. I remember when you were still in high school, you went to Times Square for New Year's Eve. Call your friends and go out! That's an order. You can't disobey your mother."

That's how I ended up in Times Square, alone, because in reality there was no-one to call in New York. When I got there, the area was filled with thousands of people. I felt good. Relieved. I let myself be carried along by the human tide. It was then that I caught sight of a woman drinking from a bottle of champagne. She smiled at me. I liked her at once.

At the stroke of midnight, I kissed her. And that's how Raegan entered my life.

*       *       *

After we met, Raegan came to see me in New York several times, and we got together in Montreal whenever I went up there to visit the set. But after three months, we still barely knew one another. We would arrange our meetings around flights and days of shooting. But on that April evening, at the Ritz bar in Montreal, I felt something immeasurably more powerful. And as we spoke—I'm not sure about what—I realized she had easily passed my mother's test. I could imagine her by my side through all the various stages of my life.

Raegan was scheduled to pilot a flight to New York–JFK at seven the following morning. When I offered to take her out for dinner, she suggested that we stay at the hotel.

"The restaurant is pretty good," I admitted.

"Your room is even better." She smiled.

We stayed in my suite all evening. For what seemed like hours, we relaxed in the oversize bathtub, admiring, through the bay window and from the shelter of our hot, foamy bath, the snow that continued to fall on Montreal. We ordered room service. It all seemed so easy; there was a kind of chemistry between us. My only regret was not being able to spend more time with her—we lived so far apart. I was in New York and she lived in a small town an hour south of Montreal, which I had still not visited. But most of all, she was limited by her schedule as a pilot. Our encounter that evening was no exception, and once again, the night was short. At five in the morning, while the hotel still slept, Raegan and I finished getting ready. I watched her from the bathroom door as she stood in her pilot's trousers and a bra, putting on her makeup while drinking a cup of coffee. We both left for New York, but separately. She flew and I took the highway, having come to Montreal by car. I drove her to Trudeau Airport. As I pulled up in front of the terminal, she asked, "Why didn't you fly here, Marcus?"

I hesitated for a moment. I couldn't honestly tell her why I'd chosen not to. "I like the road between New York and Montreal."

She didn't entirely believe my lie. "You're not afraid of flying, are you?"

"Of course not."

She kissed me and said, "I'd love you all the same."

"When will I see you again?"

"When are you back in Montreal?"

"April twelfth."

She looked at her schedule. "I'll be in Chicago that night and then I have a week of rotation in Toronto."

She saw the disappointment on my face.

"And then I have a week off. I promise we'll have time to see each other then. We'll lock ourselves in your hotel room and won't budge."

"And what if we took off for a few days? Not New York. Not Montreal. Just you and me somewhere."

She nodded and smiled. "I'd like that a lot," she whispered, as if it were a secret that couldn't be acknowledged openly.

She kissed me for a long time, then got out of the car, leaving me, now hopeful, to contemplate what we might become together. As I watched her disappear into the airport terminal, I decided to take the initiative and organize a romantic getaway to a hotel in the Bahamas that had been highly recommended: Harbour Island Resort. I checked the hotel's website on my phone. Hidden away on a private island, it looked like paradise. We would spend the week on a beach of fine sand on the shore of a turquoise sea. I made the reservation at once, then set out for New York.

I drove east until I reached Magog, where I stopped for a cup of coffee, then headed for the small town of Stanstead, along the US border, which you may have heard of because it's home to the only library in the world that straddles two countries.

As I crossed the border, the US customs agent who examined my passport asked me, routinely, where I was coming from and where I was going. When I answered that I was traveling from Montreal to Manhattan, he said, "That's not the most direct route to New York." Assuming I had gotten lost, he told me how to get back to Interstate 87. I listened politely without the least intention of following his directions.

I knew exactly where I was going.

I was going to Somerset, New Hampshire, where Harry had spent half his life before disappearing without a trace.

# The Day of the Murder

*April 3, 1999*

An unmarked Chevy Impala, lights flashing and siren blaring, sped along Route 21, which connects the small town of Mount Pleasant to the rest of New Hampshire. A black streak, it tore through a landscape of alpine wildflowers and crystalline lakes, beyond which stretched the immense White Mountain National Forest.

Sergeant Perry Gahalowood was behind the wheel. Next to him sat his partner Matt Vance, his eyes glued to a map of the area.

"It's just ahead on your right," Vance pointed out, as they passed a gas station. "You should see a small road that breaks off through the forest."

"The local police should have someone there to direct us."

The two detectives had no idea of the welcoming committee that awaited them—after their final turn onto the local road, a traffic jam slowed them to a crawl. Gahalowood bypassed it, driving down the opposite lane, not so much because there was no traffic heading the other way, but to avoid the dozens of onlookers wandering along the shoulder of the road.

"What the hell is going on?" Gahalowood asked.

"The usual circus whenever something big happens in a small town. Everyone wants a front-row seat."

After a short while, they reached a police checkpoint where the road forked for the Grey Beach parking area. Through the open window, Gahalowood flashed his badge. "Crime squad, homicide."

"Follow the dirt track, straight ahead," one of the officers told him, waving away a group of officers blocking access to the road.

A few hundred feet down the track, the Chevy Impala reached the edge of the forest, marked by a large, flat stretch of grass. A local cop was pacing back and forth.

"State police, crime squad," Gahalowood called out through the open window.

The policeman looked completely dazed by the day's events. "You better park over here. It must be one helluva mess down there."

The two detectives got out of the car and continued on foot.

"Why do these things always happen on the weekends we're on duty?" Vance asked as he walked along the dirt path. "You remember Greg Bonnet? That was a Saturday as well."

"Before I became your partner, my weekends were always nice and quiet," Gahalowood joked. "You must be bad luck, old man. Helen's not going to be happy. I promised to help her unpack the boxes tonight. But now, with this homicide on our hands . . ."

"Well, we don't know it was a murder yet. It wouldn't be the first time they sent us out to investigate a hiking accident."

They soon reached the Grey Beach parking area, which was filled with emergency vehicles. There was a frenzy of activity. Francis Mitchell, chief of police for Mount Pleasant, came up to greet them. His first words were a warning. "It's not pretty."

"What happened, exactly?" Gahalowood asked. "We were told a woman was murdered."

"It's better you see for yourself."

They followed Chief Mitchell down the path leading to the lake.

Both Gahalowood and Vance had been around crime scenes for years, and both had seen dead bodies. But when they got to the beach, they just stood there. They had never seen anything like it. A woman's body lay there, her head pressed into the loose soil, and alongside her was . . . a dead bear.

"A jogger called it in," the chief explained. "She surprised the bear as it was devouring the body."

"What do you mean, *devouring*?"

"Well, it was eating her!"

Judging by the way the woman was lying on the ground, you would have thought she was sleeping. The gentle sounds of the lake and the springtime birdsong lent the place a peaceful air. Only the presence of the bear, stretched out in a pool of blood that glistened on its black fur, marked the struggle that had occurred.

Vance turned to Mitchell and asked, "A shame about this poor woman, but I'd really like someone to explain to me why you called the crime squad for a bear attack?"

"There are plenty of black bears in these parts," Mitchell replied. "Believe me, it's something we have experience handling. We've had a number of incidents, and when they attack a human, it's to defend their territory, not to eat them."

"What are you getting at?"

"If this bear was eating the woman, then it was feeding on carrion. Because she was already dead when he found her."

Gahalowood and Vance cautiously approached the woman's body. From up close, she looked anything but peaceful. Her torn clothing revealed deep bite marks. Her hair was covered with dried blood.

"What do you think, Perry?" Vance asked.

Gahalowood looked at the victim; she was wearing leather slacks and fashionable boots. "She's dressed as if she was going out somewhere. I'm thinking she was probably killed during the night. But the wounds from the bear appear to be recent."

"In other words, she was dead when the bear found her," Vance concluded. "Probably around daybreak."

Gahalowood nodded. "This doesn't make a lot of sense. We need to call in the cavalry."

Vance took out his phone to alert the rest of the team and notify forensics. Gahalowood was still bent over the corpse. He then noticed a piece of paper sticking out of the back pocket of her slacks. Pulling on a pair of latex gloves, he retrieved what turned out to be a single sheet folded in four. He opened it and found a brief printed message:

I KNOW WHAT YOU DID

# 2

# *Memories*

*New Hampshire*
*April 6, 2010*

It was nearly midday when I arrived in Somerset. The small town, like the rest of New England, was covered in a fine layer of snow that was melting in the bright sunshine. My decision to come here and relive the memories that tied me to Harry Quebert felt right.

To be perfectly honest, I had initially thought that writing, then publishing, *The Truth About the Harry Quebert Affair* would allow me to turn the page on our abruptly broken friendship. But the general enthusiasm for the book only reminded me of the extent to which I had remained marked by the affair. Not so much because of the investigation, which has since been closed, or its conclusions, but by the questions that still remain unanswered: Where did Harry go? What happened to him? And why did he decide to disappear from my life?

I've written at length in that book about how Harry and I had met. There's no point in going over all that here; I simply want to note that Harry had enough faith in my future as a writer to invite me to his home to work on my manuscript. The first time I visited Somerset was in January 2000. I discovered both his extraordinary home in Goose Cove—a writer's home, sheltered from the world, situated next to the ocean—and his solitude, which came as a complete surprise. The famous Harry Quebert, a charismatic and highly regarded character, was in reality an astonishingly lonely man, without a wife, without children, without anyone, really. I have very clear memories of that day: his fridge was desperately empty. When I pointed it out to him, he explained that he wasn't accustomed to receiving guests. He then took me to eat at Clark's, the diner on the town's main street. That's how I discovered the place that had become an integral part of Harry's legend. It's where I met Jenny Quinn, the owner, who had had a thing for Harry for twenty-five years. He had his own table, number 17, to which Jenny Quinn had attached a plaque that read:

IT WAS AT THIS TABLE, IN THE SUMMER OF 1975,
THAT HARRY QUEBERT WROTE HIS FAMOUS NOVEL,
THE ORIGIN OF EVIL.

*The Origin of Evil*, which came out in 1976, was the book that had won Harry fame and glory. In response to my admiring questions, Harry made a face. "I'm a one-hit author," he said. "My reputation rests on this one book."

"But what a book! It's a masterpiece."

Jenny had come over to take our order. Harry said to her, "Jenny, if this young man learns to write like he boxes, he'll be a great writer."

When she had left, I asked Harry to explain what he meant.

"Everyone always expects a great writer to resemble those who came before him, without realizing that if he really is great, it's precisely because he doesn't resemble them at all."

When I looked at him doubtfully, he added, "You know, Marcus, at home earlier, I noticed how intently you examined the classics in my library. You stared at those books wondering whether people would look at yours in the same way in fifty years. Start by writing a book—that's already an accomplishment. And stop pestering everyone about posterity."

"I want to be like you, Harry."

"You don't know what you're talking about. I intend to do everything I can to ensure you don't end up like me. That's why you're here."

I hadn't understood the meaning of what Harry was trying to tell me. I was just a young man who had found his mentor. How could I foresee, back then, blinded by naïveté, the events that would erupt in the summer of 2008 in that peaceful little town and *The Origin of Evil*, a novel considered to be a major work of American literature, being pulled from the shelves of bookstores and libraries from one day to the next?

On that day in April 2010, ten years after my first visit, I parked outside Clark's. Marcus, once a dreamy student, was back, garlanded with success, but Harry was nowhere to be seen.

After the events of the summer of 2008, the restaurant was sold. I didn't recognize anyone, which was fine with me—most of the town's inhabitants had given me the cold shoulder ever since I had unearthed some of Somerset's most intimate secrets during my investigation into the "affair." But, aside from the owner, nothing much had changed. Not the décor, nor the menu. Harry's table was free, so I sat down. For the regulars, it had become something to be avoided. Only tourists sat there now. The plaque was removed after the summer of 2008, leaving only the holes from the screws, like bullet wounds, the scars of an execution. I ordered a cheeseburger and fries; I looked out the window as I ate.

As I was finishing my meal, I was joined by Ernie Pinkas, the town librarian. Ernie was my last friend in Somerset. He was a man with a big heart, a true lover of books, his only companions since he'd been widowed. Ernie ran the Harry Quebert House for Writers, a program I had set up in connection with Burrows University, which had enabled us to transform Harry's house in Goose Cove into a writers' residence for promising young authors. The scandal in the summer of 2008 had tarnished Harry's reputation, but his aura remained largely intact: candidates flocked to the house, drawn by its prestige and its comforts. Ernie Pinkas selected the writers in concert with the English faculty at Burrows, which financed the upkeep of the place. The house could accommodate six writers, who lived there together for three months.

As a result of his new role, Ernie now had a small office at Burrows, an honor that filled him with pride.

He sat down facing me. "Marcus, what are you doing here?"

His surprise stemmed from the fact that we had seen each other just a week earlier, when I was on my way to Montreal. We met for a coffee at Goose Cove, and I was introduced to the new residents, who would be there until the summer.

"I was passing by and I decided to stop for lunch."

"From Montreal?"

His intonation made it clear that he wasn't fooled by this. He knew I was there to look for Harry—or my own ghosts. "It seems you're just wandering around aimlessly, Marcus."

Ernie had put his finger right where it hurt the most.

"You know who used to do this?"

"Do what?"

"Hang around at Clark's. Harry. I always wondered what he was up to, spending all those hours here, at this table, staring into space, like you're doing. I thought he was looking for inspiration. But, in fact, he was waiting for Nola."

I sighed deeply. "I just want some kind of sign, Ernie."

"Harry's not coming back to Somerset."

"How can you be so sure?"

"He's turned the page. You should do the same."

"What are you saying?"

"Thanks to you, he moved on, Marcus. Now that he knows what happened to Nola, there's no point hanging around anymore. He finally got out. Somerset was his prison, and you freed him."

"No, Ernie, Somerset was—"

"You know I'm right, Marcus," Ernie interrupted. "You know Harry's never coming back here. You can't wait for your friends like you wait for a bus. Why do you keep coming back? Stop torturing yourself. You're a nice guy, Marcus, it's time to move on."

Ernie was right. But when I had finished lunch, I couldn't resist making a pilgrimage to Goose Cove. I walked along the beach down below Harry's house for a while and sat on a large boulder to take in the view. I gazed at the imposing structure, filled with so many memories. The gulls were hopping around on the sand. Gradually, the sky filled with gray clouds and it began to drizzle. Then, within the curtain of haze, I saw a man approach, a man I considered a dear friend: Perry Gahalowood, sergeant with the crime squad of the New Hampshire State Police. He walked toward me with a bemused smile on his face and a cup of coffee in each hand.

Those who know me and have read my books know all about how Perry and I are connected. For those who don't and haven't, I had first met Perry two years earlier, during the Harry Quebert affair. He was in charge of the investigation. Together, we had shed light on the death of Nola Kellergan. Some will say that figuring out who killed Nola helped me write my second novel. In reality, she allowed the seeds of friendship between me and Perry to germinate. He was like some hardy desert fruit: thorny, protected by a thick skin that concealed sweet flesh and a tender heart. Rough, brusque, irascible, but loyal and fair. Sometimes a man can be judged by his family, and Perry's—which I knew well—was the picture of happiness.

"Sergeant, what are you doing here?" (Since the day we met, I called him "Sergeant" and he called me "Writer," and we have maintained the tradition.)

He offered me one of the cups of coffee. "I should ask you the same question. Whenever you show up here, at least one person calls the police. You've left quite an impression on this town."

"You're worse than my mother, Sergeant."

He burst out laughing. "So, what half-assed excuse brings you to Somerset, Writer?"

"I was returning from Montreal and thought I'd stop by."

"That's a two-hour detour," Gahalowood remarked.

I pointed my chin in the direction of Goose Cove. "I loved that house," I said. "I loved this town. And when we love, we love forever. There's nothing we can do to change that."

"If you think you love this town, you're mistaken, Writer. You love the memories you have of this place. *Nostalgia* is your problem. We convince ourselves that our past was happy and that our choices must've been the right ones. Whenever we think about the past and say to ourselves, 'It was good,' it's just our sick brain distilling that nostalgia in order to persuade us that our past wasn't in vain, that we didn't waste our time. Because when you waste your time, you waste your life."

Listening to those words, I didn't realize that Gahalowood, who was never afraid of making waves, was talking about himself. I assumed he was referring to me, so I replied, "All the same, it was good at Goose Cove."

"Good for you? I'm not so sure. You're the writer of the decade and you're wandering around some New Hampshire backwater. The last time I saw you here was in October. You remember?"

"Yes."

"I thought you'd come to say your goodbyes to that house. We had a beer, more or less right here, and you mumbled something about heading off in search of love. So much for that! You still with your pilot?"

No-one was better informed than Gahalowood when it came to my love life. I called him whenever I met someone new. When I started seeing Raegan, he was the first person I told.

"I think it's getting serious between us."

"Well, good news for once. Try not to bring her here for your vacation if you want it to last."

"I'm taking her to the Bahamas."

"Now you're annoying me, Writer."

"A private island, an amazing place. Want to see some pictures?"

"I want to say no, but I feel you're going to show me all the same."

Seated on our boulder, indifferent to the rain falling on us, we talked about nothing in particular, a banal exchange between friends, which is to say that I didn't gather much about Gahalowood's life at the time. I asked him about his wife, Helen, and his daughters, Malia and Lisa, but I didn't ask how he was doing. I didn't give him the chance to open up, and we parted without me ever suspecting what was going on.

When we had finished our coffee, Gahalowood stood up.

"Time to get back to fighting crime?" I asked.

"No, I have to meet Helen. It's Lisa's birthday; we have some shopping to do. She's eleven today."

"How does it make you feel? Like an old man?"

Gahalowood's face grew sad and I began to worry.

"Everything okay, Sarge? You don't look very happy."

"Unfortunately, it reminds me of something. Something painful. Exactly eleven years ago, April sixth, 1999, the day my life was turned upside down."

"What happened?"

As he always did when it came to talking about himself, Gahalowood changed the subject. "Doesn't matter. Tonight we're making dinner at home for Lisa, the whole family. Join us. Six o'clock."

"I'd love to. I can even come earlier if you like."

"No, no, no! You are absolutely forbidden to show your face before six."

"Whatever you say, Sergeant!"

He walked a few steps, then turned to me and said, in his usual, provocative tone, "Don't go thinking I consider you a member of the family. But Helen would kill me if I didn't invite you."

"I don't think anything at all," I said, smiling.

He walked away. I stayed a moment longer on the beach, wondering what could have happened in Perry's life eleven years earlier. At the time, I had no inkling of what had been haunting him all those years—that is, until the events I'm about to relate here began to unfold.

# The Day of the Murder

*April 3, 1999*

The little town of Mount Pleasant was in a state of agitation it had never known before. Everyone was asking questions, looking for information. From store to store, the conversation was the same. Whether it was at the Season, the coffee shop well known for its breakfasts; Cinzia Lockart's bookstore; or the Carrey family's hunting and fishing store, the customers kept asking one another, "Do you know anything?" "No. You?" "Did you go to Grey Beach to see what happened?" "My wife went but the police had cordoned off the area."

The only thing they knew was that a woman had been found dead at Grey Beach. Lauren Donovan, the daughter of Janet and Mark Donovan, the owners of Donovan's General Store, had discovered the body while out jogging. As the news circulated, everyone converged on the store, supposedly to do their grocery shopping but mostly to find out what was going on. The store was busy throughout the day, and from time to time, a small crowd gathered inside. The customers would stop Mark or Janet to ask whether Lauren was there.

"No, she's not."

"Do you have any news about what happened at Grey Beach?"

"We don't know any more than you do. Lauren's still with the police. Excuse me, but we have a lot of customers to take care of."

"If you find something out, please let us know!"

While the curious continued to ask questions in Mount Pleasant, at that moment, on Grey Beach, the investigators were looking for answers.

Fifty officers from the local and state police had gone over the shore of the lake and the surrounding woods with a fine-tooth comb. On the beach, the medical examiner's team was gathered around the body, which was still lying on the ground. Back in the parking lot, experts from the forensic science department were inspecting the blue convertible. Based on the plate, the car belonged to a twenty-two-year-old woman named Alaska Sanders. And the handbag on the passenger seat contained her driver's license.

The name had caused some commotion among the local police: Alaska was a young woman from Mount Pleasant.

"I'll need to see her face to confirm it's her," Chief Mitchell explained to Gahalowood and Vance, while the medical examiner scrutinized the inert body.

"What can you tell us about her?" Vance asked.

"A girl without a history. She settled here a few months ago with her boyfriend. Worked at a nearby gas station."

"How do you know her?"

"In Mount Pleasant everyone knows everyone."

When his preliminary examination was over, the medical examiner had the body moved, revealing the victim's face. Seeing this, Chief Mitchell swore, loudly. Several of the local police officers came over and the hubbub grew louder.

"Is it her?" Gahalowood asked Mitchell.

"Yes."

Gahalowood and Vance approached the body.

"So, Doc?" Vance asked the medical examiner.

"You know me, Sergeant, I don't like to offer an opinion before the autopsy. But what I can tell you is that she died during the night, maybe one or two in the morning. Probably from a blow to the back of the head. There's a large wound there. The bear had nothing to do with it."

"So it was murder."

"That it was. She was struck with a blunt object. I can't tell you more until I've conducted the autopsy."

"And when will that be?"

"As soon as possible."

"That's not an answer," Vance remarked.

"For me it is," the doctor joked.

Gahalowood and Vance stood looking silently at the body. Suddenly, a voice called out to them.

"I hate murders in small towns. They're always the worst." It was Morris Lansdane, head of the crime squad for the state police.

"What are you doing here, Captain?" Vance asked. "I thought you were on leave."

"I'm always around when this sort of thing happens," Lansdane replied. "The director wants to know what's going on and asked me for an update. What do you have?"

"The victim is a young woman, twenty-two years old, by the name of Alaska Sanders," Gahalowood began. "Originally from Salem, Massachusetts. She died during the night after she was struck on the back of the head."

Vance took over: "We found her car in the parking lot nearby. It was unlocked. There's a travel bag with some clothing inside on the rear seat and her handbag was on the passenger seat."

"Robbery?" Lansdane asked.

"I doubt it," Gahalowood replied. "We found a message, some kind of threat, on the victim. Just a sentence printed from a computer: 'I know what you did.'"

"Hmm. Revenge?"

"Maybe. In any case, the bag leads me to believe that she was on her way somewhere. Or running from something."

"I'm going to get her parents' address," Vance added. "I'd like to alert them as soon as possible. It's a small town and the cops here are talkative. I don't want the family to learn about it from the local news."

"You're right," Lansdane agreed. "I'll let you guys get back to work. Oh, wait . . . what's this business with the bear? Everybody's been talking about it."

"The body was found by a jogger; she surprised a bear that was feeding on the corpse," Gahalowood explained.

Lansdane grimaced. "Did you talk to the jogger?"

"Not yet. She's waiting at the service station nearby. We'll head over shortly."

At that moment, a local policeman approached them. "They're asking for you in the woods. They found something. Come on, follow me."

Gahalowood, Vance, and Lansdane followed the officer onto a path through the forest. Everything was bathed in light. Winding their way among the ferns and century-old tree trunks, they arrived at an abandoned trailer, eaten away by thorns and scrub, surrounded by a clutch of police.

"We didn't go in," one of the men explained. "We just looked through the open door."

"And . . . ?" Gahalowood asked.

"See for yourself," the officer suggested, handing him a flashlight.

The trailer's windows were covered, and when Gahalowood looked inside, at first he saw only darkness. Then, in the beam of the flashlight, he saw the mess: a torn mattress, garbage, cigarette butts. And a pullover stained with purple streaks. He stepped inside to get a better look: the garment was spattered with blood. "Get the forensics team over here and have them go over this place inch by inch," Gahalowood ordered.

He and Vance then explored the surrounding area. About thirty feet away, they found a track, wide enough for a vehicle, that was used by forest rangers. On the ground Vance noticed debris from the taillight of a car and, nearby, a tree trunk that bore the traces of a recent collision. "Looks like black paint," he noted, looking closely at the dark flecks on the bark.

*       *       *

It was noon when Robbie and Donna Sanders got the call from Sergeant Matt Vance. When the conversation was over, the two parents just stood there, unable to speak, Robbie clutching the receiver. Destroyed. Their world was collapsing.

One hundred miles away, on the flower-strewn field separating the forest at Grey Beach from Route 21, Vance closed his cell phone and turned to Gahalowood, who was waiting for him by their unmarked car.

"All these goddamn flowers on a day like this," Vance swore, intentionally trampling a cluster of yellow trout lilies. "Alaska's parents will be at headquarters in a couple of hours."

"Thanks for taking care of that," Gahalowood remarked, giving him a fraternal tap on the shoulder.

"No big deal, Perry, you've got a kid on the way. You shouldn't even be here, seeing all this."

"It's my job. Speaking of which, Chief Mitchell gave me Alaska's address in Mount Pleasant. She had an apartment on the main drag, where she was living with her boyfriend. Apparently, he works at the hunting and fishing store below. He's there now."

"Let's start with the gas station; we can go to Mount Pleasant afterward," Vance suggested.

The Chevy Impala drove up the dirt road to Route 21, where Gahalowood turned on the siren to open a path among the cops, the onlookers, and the journalists. He turned left in the direction of Mount Pleasant. About a mile down the road, they reached the gas station where it had all begun that morning. A local police car was parked out front.

Inside the store they found Lauren Donovan, the jogger, and Lewis Jacob, the owner, with tears running down his cheeks. They were comforting each other as officer Peter Philipps looked on helplessly. Seeing the state police arrive, Jacob yelled, "Is it true? Is it Alaska? Is she dead?"

Gahalowood and Vance looked at one another—the news was already out. "Unfortunately, it's true," Gahalowood replied.

"Dead how? Was she eaten by a bear? That's what Peter told me. But bears, they don't eat people. Especially not the black bears around here. Last fall, I had two of them who'd come nosing around the garbage. One thing I know is that if you yell at them loud enough, they'll run away."

"She wasn't killed by a bear," Vance told him.

"So, how did she die?"

Vance avoided the question. "When did you last see Alaska?" he asked.

"Last night. I left here at seven thirty. She was supposed to close up at eight."

"And did she?"

"Yes. When I arrived this morning, the alarm had been set, everything looked normal."

"How did she seem to you yesterday?"

"Same as always. Nothing special. You know, she was always friendly, always had a kind word for everyone, never moody or angry. That girl was something else."

"Did she have plans for the evening? Did she mention anything?"

"She said she had a 'romantic dinner.' Those were her words."

"With her boyfriend?"

"I asked but she didn't answer. I know they've been having problems lately. Did you talk to Walter?"

"Walter is the boyfriend, right?"

"Yes, Walter Carrey."

"We'll get to him later."

Gahalowood looked up at the ceiling and noticed a surveillance camera. "Can we take a look at the footage?"

"That's what I was just explaining. I don't know how to make this thing go backwards," Jacob admitted. "Never had to try before. But I know it can be done. My nephew installed the thing. I called and asked him to come down—he's spending the weekend in Vermont."

"We'll take the hard drive, if you don't mind."

"Take whatever you like, Sergeant."

*    *    *

Until the murder of Alaska Sanders, Mount Pleasant had been a quiet, peaceful place, a charming town on the border with Maine and two hours' drive from Canada, surrounded by the White Mountain National Forest.

Main Street was bordered with tall maple trees that were covered in snow in winter and provided generous shade in summer. On either side of the wide sidewalks were stores well known throughout the area: Donovan's General Store, whose goods, selected with care, were unlike any stocked by the supermarkets; Lockart's Bookstore, owned by Cinzia Lockart, which drew writers from around the East Coast for book signings; Carrey Hunting & Fishing, run by the Carrey family and appreciated for the quality of its gear and its expert advice; and the sports bar, the National Anthem, which showed major-league football, baseball, and hockey games, of which the owner was a great fan.

But today, along that same street, the passersby mostly gossiped. Word had gotten around it was Alaska Sanders who had been found dead. Several women had gotten the news from their husbands on the local police force. Suddenly, everyone grew quiet as they watched the unmarked Chevy Impala—recognizable as a police vehicle by the flashing lights on the roof—drive down the street. The car stopped in front of Donovan's. Sergeant Gahalowood got out to open the door for Lauren Donovan.

"Thank you, Sergeant," she said.

"Take care, Lauren. If you have any questions, you have my card."

She nodded and rushed into the store, avoiding the eyes of the onlookers. Inside, she ran behind the counter to her mother, who held her tight.

"Oh, honey . . ."

"Mom, it was awful!"

The customers who happened to be in the store crowded around Lauren. "Was it Alaska they found?" "What did you see?" "Did something happen at Grey Beach?"

Janet Donovan led her daughter to the storeroom, where she was sheltered from the crowd. Mark, her father, made sure that the customers didn't try to follow them in and shooed away anybody who hadn't come to do their shopping.

In the storeroom, Janet made her daughter a cup of coffee and helped her into a chair. Eric, Lauren's older brother, who worked in the store with their parents, joined them.

Her voice trembling, Lauren told them, "It was Alaska. She's dead."

"What?" Eric blurted out in shock. "I can't believe it!"

"Eric, what I saw on the beach was horrible. I didn't even recognize her right away, but luckily, I didn't see very much."

"Alaska's dead?" Eric repeated incredulously. "I have to find Walter!"

"The cops are headed there now."

Down the street, the Chevy Impala had parked in front of Carrey Hunting & Fishing. When Walter Carrey saw the two men enter, badges on their belts, he hid his face in his hands. So, the rumors were true. Alaska was dead.

Walter took refuge in the back room to escape the eyes of the curious onlookers who had crowded into the store. He was a man of about thirty, solid and well built. For a second it looked as if the old armchair in which he was curled up was about to give way under him. Distraught, he kept repeating: "Murdered? Murdered? But who could have done something like this? And why?" It was a while before he was able to answer the investigators' questions.

"You lived with Alaska Sanders, is that correct?" Vance asked.

"Yes, in an apartment above the store."

"You weren't surprised when she didn't come home last night?" Gahalowood asked.

"She'd left for the weekend."

"Left for where?"

"Her parents', I think. Did you talk to them?"

"Yes," Vance replied. "And they never said they were expecting her."

Walter Carrey ran his hands through his hair, muttering, "It's not possible. It's not possible," over and over.

"Walter," Vance asked. "When did you last see Alaska?"

"Yesterday. Late afternoon."

"And did you notice anything out of the ordinary?"

"Yes! I would even say that she didn't appear to be her normal self. I went up to the apartment for a while, at around five o'clock. I was cold and wanted to grab a sweater. When I walked in, there she was. I wasn't expecting to see her because she usually worked at the gas station until eight. I thought maybe she wanted to surprise me. Talk about a surprise . . ."

\*         \*         \*

*The previous day, five fifteen in the afternoon*
Walter opened the door of the apartment and saw Alaska standing before him. She was wearing skin-tight black leather slacks, a lace shirt that revealed her bra, and those little black boots that made her look so good. She was observing herself in the large mirror in the hallway.

"Alaska." Walter smiled, thinking she was getting ready for him.

"Oh, you're here," she said.

By her tone, he understood that she hadn't expected to see him.

"What are you doing?" Walter asked, disappointed. "And why are you dressed like that?"

"No reason. I'm trying something out."

She took off the clothes at once and put her jeans and gas station polo shirt back on, before stuffing the clothes and the boots into a large leather bag.

"What are you up to?" Walter insisted.

48

She looked at him with bitter disappointment. "Walter, please. Don't pretend you don't understand."

"Understand what?"

"I'm leaving. I'm leaving you."

"What? What do you mean, *you're leaving me*?"

"It's not working out, Walter. And I'm tired of living above your parents' store. Where are we going to end up if we stay together?"

"Alaska, you can't leave! Not without giving me a chance!"

"I'm sorry."

"Where are you going?"

"Back to my parents. It's time to take stock of my life."

\*　　\*　　\*

"And that's how it ended," Walter explained. "She grabbed her bag and left. I followed her down to the street, to try to talk her out of it, but she wouldn't listen. She got in her car and took off."

"And what did you do?" Gahalowood asked.

"We had a customer. I had to go and take care of them."

"You were alone in the store?"

"Yes, it's just me right now. My parents are on vacation; they're coming back tomorrow."

"So, you had no idea that Alaska was going to leave you?"

"No! We had our ups and downs, like every couple. But to just pack up and leave like that, without warning . . ."

"Was there someone else?" Vance asked.

"No!" Walter replied, wounded by the suggestion. "Well . . . I have no idea . . . no idea . . . it doesn't feel real."

"And what did you do?"

"I was stuck in the store until closing time. I didn't want to lock up early; my parents call from time to time, to get the news, they say, but really to check up on me. They want to know that I'm serious and ready to take over. They say that their retirement depends on me—they put a lot of pressure on me that way. So I guess I was just hoping she'd come back, but she didn't. At closing time, I locked up and went upstairs. I was in a bad way. Then I went out to meet my friend Eric—Eric Donovan; we had a hamburger and watched the hockey game at the National Anthem. I got back late."

"What time?"

"I don't know. I drank a lot. I went to bed and slept till noon."

"Did you go to the gas station to try to talk with Alaska?"

"No."

"Why not?" Gahalowood asked. "If my girlfriend left me, I would want to find her and ask for an explanation."

"What was the point?" Walter grumbled. "When Alaska made up her mind, that was it. Besides, I didn't want to look pathetic. I wasn't going to beg. I could just see myself trailing along behind her in front of all the customers at the gas station."

"You preferred to tough it out," Vance remarked ironically.

Walter shrugged. "I tried to call her at least twenty times. I bombarded her with messages."

"To her cell phone, you mean?" Gahalowood asked.

"Yes, of course, to her cell phone. Why?"

"Because we didn't find it. Not on her and not in the car. We found everything else, but not her phone. Walter, can we take a look at your apartment?"

"Sure."

He led them through a service door. Outside, an exterior staircase led to the floor above. The three men entered the apartment, where Gahalowood and Vance made a preliminary search.

"What are you looking for?" Walter asked.

"Nothing in particular. It's routine in this type of situation."

"You mean a murder?"

"Yes. Where are Alaska's things?"

"In the bedroom."

Walter Carrey led the two policemen through. Gahalowood noticed a beat-up video camera on a shelf. "Whose camera is that?"

"Alaska's."

Gahalowood opened the cassette compartment and saw that it was empty. "What happened to it? Looks like it's seen better days."

"I have no idea," Walter replied. "Alaska told me she dropped it. It didn't matter; she never used it anyway. It was for her casting calls. She wanted to be an actress. She even had an agent in New York and all that. But she put it all on hold when she moved here."

"If she never used it, why is it so beat up?" Vance asked.

"I really have no idea."

Gahalowood opened the closet and inspected the clothing. "Is anything missing?"

"Hard to say. Like I told you, she left with a bag; there were some clothes in it, I guess."

Gahalowood lifted a pile of slacks and stopped suddenly. Two messages, identical to the one in Alaska's pocket.

I KNOW WHAT YOU DID

"Did anyone ever try to blackmail Alaska?" Gahalowood asked.

"No, why?"

"Because it looks like she was being threatened," Gahalowood replied, showing Walter the messages.

"What the hell?" Walter thought he was losing his mind.

"Alaska never mentioned it?"

"No, never! I feel like I'm in some kind of nightmare."

\*　　\*　　\*

By late afternoon, the commotion at Grey Beach had died down. Alaska's body had been taken away and the markers around the beach removed.

The police cars were leaving one after the other, while the crowd of journalists and onlookers had thinned. There was nothing more to see.

Gahalowood and Vance had returned to New Hampshire State Police headquarters in Concord. There they undertook the essential ritual that marked the beginning of every new case. They pulled out the large magnetic whiteboard from behind their desks and began to lay out the first elements of their investigation.

Gahalowood wrote in red marker: *Alaska Sanders*. Below that, Vance positioned the forensics photos that had just come through: Alaska's body on the beach, the dead bear by her side, and disturbing close-ups of the young woman's face. There were photos of the note—I KNOW WHAT YOU DID—the blue convertible, and the leather bag found in the trunk containing clothing and toiletries. There were also photographs of the forest. The abandoned trailer. The gray, bloodstained sweater bearing the letters *MU*. The trail through the forest. The tree with the black paint on it. The debris from the broken taillight.

A phone call from the reception desk interrupted their work: Alaska's parents had arrived.

"I'll take care of it," Vance suggested to Gahalowood. "You should go home."

Gahalowood looked at his watch. "I'm not going to play the nine-to-five when we have a murder on our hands."

"You know as well as I do that nothing's going to happen before tomorrow, and even then, the medical examiner won't complete the autopsy before Monday. I'm going to take Alaska's parents to the morgue to identify the body. You should go home and take care of Helen and start unpacking. And don't let her carry any boxes. I can stop by later if you need a hand."

Gahalowood returned home. As he parked in front of his new house, he was at once flooded by a sense of relief. As if the day's emotions had been washed away. He switched off the engine and waited in the car awhile, admiring his new home, small but pretty. He and Helen had fallen in love with it three months earlier. Ever since they discovered she was pregnant, they had been itching to leave their cramped apartment and buy a house. They would soon be four; they needed more room. He wanted a small garden. They had toured a number of places, but none of them felt right, except for this one. It was pouring that day but, despite the bad weather, from the outside they liked it immediately. Once inside, they were sold: they could imagine it filled with life. And the price was right, even if it did need a bit of work. A month later, the renovations were underway but, as always, they dragged on, and they hadn't been able to move in until the previous week, a few days before Helen was due.

Gahalowood stepped through the door; a joyous disorder reigned within. But he didn't care. He was happy. Helen was lying on the couch. He woke her gently; she pulled him toward her round belly.

"It feels really good to be in this house," she said.

"I know. Where's Malia?"

"She's with my mother. She's sleeping there tonight."

"I'm sorry I didn't get a chance to call you during the day."

"Don't worry about it, I assumed you were busy."

"There was a murder. A twenty-two-year-old girl, found in the forest."

Gahalowood struggled to drive the images of Alaska out of his mind.

"And your day?" he asked his wife, hoping to change the subject.

"I went to that decorating store on Isaac Street. Look what I found."

She got up and pulled from a paper bag a wrought-iron wall plaque that read:

*JOIE DE VIVRE*

"I want to put it outside, next to the front door," she explained.

"And what's it supposed to mean?"

"Us! That's us in this house."

Gahalowood smiled. After dinner, he attached the plaque to the front wall, by the porch. He had just finished when a car turned in to his driveway. It was Vance.

"So?" Gahalowood asked when Vance joined him by the front door.

"The parents have formally identified their daughter. They're devastated."

Gahalowood went to get two beers. They sat on the steps and Vance lit a cigarette.

"Nice place," he said.

"Thanks."

"But I don't know where you got the idea to move right before your wife was due to give birth."

Vance noticed the wrought-iron decoration on the wall, which now greeted visitors. "Joie de Vivre," he read out loud.

"Helen's idea," Gahalowood said.

"I like it," Vance replied. "It's an invitation to leave all the horrors you have to deal with at the door."

The two men remained silent. Vance finished his cigarette and lit another. He was nervous. After a few drags, he felt it was time to share his decision with his partner. He had been thinking about it for a while, but that morning, discovering Alaska's body, he knew the moment had arrived.

"I started out as a cop in Bangor, Maine. One of my first cases was a seventeen-year-old kid who was murdered walking home after a night out with a girlfriend. Gaby Robinson was her name. I'll never forget it. We never found the guy who did it. This morning, when I saw that body on the beach, a lot of bad memories came back to me. This is going to be my last case, Perry. We'll get the person who did this. We'll take care of it. I promise. I want to be able to look Alaska's parents in the eye and tell them that justice has been served. And then, I'm quitting."

# 3

## *Joie de Vivre*

*New Hampshire*
*April 6, 2010*

I arrived early on the doorstep of the Gahalowood home, carrying flowers, wine, and a gift for Lisa. As with all of my visits, as I rang the buzzer, my gaze fell upon the wrought-iron plaque that greeted visitors: *JOIE DE VIVRE*.

For a little more than two years, the house had been the cradle of our friendship. My first few visits took place in the summer of 2008, while we were investigating the Harry Quebert case. It was then that I met Helen, Gahalowood's charming wife, and their adorable daughters, Malia and Lisa. The real turning point in my relationship with them took place around Christmas 2008.

\*        \*        \*

*December 2008*

A few months had gone by since the conclusion of the Harry Quebert case, and Perry and I had been in touch only sporadically. But, as always when it comes to such strong bonds, the scarcity of our exchanges hadn't affected the depth of our friendship. I realized this one morning during the holidays, when time seems to be suspended. I received a small package in the mail from Helen Gahalowood, containing a few culinary delicacies from New Hampshire and a greeting card.

It included a vivid portrait of the family: Perry, wearing one of his awful ties, stared at the lens like a sulky buffalo, while Helen, radiant, embraced the two girls. Inside were a few lines in Helen's handwriting:

> *Happy New Year, dear Marcus, the best thing to have*
> *come our way in 2008.*
> *Helen, Perry, and the girls*

And just below that, in Perry's handwriting:

> *I'm not signing! But Happy New Year all the same, Writer!*
> *Perry*

These marks of affection touched me deeply. They made me aware of my feelings for Gahalowood's family. Gripped by an immediate need to reciprocate, I started preparing a cake for them. I made the only dessert I knew how to make, a banana bread that my aunt Anita always baked at this time of year, whose success depended on the use of very ripe bananas. An hour later, when the bread was done, I jumped into my car and drove the more than four hours it takes to get to Concord.

It was mid-afternoon when I rang Gahalowood's bell, holding my dessert and a few trinkets I had picked up at a mall just off the highway. I had no intention of staying. Driving all that way simply to drop off my miserable cake was nothing more than my response to their greeting: "You too, you're the best thing to have happened to me in 2008." We don't simply find our friends: they reveal themselves to us. That's what happened with the Gahalowoods. They were true friends, like I had never had, or, rather, like I no longer had since "fame" had arrived. Except for Harry.

I recall Helen's smile when she opened the door and saw me with my strange gift. After a moment's shock, she hugged me.

"Marcus! Marcus, what are you doing here?" Turning to the interior of the house, she called out, "Perry, come here, it's Marcus!" Then, turning back to me, "It's freezing out, come inside."

"I don't want to disturb you. I was only passing by."

"Oh, please, come in for a bit."

I obeyed and stepped into the house. The mood was one of joyous agitation—the family was playing a board game. Perry came over and shook my hand firmly. "Well, this is a surprise! What are you doing in these parts?"

"Nothing special, I was just passing by to bring you a dessert I made. Then I have to get going. Thanks for the package. And especially the card. I was very moved. Here, Sergeant, this is for you."

I offered him one of the four small packages. Perry unwrapped it and stared, slightly disgusted, at the tie I had bought for him. "It's really ugly," he noted.

"Just the way you like them, Sergeant."

He thanked me and suddenly frowned. Like the practiced sleuth that he was, he had figured out what I meant by my previous remark. "Wait a minute! When you said you have to *get going*, you mean you're headed back to New York?"

"Yes," I replied, as if there were nothing out of the ordinary about it.

"Damn it, Writer! You mean to tell me that you drove four hours to drop off an overcooked cake and you're going to drive another four hours to go back?"

I nodded. "It may look overcooked, but that's the way it's supposed to be. It's soft inside, you'll see."

Perry rolled his eyes. "I think you're completely nuts. Come on, give me your jacket and take off your shoes—you're going to get snow all over the place. Do you like eggnog? I make a mean one."

I smiled. "I never say no to eggnog."

I stayed at the Gahalowoods until well into the night, playing Trivial Pursuit, Monopoly, and Scrabble and sipping eggnog, as Perry kept refilling our glasses with his concoction. I stayed for dinner as well. And when it was time to go, Helen and Perry were worried that I would try driving back to New York at such a late hour.

"I'm going to stop at a motel, don't worry. I saw one near the highway."

"The motel is downstairs," Perry decreed. He took me down into the basement and unfolded the sofa bed, which nearly filled the narrow room. He opened a closet and pointed to some sheets.

"If Helen asks, tell her I prepared the bed. Otherwise, she's going to grumble and tell me I don't know how to be a good host. Good night, Writer."

"Good night, Sarge. And thanks. Thanks for everything."

His only response was to snort like a buffalo, which in his gruff language meant *Don't mention it*. How grateful I was to have met these good people, who had become my closest friends in the world.

*     *     *

On that spring day in April 2010, as I stood outside the Gahalowood family home, it was that happy memory that came back to me. And yet Perry's greeting wasn't all that warm. Seeing me before the door, he grumbled, "What the hell! What the hell are you doing here? I told you six o'clock!"

"I came to help."

"No-one needs your help."

Helen appeared beside her husband, with her ever-present warm smile. "Marcus, what a pleasure to see you." She pushed her husband aside to hug me.

"I'm early, but I've come to lend a hand," I explained, offering her the flowers.

"Marcus, you're adorable." She sniffed the bouquet and invited me to follow her to the kitchen. Perry stood in the way.

"Your wife said I was adorable," I chided.

"Oh, please shut up!"

"Sarge, explain to me how this extraordinary woman ended up marrying a guy like you?"

"You tell me!"

"Pity, no doubt."

"We'll see about that."

"Here, the wine is for you. I believe you like this one."

"Thanks, Writer."

Helen and Perry were planning to make fajitas, which Lisa was crazy about. They were expecting about twenty guests, and to help out, I started cutting up the chicken and peppers, grating the cheese, and mashing ripe avocados for the guacamole. We put together two platters, which Perry and I decorated with a modest degree of talent.

Helen took advantage of my presence to ask me about my love life. "So, Marcus, still single?"

"He has a girlfriend," Perry chimed in.

"Oh?" Helen said, surprised, pretending to be offended that I hadn't informed her. "Tell us, Marcus."

"It's very new—it's not like we're getting married."

"So, your interviews managed to bear fruit?" Helen teased. "Did your mother's spirit approve of your choice?"

"Sarge," I shouted, "I can't believe you told her about that!"

"She's my wife, I tell her everything. Besides, the business about your mother showing up in your head to give advice, that's pretty crazy."

"Her name is Raegan," I told Helen.

"Your mother?"

"No, my girlfriend. She's an airline pilot. She lives near Montreal."

"How long have you been seeing her?"

"They've been together for three months already!" Perry blurted out.

"Three months? So, it's serious," Helen remarked.

"I have no idea. We haven't had a chance to spend much time together."

"It's very serious," Perry interjected. "He's taking her to the Bahamas for a vacation."

"Sergeant, please, let's not make a big deal of it!"

"The poor girl," Perry teased. "If she only knew what was in store for her."

We burst out laughing.

Malia and Lisa arrived one after the other. They rushed over and wrapped their arms around my neck, happy and surprised to find me in their kitchen. Both of them had grown since the last time I had seen them. Lisa was eleven and finishing grammar school. Malia was nineteen and had finished high school the previous year, and was taking a prep course before going to college. I had a very close relationship with the girls, and they affectionately referred to me as "Uncle Marcus."

Around six, the grandparents, uncles, aunts, and cousins arrived. I have lasting memories of that evening—the lively conversations and the laughter; Lisa blowing out the candles; Perry and me judging the most beautiful cake; Helen, more stunning than ever, sitting at the piano and singing jazz standards for us.

It was after eleven when I left. How could I imagine that, when I next returned to that home, it would be torn apart by sorrow?

Gahalowood walked out with me as I was leaving. "You're sure you don't want to stay, Writer?"

"No, thanks, Sarge, I'm going back to New York."

"You'll arrive in the middle of the night."

"I'm not afraid of the dark."

We exchanged a fraternal embrace. "I'd like to be like you, Sarge."

"The grass is always greener on the other side, Writer."

"I know . . . but I envy your life with Helen. You seem so happy together."

"A marriage is a lot of work. You have your whole life ahead of you. Be glad you can play the field; consider yourself lucky."

He looked at me a long time, as if he wanted to emphasize the seriousness of his remark.

"What were you talking about earlier?" I asked. "This afternoon, on the beach, you mentioned something that happened exactly eleven years ago, the day Lisa was born."

He avoided answering me, changing the subject. "And what about you, Writer? What are you keeping secret?"

"What happened to my cousins, Woody and Hillel."

"You never mentioned that before."

"I just did. Now, tell me, what happened on April sixth, 1999?"

"You know, Writer, the real wounds are hidden. They need to be kept secret. They only heal if you keep them to yourself."

"I'm not so sure."

There was a long silence. Then Gahalowood made a curious remark: "White Mountain Forest—does that mean anything to you?"

"No, why?"

"Don't worry, Writer. Go on, let's not ruin this beautiful evening with these old memories. Drive safely and send me a text from New York to let me know you've arrived okay."

"Yes, Mother."

He smiled and went inside. Back in my car, I used my phone to check the web. I searched for "White Mountain Forest" and the date "April 6, 1999." But nothing of interest came up. What was Gahalowood alluding to?

My search was interrupted by a message from Raegan. That afternoon, I had sent her an email with her plane ticket and a link to the Harbour Island Resort website. She wrote that I was crazy. I called her at once.

"We're going to the Bahamas?" she blurted out, incredulous and excited.

I had arranged it so we would be able to leave together from Montreal. I would go up to spend a few days on the film set, then we'd fly off to our little paradise.

"Do the dates work for you? I can still change the reservation if we need to."

"The dates are perfect. Everything is perfect. You're the perfect guy, Marcus Goldman. I'm very lucky to have met you."

I smiled. I felt lucky too. "We leave in ten days," I said. "It feels so far away."

"I know. I miss you."

"I miss you too. You going to bed?"

"Yes, I'm under the covers. Are you in New York?"

"No, I stopped in New Hampshire. I had dinner with some good friends. I think I told you about them."

"The Gahalowoods?"

"Yes. I'd really like you to meet them."

"I'd be happy to."

"Sleep tight. Let's talk tomorrow."

We hung up.

Raegan wasn't in her bed. Raegan was lying. She was outside, wandering around a deserted street in her neighborhood under the pretext of walking her dog. Our conversation concluded, she closed her phone or, rather, the prepaid phone she used only to call me, put it in her pocket, and returned home. Her husband was watching television in the living room. She walked over and sat down beside him. He thought she looked strange.

"Everything okay, dear?"

"Everything's fine."

She sat for a moment staring at the TV without watching it, then went upstairs to tuck in her two children.

# Excerpt from the Police Report
# Interview with Robert and Donna Sanders

*[Robert, known as Robbie, and Donna, are the parents of Alaska Sanders, their only daughter. This interview was recorded in the offices of the crime squad of the New Hampshire State Police on Sunday, April 4, 1999.]*

*Can you introduce yourselves briefly—your age, what you do, where you live?*

ROBBIE SANDERS: I'm fifty-three years old. I'm an electrician, I run my own business.

DONNA SANDERS: I'm forty-eight years old. I'm a medical secretary.

ROBBIE SANDERS: We live in Salem, Massachusetts. Alaska was born and grew up there. We're an ordinary middle-class family. Alaska went to public school. Nothing special.

*How would you describe your daughter?*

ROBBIE SANDERS: Alaska was a wonderful girl. Enthusiastic. Happy.

Donna Sanders: Everybody felt the same way about her. Everybody liked her. She dreamed of becoming a famous actress. They said she'd have a great career.

*Did she appear in any films?*

DONNA SANDERS: No, but she went on a lot of casting calls. She was on the right track. She even had an agent. It was serious.

*What was her life like when she was young?*

ROBBIE SANDERS: She went to school in Salem. In high school, she entered a few beauty pageants. She became successful very quickly. She was a beautiful girl and had a great deal of personality. She continued along those lines and it worked out well. She was asked to appear in ads for some local brands.

*So she was a model?*

ROBBIE SANDERS: You could put it that way.

DONNA SANDERS: She didn't like people to call her a model. She felt the pageants and the adverts were stepping stones for her acting career. She was right too. That's how she found her agent in New York.

*You mentioned New York several times. How did she end up in Mount Pleasant and not in New York?*

DONNA SANDERS: Mount Pleasant was temporary. Last summer she met a guy, Walter Carrey, who comes from there. They met at a bar in Salem. Walter was in the military—a country boy and a bit of a brawler. I guess she liked that about him and decided to join him there without giving it too much thought. I think she was under pressure because of her career.

*So it didn't work out?*

DONNA SANDERS: On the contrary, it worked out very well. She had just won her first major beauty contest—she'd been chosen as Miss New England. I think it stressed her out. My husband and I found out that she had started smoking pot. To relax, I guess. I suppose that leaving for Mount Pleasant was an opportunity to get away from Salem, to leave it all behind. To find herself. But it was only temporary. And when I spoke to her on the phone just last week, she told me she wanted to move to New York in the near future.

*Was it a normal conversation?*

DONNA SANDERS: Yes, well . . . in a sense.

*What do you mean,* in a sense? *Did she sound worried, mention any threats?*

DONNA SANDERS: No, nothing like that.

ROBBIE SANDERS: Sergeant, I should mention that ever since she left, our relationship with Alaska has not always been the best. When I found pot among her things, we had an argument. She took the opportunity to take off, cut the cord, so to speak. I guess it was something she needed to do.

DONNA SANDERS: We were close in spite of everything. I'd say that her moving away was good for all of us.

*When did you see her last?*

DONNA SANDERS: February. We went to visit her in Mount Pleasant.

*And how was your relationship with Walter Carrey?*

ROBBIE SANDERS: Cordial.

DONNA SANDERS: At first we didn't take to him. When Alaska moved to Mount Pleasant and started to work at a gas station, we felt he was controlling her. He was older, more mature, more experienced. But she seemed to be happy there.

*Apparently, things between Alaska and Walter weren't going all that well. In fact, the day before she was killed, she was getting ready to leave him. Did she mention that to you?*

DONNA SANDERS AND ROBBIE SANDERS: No.

*Do you have a recent photo of Alaska?*

DONNA SANDERS: Yes, of course. I brought one with me, just like you asked.

ROBBIE SANDERS: Why?

*We'd like to send it to the papers for distribution. We're looking for witnesses who might be able to help us sort things out.*
ROBBIE SANDERS: Do you have any leads?

*Not at the moment.*

# The Day After the Murder

*Sunday, April 4, 1999*

Once the interview with Alaska Sanders's parents was over, Gahalowood and Vance accompanied them to the entrance of police headquarters.

"We're staying at a hotel not far from here," Robbie Sanders informed them. "We don't feel much like returning home right now."

"Don't hesitate to call us. Really, for anything," Vance replied.

"You have our numbers and we're always available," Gahalowood insisted.

"We need answers," Donna Sanders said quietly, holding back her tears. "We need to know what happened. Who could have done this to our daughter?"

"We have fewer staff working on weekends, but the medical examiner has assured me that we'll have his report by tomorrow afternoon. We'll let you know as soon as we hear something. Promise."

"I guess it's better to be murdered on a weekday," Donna Sanders replied bitterly.

The young woman's parents left. As Gahalowood and Vance watched them go, they could tell from their bearing how they must be feeling. Gahalowood was holding the photo of Alaska, the one her mother had given him, along with a newspaper clipping from September. There she was, in a muslin dress, flanked by her parents. The headline read: "Alaska Sanders Elected Miss New England."

"What a shame," he said, looking at Alaska's smile. "I'll send the photo to the papers right away."

They walked up to the second floor, where the offices of the crime squad were located. There, a third agent, Nicholas Kazinsky, sent by Lansdane to assist them, was waiting. Another investigator was a welcome development, especially since Kazinsky was an expert in computers.

"You got a call from someone by the name of Lewis Jacob," Kazinsky announced, as his colleagues entered the room. "He'd like you to come round."

"What for?" Vance asked.

"He wants to show you something; he didn't say what. He just said that he'd be at the gas station all day."

"We'll take a ride over. About the gas station, did you manage to access the footage from the security cameras?"

Kazinsky smiled triumphantly. "Child's play. Take a look."

On his computer screen, Kazinsky had arranged, side by side, two windows corresponding to the two cameras at the gas station: one outside, which monitored the gas pumps, and one inside the store, which filmed customers at the register. Kazinsky started the video and fast-forwarded through the footage for Friday, April 2.

The first thing they saw was a family of raccoons making their way across the parking lot at six in the morning. Then, at seven, Lewis Jacob arrived at the station and opened the store. They could see him inside, preparing coffee. Over the next hour, he served a handful of customers. At eight, Alaska's blue convertible made its appearance in the parking lot. It was definitely Alaska who got out of the vehicle. She entered the store, greeted Lewis Jacob, and they chatted for a while. She then disappeared into the back room, probably to change, and returned wearing a polo shirt with the station's logo. She settled herself behind the counter. That began a day of apparently monotonous work without much of any note happening. Alaska divided her time between working the register for customers who bought gas and serving coffee from a small bar set up at the back of the store. Customers came and went; the exchanges were brief.

On two occasions, Alaska took a ten-minute break in the parking lot to drink some coffee. She typed on her cell phone. Around noon, she disappeared into the back room for thirty minutes, probably to eat lunch. She then returned to work. Nothing out of the ordinary. Then, at four forty-five, after a short conversation with Jacob, Alaska left the gas station and took off in her convertible. She returned a little before five thirty. She got out of her car holding a brown leather travel bag, which she took with her into the store. She left it in the back room and resumed working.

"That's exactly what Walter Carrey told us," Gahalowood said, looking at his notes. "He found her in the apartment at five fifteen, and she left with a brown leather bag a few minutes later."

The rest of the footage showed the last few hours of the day to be very like what had come before. Alaska behind the register, Alaska behind the counter, Alaska arranging the bags of potato chips on display. At seven twenty, Lewis Jacob disappeared into the back room. At seven thirty, he reappeared wearing a tie. He spoke for a short while with Alaska, arranged his tie while looking at his reflection in the window, and then left. The outside camera filmed him leaving at the wheel of his car. Night was about to fall. It grew dark and not much could be seen, except for the gas pumps, which were illuminated. At exactly eight p.m., Alaska disappeared into the back room, then reappeared in an entirely new outfit—wearing leather slacks, a stylish top, and low boots. She was dressed for an evening out.

"Stop!" Vance said to Kazinsky. "That's the way she was dressed when we found her."

A brief glance at the picture of the young woman's corpse on the board confirmed this.

"She's dressed for that 'romantic dinner' Lewis Jacob mentioned," Gahalowood said. "She was leaving."

"Who was she going to meet?" Kazinsky asked.

"That's the million-dollar question," Gahalowood replied.

The video resumed. Alaska reached for the light switch and the store went dark, save for the glow from the refrigerators. She stepped outside, carrying her large, leather bag, and locked the door. She slipped the store keys into the mailbox, got into her car, and drove off.

"Why'd she put the keys in the mailbox?" Kazinsky asked.

"Maybe that was the routine for closing up," Gahalowood reflected. "We'll check with Jacob when we head over."

"So she leaves the gas station and goes where?" Vance wondered aloud.

"It's a mystery," Gahalowood said. "The camera's field of view doesn't show us which way she was heading. Nicholas, were you able to reach anyone at the phone company?"

"Yeah, but unfortunately, Alaska had a prepaid cell phone. We contacted the phone company, but they were unable to trace her calls, so we have no record of who she spoke to."

"Shit," Vance grumbled. "Would've been too easy! So there's no way of knowing who she talked to before she died. But since her phone disappeared, we can assume she knew the killer and that they'd talked on the phone. He took her phone to prevent us from tracing the murder back to him."

"And was it the murderer who sent the threatening notes to Alaska?" Kazinsky asked.

"Probably," Gahalowood answered. "There was presumably some kind of logic in doing so."

"'I know what you did,'" Vance said, rereading the message displayed on the board. "What could she have done?"

Given their experience, the detectives didn't want to waste their time on conjecture. They had to begin with the most likely and most obvious possibilities, and for Gahalowood the most likely suspect at this stage of the investigation was the boyfriend.

"Walter Carrey suspected Alaska of cheating on him. He sent the messages to scare her. He refused to accept the fact that she was leaving him. He arranged to meet her on Grey Beach and he killed her. When he was done, he got rid of his bloodstained sweater and got in his car to leave, but, in his haste, he hit a tree."

"For your theory to work out," Vance remarked, "Carrey would have to drive a black car."

"We can check the police database," Kazinsky said. "Let's see if Walter Carrey has a car registered in his name."

Kazinsky typed on his computer's keyboard. After a few moments, he said, "Walter Carrey owns a black Ford Taurus."

"Bingo!" Vance exclaimed. "Why don't we go to Mount Pleasant to see if Carrey's car is missing a taillight?"

\*     \*     \*

"Intact," Kazinsky noted. The three detectives observed the black Ford Taurus parked in front of Carrey Hunting & Fishing. The two taillights were undamaged, and the body showed no traces of a collision.

"Is it the same car?" Gahalowood asked.

"Yeah, the same plate," Kazinsky assured him.

"There goes my theory," Gahalowood replied.

At that moment, Walter Carrey, who had just noticed the detectives in front of his apartment, called them from the window. "Hey—any news?"

"Can we come up?" Gahalowood asked.

"Sure."

Moments later, the investigators found themselves in Carrey's living room. His parents were also there, having returned suddenly from their vacation in Maine to be with their son. Pictures of Alaska were scattered about on a coffee table. Walter's mother, Sally Carrey, piled them up and placed them on the sideboard. "There's no point torturing yourself," she said to her son.

The man looked utterly defeated. "I feel empty," he confided to the policemen. "This is all surreal."

"I can imagine," Gahalowood said.

"Do you have any leads?"

"Not yet. But we were wondering about the reasons for your breakup. Yesterday, you told us you two weren't getting along so well. Alaska's employer, Lewis Jacob, seemed to notice it as well."

"Alaska had big dreams. She wanted to be an actress, make movies, become a star! Me, I'm fine where I am. Obviously, that created tension. And it wasn't always easy to find time for one another. On Saturday I was often busy in the store, and on Sunday she would just go off somewhere. She said she needed time for herself."

"Where'd she go?"

"I don't know—though the last two months she was helping Mr. Jacob at the gas station on Sunday because the other employee just quit overnight."

"We spoke with Alaska's parents. They couldn't understand why she decided to move to Mount Pleasant."

"I guess they mentioned New York."

"It came up."

"Alaska needed to put some distance between herself and her parents. That's why she left Salem."

"She would've put more distance between them by going to New York," Vance remarked.

"Not necessarily. In New York, her parents would've been in her hair the whole time. They were always on her case. Here, she was with me. She knew they wouldn't interfere."

"Do you think she was seeing someone else?" Gahalowood asked.

"Was she cheating on me? No! Well . . . I have no idea. You think she left because of another guy?"

"I thought so," Sally Carrey interjected. "I think she was having an affair with Eric Donovan. That's the first thing I said to Walter when he called me yesterday to tell me that Alaska had left him."

"Ma, stop! You don't know what you're saying. There's never been anything between Eric and Alaska."

"Well, I'm telling you I saw them."

"You didn't see anything."

"What did you see, Mrs. Carrey?" Gahalowood asked.

"Two weeks ago—Walt was away. He had left for a few days to attend a trade fair for fishing equipment in Quebec. I was in the store, and I saw Eric and Alaska on the sidewalk. They were arguing."

"What kind of argument?"

"The kind that couples have," Sally Carrey emphasized. "Alaska told Eric something like 'After what we went through . . .' and he said, 'Should we talk to Walter about it?' I saw them again the next day, still fighting. That's not nothing."

"Stop, Ma!" Walter insisted.

Vance steered the discussion back on course. "Walter, I know we already went through this yesterday, but can you tell us again about Friday night?"

"I closed the store at seven. By the time I'd cleaned up and checked the register, it was seven thirty; then I went upstairs. I felt lost, just lost. Disoriented. My parents called. I told them Alaska had left me."

"Walt was in such a state!" his mother interjected again, clearly needing to be heard. "I didn't want him to be alone. I told him to call a friend and go out."

"And that's what you did," Gahalowood said to Walter. "You went to watch the hockey game at the National Anthem. That's what you told us yesterday."

"Yes."

"Who was the friend?"

"Eric Donovan."

"The same person your mother believes Alaska was having an affair with?"

"There was never anything between them!" Walter shouted. "Eric is my best friend. I've known him forever. His parents own the grocery store down the street. Yesterday afternoon, between customers, I went to see him to tell him what had happened. He suggested I come watch the game that evening at the National Anthem, that it would help clear my head. And that's what I did. I went to the bar."

"How did you get there?"

"On foot. It's only five minutes from here."

"What time was it?"

"I left here around eight, maybe eight fifteen. I'm not sure. The game had already started."

"Was anyone else with you?"

"Eric's sister, Lauren. She goes to school in Durham, but she'd come back to Mount Pleasant for the weekend."

Gahalowood and Vance exchanged glances: Lauren Donovan was the jogger who had discovered the body.

"How late did you stay at the bar?"

"Until closing—it was after two. I had nothing better to do."

"And then?"

"I went home and went to bed right away. I was in a bad way. Yesterday morning, soon as I opened the store, all the customers were talking about a woman being found dead at Grey Beach."

"Did you think it was Alaska?"

"Not for a second. I thought she was in Massachusetts with her parents."

Walter couldn't hold back his tears any longer. Gahalowood put a hand on his shoulder. "I'm sorry to have to ask you this, Walter, but could you come down to headquarters tomorrow to make a statement? We need to have an official record."

"Okay. I'll be there first thing in the morning if it's alright with you."

Vance and Gahalowood wondered why Lauren Donovan hadn't told them she had spent the evening with the victim's boyfriend. As they were leaving Carrey's apartment, they decided to go and ask her.

The grocery store was closed on Sundays, so the investigators went to the home of Eric and Lauren's parents, Janet and Mark Donovan. They lived in a quaint clapboard house in a residential area of Mount Pleasant. The family was gathered for lunch, which the police interrupted. Yet, they were warmly received and had to insist that they didn't have time for the chili con carne Janet Donovan wanted to serve them.

"We won't keep you long," Vance promised. "We just have a few questions about Friday evening." Turning to Eric, he said, "Walter Carrey told us that you went to the National Anthem together to watch the hockey game."

"That's right," Eric replied. "My sister was there too."

Vance then turned to Lauren. "When we questioned you yesterday at the gas station, why didn't you mention you'd spent the evening with the victim's boyfriend?"

"I was in a state of shock, I guess. I could only think of the sight of that bear over her body. Peter Philipps, the policeman who killed the bear, told us what was going on that morning—he told us just about everything. He was nervous and kept wondering if he'd get in trouble for killing a bear. Then there was another call, and he told us that it was Alaska who had been found dead. Lewis Jacob, the gas station owner, collapsed. I just couldn't believe it. Like I said, I was in shock."

"Did you know the victim well?"

"Well? No. But Mount Pleasant is a small town and everyone knows everyone, more or less. I'm not here that often; I'm studying biology at the University of New Hampshire in Durham."

"How often do you get back to Mount Pleasant?"

"From time to time. A bit more now because Eric and I are training together for the Boston marathon in three weeks. I generally arrive on Friday and leave first thing on Monday. I have no classes that morning."

"Let's go back to Friday evening."

"I got here late. The trip from Durham took forever. I went directly to the National Anthem."

"What time did you get to the bar?"

"Eight thirty," Lauren replied with assurance.

"You seem pretty sure about that," Vance said to her. "You're certain about the time?"

"Yes, because I'm always late. I'd told Eric I'd be there at six thirty. When I walked in, I saw the clock on the wall, it's shaped like a beer bottle, and I said to myself, 'You're two hours late.'"

"Was Walter there?"

"No."

*     *     *

*Two days earlier, the evening of Friday, April 2, 1999*
It was eight thirty in the evening. The National Anthem was packed. One of the two giant screens was broadcasting the hockey game between the New Jersey Devils and the Tampa Bay Lightning. Sitting at the bar, Eric Donovan struggled to keep the two stools next to him free. Finally, his sister arrived, making her way through the crowd.

"Sorry I'm late," she said, giving Eric a quick peck on the cheek. "The traffic was insane."

She sat on one of the empty stools and ordered a beer.

"Who's this seat for?" Lauren asked, seeing Eric jealously safe-guarding the third stool.

"Walter. I don't know what he's up to. His girlfriend just left him. I told him to come down; I thought it would take his mind off things."

"So, it's over between him and Alaska?"

"Apparently. It was never going to work, anyway. She wanted to be some great actress and he sells fishing rods in Mount Pleasant."

There was a shout from the crowd. The Devils had just scored. Walter arrived at that very moment. He looked terrible. He briefly told them about Alaska, but when Lauren tried to ask him a question, he simply said, "Don't want to talk about it."

They ordered hamburgers, and Eric and Walter drank several beers. Lauren was more cautious. She and her brother planned to train for the marathon in the morning, and she wanted to be up to it.

76

When the game ended, and after a final beer, Eric and Lauren left the bar. It was eleven by then. They returned to their parents' home.

At six fifteen the next morning, Lauren didn't find Eric in the kitchen—he was still in bed with a hangover. She decided to go running anyway. She tied her sneakers and left.

*    *    *

"You know what happened next," Lauren said to the police.

"So, Friday night, you left the bar at eleven."

"Yes, eleven fifteen at the latest," Eric said. "We were back here by eleven thirty."

"And did Walter Carrey leave with you?"

"No. He stayed. He said he didn't feel like being home by himself."

Gahalowood studied Eric, a handsome man who had just turned twenty-nine, well built, with light red hair. "You live here, with your parents?" he asked.

"Yes, but it's temporary."

"Long-term temporary," Lauren teased.

Eric felt the need to justify himself. "I went to college in Massachusetts, then I found a job in Salem. I worked on developing a small chain of supermarkets. But I didn't get along with my boss, and he fired me last fall. So I returned to Mount Pleasant to work on my parents' store. I'd like to create a regional chain, high-quality merchandise. There's a gap in the market for it. Besides, my father isn't in the best shape. I'm happy to help out and make things a bit easier for him."

Eric's father, Mark, added, "I had a small health problem but I'm fine now. Having Eric around last fall was a big help. It would've been hard without him."

Gahalowood turned to Eric. "So you were living in Salem?"

"Yes, for almost five years."

"Like Alaska . . ."

"Yeah, that's where we met, last spring. We went to the same bars.

She was old enough to drink and always going out with the same group of girlfriends. Walter came to see me in Salem from time to time. One night they met and hit it off."

"Were you the one who introduced Walter to Alaska?"

"They introduced themselves, but they met through me, yeah."

"Was there anything between you and Alaska?"

Eric appeared to be very surprised by the question. "If you're implying that we had an affair, no, that didn't happen. There was absolutely nothing between us. She was just a nice girl, a bit out of the ordinary, and I liked her a lot. Why would you think there was something going on?"

"Sally Carrey has that impression," Gahalowood said.

"Sally? Why would she say that?"

"Something to do with your behavior. About two weeks ago, she saw you and Alaska arguing, twice."

Eric found the remark amusing. "I have no memory of any argument. Alaska is the way she is, you know. She says what she thinks . . . well, what she thought."

"You have a girlfriend?" Gahalowood asked.

"No. There was someone in Salem, but it ended last fall. Between that and getting fired, it was time to leave."

# The Day After the Murder

*Sunday, April 4, 1999*

The visit to the Donovans shed new light on the night of Friday, April 2: Walter Carrey claimed that he had stayed at the bar until closing, but the Donovans, having left earlier, couldn't confirm it.

Gahalowood, Vance, and Kazinsky decided to pay a visit to the National Anthem. It was the middle of lunchtime service and Steve Ryan, the owner, was busy preparing for the evening, which marked the beginning of the baseball season. The opening game was between the San Diego Padres, playing at home, and the Colorado Rockies.

"We won't take up much of your time," Vance assured him. "We just want to be certain a customer was here on Friday night."

"If you knew how many people were here last Friday night . . . But, sure, who?"

"Walter Carrey. Do you know him?"

"Walter? Of course I know him. Yeah, he was here Friday night. That, I do recall. He wasn't doing too well—Alaska had just left him. He wanted to talk, but I really didn't have time. Who would've thought they'd find her dead the next morning? Wait . . . you don't think Walter killed her, do you?"

"We're not accusing anyone at this point. We're simply conducting our investigation."

"Walter wouldn't hurt a fly. Well, a fly, yes, he loves fishing. But he's a softy. He's not the type of guy to kill his girlfriend. And he loved that girl."

"Walter stated he was here until closing."

"That's possible, but I couldn't say for sure. There were still so many customers around, my bouncers had to ask for police assistance to herd everyone out."

"Could you ask the staff who worked that Friday night if they saw Carrey in the bar at closing time?"

"No problem."

After the National Anthem, the detectives walked down Main Street to Carrey Hunting & Fishing. At that moment, a police car stopped next to them. Chief Mitchell was at the wheel. "Oh, it's you," he said as he stepped from the car. "We got a call that three suspicious characters were walking down Main Street. Since yesterday, everybody's been a little jumpy. Not too surprising though. Any news?"

"Not much," Vance replied. "We were just at the National Anthem. The owner says he had to call the cops Friday night to empty the bar at closing time."

"Yup. The place was a madhouse. Well, kind of. Ryan really asked us to stop by so that we wouldn't give him a fine for staying open past the legal closing time. He's a smart guy. He calls the cops and that gives him a few more minutes to take those final orders, which go straight into the register. What did you need Ryan for?"

"We're trying to determine if Walter Carrey was at the bar at closing time."

"You suspect him of killing Alaska?"

"We're trying to untangle this mess."

"You want my advice?" Mitchell said. "Your intuition is sound. Walter's a nice guy, but he can be aggressive and violent when he's been drinking. Go talk to his ex-girlfriend, Deborah Miles. She's still here. A few years ago, I got a call to go to her place, well, her parents' place, where she was living at the time."

"What happened between her and Carrey?" Gahalowood asked.

"She left him and he couldn't take it. He nearly beat her up. Not exactly irrelevant, especially when we know that Alaska broke up with him the day she died."

Gahalowood took down the name and address of Deborah Miles and then turned to Mitchell. "Tomorrow we'll send out a call for witnesses to all the regional papers. Maybe that will jog someone's memory. Let us know if you hear something."

"Sure thing. People talk, you know, but mostly to make themselves look interesting. Until now, the only real piece of information we got was from Cinzia Lockart at the bookstore."

"What did she see?"

"Early Saturday morning, around one forty-five, she noticed a blue car with Massachusetts plates, which took off at high speed near the Carrey store."

"A blue car like Alaska's?"

"Yes."

The bookstore was open on Sundays, and the detectives only had to cross the street to find Cinzia Lockart. The store was small but very well stocked. Behind the register was a wall of photos with pictures of literary celebrities who had stopped by to sign their books.

Cinzia Lockart explained to the detectives that she lived with her family in a building adjoining the bookstore. It was a former workshop with a good deal of character. You entered from a parallel street, but the living room looked out onto the town's main drag.

"I couldn't sleep Friday night. It's often like that. That's why I read so much. Whenever I have insomnia, I sit on the couch in the living room, make myself some herbal tea, and read. That night—it was around 1:40—I heard what sounded like breaking glass coming from the street. Obviously, that drew my attention. When I got to the window, I saw a car driving away at high speed. It was too far to read the numbers, but I could make out that it was a Massachusetts plate. The car was blue; I could see that much in the light from the streetlamps."

"And you say it was 1:40?"

"It was 1:39 exactly. I know because I immediately went to check the kitchen clock. Just in case."

"*Just in case* of what?"

"There was something a little suspicious about it, if you ask me. But when I told my husband, he said I was making a big deal out of nothing."

"Could you identify the make of the car?" Gahalowood asked.

"Unfortunately, no," she replied.

"Was it a convertible?"

"Impossible to say."


When they left the bookstore, Kazinsky asked, "A blue car with Massachusetts plates. Did Alaska come back to get her things?"

"That would make sense," Vance admitted. "According to Walter, he surprised her that day, at around five p.m., as she was gathering her belongings. Maybe, because she was interrupted, she returned later to pick up the rest."

"At one forty-five in the morning?" Gahalowood said doubtfully.

"I guess she figured Walter would be asleep by then. But he was at the National Anthem—or, at least, that's what he claims. Did she go up to the apartment? Or did she give up on the idea? In any event, she left in a hurry. A short while later, she was killed at Grey Beach. What was she doing by the lake at two in the morning?"

"What it does suggest," Gahalowood replied, "is that Alaska didn't leave the area that night. Did she go to her 'romantic dinner'? And who was her date, since we know it wasn't Walter Carrey? We should go round to the local restaurants with her picture. Maybe someone saw her."

"There are a lot of restaurants around here," Kazinsky noted.

"Not if we limit ourselves to the kinds of places where you'd want to have a romantic dinner. We should check with the tourist offices. Starting with the one in Mount Pleasant."

Vance, Gahalowood, and Kazinsky had arrived in Mount Pleasant in two cars so they could split up when necessary. Kazinsky took charge of the restaurants, while Gahalowood and Vance went to the gas station to pay a visit to Lewis Jacob, who had asked to see them, and then to Deborah Miles, Walter's ex.

When Lewis Jacob saw Gahalowood and Vance enter his store, he looked relieved. "Finally! I thought you'd never get here."

The reason he had asked them to stop by was in the back room. "I didn't touch anything," he informed them, as he led them through to his office, a small, narrow room at the back of which stood a large safe.

"Look what I found this morning," he said, pulling on the reinforced door.

He pointed to an article of clothing, a handwritten note, and a wad of cash. Gahalowood and Vance put on plastic gloves. Gahalowood grabbed the garment—Alaska's gas station polo shirt with her metal name badge pinned to the chest. "She must've left it Friday night when she closed the place," Jacob said. "I didn't notice it yesterday. With all that was going on, we were closed so I didn't open the safe. I hadn't even opened it when Lauren came running up to the store."

Vance read the note.

*Dear Mr. Jacob,*

*I didn't have the courage to tell you I was leaving in person. I'm not coming back. Thanks for everything you've done for me. I'll write to you, promise. I left my key to the store in the mailbox.*

*Affectionately,*

*Alaska*

*p.s.: Don't say anything to Walter, please.*
*p.p.s.: I'm sorry for all the trouble I've caused you.*

"On the security camera footage, you can see her put something in the mailbox," Gahalowood recalled.

Jacob confirmed that it was the key.

"So, she was planning to leave," Vance said. "What trouble was she referring to?"

Jacob shrugged. "Nothing I can recall. Look, she was a perfectionist. And perfectionists make a big deal out of everything. Alaska was always there when I needed her. When Samantha, my Sunday employee, quit about a month ago, Alaska worked extra shifts to help me out. From time to time, yes, there was a small problem with an order or the register, and she would call me, but she didn't like to bother me. She'd say, 'I'm supposed to be helping you, not giving you more work.' She was that kind of girl."

Gahalowood gathered the money and counted it. "Did Alaska put this money here?"

"Yes," Jacob replied. "I never leave money lying around like that; I put it all in the metal box. How much is there?"

"Four hundred dollars."

The attendant smiled. "When she worked all that overtime after Samantha left, she refused to be paid. I insisted, but she told me it was normal to help out. I ended up putting four hundred dollars in her bag. And here it is."

Talking about Alaska brought tears to his eyes. He was visibly upset. "Sorry. I didn't mean to make a scene, but it's just so hard accepting that she's gone."

"You don't have to apologize, Mr. Jacob," Vance said, trying to comfort him. "Did you have any idea she was planning to quit?"

"Not in the least. Sure, sometimes she would talk about New York and her dreams of becoming an actress. I didn't think she'd stay in Mount Pleasant all her life. Alaska was a girl who needed the bright lights of a big city. But why leave from one day to the next? It's almost like she was running away from something."

"On the video footage for Friday, Alaska leaves for about a half hour and comes back with a travel bag."

"She told me she had forgotten her things and asked to go back home for a bit. I agreed, obviously."

"Did she do that kind of thing often?"

"No, that was the first time. I didn't have any reason to refuse her. She was a model employee—motivated, available, a hard worker, always smiling, never sick, never complained. Nothing. Simply wonderful."

"And when you saw her return with the bag, did you ask her anything?"

"To tell the truth, I didn't really pay much attention. I don't spy on my employees, you know. She had forgotten her things, she returned with a bag, it all made sense."

"Yesterday," Gahalowood resumed, "you told us that Alaska and Walter were having problems."

"Yes, that's true. To be honest, I don't think she ever really loved the guy. I always wondered what she was doing with him."

"Did you know that while she was away from work on Friday, she told Walter she was going to leave him?"

"I found out yesterday. Everyone in town is talking about it."

Vance took over. "You mentioned a romantic dinner. Alaska had a date with someone and we now know it wasn't Walter. Do you have any idea who it could've been?"

"Nope. I would've mentioned it already if I did."

"Alaska never spoke to you about a lover?"

"Never."

"In the note she left you, she asks you not to say anything to Walter. Any idea why?"

"Because she didn't want to hurt him, I guess. And perhaps . . ." Jacob trailed off. He looked suddenly pensive.

"What is it, Mr. Jacob?" Gahalowood asked.

"Did you hear anything about Deborah Miles?"

"Funny you should mention it. Chief Mitchell just spoke to us about her; he suggested we pay her a visit."

"He's not wrong."

*

Deborah Miles was not home. That Sunday, she was working at the Wolfeboro supermarket, open seven days a week, twenty-three hours a day. Gahalowood and Vance went to find her. She was on a break and suggested they step out into the parking lot for some privacy. Deborah was a young woman of about thirty, but looked much older.

"Who told you about Walter and me?" she asked.

"Chief Mitchell of the Mount Pleasant police," Gahalowood replied. "Sounds like it didn't end very well."

"We went out together—that was about five years ago. He had just returned to Mount Pleasant."

"Where was he before that?"

"The service."

"So he was a soldier."

"Yes. After high school he joined the Marines. He was in the Gulf War and Somalia. After that, he decided to return to civilian life; I think he wanted to take over his parents' store. Hunting and fishing was his thing. Walter and I knew each other back in high school. I was happy to reconnect. We clicked and we started dating. He was nice, at first."

"When was that?"

"Autumn of '94. It didn't last long."

"What happened?"

"I really liked him. Deep down he's a good guy. But I quickly saw that our relationship wasn't going anywhere. I was still young, but I wanted to get married and have kids. And I knew I could never make a life with Walter."

"Why?"

"I wanted to leave Mount Pleasant, to see other things. I don't know how, or why, but five years later I'm still here, married to a local guy, with two children who'll no doubt spend their lives here like me."

"It's a pretty little town," Vance noted.

"Pretty little towns are often filled with narrow-minded people. Sooner or later, you have to know it's time to leave."

"So you had plans to leave Mount Pleasant. Is that what led to your breakup with Walter?"

"No. Although like I told you, I couldn't see myself spending my life with him, so after a few months, I decided to break up with him. It was shortly before Christmas. He took it badly. It was strange, because, at first, he didn't really react. We had gone to get a coffee at the Season. I told him I wanted us to split up, and all he said was 'Okay.' He looked like he didn't care at all. I returned home, very relieved that he'd taken it so well. That evening, my parents weren't home. I was watching television in the living room when I heard someone knocking on the door."

*    *    *

*Mount Pleasant*
*December 1994*
Deborah Miles wondered who was pounding on the door rather than using the bell. She wasn't worried though. Mount Pleasant was a peaceful town. She opened the door and saw Walter. He looked frozen. The Mileses' house was off the beaten path. It was a dark winter's evening, and snow covered the ground.

"Walter, what are you doing here?"

He glowered at her. He looked furious. "There's someone else, isn't there?" he said, looking disgusted. "You've been sleeping with some other guy. You've been cheating on me."

"What are you talking about, Walter? I didn't cheat on you."

"Don't lie to me, you bitch!"

"Stop it, Walter, you're frightening me. What's gotten into you?"

But Walter wouldn't let up. "You're waiting for him, aren't you?"

"I'm not waiting for anyone."

"That's why you're all dolled up, isn't it?"

Deborah had never seen Walter in such a state. She needed to calm things down and persuade him to leave. "Walter, I was watching TV, that's all. I swear. You should go home."

"You're a whore, Deborah!"

She was starting to feel afraid now. She had to get rid of him. She would have shut the door in his face, but he had wedged himself into the opening. She decided to play her last card. "Walter, you should go home. My parents are here and you know my father. He's not going to be happy about this."

He sneered, "Your parents aren't home. They left a half hour ago."

"Have you been spying on me?" she asked, genuinely frightened now.

"I was waiting to see if your Prince Charming would show up, but it must be too cold. Let me in, we need to talk."

Desperate now, Deborah pushed Walter away hard. Surprised, he fell back into the snow. She managed to shut and lock the door before he could get up. When he did, he threw himself against the door as hard as he could. "Open up!" he screamed. "Open up, you bitch!" Deborah had already gone upstairs and locked herself in her parents' bedroom. Suddenly, she heard a window breaking. She grabbed the phone and dialed 911.

*     *     *

"Walter was arrested as he was leaving our property," Deborah told the police. "He'd been drinking—a lot."

"Did you file charges?"

"No. He paid for the repairs to the window and wrote a letter, apologizing to my parents and me. My dad, who had been in Vietnam, always had a soft spot for veterans. Walter's real punishment was that none of the girls in the area wanted anything to do with him after that. He was done. That's why he went to Salem so often to see his friend Eric. He was hoping to meet someone who didn't know about his past. When he came back with that pretty blond, Alaska, everybody wondered what the poor girl was going to do in this hole. I regret not bringing charges against him. I should have—not for me but for the others. Maybe I could have prevented all this."

"Prevented all what?"

"His killing Alaska."

# 4

## *Paradise Lost*

*April 17, 2010*

My romantic getaway on the island paradise in the Bahamas didn't go at all as I had planned. Problems began when we were supposed to leave—Raegan didn't show up at the Montreal airport.

I had been waiting a long time at the Air Canada check-in counter. I tried to call her, but her phone was turned off. Finally, she sent me a text message:

—Sorry. I won't be coming. Forgive me.

I tried calling her again, but there was still no reply. Obviously, she had only turned it on to send me those few terse words. Our last exchange had been the night before last, also by text. When I asked how she was doing, she told me her flight from Chicago to Montreal had been delayed and she was packing her bags.

But in reality, she had never intended to go with me to the Bahamas.

Only later did I receive an explanation in a handwritten letter left at the reception desk of the Ritz-Carlton, which told me that Raegan was married and had two children. I was merely an extramarital fling following a wild layover in New York with her girlfriends. For the two times she had stayed with me, she used the excuse of a sick grandmother in the Ontario countryside. She hadn't known how to tell me. She'd let herself get carried away before realizing that she wasn't going to turn her life upside down for a brief infatuation.

At the time, in the Montreal airport lobby, I simply stared dumbly at the screen of my phone until an airline employee shook me from my stupor. "Sir, we're closing check-ins for this flight . . . What do you want to do?"

I decided to go anyway. Maybe it was an attempt to escape. I found myself alone on a flight to Nassau. To celebrate my reunion with my dear friend Solitude, I chugged a bottle of champagne followed by several of the tiny whiskey miniatures to which commercial airlines have condemned us.

Once in the Bahamas, I boarded a small, rickety old plane. After twenty minutes in the air, we arrived at a diminutive island floating in a turquoise sea. I had arrived at Harbour Island Resort. This small paradise would be my new hell. Try to imagine a luxury hotel nestled in the midst of tropical vegetation. The main building was surrounded by a park, more like a botanical garden, where small ponds covered with water lilies served as a kingdom for multicolored fish and turtles. The rooms were small bungalows, isolated from one another and only a few feet from the water, providing their occupants with the illusion of absolute privacy.

The clientele appreciated the high-end service provided by the staff but not as much as the hotel's extreme discretion—because no-one came to Harbour Island Resort alone. I was surrounded by twosomes: lovers, adulterers, purring older couples, newlyweds kissing in the restaurant who tested the patience of their servers as they waited for them to untangle their tongues so they could articulate their order. I even caught sight of a threesome, secure in their nonconformity. And in the midst of all that, I ate solo. I must have been the first moron in the history of the hotel to show up alone.

I could have packed my bags then and there and returned to New York, yet I was weak enough to think that the palm trees and the sea would do me good. But whether you face heartbreak on your couch or on a beach chair, the result is exactly the same: depression. The boredom of an island vacation didn't help matters. On the beach all I could do was think about Raegan. My head was swarming with images. I needed company, and so I went in search of a sympathetic ear. I ended up at the hotel bar. But the bartender didn't have time, while his colleague avoided me, assuming I wanted to flirt with her. Seated at the bar in the company of my beer, I imagined Harry Quebert sitting by my side wearing a flowered shirt. He would have tapped me on the shoulder and tutted, "Marcus . . . Marcus . . . Marcus," which would have been the preamble to a little life lesson whose secret he possessed and which I desperately needed at that moment. What would he have said? Something like, "Marcus, what are you doing sitting at this bar sulking? Just because you're alone on an island doesn't mean you can't be with someone. Do you know that little device in your pocket called a phone? You can use it to call people far away from you. Friends, for example. A friend, Marcus, someone you can talk to who isn't your shrink or your mother. Leave the poor bartender alone, will you, and call a friend. It'll do you good."

There was only one person I felt like opening up to, and that was Sergeant Perry Gahalowood. But until that point, something had held me back. I think I felt ashamed of being dumped. But encouraged by the phantom Harry's advice, I decided to call him anyway.

"Writer!" he answered, with an unusually lively inflection.

I should have realized that something was up. Gahalowood was never jovial, especially with me. That was part of his charm. If I happened to call him twice in the same week, he'd say, "There must be some emergency if you're calling me again." That day, I should have understood that his unusual demeanor betrayed a need to unburden himself. But I didn't. I was too wrapped up in my own pathetic story.

"Hello, Sarge, how are you?"

"I should ask you that question, Writer. How are things in the Bahamas? Let me dream a little: it's raining cats and dogs here, and it's cold."

I considered the idyllic setting in which I happened to find myself and suddenly felt uncomfortable complaining. I didn't dare tell him what had happened with Raegan. "Everything's going well," I lied. "Tropical heat, gorgeous location. Who could ask for more? I'm at the hotel bar sipping a beer. I thought about you and felt like giving you a call."

There was a strange silence on the other end of the line. Then, in a halting voice, Gahalowood said, "You know, when you came over the other night for my daughter's birthday . . ."

He hesitated. I had the feeling he wanted to open up to me, but he caught himself and merely said, "I was glad you came."

"Everything okay, Sergeant?"

"Everything's fine."

We hung up. The call had been a missed connection from a thousand miles away. We needed each other, but we were incapable of acknowledging it.

I didn't know it at the time, but Gahalowood had picked up from his car. He was parked on a street in downtown Concord, where—through the glass front of a restaurant—he was watching his wife having dinner with another man. She had lied to him yet again about staying late at the office. Gahalowood had suspected something like this for weeks, and now he had proof. Helen was cheating on him.

*     *     *

The days passed and my stay at Harbour Island Resort came to an end. I spent the last evening in my bungalow. Gathering my belongings, I discovered a notebook at the bottom of my bag that I had long forgotten about. Flipping through it, I found, stuck in the leather binding, a twenty-year-old photo. I was with my family in Baltimore: my uncle Saul (my father's brother), my aunt Anita, and my cousins Woody and Hillel.

I smiled at the faces on the glossy paper. I had loved them all so much. I stared at the picture for a long time, thinking about what had happened to them. Later that night I went to the beach. On the sand, I could make out crabs scuttling between the trees and the ocean, and in the distance, a series of bright points on the horizon. It must have been

Florida, which, although quite near, was still too far. Yet, it made me happy to think Miami was out there, a place that had held many family memories. Uncle Saul was still living there, in his little house in Coconut Grove, surrounded by mango trees. I used to go there often, but ever since the publication of *The Truth About the Harry Quebert Affair* and the film shoot, I hadn't been able to find the time. I wanted to hear his voice again, and so I called him. He had a good voice.

"Uncle Saul. It's been a while."

"I know—time flies."

"You didn't come out to the set."

"It's better this way. Thanks again for the plane tickets; I hope you're not angry with me."

"I understand. Uncle Saul, I'd like to stop by, pay a visit."

"Of course. When?"

"Tomorrow?"

"Tomorrow . . . sure, if you like," he said, somewhat surprised. "That would be wonderful."

My uncle and his family had meant a great deal to me. We called them the Baltimore Goldmans, the ones who had made it, unlike my parents and myself, the Montclair Goldmans. This book is not about the Baltimore Goldmans, but I have to mention them here because I now understand that it was on Harbour Island that I first had the idea of writing about them. The book appeared two years later. It was called *The Baltimore Boys*.

# Excerpt from the Police Report
## Interview with Walter Carrey

*[Recorded at the state police crime squad headquarters on Monday, April 5, 1999.]*

*Walter, does the name Deborah Miles mean anything to you?*
Yes, of course. We went out together five years ago. You already know that since you're asking about her. I guess you know about my little tantrum as well.

*We do. Can you talk about that night in December when you tried to break into her house?*
I wasn't trying to break in, I wanted to talk to her. She shut the door in my face. That set me off and I threw a rock through the window. It was stupid of me. I'm not proud of what I did. Obviously, I'd had too much to drink, but that's no excuse either. But I had no intention of hurting her or breaking into the house. If she had asked me to leave, I would've left at once. The whole thing just made me look ridiculous. Luckily, my friend Eric was around. I was able to spend a few weekends with him in Salem and clear the air.

*You seem to be very close to Eric Donovan.*
He's a childhood friend. We grew up together.

*And it's through him that you met Alaska, is that right?*
That's right. Alaska was part of a group of girls we would hang out with

in Salem. Eric went out with one of them. He was very attached to her. She acted like a bitch though and dumped him. It broke his heart, poor guy. That was one of the reasons why he came back to Mount Pleasant.

*Yes, he told us about it. So, if I'm not mistaken, he returned to Mount Pleasant before Alaska joined you here.*
Yeah. I don't have the exact dates in my head, but Alaska came to live with me here a few weeks later.

*Why did Alaska leave Salem?*
We already talked about this before . . . She wanted a change of scenery.

*I'm wondering if she might have wanted to join Eric?*
Stop with that! There was nothing between Alaska and Eric. You shouldn't listen to my mother, and I should know.

*Tell us how you first met Alaska.*
The first time I saw her was in the spring of 1998, at the Blue Lagoon, a bar in Salem. I didn't know what hit me. I couldn't take my eyes off her.

*Were your feelings reciprocated?*
She let me stew awhile. I could see she liked me, but she played hard to get. Which I didn't really mind anyway. I remember the night she finally kissed me. She was the one who initiated it. We were outside. She grabbed me by my jacket collar and pressed her lips to mine. Damn it . . . I can't believe she's dead.

*You want to take a break?*
No. I'm okay. Well, not really, but I don't need a break.

*Did Alaska have any reason to feel threatened?*
No.

*Yet she was getting threatening messages.*
You were the ones who told me that.

*She never talked to you about it?*
Never.

*Did you notice any recent changes in her behavior?*
I told you, we had our ups and downs. Sometimes she was in a bad mood, pissed with me . . .

*I was thinking more about nervousness, anxiety. Did it seem like she was acting strange to you?*
No.

*Walter, it appears that on the night of her murder, Alaska returned to your apartment. Probably right before she went to Grey Beach.*
What are you talking about?

*A witness claims to have seen her car at 1:40 a.m. Could she have come back to get her things?*
I have no idea.

*Where were you at 1:40 that morning?*
At the National Anthem, like I already told you.

*The problem is that nobody recalls you being at the bar at closing time.*
That's not surprising, the place was packed. And how would I know that if I hadn't been there? The crowd didn't want to leave, so the police showed up.

*With your permission, we'd like to take a DNA sample.*
Sure. Go ahead.

# Two Days After the Murder

*Monday, April 5, 1999*

The DNA sample was taken in the interview room. It only took a moment, just long enough for a technician from forensics to swab the inside of Walter Carrey's mouth. Once concluded, Walter put on his jacket and grabbed the paper he had brought with him. That morning, Alaska was headline news in all the New Hampshire dailies. "She always dreamed of making the front page . . ." he said as he left.

The young woman's smiling face was now in everyone's hands, in kitchens, coffee shops, waiting rooms, and on buses. Her name was on everyone's lips. And all the articles concluded with the same appeal to readers: "If you saw Ms. Sanders on Friday evening, April 2, or have any information about her, please contact the police at once."

The investigators were hoping that someone would come forward to help move the case along. The day before, Kazinsky had visited all the restaurants in the area, but without success. No-one had seen Alaska. The police were hoping that distributing her photo across the region would help jog someone's memory. And that's what happened. The manager of a supermarket in Conway, a town twenty minutes to the north of Mount Pleasant, claimed to have seen Alaska arguing with a man. His testimony sounded convincing; Vance and Gahalowood decided to drive there to question him. The supermarket was situated in a sprawling shopping center, with various stores grouped around a single parking lot.

"I don't recall the exact date," the manager told them. "It must've been two weeks ago. I hope you don't think I'm a creep, but I won't lie, I noticed her because she was a knockout. Don't get the wrong idea, I have a family of my own and a daughter about her age. Just . . . there was something about the way she looked. I got the impression everyone was staring at her. Then, a little while after she left, someone told me there was an argument out front. I went to see what was going on. She was there, in tears, with some tall guy who was saying something like, 'You can't do this to me.' I asked her if she was alright, but he answered for her and told me to stay out of it. So, I went inside to call the police. When I came back out, they were in the parking lot. She was yelling at him, 'I want to leave!' The guy got into a car and she climbed into the passenger seat. It was a strange scene. I wondered if she got in the car willingly. And then the police arrived."

"And . . . ?"

"Just a quick word. The cop let them go right after that, said it was nothing. But I saw it, and it wasn't nothing."

Gahalowood looked up and saw the cameras trained on the supermarket entrance. "Can we see the footage from that day?"

"Unfortunately, the tapes are recorded over every forty-eight hours."

Was it definitely Alaska in the supermarket parking lot? And who was the man she was arguing with? At the Conway police station, with the help of the precinct call center, Gahalowood and Vance were able to find a record of the incident, which happened on March 22. The officer who had responded had only a vague recollection of events.

"Well, the fact I can barely remember it means it can't have been very important. This kind of thing happens every day. Since we spend our time telling people that it's better to call us too often than too late, we get calls for just about anything."

Gahalowood showed him Alaska's picture again. "Take another look. Are you sure you don't recognize her? She was arguing with a man in the supermarket parking lot."

The officer sat down behind a computer screen. As he typed on the keyboard, he asked, "Did the call center send you the report?"

"What report?" Vance asked.

"Every 911 gets an incident report, even if it's only a couple of lines we enter directly into the computer terminal in our patrol vehicle."

"And can you access it?" Gahalowood asked.

The officer clicked the mouse a few times and then went to the printer to grab the sheet of paper it had just spat out. "Here it is," he said, as he scanned the page. "An argument in the parking lot. Now it comes back to me. A young guy at the wheel, a girl in the passenger seat. Her eyes were puffy. She'd been crying. I questioned them. The girl said they'd been arguing but that everything was alright. Now I remember. She said, 'Don't you ever argue with your wife, officer?' She tried to joke about it, saying, 'If you can't argue in public anymore without the police showing up . . .' It was clearly a false alarm. I took a look at the guy's driver's license and it was valid. And I see from the report that I even went so far as to check the vehicle in the database to make sure it wasn't stolen and it had insurance."

"Can I have a look?" Gahalowood asked.

"Of course."

**Monday, March 22, 1999—14:25 p.m.**
**Reason for call:** Public disturbance.
**Note:** Couple in a car, no visible signs of violence. No intervention necessary. Action: Checked the driver's license and registration. Black Ford Taurus, registered in New Hampshire, No. SDX8965. Insurance valid. Not indicated as stolen. End of intervention at 14:33 p.m.

His eyes riveted to the paper, Gahalowood asked Vance, "You still have the plate number for Walter Carrey's car?"

Vance looked at his notes. "New Hampshire SDX8965."

"So, she was with Carrey."

\*       \*       \*

"Carrey and Alaska Sanders having an argument when they went shopping isn't much to go on," Vance reflected as they were leaving the police station.

"At least we know the breakup on April second wasn't unexpected, contrary to what he told us. He's playing dumb: nobody calls the cops for an innocent argument. At that point you're pretty much on the brink, right?"

"Yeah. I get the impression that he's been lying to us from the start."

In Conway, Gahalowood and Vance would also discover important information about the forest path where the debris from the taillight and the traces of paint were found. Conway happened to be the location of the regional office of the US Forest Service, which was responsible for the management of White Mountain National Forest, where Alaska's body had been found.

Kazinsky, who had managed to make some headway in the face of federal government bureaucracy, explained the situation to them over the phone. "To put it simply," he said, "the forest is run from Washington."

"Practical," Vance remarked, ironically.

"Actually, yes, because it's the local Forest Service offices that make the decisions. The guy in charge of the Conway office is waiting for you; I just had him on the line. He's very familiar with that road; he said he's been complaining about it for years. Calls it the 'asshole's highway.'"

Those words were verbatim from the head of the Conway office. He opened a map and pointed out the road to Gahalowood and Vance. It broke off from Route 21 at Mount Pleasant, then cut through the forest for a distance of about eight miles before joining Route 16.

The asshole's highway, he explained, was created after the big fires in Yellowstone in 1988. The Forest Service felt it had to provide rapid access to the interior of the national forests so that responders could quickly get around a fire. The road allowed forest rangers to trim the undergrowth, which is generally left to grow wild because it's so hard to get to. It was a good idea, but the road, which was intended for the use of the fire department and the Forest Service, began to be used by everyone.

"It just doesn't stop: cars, quads, motorcycles—you name it. Some guys even drag their boats to Lake Skotam along it! That's how that abandoned trailer wound up there. My team complains about it all the time. What am I supposed to do? I notified the mayor of Mount Pleasant, who told me that it's not his problem since it's a national forest and under federal jurisdiction. Now, do you think Washington gives a damn about some trailer rotting by the shore of a lake in New Hampshire? I wanted to put a gate at each entrance but that was rejected because, if there ever was a fire, the fire brigade might have trouble getting in if they couldn't find someone with the key. The only thing I can do is take down the names of the offenders. We record the plate number, write a brief statement, and enter it into the system with a detailed report. After that, Washington takes care of it and sends them a ticket. You see the problem? Besides, my guys are forest rangers, not traffic cops!"

"So do you have a file with all those reports?"

"Yes."

A few minutes later, Gahalowood and Vance were seated at a computer screen. Before them was a list of the statements prepared over the previous few weeks by the forest rangers. There were very few. This allowed them to quickly pick out a vehicle that had been written up on Saturday, March 20. A car they were beginning to know well: a black Ford Taurus with New Hampshire plate number SDX8965. Walter Carrey's car. A note read: "M1, vehicle parked without occupant."

"M1?" Gahalowood asked the regional manager. "What does that mean?"

"That means the car was found on the first mile of the road. That helps us identify the location in case of any disputes—once Washington sends the ticket, the driver can challenge it and then we have to resolve it. We have to provide these 'updates.' It's a pain in the ass, this stuff."

"Which is the first mile?" Vance asked him. The manager returned to his map and pointed to a discrete line. "It's around here—the same stretch where the abandoned trailer was left."

The file showed that a second vehicle had been recorded on March 20, also on M1: a black Pontiac Sunrunner. Vance called Kazinsky and asked him to enter the plate number into the national registration database.

"Well, damn!" Kazinsky remarked when he read the owner's name on his screen. "It's Eric Donovan's car."

Gahalowood and Vance left at once for Mount Pleasant to question Eric Donovan about his car. He was at the checkout in the grocery store. He took the detectives to the back room so they could talk in peace.

"What's going on?" he asked, visibly uneasy.

"You drive a Pontiac Sunrunner, right?" Gahalowood asked.

"Yeah, why?"

"You were identified as taking the forest road near Grey Beach, right?"

"Yeah, I was written up by those idiot rangers. We've been using that road for ten years to go fishing, and from one day to the next they started adding restrictions. What's the problem?"

"What were you doing there on that day?"

Eric seemed surprised by the question. "Walter and I were going to Trout Paradise. It's a well-known fishing spot. When we were kids, we'd go by bike or on foot. Now that they've torn up the forest with that useless road, why shouldn't we take advantage of it? We can park right by the lake with our equipment. They're not going to take that away from us."

"So you're both familiar with that part of the forest?"

"Everyone knows the area around Grey Beach. It's a popular spot."

"Eric," Vance asked, "did you have an accident with your car recently?"

"No, why? Wait, is this about the debris from the taillight you found in the forest?"

"How did you know about that?" Gahalowood asked.

"How do you think? The local cops talk. And everyone in town's been talking about it. You don't think I had anything to do with Alaska's death, do you?"

"Mind if we take a look at your car?"

Though surprised by the request, he led the police to his black Sunrunner, parked in the store's parking lot. It was intact.

Gahalowood and Vance were about to leave when they received a call from Kazinsky: "We got the preliminary findings from the medical examiner and the forensics team. Alaska didn't die from the blow to the head."

*　　*　　*

At state police headquarters, Gahalowood, Vance, and Kazinsky listened closely as the medical examiner presented the conclusions of the autopsy report: "Alaska Sanders died from strangulation. Probably with someone's bare hands, to judge by the bruises on her neck."

"Strangled?" Vance repeated, surprised. "I thought she was struck on the head."

"She was," the examiner replied, "but that wasn't the cause of death." He laid out some photographs. "You can clearly see that there's a cranial trauma near the occipital bone. But it wasn't fatal."

"So she was struck on the head and then strangled?" Gahalowood said.

"Exactly."

"What was she struck with?"

"Judging by the wound, the blow was very violent; clearly there was a great deal of force behind it. A great deal of inertial force, which means that the murderer struck her with a heavy object, which acted like an extension of his arm. An iron bar, for example."

"Or a heavy club?" Vance asked.

"No, or I would have found traces of wood in the wound. I'd say it was an iron bar or a similar object."

"Are we certain she died on the beach?" Gahalowood asked.

"Yes, the body wasn't moved. We found traces of blood at the location, which shows that she was struck on the beach. But we also found traces of larvae in her nostrils and in her ears, from flies that are common to the area around Lake Skotam. And they would've laid their eggs only after she was dead. Thanks to that, I can confirm that the murder took place between one and two in the morning. Toxicology was normal. She wasn't drugged, but there were traces of alcohol."

"Was she raped?" Vance asked.

"No, no sign of rape or any sexual activity."

After the medical examiner, they heard from Keith Benton, head of the forensics team. He began by presenting them with a photo of the gray pullover with the letters *MU* on it. "The sweater found in the trailer is stained with Alaska Sanders's blood," he told them. "We found traces of two other DNA profiles in addition to hers."

"Are you saying there could have been two murderers?" Gahalowood asked.

"It's a possibility."

"I assume those DNA samples don't match anything in the database."

"That's correct, Sergeant. They're unknown. But their sequences contain X and Y chromosomes, which means they're male. The sweater is a men's size XL."

"So, it could have been worn by the murderer or one of the murderers?"

"Very possible," Benton confirmed. "The medical examiner tells us that the victim was struck and then strangled. It's likely that when she was strangled, the murderer was stained by her blood."

"Any idea what *MU* might refer to?" Vance asked.

"None. To be honest, we focused on the analyses we had to perform."

"We took a DNA sample this morning from a male by the name of Walter Carrey," Gahalowood said. "Could you compare it to those you took from the sweater and see if it's a match?"

"Of course. I'll try to have it for you by the end of the day. Tomorrow morning at the latest."

Benton continued with a photograph of Alaska's blue convertible, which had been found in the Grey Beach parking lot. "In the car there was no DNA but the victim's. As you know, we found her handbag along with a travel bag containing personal effects that we've listed here: clothing and toiletries. Enough for a few days. Unfortunately, there's not much there to go on. However, those threatening notes did give us something."

Benton then presented the analysis of the messages found in Alaska's pocket and those found in her home. "They're all very similar. The paper used is the same in each case. The kind you can buy in any supermarket. No DNA was found, but there were fingerprints, all of which match those of the victim. I can state with confidence that all three notes were printed from the same printer. They all have the same slight print defect, almost invisible to the naked eye. It indicates that the printer had a faulty print head."

"If I understand you correctly," Gahalowood said, "we should be able to identify the printer used for those messages?"

"If I had the machine here, I could determine if it was used to print them, yes. Find me a suspect, and his printer will tell me if he's your man."

"What about the debris from the taillight?" Vance asked.

An amused smile flickered across Benton's lips. "Gentlemen, I had some of my team working over the weekend to get you these results. I know time is running short for you, but analyzing the debris from the car could take months. We're talking about identifying a car model from a shard of glass."

"And what if we gave you the model and all you had to do was tell us if the broken light matches that type of car? Would that make your job easier?"

"Much easier. The state police have compiled a shared database cataloguing paint samples and sealed beam lights. If the car you have in mind is a recent model, it could be no more than a few hours' work."

"We'd like to know if it's either a black Ford Taurus or a black Pontiac Sunrunner," Gahalowood specified.

Benton wrote down the information and looked at his watch. "Give me until tomorrow morning and I'll come back to you on Walter Carrey's DNA sample and the car model."

That evening, at Helen's request, Vance and Kazinsky went over to Gahalowood's home for dinner. It was a moment of joyful camaraderie. For the duration of the meal, the three detectives were able to forget about the case. Helen had prepared a pot roast. Vance, taking his third helping, pretended to bemoan the trouble she had gone to. "Helen, you promised you would order pizza!"

"I lied so that you'd show up. I'm pregnant, Matt, not an invalid."

"Looks like it's going to pop out any minute now," Vance observed.

"Take it from me, Matt," Gahalowood advised, "don't argue with a pregnant woman."

"In any case," Kazinsky interjected, "I like the plaque outside: *Joie de Vivre*. That sums up your house in every way—warm and welcoming. I should bring my wife over to take lessons. We argue all the time."

"Perry and I argue too," Helen remarked.

"Well, now I know how you make up," Vance joked, pointing to her round belly.

Everyone laughed. "Helen is more than a match for me," Gahalowood added.

"Maybe," Vance replied. "I never got married, never had kids, and I don't regret it. Well, except when I see the two of you together."

The atmosphere remained relaxed throughout dessert. Gahalowood offered the others a beer. Kazinsky accepted, but Vance remained silent, staring into space. He looked troubled.

"What's up, Matt?" Gahalowood asked him.

"I've been thinking about the case." The men's faces darkened. Now it was back to business.

"Cops will always be cops" Helen sighed. "I'll leave you men alone.

106

I don't want to hear any more about that poor girl." She kissed her husband and went upstairs.

"What's up?" Gahalowood asked.

"I've been thinking about what the medical examiner said: Alaska was struck first and then strangled."

"And . . . ?"

"And I'm wondering why the murderer would do that."

"What do you mean, exactly?" Gahalowood asked him.

"He struck Alaska violently with some hard object. In fact, he hit her so hard that he fractured the back of her skull. He wanted to kill her. But she survived. And he knew it. He had to finish her off, so he strangled her. Why strangle her rather than hit her again? Why not keep going? Why complicate matters by strangling Alaska rather than finishing her off the way he started?"

"Whenever you ask those kinds of questions," Gahalowood observed, "it's because you already have the answer."

Vance nodded.

*　　*　　*

*Saturday, April 3, 1999, between one and two in the morning*
*(according to Sergeant Matt Vance's hypothesis)*
The sand at Grey Beach was bathed in moonlight, which glittered off the surface of Lake Skotam. Alaska, alone on the shore, didn't hear her murderer approach. The lapping water, the croaking frogs, and the noises of the night covered his footsteps along the rocky shore.

When the heavy object struck her skull, the only sound was the dull crack of bone. She didn't even cry out. There was a muffled noise and then the thud of her body as it hit the ground. It all happened very quickly. The murderer looked at the body and then, with all his strength, hurled the iron bar far into the lake. It was too dark for him to see it fall, but he heard it cleave the surface of the water. It was all over. It was time to go.

But as he stepped away from the body, he heard a moan. He turned and saw that Alaska was trying to move. He was terrified. A groan escaped her lips. The murderer shivered with disgust and then panic. Surely she would die from her wound, but how could he be certain? Besides, now she had seen him. Her eyes were open, staring up at him. He had to finish what he had started.

He at once regretted having thrown away the metal bar. He looked around, but there was nothing heavy enough to use as a bludgeon. He looked for a rock, but the stones along the shore were little more than pebbles. He had no choice but to strangle her. He got behind Alaska and wrapped his hands around her neck. He squeezed as hard as he could. His movements were clumsy, however, and he had to hold her body against him to gain leverage. His sweater was soon stained with blood.

The moment he was sure she was dead, he took off through the forest. When he reached the forest road where he had parked his car, he noticed the abandoned trailer. He took off his sweater and threw it inside. Then he got into his car, turned the key, put it in reverse, and stepped on the gas. In his haste, he failed to see the tree behind him and struck it. He swore and shifted into drive, disappearing into the night.

*     *     *

"According to your theory, the murder weapon must be somewhere in the lake," Gahalowood said.

"It's just one possibility," Vance acknowledged.

"Why would the murderer get rid of it so near the scene of the crime?" Kazinsky asked as he opened his beer.

"You know as well as I do," Vance replied, "half the time, we find it in a nearby garbage can. Why? Because murderers don't want to risk getting busted during some routine inspection. Same with the sweater. Alaska's murderer was covered with blood, something he hadn't planned on. So, he got rid of his sweater to avoid drawing attention and to not leave traces of blood in his car if he became a suspect and his vehicle was examined."

"It makes sense," Gahalowood said. "We need to search Lake Skotam to see if we can find that iron bar."

The next day, upon arriving at police headquarters, the three detectives requested that a team of divers be dispatched to Grey Beach as soon as possible. At the same time, Keith Benton from forensics showed up at their office. "I just received your DNA results," he said, waving the reports he held in his hand.

"And?" Gahalowood asked.

"Walter Carrey's DNA matches one of the two samples found on the gray pullover."

Without wasting a second, the detectives left the office and drove to Mount Pleasant. They drove down Main Street at high speed but could go no farther than Donovan's General Store. The road was blocked. Several fire trucks could be seen up ahead. Gahalowood, Vance, and Kazinsky jumped out of their car and ran down the street. When they reached Carrey Hunting & Fishing, they stopped: Walter Carrey's apartment, on the upper floor, had burned during the night.

# 5

## *The Goldmans of Baltimore*

*Miami, Florida*
*April 24, 2010*

Only a fifty-minute flight separated Florida and the Bahamas. I left the island in the morning and landed in Miami before noon. I rented a car and drove to Coconut Grove, where my uncle Saul lived.

While on the highway, I received a call from my mother. "Hello dear, how was your vacation?"

"Excellent."

"Were you alone?"

"Yes."

"I hope you're lying to your mother. I hope you were there with a charming young woman who put sunscreen on your back and will soon give you beautiful children. Are you in New York? Would you like to have dinner at the house tonight?"

"I stopped in Florida, Mother. I'm going to pay a visit to Uncle Saul."

"These trips to Florida aren't good for you," my mother said after a disapproving silence. "All they do is make you think about the past and what happened to your cousins."

I was tempted to reply that maybe that was what I needed, but I preferred to cut our conversation short. "Don't worry, Mother, I'll be back in a few days. I'll call you from New York."

I had barely hung up when the phone rang again. I had connected it to the car's speakers and answered without noticing the call number. "Mother?" I asked, thinking she had forgotten something.

"No," answered the voice of Roy Barnaski, "but you can call me that if you like."

"My apologies, Roy. I'm on the road, I didn't check the number."

"Goldman! Tell me you're in New York. We can have dinner at the Pierre."

"I'm in Florida."

"Florida!" Roy lamented. "You move around too much."

"I needed to get away."

"Something bothering you?"

"Heartbreak."

"Well, it's your lucky day because I have an excellent remedy: two million dollars."

"For the screen rights to *Harry Quebert*?"

"Yes."

"No. I told you—I have no desire to make it into a film."

"You're unbelievable, Goldman! Who says no to two million dollars?"

"Me."

When I told Barnaski that wealth doesn't equal happiness, he replied, "Nor does poverty!"

I hung up on him.

In Coconut Grove, Uncle Saul was waiting for me on the porch of his small house. We exchanged greetings. He looked thinner. His beard, which he had allowed to grow since the tragedy, had thickened. Uncle Saul had had everything and lost everything. When I looked at him, I still saw the great Baltimore lawyer, surrounded by the trappings of success: his luxurious mansion in Oak Park, his summer house in the Hamptons, his winter apartment in an exclusive complex in Miami. But today he was a loner whose only asset was this small clapboard house, purchased four or five years earlier with what remained of his savings. He lived frugally, working as a stock clerk in a supermarket in Coral Gables, where he bagged customers' purchases at the register.

I liked the house in Coconut Grove very much. I loved the peace and quiet, in spite of everything my uncle had gone through. We spent a good part of the afternoon on his porch, in the shade of mango and avocado trees.

"Yesterday evening, by chance, I found this photo," I told him, showing him the picture. The image had been taken at the height of the Baltimore Goldmans' success. Uncle Saul looked at it attentively before commenting. I didn't know if he was addressing his words to me or to himself.

"The thing about money, Marcus, is it can buy every kind of emotion but never any real feeling. It can give the illusion of happiness but not true happiness, the illusion of love but not real love. Money can put a roof over your head, but it can't provide the feeling of home."

He ran his finger over the faces of those who had been his family. I wondered what memories he was reliving at that moment. He placed his index finger on the woman who had been his wife and whom he had loved deeply, my aunt Anita.

"She was really beautiful," I murmured.

"She was marvelous," he added.

"You know, that's what I'm looking for in a woman."

"A woman like Anita in this picture?"

"That we're a couple like you and Aunt Anita." I stopped there, realizing what I'd said.

"You mean before her tragic end?" he asked, picking up on my slip.

"You know what I meant, Uncle Saul. I'm sorry, I . . ."

"Don't worry about it, Marcus."

We didn't mention her again. But that night, in the guest room where I was sleeping, Aunt Anita dominated my thoughts. I stayed awake for a long time, my eyes fixed on the photograph. Even when I turned out the light, I couldn't sleep. It was sweltering and the air-conditioning didn't work very well. I was overcome by a flood of memories. At some point during the night, I found myself in the kitchen. And standing in that dark room brought back memories of my visits to the Baltimore Goldmans.

*     *     *

*Baltimore, Maryland*
*September 1995*

It was five in the morning when the small watch on my wrist began to buzz softly. With a reflexive gesture, I stopped the alarm so I wouldn't wake my cousins, Hillel and Woody, who were sleeping in the same room. It was Labor Day weekend, and as with all school holidays, I had come to stay with the Baltimore Goldmans. I felt the same sense of wonder whenever I visited them, the same happiness in becoming, if just for a weekend, a member of what seemed to be the perfect family.

My arrival always followed the same pattern: Aunt Anita came to get me at the train station. All my life, I will cherish the memory of her silhouette as she waited for me on the platform—her beauty, her soft features, her way of folding me in her arms, the scent of her perfume. Aunt Anita took me to their home, a very large house in Oak Park, an upscale residential neighborhood, where everything seemed finer and grander than anywhere else—the trees, the sidewalks, the people on the street, the gates and front yards. It's where I found the two boys who were, for me, the brothers life had never wanted me to have: Woody and Hillel. And a man who, along with Harry Quebert, had the most profound influence on my life: my uncle Saul. Always handsome, elegant, witty, and good-humored.

My vacations in Oak Park always seemed too short to me. To avoid wasting precious time, I got up at dawn and went quietly to the kitchen. I behaved as one of the family. I squeezed some oranges, turned on the coffee maker, then stepped outside to get the paper, which was delivered early every morning. I sat at the kitchen counter, unfolded the *Baltimore Sun*, and scanned the headlines while eating a piece of toast spread with peanut butter. And I wondered what it would be like to live in Oak Park forever.

What made me happiest, however, was spending time alone with Aunt Anita, who was an early riser. She would join me in the kitchen, mussing my hair and saying "Good morning, Marcus dear." She poured herself a cup of coffee and sat down at the counter next to me, scanning the newspaper. Sometimes—and this always delighted me—she would grab one of my slices of toast.

Having finished with the paper, Aunt Anita began to prepare breakfast, usually pancakes or a simple cake of some kind. I've never been much of a cook, and I always admired her ability to prepare all kinds of desserts without consulting a recipe. There was one, quite simple, which she managed to teach me—her famous banana bread, which required only flour, eggs, sugar, a pinch of salt, and, of course, very ripe bananas.

\*       \*       \*

The sun had risen over Coconut Grove when Uncle Saul entered the kitchen, drawn by the aroma of the banana bread that was cooling on the rack. "Is that your aunt's recipe?" he asked, his eyes shining.

"The only thing I know how to bake."

He burst out laughing and poured himself a cup of coffee. "Have you been up long?"

"No," I lied, "I slept like a log."

He sat down at the table with a slice of banana bread and his cup, then he did what he always used to do at Oak Park: he dunked a corner into his coffee.

"I've made a lot of friends thanks to this banana bread," I told him.

"Like who?"

"The cop I interviewed for the Harry Quebert case and his family. Lovely people."

Whether it was a coincidence, an accident, or a twist of fate, I was to meet up with the Gahalowood family later that day. At lunch, while browsing social media, I came across a photo that Malia Gahalowood had just posted on Facebook. The entire family was having lunch on the terrace of the Cheesecake Factory in the business district of Aventura, north of Miami.

I called Perry at once. When he picked up, he still had his mouth full. "Sergeant, how's your steak? Have you tried the cheese fritters? They're outstanding."

"Writer?" he answered, sounding shocked. "How the hell did you know that—?"

"The magic of social media, Sergeant."

He began to grumble something to his daughter before getting back to our conversation, adopting his customary tone of affected bad humor.

"Do you have anything to say that isn't about my steak?"

"Whatever you do, don't move, Sergeant. I'm on my way."

I joined the Gahalowood family just in time for dessert. It gave me immense pleasure to see them again. They were using their spring vacation to spend a few days in Florida. "Your weekend in the Bahamas inspired us," Gahalowood confided. "We were missing the sun."

When lunch was over, the girls wanted to go shopping. I joined the family in the shopping center, and then when Gahalowood had had enough, the two of us sat down for a cup of coffee.

"I'm worried about you, Writer."

"Worried?"

"First I find you in Somerset, at Harry Quebert's, then in Florida at your uncle's."

"So?"

"So, you're never at home. Are you okay?"

"Yes, perfectly okay."

"Someone who's 'perfectly okay' doesn't spend all their time hanging out at other people's houses."

He gave me that look, a cop's look, the one that meant "I know everything, it's time to tell me the truth," the look that made you want to unburden your conscience and had persuaded dozens of criminals to confess. I decided to open up to him about Raegan and my doomed vacation in the Bahamas. He listened as only he could. Perry was like that. The type of guy who, when I most needed someone to talk to, always showed up, as if by magic. The kind of guy who listens without judging. I didn't mind telling him how lonesome I felt. Millions of people fell asleep with me, but I always woke up alone. He showed all his usual concern. I, on the other hand, had no idea that he was the one who really needed someone to talk to.

That day with the Gahalowood family has remained with me. When they left, I felt something like heartache. It was almost painful—as if I somehow knew that it was the last time I would see them all together.

I returned to New York. About a month went by without any news from Gahalowood. Then, one evening in May, tragedy struck.

# Three Days After the Murder

*Tuesday, April 6, 1999*

Statistics show that murders committed by someone close to the victim are resolved within seventy-two hours. The Alaska Sanders case was no exception.

That morning in Mount Pleasant, Gahalowood, Vance, and Kazinsky arrived to find that there wasn't much left of the upper story of the building that housed Carrey Hunting & Fishing. And although the flames hadn't reached the store on the ground floor, smoke and water had caused extensive damage. Chief Mitchell summarized the situation for the three detectives.

"A squad car discovered the blaze at four in the morning. They notified the fire department immediately. No-one was injured—Walter Carrey doesn't appear to have been home."

"What was the cause of the fire?" Vance asked.

"We don't know yet, but there's a fire inspector in there now. Who told you about it?"

"No-one," Gahalowood replied. "We were coming by to interview Carrey. His DNA was found on the sweater covered in Alaska's blood."

"Shit," Mitchell grumbled. "I can't believe it. At heart, he's not a bad guy, Walter. What was he thinking?"

"That's what we want to know. But first we have to find him."

"You should ask his parents," Chief Mitchell advised.

Sally and George Carrey were standing on the sidewalk, staring at what remained of their store. Gahalowood went over to them. "I'm very sorry for what's happened here."

Sally remained speechless. George, more pragmatic, was wondering about the insurance.

"We're looking for your son," Gahalowood said to him.

"I don't know where he is," Sally replied. "Thank God, he wasn't home when the fire started."

"It was four in the morning; where could he have been?"

"I don't know. I tried to call him, but his phone was off."

"When did you last see him?"

"Yesterday evening. He came over to the house for supper."

"And after that? Where did he go?"

"I have no idea, Sergeant. I'm terribly sorry, but I'm a mess right now."

A short distance away, in front of the store, Eric Donovan was watching the firefighters at work. Gahalowood walked over. Eric didn't have any news about Walter either. He had run into him briefly the day before, but that was all.

"How was he?" Gahalowood asked.

"Not so good, as you can imagine."

Vance came over and took Gahalowood aside. "Perry, you have to see this."

The two detectives went over to the damaged building. The staircase was still intact. They went up to the second floor, where they joined Kazinsky. The walls in the hallway had been defaced with broad bands of paint:

UNFAITHFUL WHORE

The detectives entered the apartment. The living room was a charred ruin, the wooden walls blackened and scorched. On the floor they found pictures of Alaska, curled by the flames. Access to the bedroom was barred by tape; the floor had been badly damaged and there was a risk it might collapse. From what they could see, this room had been especially affected. Almost nothing remained of the bed.

118

The fire inspector gave them an update on their investigation: "It was definitely deliberate, which isn't surprising when you consider how quickly it spread. From the looks of it, an accelerant was used, probably gasoline."

"The front door looks intact," Gahalowood noted. "How did your crew get inside?"

"It was open when they got here and there were no visible signs the lock had been forced."

"So there was no break-in. Whoever started it had a key."

"There's one thing that bothers me," the fire inspector remarked. "Whoever did it set fire to the bed."

"The bed?"

"Yes. I've never seen that before. In general, they set fire to the curtains and it spreads to the rest of the room. But look—there's nothing left of the bed. That's got to be symbolic: whoever did this wanted to destroy it, there's no doubt about it, especially given what's on the wall."

The bedroom wall was daubed with the same message found in the hallway:

UNFAITHFUL WHORE

"Alaska was cheating on him and Walter knew it," Vance said.

"But why write that when she's already dead?" Kazinsky wondered aloud.

"He killed her in a rage and now he can't cope with the guilt."

Gahalowood ordered that an alert be issued—they needed to find Walter Carrey without delay. The search covered a large area. Police across New Hampshire and the neighboring states were mobilized. Sally Carrey gave them a recent photo of her son, which was distributed along with his personal information. Less than an hour later, the local television stations in New Hampshire interrupted their programming with a news bulletin: Walter Carrey, whose picture was displayed on-screen, was being sought for the murder of Alaska Sanders.

Mount Pleasant was in an uproar.

As the detectives were leaving Carrey's apartment, Gahalowood received a call from Keith Benton in forensics. "Your hunch was right," he said. "The debris found in the forest is from a Ford Taurus, manufactured between 1995 and today. We tested the paint with a colorimeter and it's definitely black. So, it looks like it was a black Ford Taurus that hit the tree."

Gahalowood hung up and shared the information with Vance and Kazinsky.

"So, was it Carrey's car in the forest?" Vance asked.

"But the car shows no sign of a collision," Kazinsky added. "There's no damage to the bumpers, and the taillights are intact."

"I bet he had it fixed on the sly," Gahalowood said. "We should contact all the repair shops in the area. The accident happened over the weekend, so it must've been someone nearby who could do the repair on short notice. We can start in Mount Pleasant; it shouldn't take long."

Chief Mitchell took them around the local repair shops. The first two visits came up empty. The third shop had a Ford concession. Mitchell introduced himself to the owner and asked if he could talk to the mechanics. After considering his options, he walked over to one of them, Dave Burke, a tall, thin man, in oversized overalls, around the same age as Walter.

"Dave," Mitchell asked the young man, who looked especially ill at ease, "I've seen you hanging around with Walter Carrey, right?"

"Maybe."

"*Maybe?*" Mitchell snapped at the mechanic. "Is it yes or no?"

"Yes," Burke replied, his head lowered.

"Did Walter ask you to lend a hand this weekend?"

"I have no idea . . ."

"Listen, Dave," Mitchell replied, annoyed. "You must be aware that Walter's being sought for the murder. If you don't want to make trouble for yourself, now's the time to speak up."

Burke hesitated, then said, "He came to see me on Saturday."

*     *     *

*Three days earlier, Saturday, April 3, 1999*

It was the middle of the afternoon. Dave Burke was smoking a cigarette in front of the shop when he heard someone quietly call his name. "Dave! Psst! Dave!" He looked around, then caught sight of Walter Carrey on the other side of the street, partly hidden by the cars parked along the sidewalk. Walter gestured for him to cross over.

"What are you doing here, Walter?" Burke asked.

"I need your help."

"I'm listening."

"I banged up my car this morning, in front of the store. I was unloading some supplies and I wanted to back up to the entrance, but I hit a post for the porch."

"Shit. A lot of damage?"

"A broken taillight and a dented bumper. My parents are back from vacation tomorrow and I don't want them to know what I did. My mother's liable to repaint the entire front of the store and deduct it from my salary."

Burke burst out laughing. "I get it. Bring your car over to the shop and I'll see what we can do. It's pretty quiet today."

"I can't bring it down here, my folks will find out. My father plays poker with your boss, remember."

"What do you suggest, then?"

"You have the parts in stock?"

"For a Taurus? Yeah, we have plenty of spare parts."

"Great. Grab what you need and come over to my parents' place tonight. I put the car in their garage. You can repair it there; no-one will bother you."

*     *     *

"And so you went?" Gahalowood asked him.

"Yeah, it didn't take more than half an hour. I changed the light, readjusted the bumper, and touched up the paint. It wasn't a big deal. The car looks like new."

"And you weren't suspicious?"

"Suspicious, why?"

"His girlfriend was found dead that morning."

"I don't see the connection between his car and the murder. I helped a friend out, that's all. I tell you what did surprise me, though. He didn't even mention Alaska. He didn't appear to be very upset."

Leaving the garage, Vance couldn't help himself. "We bought Walter's story hook, line, and sinker. We should've brought him in right away."

"Any decent lawyer would've had him out within an hour," Gahalowood remarked. "We still don't have anything solid."

Late that morning, a team of state police divers arrived at Grey Beach to search the lake. Gahalowood, Vance, and Kazinsky observed the activity from the shore. After less than half an hour in the water, the divers brought an object up to the surface. They came to shore and one of the men showed the detectives what they'd found: a telescopic metal baton.

"Looks like you were right," Gahalowood told Vance. "He got rid of the weapon right after he hit Alaska. He had to strangle her to finish her off."

*　　*　　*

Seven p.m. The search for Walter Carrey had come up empty-handed. At state police headquarters, Vance, Gahalowood, and Kazinsky were pacing the office in agitation.

"We may as well call it a day," Vance suggested. "We're not going to spend the night here."

At that moment, Gahalowood's phone rang. His colleagues froze, trying to listen in: ever since early afternoon, whenever a phone had rung, they'd hoped it was to announce that Walter Carrey had been arrested.

"It's Helen, sorry to disappoint you," Gahalowood told them.

"Why disappointed?" she asked on the other end of the line.

"We've identified the murderer, but we can't find him. How are you feeling?"

"I'm fine, but I think it's going to be very soon."

Gahalowood shouted to Vance and Kazinsky, "Helen's about to give birth!"

Vance grabbed his coat and keys.

"I don't mean right now," Helen said, "but I can feel some slight contractions."

"Has your water broken?" Gahalowood asked.

"Her water has broken!" Vance cried out, jumping from foot to foot.

"Everyone please calm down," she said. "Nothing's broken. I'm going to take a bath and relax."

"I'll be home soon," Gahalowood promised. "I'll see you there." He hung up.

"Go be with Helen," Vance told him. "And keep us informed—we want to be the first ones to get a picture of the baby!"

But Gahalowood didn't set off for home. His phone rang again, followed immediately by those of Vance and Kazinsky. Walter Carrey was being held at Wolfeboro police station.

An hour later, Walter arrived, under guard, at state police headquarters. He was taken at once to the offices of the crime squad, where Gahalowood, Vance, and Kazinsky proceeded to question him.

"You've lost your minds," Walter protested. "I could never hurt Alaska!"

"We found your DNA at the scene of the crime. When you fled, you smashed a taillight on your car, which you rushed to get repaired on Saturday afternoon. We know what you've been up to."

"I wasn't at Grey Beach! I spent the evening at the National Anthem—how many times do I have to tell you? As for the car, that was stupid. Saturday morning, I realized that my taillight was broken. Don't know how it happened. Someone must've hit my car. I don't spend my time staring at the taillights. And that Saturday afternoon, talking to a friend who's a cop, I learned that you'd found a broken taillight at Grey Beach and traces of black paint. I figured I'd be blamed and started to panic. So I asked my friend Dave to help me out."

"Why would you go to all that trouble if you weren't guilty?" Gahalowood asked.

"I don't know! You scrambled my brains. The way you were questioning me, I just knew you were going to trap me."

"Trap you?"

"We've all heard stories about cops who hide drugs in some innocent guy's car to take him down."

"Stop, Walter!" Vance shouted. "Are you also going to blame us for setting fire to your apartment?"

Carrey looked distraught. "No, I did that."

"Why?"

"I wanted to torch that rotten place. Torch the bed where she let him fuck her, that bitch . . ."

"Who? Alaska? She had a lover, is that it? She had a lover and you couldn't bear it, so you killed her? Is that how it went?"

"I didn't kill her!"

"So why did you run?"

"I spent the night drinking, and early in the morning, I got this . . . this urge. I wanted to destroy everything. I tagged the walls, set fire to the bed. I thought it would burn out quickly. When I saw it was getting out of control, I fled. I found a motel on Route 28 and took a room. I just collapsed on the bed. When I woke up, it was past noon. I turned on the TV and saw my picture. At first, I stayed indoors. What was I supposed to do? But since I knew I wasn't guilty, I decided to turn myself in. If I had killed Alaska, why would I go to the police?"

"Because you were cornered and you figured that playing dumb would save you."

"You told me I had the right to an attorney. I'm not saying any more until I get one."

Walter didn't have a lawyer of his own, so he asked for a public defender. Gahalowood and Vance left the room. They were joined in the hallway by Kazinsky, who had followed the exchange from an adjacent room behind one-way glass.

"I guess he wants to buy time," Vance surmised. "I might as well call legal services; maybe they can find someone who can get over here quickly." Vance disappeared to make the phone call.

When he returned he found his colleagues still in the hallway. "They're sending someone 'as quickly as possible,'" he told them. "God knows what that means. We'll be waiting a couple of hours at least."

"Can we maybe get something to eat in the meantime?" Kazinsky asked.

Vance, however, had other ideas. "What if we call the prosecutor's office?" he suggested. "We could put the fear of God into Carrey by telling him his only chance of avoiding the death penalty is to admit everything now."

"Not without a lawyer by his side," Gahalowood objected. "Otherwise, we're going to end up with a mistrial on our hands."

Gahalowood looked at his watch. It had been a while since Helen said she was feeling contractions. He didn't want to wait any longer.

"Go," Vance told him, as if he had read his mind. "Don't miss the birth of your daughter for that lowlife. There's no sense in all three of us hanging around here."

"You sure?"

"I'm as sure as I'll ever be," Vance insisted. "Kazinsky and I can hold the fort."

"Okay," Gahalowood said, "but keep me posted."

"No." Vance smiled. "*You* keep *us* posted."

Gahalowood left the crime squad's offices and ran down the stairs and out to the parking lot. He had no idea what was about to happen on the second floor of state police headquarters.

# 6

## *Sorrow*

Helen Gahalowood was buried on Thursday, May 27, 2010. It was a beautiful afternoon. The sun was shining. Birds were singing in the nearby trees. Nature inflicted the insolent promise of its beauty upon us.

Seated on folding chairs facing the coffin, surrounded by bouquets of white roses, the Gahalowood family and their friends listened to the pastor's oration. Perry, in the front row, wrapped his daughters in his thick arms. At his request, I had taken the seat behind him. I couldn't see his tears, but I knew they were there from the movements of his body. I kept my hand on his shoulder as if, with that insignificant gesture, I could ease his pain.

What always strikes me about funerals is the dignified sorrow of the assembled mourners. It was the most vibrant of eulogies. The most eloquent homage. It revealed the love the deceased had inspired—both for what she had been and for what we would no longer be without her.

Malia and Lisa sang "Amazing Grace." Perry was supposed to speak, but instead of getting up to stand before the small platform, he turned to me and handed me a piece of crumpled paper. It was his speech. He was unable to manage a word of it. So it was I who stood before Helen's coffin, facing the crowd. Taking in the scope of that flower-filled cemetery, I considered how that moment was like Helen, disarmingly perfect, at once sublime and unsettling. Then I looked at the paper, stained with tears that had streaked the ink.

I clung to the wooden lectern to steady myself, reading Perry's words aloud. Recalling what Helen had gone through suddenly brought to mind a very difficult chapter in my own life—the death, a few years earlier, also under tragic circumstances, of my aunt Anita.

After the ceremony, there was a reception at Perry's home. The house was filled with people. The caterers were overwhelmed, so I helped them out. A platter of hors d'oeuvres in one hand and a bottle of wine in the other, I wandered through the ground-floor rooms, where the guests were standing in small clusters.

I met Helen's family and her colleagues. I was touched to discover that they all knew of me, not as a famous writer, but as a friend of the family. I hadn't felt so at home in a long time, freed for a few hours at least from my Marcus Goldman persona.

All the conversations revolved around one subject: Helen. She called to mind distinct memories in everyone. When it came to me, I was asked to say a few words about how we had met. To master my emotions, I attempted humor.

"Helen was an extraordinary woman. But before I could get to know her, I first had to get to know Perry." The guests laughed nervously. "The first time I met Perry was two and a half years ago, at the start of the Harry Quebert investigation. I still remember the date: June 18, 2008. It's hard to forget that day. Perry surprised me as I was stomping through a crime scene and pointed his gun at me. Just like that. And then he complained that my book was pathetically bad and demanded that I reimburse him the fifteen dollars he'd paid for it."

"It's true!" Perry confirmed, causing everyone to burst out laughing.

"I gave him a fifty, but he didn't have any change."

"I had the change, but you were getting on my nerves!"

The guests were in hysterics now.

"Not long after this," I continued, "Perry finally realized I was a wonderful guy and invited me over for dinner."

"Only because I felt sorry for you. You were being threatened."

"I remember that summer evening, right here in this house, when Helen entered my life. She opened her heart to me, the way few people have. She was kind and tender. She was generous. She made the world a better place. Today, my friends, recalling Helen before you, I feel despair at having lost her and thankful to have known her. We can't tame death. It's a part of life. And we have to speak of the dead so they remain a part of us. If, out of a sense of propriety, we fail to keep their memory alive, we bury them for good. A few weeks ago, I had the good fortune to meet up with the Gahalowood family in Florida. We had dinner with my uncle Saul, a man dear to my heart. I was very happy that my uncle was able to meet Helen. And, if you'll allow me, I'd like to quote here the words he spoke at the burial of my aunt Anita: 'The great weakness of death is that it can only destroy matter. It can do nothing to harm our memories and our feelings. On the contrary, it brings them to life and binds them to us forever, as if seeking our forgiveness, saying, *It's true, I have taken much from you, but look what I have left you.*'"

What I found curious about that day at the Gahalowoods' was that I didn't meet any of Perry's colleagues. The only representative from the police force was Chief Lansdane of the New Hampshire State Police, whom I had met during the Harry Quebert affair. I had expected to see dozens of police there, united in their grief, all in dress uniform. I was so surprised that I had to ask Chief Lansdane about it.

I tried to be subtle by offering him a platter of salmon canapés, which I had seen him eating previously. "Aside from yourself, I don't see any police here," I remarked as he helped himself to more hors d'oeuvres.

He took the time to swallow before replying. "Does that surprise you, Marcus?"

"Yes. Where are Perry's colleagues?"

Lansdane looked at me quizzically. "During the Quebert affair, did it never surprise you that Perry conducted the investigation by himself?"

"It didn't really register at the time, but now that you mention it . . ."

"In general, officers work in pairs. Never alone. Except for Perry Gahalowood."

"Why?"

"He never told you what happened eleven years ago?"

"No."

"It's not important. But you should know that Perry was never very close to the other members of his department and that the Quebert case didn't help matters."

"What's it got to do with Harry?"

"Let it go, Marcus. This is neither the time nor the place."

"You've either told me too much or not enough."

Lansdane looked around; there was no-one in the vicinity who might eavesdrop. "Perry had to fight to get the Nola Kellergan investigation, which had initially been given to two other detectives. It was a tough case. Harry Quebert was a very well known individual. Perry convinced me to let him handle it. We knew each other well, me and Perry. Before becoming chief of the state police, I was his supervisor on the crime squad. I arranged for him to get the case, and his colleagues never forgave him for it."

"But why was he so intent on investigating the murder of Nola Kellergan?"

"He saw it as a way to redeem himself. You know, that's why I like you, Marcus. You caused one helluva mess with the Quebert case, but you helped Perry fix something inside him."

"Fix what?"

"I can't say any more. If Perry's never mentioned it, he must have a good reason. He should be the one to tell you."

And with that, Lansdane turned and walked away.

\*       \*       \*

When the last guests and the caterers had left, I stayed around to help straighten up the house. I wanted the family to find the place clean in the morning. The girls had gone to bed and I thought Perry had as well. I was alone on the ground floor, or so I thought. I emptied the dishwasher, cleaned the ashtrays, and put away the plates that had been left to dry before getting ready to leave. I was planning to spend the night at a nearby hotel—that way I would be available to help Perry the following morning if he needed me, but I wouldn't be getting in the way.

As I was about to leave, Perry burst into the kitchen, looking as if he had just climbed out of the depths of hell. Pale and defeated. His eyes betrayed his broken heart. We stared at one another. I knew at that moment that I was going to stay with them for a while. Perry simply said, in a quiet voice, "You know where the sheets are."

Then he pulled up a chair and sat down. In his language, that meant he needed to talk. I poured two large glasses of Scotch. With a hollow voice, he began to tell me about Helen's death. I had already heard part of the story. He must have repeated it dozens of times, and he would continue to do so. For months to come, whenever he spoke to someone he knew, even for the smallest things, at the barber's, at the supermarket, with an old friend he met by accident on the street, he was asked to return to that tragedy. "Helen died? But what happened?" What happened is that one evening, returning home late from work, Helen had stopped in the parking lot of a fast-food restaurant, presumably to get something to eat. She had parked her car but hadn't gotten out yet. Two hours later, a passerby noticed Helen's body in the car, slumped strangely against the wheel, and called 911. Their attempts to revive her were fruitless. It was too late.

Helen had had a heart attack. In fact, it had started a few hours earlier. She had complained to her colleagues that she was having back pains and was feeling nauseous. One of them even joked that she was too old to be pregnant, and Helen laughed. She thought it was just fatigue, no doubt from overwork.

"She hadn't been feeling well for a while," Perry explained. "The trip to Florida was supposed to help her recharge her batteries. We had to conduct an autopsy, it's the law. The doctor told me that one out of every two women who have a heart attack show very few prior symptoms."

I had the impression that Perry was feeling guilty about something.

"It's not your fault, Sergeant. What could you have done?"

He grimaced. "It's not that simple, Marcus. The evening she died, Helen tried to reach me several times."

"Yes, I know, the girls told me. You dozed off and you didn't hear the phone. It could have happened to anyone."

"I wasn't sleeping, Marcus! I lied to everyone about it. That night, I was here in this kitchen, and I watched my phone vibrating on the table. I deliberately ignored those calls."

I was stunned.

"Since I didn't pick up, she left me a voice message."

He took out his mobile phone. An electronic voice announced that a message had been received on May 20 at 9:05 p.m., then, suddenly, Helen's voice was in our ears: *Perry, where are you? Call me. Call me, please. It's urgent.*

"I'll never forgive myself," Gahalowood sobbed. "If I had picked up, if I had listened to her damn message . . ."

"Sergeant, what happened between you and Helen?"

"She was cheating on me."

"What? Are you sure?"

"Almost certain."

"I can't imagine Helen having an affair, Sergeant."

"That's because you're naïve."

Perry remarked that his wife had been behaving strangely for the past few weeks. "She was out more than usual. She stayed late at the office, which had never happened before. When I asked about it, she told me that her new boss was much more demanding than the old one. I suspected she wasn't telling me the truth. That she was avoiding me. That was the start of the trouble between us."

"When did all this happen?"

"In April, shortly after you stopped by for Lisa's birthday."

"So, when we met in Florida, you were in the middle of this?"

"Yeah, right in the middle."

"But you both looked so relaxed."

"Appearances, Writer. The glue in our social lives. But in the intimacy of the home, it all collapses. And it was right before we left for Florida that I discovered the truth. You remember that night when we spoke on the phone? You were on your island paradise, spilling your guts . . ."

"You didn't sound so good yourself."

"That day, Helen told me she had to stay late at work to finish a presentation. I was doubtful so I drove to her office. It must've been around nine o'clock. When I reached her floor, all the lights were out; only the cleaners were still working, and they were getting ready to leave."

"That doesn't prove anything."

"I called Helen but there was no answer. So I took a walk around the neighborhood. I didn't have to walk long before I found her, sitting in a restaurant having a cozy meal with her boss."

"So what did you do?"

"Nothing. I felt my legs buckle. I didn't want to believe my eyes. I drove home. Helen didn't get back until late that night. The next morning, when I asked her how her evening had been, she told me, without breaking a sweat, that she'd spent it in front of her computer."

"And then?"

"We were scheduled to leave for Florida in a couple of days, so I decided not to say anything. Maybe I was a coward, maybe I was hoping that our vacation would help us put the pieces back together."

"But Sarge, why didn't you tell me when we met?"

"Too hard. I didn't know where to begin. You know, we swear that if our partner cheats on us, we'll leave at once. But, in reality, it's not that easy. You're alone, with this knot in your stomach, hoping it'll all disappear. And then there's the children. When we got back from Florida, Helen and I were more distant than ever. Especially since I had proof that she was lying to me."

"What sort of proof?"

"She was driving a lot. I'm a cop, so I started checking the mileage on her car to try to figure out what she was up to. If she was really spending her evenings at the office as she claimed, she wouldn't have had to drive much more than the round-trip distance between our house and downtown Concord."

"I assume that wasn't what you found."

"You assume correctly."

"And so, what happened the night she died?"

"She was supposed to be at the office. She told me at the last minute. I had dinner alone with the girls and then stayed in the kitchen, thinking. Waiting for her to return. I even promised myself I'd confront her this time, put an end to the lies. That's why I didn't answer the phone when she called. I didn't want to listen to any more of her stories. I didn't want her to make excuses for staying late and tell me she had to finish up some work, and that I should go to bed without waiting up for her. I didn't want to give her the chance to slip away. So I didn't pick up. I watched the phone vibrate. I even heard her message. Later, Chief Lansdane came over and rang the bell. It wasn't some stranger who found Helen, like I told everyone. She had called Lansdane—I don't know why. Maybe she was desperate, but he got there too late. That's the truth, Marcus. I watched that damn phone as it rang and I let Helen die."

"Don't think like that, Sergeant."

"For God's sake, how should I think?" In his anger, he hurled his glass at the wall, then slumped over the table, his face in his hands.

"Go to bed, Sergeant. You need some sleep. I'll clean up in here."

He listened. Without saying a word, he went upstairs to his bedroom like a shadow. That night I couldn't sleep. I kept thinking about Helen's message. She had told Perry, "It's urgent." As far as I was concerned, that didn't sound like a medical emergency, but rather, she needed to tell him something. What had happened that night in the life of Helen Gahalowood? What had she found?

*

The following morning, as I was trying to recover from my sleepless night by drinking a cup of coffee on the front porch, a mail carrier stopped at the mailbox. She waved to me. I walked over.

"Are you related to Helen Gahalowood?" she asked.

"In a way."

"It's a shame, what happened. Such a young woman, so nice. She was the only one in the neighborhood who always said hello to me and gave me a gift at the end of the year. Please give my condolences to her husband and daughters. My name is Edna."

"I'll make sure of it, Edna."

After a moment's hesitation, she asked, "Did Helen talk to you about the letter?"

"What letter?"

\*　　　\*　　　\*

*A few weeks earlier*

That morning, as Edna was making her daily rounds, she found Helen Gahalowood standing next to the mailbox waiting for her. Helen looked agitated, and Edna saw she was holding a blue envelope.

"Edna, were you the one who put this in the mailbox yesterday?" By her tone of voice, she seemed annoyed.

"I deliver hundreds of letters a day," Edna explained, slightly taken aback. "I don't remember each and every one that passes through my hands. But let me take a look just in case."

Edna took the envelope and saw that it had no address on it and no stamp. "We wouldn't have delivered it, Helen. There's no name, no address. How would we know that you're the recipient? We're not mind readers."

"So, if you didn't put it here, who did?"

"Someone who knows you and came here to make sure you got it. Maybe a neighbor? A secret admirer?"

\*　　　\*　　　\*

"She didn't laugh at that," Edna remarked. "In fact, she seemed irritated."

"And what was in the envelope?"

"Helen never said. That was the last time I saw her."

"And when was that?"

"I don't remember exactly, time goes by so fast. It must have been about two months ago."

"Could you be more specific? Any detail you can recall. Was there anything special about that day?"

She thought about it for a while, then suddenly, she said, "That was the same day we got a bomb alert at the New Hampshire Capitol building! What a mess that morning was. The entire city was shut down. I was late for my shift. Yes, I'm sure of it now. It was the same day."

After a quick internet search, I easily found the date of the alert—April 7. Helen had complained about a piece of mail she had received the day before, on the sixth. That was when I showed up at the Gahalowood home for Lisa's birthday. Coincidence? What was in that envelope? Was Helen's call to Perry the night of her death related to the letter?

My first thought was to connect Perry's suspicion of adultery with the letter. Was someone blackmailing her? I had to sort this out, and the first person I needed to talk to was Helen's boss.

I drove to her office in downtown Concord without saying a word to Perry. Helen's boss was a man named Mads Bergsen, a nice Danish guy I had met at the cemetery. He saw me into his office.

"What brings you here, Marcus?" he asked as he pointed to a leather armchair.

"I wanted to talk about Helen Gahalowood."

"I'm listening."

I didn't want to ask him directly about a possible affair between them, so I tiptoed around it for a while.

"Her husband found her distant these past few months," I explained. "Her behavior was strange; it seems like she was spending all her evenings at the office. She was supposed to be working on an important project. Is that what it was?"

Bergsen uttered an embarrassed sigh. "As you know, Marcus, I'm Danish. And in Denmark we're not fond of this kind of stupidity."

He had me at my own game. He was alluding to something I couldn't grasp.

"Which stupidity are you referring to?"

"The stupidity of staying late at the office. You Americans invented it. Trying to demonstrate one's value by working all hours, sending emails in the middle of the night and on weekends. It makes no sense. If you have to work overtime, it's because you didn't finish everything when you were supposed to and so you should be fired. That's what I always told my staff, and Helen as well. I am always the last one to leave, around seven. No-one stays late here. That's not how we operate."

"Are you suggesting that Helen wasn't at the office and was lying to her husband?"

He nodded.

"So what was she doing?"

"I have no idea."

I had the feeling that Bergsen wasn't telling me the whole truth and decided it was time to play my ace. "Yet there's one night you do know about," I interjected dryly, "because you took Helen to dinner. Her husband saw you together. Do you do that with all your employees? Maybe that's how things are done in Denmark."

Bergsen stood up and grabbed a picture frame on his desk, which he handed to me. It was a photo of him in a suit, kissing another man, presumably at their wedding. "Benjamin and I got married two months ago," he said. "We were one of the first couples to tie the knot after gay marriage was legalized in New Hampshire."

"I'm an idiot." I sighed.

"No, Marcus, you're a good friend who's concerned about the people he loves. Helen often spoke of you. She said you were a decent man.

136

And I can see that. She was happy that you had entered her husband's life. Helen had problems, Marcus. I invited her to dinner because I was worried about her."

*    *    *

*April 19, 2010*

It was seven o'clock when Mads Bergsen closed the door to his office. As he did every other evening, he made a quick check of the premises before leaving. He greeted the cleaners, who were just starting their shift, and then headed for the elevators. Walking by Helen's office he saw her through the glass divider. She was at her desk, crying. He stuck his head through the door.

"Helen, what's going on?"

She wiped her tears. "Nothing, Mads. Sorry, I'm okay."

"You don't have to apologize, I can see that you're not okay."

"I didn't know you were still here."

"Good, this way you can tell me what's bothering you."

She rose and grabbed her coat. "Don't worry. I have to go."

"Where's that?"

She stopped and turned to Mads, then burst into tears. "I'm a nervous wreck, Mads," she said.

He placed his hands on her shoulders. "I'm not letting you go like this. Come on, I'll take you to dinner."

They ate at an Italian restaurant not far from the office. It was clear that Helen needed to confide in someone, but she wasn't yet ready. Bergsen thought she was having trouble at work. He asked the question, but Helen assured him that everything was fine. Instead, she said, "It's about Perry."

"What happened?"

"He doesn't know about it yet."

*    *    *

"*He doesn't know about it yet?*" I repeated after Bergsen told me what had happened.

"Those were her exact words. She didn't want to say any more. And I never found out what she was referring to. But that night, she asked me to cover for her if Perry came to the office to ask about her hours. But he never did."

"Perry thought she was having an affair. With you."

"Well, obviously, it wasn't me. But I doubt she was seeing anyone else either. She was worried about Perry. At least, that's how I understood it. After the dinner, we never talked about it again."

"Did she mention a letter?"

"A letter? No, why?"

"Nothing. Would you mind if I took a look around her desk?"

Helen's desk had remained just as it was. Bergsen had been tactful enough to leave things untouched until Perry stopped by to collect his wife's personal belongings. I had hoped he would leave me alone for a moment, but he hovered by the door, watching me as I opened the drawers and rummaged through the papers on her table. He appeared somewhat less sympathetic now and probably wondered what I was looking for, regretting his offer to let me look around.

"What are you looking for that's so important?" he finally said, sounding annoyed.

"A personal document Helen might have left here."

But I didn't find anything. I had nothing.

*    *    *

After my visit to Helen's office, I drove to where she had died, in the parking lot of Fanny's restaurant, near a highway exit. I came as a kind of pilgrim, for I had little hope of finding anything. I stayed for more than an hour, staring at the rows of anonymous cars and trying to imagine the exact spot where Helen had found herself so desperately alone as her heart gave out. Before leaving, I went inside to order a coffee. After the man at the counter had taken my order, he asked me, "Are you a cop?"

"No, why?"

"No reason. I saw you outside, looking around where that lady died. I thought maybe there was some connection."

His remark intrigued me. Why would police return to the place where someone had merely had a heart attack? I felt there was something worth pursuing here.

"I'm a close friend of the woman you mentioned. I wanted to see where she died."

"My condolences."

"Thanks. Were you working that night?"

"Yeah, I even talked to her—to that lady. It's terrible. You could see she wasn't doing well."

"You mean physically?"

"No, emotionally. There weren't many customers, so I was just standing behind the counter. She walked in and sat at a table without ordering anything. She looked desperate. As if she had just heard some really bad news or she was afraid. I went over to her because house policy is 'no food, no table.' But, you know, I was a little embarrassed. She was playing nervously with her phone. She looked lost. I told her she had to order something to sit at a table. She just said, 'Bring me whatever you want.' I told her she had to order at the counter, that I couldn't provide table service, because there were cameras and my manager would see it and I could lose my job. She mumbled something and finally left."

"What time was it?"

"About ten o'clock."

"And then?"

"Then this cop showed up. A little while after the lady left the restaurant. He looked at all the tables, then came to the counter and flashed a badge. He told me he was supposed to meet a woman there and described her to me. It was the same lady. I told him what I told you—and that he'd just missed her. Then he went out to the parking lot and I guess he found her in her car, but she was dead."

"You wouldn't have the name of that cop by any chance, would you?"

"Yeah, he left me his card . . . I think he's some kind of big shot. Hold on."

The guy went over to the board for the service schedule and removed a card. I looked at the name: Chief Lansdane. I was stunned.

"This man told you he was supposed to meet her here?" I asked.

"Absolutely."

Something wasn't right. Perry had told me that Helen had contacted Lansdane right before she died. But if Lansdane had showed up at the restaurant, it was because she had asked him to meet her. She hadn't called him because she was feeling unwell—she wanted to tell him something. But before Lansdane got there, Helen was asked to leave by the server and had returned to her car, where she had a heart attack. Lansdane knew something about Helen that Perry and I didn't.

I called Lansdane and had barely said a word when he interrupted me. "I'd prefer it if we discussed this face-to-face. Will you be free in an hour?"

We met in a public park in downtown Concord. It was a hot day, an early glimpse of summer. The esplanade was bathed in sunlight. He was waiting on a stone bench facing a large fountain.

"First, I should tell you that I don't know much about this. I really like Perry, but I couldn't say that we're particularly close. A few weeks ago, Helen asked to see me. We grabbed a coffee. She looked terrible. To be honest, she wasn't very coherent. She told me she was going through a rocky patch, that she was worried and she couldn't tell Perry about it."

"Why couldn't she tell him?" I asked.

"I asked her the same question. And you know what she told me? 'To protect him.'"

"Protect him from what? From the letter she received?"

Lansdane looked at me, surprised. "You know about the letter?"

"I spoke to the mail carrier. Helen received a letter and was beside herself with worry. But obviously, you knew that."

"I didn't find out until the night of her death. After we met, I had no further news from Helen until that terrible evening. She called me; it was late. I had left her my number in the event she needed to get in touch. And that was obviously the case—she was beside herself. She told me she couldn't reach Perry and needed help. That she'd received an anonymous letter and had identified the sender. She asked me to meet her at Fanny's. When I got there, she wasn't in the restaurant. I finally found her in her car. She was dead."

"And what about the letter? Did you get ahold of it?"

"No. I searched the car, the map pocket, the glove compartment. Nothing."

"Do you know what the letter was about?"

"All that Helen told me was that it concerned Alaska Sanders."

"Alaska Sanders?"

"Eleven years ago, in the spring of 1999, a young woman was found murdered by a lake in New Hampshire. Perry was in charge of the investigation, with his partner, Sergeant Matt Vance. It wasn't long before they arrested a suspect, the dead girl's boyfriend. That's when the trouble started."

I was speechless.

# Three Days After the Murder

*Tuesday, April 6, 1999*

It was ten forty-five p.m. Perry Gahalowood was a father for the second time. In an empty hallway of the maternity ward of Concord Hospital, he phoned his in-laws to share the news about Lisa's birth. Helen was doing well and was resting. And little Lisa had come into the world as healthy as could be.

He grabbed a coffee from a machine and ate a chocolate bar, his dinner. He wanted to call Vance to tell him the good news and find out how Walter Carrey's interrogation had gone. But before he could do so, his phone rang. It was Lansdane. Gahalowood, certain the man wanted to congratulate him, proudly said, "Her name is Lisa!"

At the other end of the line, Lansdane remained silent for a moment. Then, in a hollow voice, he said, "Perry, you've got to come down to headquarters right away. Something has happened. It's serious."

When he got to the state police building, Gahalowood found a cluster of vehicles lighting up the night with their blue and red emergency lights: SWAT and forensics team vans, ambulances.

He crossed the police cordon securing the entrance to the building. When he asked, "What happened here?" they simply replied, "Crime squad offices." He climbed the stairs four at a time until he got to the second floor, then ran down the hallway, guided by his nerves. He saw Lansdane, who was blocking access to the interrogation room. "What's going on?" Gahalowood asked. Lansdane remained silent, and Gahalowood, his heart beating strongly, stuck his head through the open doorway. He was horrified by what he saw. In the center of the room, Matt Vance's body lay in a pool of blood, his head torn apart by the impact of a bullet. Next to him lay Walter Carrey. Gahalowood thought he was going to faint. Lansdane, anticipating his reaction, pulled him aside and sat him down. It was a while before Gahalowood managed to regain his senses.

Later that night, Kazinsky told him what had happened. It began when he and Vance were waiting for Carrey's lawyer so they could continue the questioning, as required by law.

"Carrey was handcuffed in the interrogation room, alone," Kazinsky explained. "Vance and I were watching him from behind the glass. The lawyer was late, and Vance and I took the time to work on our strategy. With a lawyer in the room, we had to be a bit more subtle. I would play the bad cop and Vance the good. When Carrey asked for some water, Vance took him a glass, which gave him an opportunity to befriend him. Vance walked into the room with the glass of water, then unlocked Carrey's cuffs. It was then that I noticed, under Vance's jacket, the grip of his service revolver. He'd forgotten to take it out before going in the room. Well, to be honest, it's not a rule we follow religiously—you know as well as I do.

"At that moment, Carrey started to talk. He said, 'I killed her, that bitch.' Vance reacted calmly: he wanted to get a voluntary admission of guilt. Knowing how things worked, he said to Carrey, 'Your lawyer is on his way. Are you saying that you don't want one?' Carrey was unrecognizable: it was as if he was possessed. He just laughed. 'I hit her,' he said, 'that bitch, that unfaithful whore. She cheated on me in my own bed. What do you think a lawyer's going to do for me? I'm going to get the death penalty anyway.' Then he started to cry. He was like a child. He talked about his parents, witnessing the execution. Vance assured Carrey that he could avoid all that; he even gave him a friendly pat on the shoulder to encourage him to keep talking. He asked him if he could record their conversation, and Carrey agreed.

"Vance turned the camera on—it was on a tripod facing the table—and said, 'Can you repeat what you just told me, Walter?' Carrey burst into tears. 'I killed her,' he said again. 'I killed Alaska.' He paused, then added, '*We* killed her. I wasn't alone. Eric Donovan was with me.' Vance and I were stunned. 'Eric Donovan took part in the murder?' Vance asked. 'Yes, I didn't kill her all by myself. We did it together. That sweater you found—it's his. The initials, *MU*, that's for Monarch University, where he went to school. Check it out, you'll see I'm telling the truth.'

"Vance turned the camera off, turned to the glass, and looked at me. Suddenly, Carrey leaped at Vance and grabbed his gun. It all happened so quickly, I didn't even have time to think. Vance tried to snatch it back and a shot went off. The glass shattered. I took cover and unholstered my weapon. When I got up, I saw Carrey was holding Vance, and before I could react, he shot Vance in the head. I screamed and aimed my gun at Carrey, but before I could shoot, he pressed Vance's gun to his temple and pulled the trigger. I pushed the emergency button and ran over to Vance. He was dead. I screamed, screamed for someone to come and help. Where the hell were you?"

It was already late when the murder happened. The building was almost empty. Kazinsky had to wait until help could arrive.

Recalling what he had just been through, Kazinsky unthinkingly touched his suit, covered with blood. He looked at his fingers and started to retch.

Gahalowood was shocked. Terrified. He realized that it could have been him that night, stretched out on the floor in the interrogation room, his brains splattered across the tiles. And then he was overcome with guilt. For had he been there, he might have been able to prevent it. He had left his partner. He would never forgive himself.

*     *     *

The next morning at dawn a line of police vehicles crossed Mount Pleasant and circled the home of Janet and Mark Donovan. Eric Donovan was arrested in his bed.

The commotion woke the neighborhood. Everyone would remember Eric, looking tired, being dragged through the street, handcuffed, visible to all, before being shoved into a police car. Janet Donovan, who had to be restrained by two burly officers, screamed at them to let her son go.

Eric Donovan left the family home that day and was charged and found guilty in the death of Alaska Sanders. He believed he would never again see that street, never again drink his coffee on that flower-filled porch. He would never greet his neighbors, charming people, every one of them shocked to discover that this nice young man was a murderer. Eric, always friendly, always well dressed, now, as police led him away, unshaven, dazed, panicked like a trapped animal, wearing the sweat pants and shirt he hastily threw on and that he would continue to wear until they gave him an orange jumpsuit.

He was a man who loved freedom: he loved the forest, fly-fishing, and open spaces. He was transferred from the police car to an interrogation room, then to a holding cell, then to a Black Maria, which took him to the bowels of a prison where he would be condemned to spend the rest of his life for the murder of Alaska Sanders.

\*      \*      \*

At first, Eric denied his involvement in Alaska's murder. To refresh his memory, Gahalowood showed him the video of Walter Carrey's confession. Eric was stunned when he saw his friend's face in close-up on the screen, confessing to the murder and implicating him directly.

"What's this all about?" he protested. "I didn't kill Alaska!"

"Isn't this your sweater?" Gahalowood asked, waving the garment in its transparent plastic bag.

"I don't know if it's my sweater. Sure, I have one like it, like thousands of students at Monarch University."

"Walter claims it's yours."

"If he says so, then it's the sweater I lent him."

"When was that?"

"Two weeks ago. It was a Saturday, March twentieth. I remember because that's the day Walter and I were ticketed by the forest rangers. We went fishing together in the river that runs near Grey Beach. The place I told you about on Monday. We got caught by some bad weather. We thought it would be a brief storm, so we took cover under a tree for a while. Walter was slow about it and got soaked and started to shiver. The poor guy's teeth were chattering. I wasn't especially cold, and besides, I'm less sensitive than he is, so I gave him the sweater I was wearing. This sweater! The rain didn't stop, so we packed up our gear and ran back to our cars. I saw Walter, in his car, take off my sweater, now soaked from the rain, and throw it on the back seat. He said to me, 'I'll wash it and give it back to you.' I told him it wasn't necessary, but he insisted."

"And did he return it?"

"No."

"That's a nice story," Gahalowood said, "but I'm not convinced."

"Look, it's the truth! I even tried to get the sweater back a few days later. I talked to Alaska—she got upset about it. I think that was the so-called argument Sally Carrey mentioned to you."

"Oh, so you *did* have an argument! Why did you lie to us?"

"I didn't lie. It wasn't even an argument. I wanted my sweater back. Walter was away from Mount Pleasant for a few days, I asked Alaska to let me have it, and she got angry because I was so insistent, that's all. She told me to call Walter, which I did. He said he'd put my sweater in the trunk of his car before leaving, and since his car was still in Mount Pleasant, I asked Alaska if she could take a look. But the sweater wasn't there."

"Sorry, Eric, but I don't believe a word of this. Why didn't you mention it the other day?"

"How was I supposed to know the sweater was connected to the crime?"

146

When Gahalowood still didn't seem convinced, Eric added, "I'm telling you the truth, Sergeant. I swear! Ask Walter, he'll confirm everything I just told you."

"Walter is dead," Gahalowood suddenly announced.

"What? *Walter's dead?*"

The questioning continued. Eric insisted that he hadn't killed Alaska Sanders and had no connection with the murder. He wanted an attorney and contacted Patricia Widsmith, a young criminal lawyer from Boston. But the evidence against him was starting to pile up: first, his DNA matched the second DNA sample found on the sweater. "Since it's Eric's sweater," Widsmith stated, "it's perfectly logical that his DNA would be on it. My client told you he was wearing it before he lent it to Walter."

Then, Eric had no alibi for the exact time of the murder. He had returned from the National Anthem to his parents' place with his sister around eleven thirty p.m. He claimed he had gone to bed, but he very easily could have left when the rest of the family was asleep without anyone noticing his absence.

The final nail was driven in with the discovery, in Eric's bedroom, of a printed note:

I KNOW WHAT YOU DID

The message was identical to those received by Alaska. Eric's printer, after analysis, revealed a very specific defect: the print head was worn and left an impression similar to the one found on the messages Alaska had received.

"Anyone could have gotten into my parents' place and used my printer," Eric argued. "We don't even lock the doors during the day. That's how it is in Mount Pleasant—we trust people. It's a quiet town."

But his arguments didn't hold much weight compared with the evidence against him, and his attorney found it difficult to demonstrate his innocence. Overwhelmed, Eric reverted to silence. Shortly before his trial he pleaded guilty to the murder of Alaska Sanders. He was given life in prison, without parole.

The day of Eric Donovan's sentencing, Gahalowood went to see Lansdane in his office. He handed him a letter.

"What's this?" Lansdane asked.

"My resignation."

Lansdane looked at him, confused. "I'm not accepting this. You're the best cop I've met in my career."

"I'll stay on one condition . . ."

"You know, Perry, I'm not a fan of blackmail."

"It's not blackmail. It's a condition for me to stick with the department."

"Go on . . ."

"I don't want a partner."

"Perry, you can't conduct investigations by yourself!"

"It's better if I do it alone. That way there's no risk of getting my partner killed."

"Perry, you had nothing to do with that."

"I want to work alone. Regulations allow it."

Lansdane accepted, unwillingly, believing it was nothing more than a passing fancy of Gahalowood's. As Gahalowood was about to leave the office, Lansdane said, "By the way, Perry, congratulations all the same. The Sanders case is officially closed."

"A case is never really closed," Gahalowood replied.

"What do you mean?"

"They'll always be after me. The dead and the living."

# 7

## An Anonymous Message

*Saturday, May 29, 2010*

I was stunned by Lansdane's story about the events of April 6, 1999. After our meeting, I had only one thing in mind—to find the letter Helen had received.

That morning I took advantage of Perry's absence to search the house—he had gone to the cemetery with his daughters. Where could Helen have hidden the letter? It wouldn't be in one of the common areas; it had to be somewhere more private. So, I looked through her closets, her personal effects, her makeup case. I hated doing this, but I felt I had no choice. The search was in vain, but I wasn't all that surprised. If Helen had wanted to hide that letter from Perry, her police husband, she wouldn't have left it where he could find it. Since I hadn't found anything at her office, my last guess was her car. Lansdane had had the opportunity to inspect it the night Helen died, but did he do it thoroughly, given the overall confusion? I had to check again.

I walked to the garage, where the bikes, an exercise machine, and Helen's gray Toyota Camry were kept. I looked at the vehicle. I could imagine Helen, lifeless, in the driver's seat. Steeling myself, I opened the door and sat down. Where could the letter be? I started with the glove compartment, then the center map compartment. Nothing. I checked the sun visors, the space between the seats. Still nothing. In a last effort, I lifted the floor mats. I don't know why I hadn't thought of it earlier. Beneath one of them, I found the blue envelope the mail carrier had spoken of. Inside it was a sheet of paper folded in two with a message. The individual letters had been cut from newspapers and glued on:

CARREY AND DONOVAN ARE INNOCENT

When I showed the letter to Chief Lansdane, he was speechless. He examined it closely, and I couldn't decide whether his face expressed astonishment or caution. "Have you spoken to Perry about this?" he asked.

"Not yet."

"'Carrey and Donovan are innocent,'" he read aloud, as if trying to grasp its meaning.

"Innocent of Alaska's murder, surely?" I suggested. "It seems the letter arrived at Gahalowood's home on April sixth, eleven years to the day after Walter Carrey's death."

"To be honest, I'm as confused as you," Lansdane admitted. "I was expecting . . . well, anything but this."

"It could be the work of some prankster," I remarked.

"I doubt it."

"Why?"

"The fact that the letter was sent to Perry. Helen was the one who found it, but clearly the letter was intended for him. And it's no joke. For one thing, Perry is connected to the Sanders case and he's a good cop. Whoever sent this message wanted Perry to reopen the investigation. There's nothing funny about that."

"But why now? The case is eleven years old."

Lansdane smiled, amused by my question. "You're a smart guy, Marcus, but a little naïve. You seem to forget that ever since your Harry Quebert book appeared, the whole world has learned of the existence of our gruff but tireless detective. Because of you, or thanks to you, millions of readers now know who Sergeant Perry Gahalowood is. Maybe someone woke up. And maybe you're indirectly responsible."

Lansdane's remark hit its target. Until that point, I had wondered why Helen hadn't asked for my help. The answer was simple: she probably wanted to keep me out of it.

"Helen knew that if Perry found out about the message, he would reopen the investigation. She didn't want him to dive back into a case that had already shaken him up so badly. But given her temperament, she wasn't the kind of woman who could simply ignore it. She probably tried to find out as much as she could so she could decide whether she should speak to her husband in spite of everything. Through her research, she found enough information to make her want to alert Perry. But she died before she could do that. The evening of her death, Helen discovered something, I'm sure of it. But what? The answer is in this message."

Lansdane nodded, then asked me, "So where do we begin?"

"You're the cop," I noted. "You could analyze it . . ."

"Pointless to try to find fingerprints. Between the two of us, the mail carrier, Helen, and I don't know who else, half the town will have their prints on it. I think we should move forward on our own before talking to anyone else, unless you want this to get back to Perry. But are you sure you want to keep him in the dark?"

"I'm positive."

It wasn't the time to give Perry more to worry about. He had taken a leave of absence "for at least a few weeks" and spent his days wandering around the house. He needed to focus on his daughters. Most of all he needed to reconnect with himself rather than confronting the ghosts of some old case.

Over the next three days, I took advantage of Perry and the girls' absence to pursue my investigation as discreetly as I could. I took a look at the GPS on Helen's car to find out where she had gone; unfortunately, no data had been recorded. I rummaged through the family computer but found nothing of interest. I retraced her steps by studying her planner, which I found in her handbag, but that was a dead end too.

I also decided to conduct my own investigation into the Alaska

Sanders murder, but the information I found online was limited. However, I did discover the existence of an association seeking to free Eric Donovan. At an internet café in Concord (I didn't dare conduct my research from the Gahalowood home), I printed a few articles as well as a photo of Alaska Sanders, which I hid inside the sofa bed in my room. I don't know why I felt the need to keep a picture of her. Maybe to remind myself that at the root of all this was a twenty-two-year-old woman who had been brutally murdered. Or maybe because I was making an unconscious connection with Nola Kellergan, the girl at the heart of the Harry Quebert case. Lansdane had told me that the Quebert investigation had served as a form of redemption for Gahalowood, and whoever delivered the anonymous letter knew that.

When I wasn't busy thinking about the Sanders case, I spent my time concerning myself with what remained of the Gahalowood family. Perry was a shadow of his former self. Laconic by default, he now buried himself in total silence. The girls were making the best of it. I tried to spend time with them, make up for their father's silence, look after them. I did what I could to add a bit of cheer to the house, once so joyous. I even attempted something I'd never attempted before: cooking. At first, there were a bunch of Aunt Anita's banana breads. But I had to shift into a higher gear and try my hand at preparing meals. Alone in the Gahalowood kitchen, I thought about Aunt Anita. She was the inspiration for my culinary adventures. And now there was a new ghost by my side: Helen. I don't know if I spoke to her audibly or silently, but I kept repeating this sentence, so unsettling for its naïveté: *Helen, I wish you weren't dead.* And as one memory led to another, I recalled the day I had met her.

*　　　*　　　*

*Two years earlier, July 2, 2008*
The Harry Quebert investigation was in full swing, but the case had taken a wrong turn. Gahalowood and I had gone to question Nola Kellergan's father, and the interview had degenerated somewhat, essentially because

of me. Perry and I had a sharp exchange outside Reverend Kellergan's house, after which he invited me over for dinner.

When I got to his house, I said, "I hope your wife isn't annoyed that I'm coming unannounced."

"Don't worry about it, Writer, her sense of compassion is very well developed."

"Thanks, Sergeant, you do know how to cheer me up."

Helen Gahalowood had just gotten back from the supermarket and was unpacking the large bags of groceries and trying to fit their contents into the fridge. Perry announced my arrival with his usual delicacy: "Darling, sorry to bother you, but can you set an extra place? I found this poor guy in the street. He looks exactly like that mug on the cover of the book on our nightstand, don't you think?"

Her smile was extraordinary and said everything there was to say about her kindness. She offered me her hand. "What a pleasure to finally meet you, Marcus! I loved your book so much. So are you really helping Perry with the investigation?"

"He's not exactly part of my team," Perry said, annoyed. "He's just some amateur who's decided to make my life difficult."

"Your husband insisted that I reimburse him for the cost of the book."

"Don't pay any attention to him," Helen said. "Deep down, he's a very kind man."

I suggested helping her and took the vegetables from a bag. Perry looked at me wide-eyed. "You see," he said to his wife, "he thinks he's helping, but in reality he just makes a mess of things. If you only knew what he's done to my investigation!"

Helen turned to me. "That means you're doing a good job."

"You see, Writer, she feels sorry for you."

"Perry doesn't have a partner," Helen continued. "He can't stand people. Want to know how many co-workers he's brought home these past years? None."

"That's because I'm very happy at home," Perry said, grabbing two beers from the fridge and offering me one. Helen winked at me conspiratorially.

"You see, Marcus, he likes you."

"Oh, no, I don't!"

"Call me Marcus too, Sergeant, we're practically friends."

"We're not friends. You call me 'Sergeant,' I'll call you 'Writer.' That way we'll keep it professional."

Helen rolled her eyes. "Welcome to the Gahalowood family, Marcus!"

That evening, after dinner, when I was alone with Perry on the porch, I said to him, "Sergeant, your wife is amazing. Her only drawback is that she's married to you."

Gahalowood burst out laughing.

*     *     *

Malia and Lisa burst out laughing when I described over dinner how I first met their mother. My osso buco was so bad we ended up ordering pizza. It was just the three of us; Perry hadn't come downstairs. When he finally joined us, he looked gloomier than ever. The girls were returning to school the next day. Seeing their father's face, I felt it was probably for the best.

Perry grabbed a slice of pizza and ate it in silence. Then the girls went up to their rooms, while he and I remained in the kitchen. We had hardly found ourselves alone lately, and I felt he was avoiding me. I put the dishes in the dishwasher as he struggled to shove the pizza boxes into the garbage can.

"They go in the recycling," I said.

"I never recycle."

"You have to start somewhere, Sergeant."

He placed the boxes on the counter and walked off, grumbling to himself. When I had straightened out the kitchen, I went downstairs to my room. I lay down on the bed, studied the photo of Alaska Sanders, and then examined the anonymous letter. It had led Helen to make a discovery, but what?

I continued to stare at the sheet of paper as if some sign would magically emerge. Suddenly, something caught my eye that had escaped me before: given the message consisted of a collage of letters making up the words CARREY AND DONOVAN ARE INNOCENT, the typography was pretty uniform. Whoever sent it had used letters cut from the same newspaper. That was a curious detail: why not use different ones to cover your tracks?

Since I was lying down and holding the message at arm's length toward the ceiling, I unwittingly positioned it between me and the overhead light. An inscription appeared through one of the letters. Ungluing the letter, I discovered, on the back, an enigmatic sequence of numbers and letters:

10 Nor

What did these printed characters correspond to? The answer came to mind at once: it was a fragment of an address label. The address of a subscriber to the newspaper, a piece of which had been on the reverse side of the letter that had been cut out to create the message to Gahalowood. I finally had my clue.

\* \* \*

The following day I met Lansdane in a coffee shop in downtown Concord to share my discovery with him. "We find the subscriber, we find the author of the message," I said.

He quickly put the brakes on my enthusiasm. "Not so fast, Marcus. You have no idea how many coffee shops, restaurants, medical offices, and who knows what take out subscriptions for their customers to read. Whoever sent that letter could've picked the newspaper up anywhere, maybe from the street, even a garbage can. Can you picture someone sending an anonymous letter with his address on it?"

"It's not that easily visible. He could've just been careless."

"Marcus, who would use a paper they subscribe to for an anonymous message? It doesn't make sense."

"I already thought of that. It could be someone who didn't have access to other papers. Someone who was locked up, for example. Like someone in prison. Maybe his cellmate, arrested for something unrelated, confesses to him that he killed Alaska Sanders. Our man then writes an anonymous message to Gahalowood. Or maybe he was sent a package wrapped in newsprint and he used it to write the message."

"Any mail that prisoners send is subject to screening. The letter would've been intercepted."

"Not if he sent it through his attorney."

"And the attorney is going to agree to playing mailman and dropping the letter off at Gahalowood's home? I have a hard time believing that, Marcus. Still, I do appreciate your fertile imagination."

"I'm still convinced that this address led Helen somewhere."

"It's possible," Lansdane conceded. "So let's try to find it before you get lost in any more of your wild conjectures."

Lansdane was clearly ambivalent about the implications of what he was saying. From the looks of it, he had little desire to get involved. But neither could he ignore it. As he was rising, he said, "Good luck with your research, keep me posted."

I blurted out, "*Good luck?* What do you mean, *good luck?* Are you just going to leave me to figure this out on my own?"

"Marcus, you're putting me in an impossible situation. I'm the head of the state police; I can't get involved in a parallel civil investigation."

"So why don't you transfer the case to one of your departments?"

"Because you're insisting that Perry be kept out of it. And you wouldn't be part of any official investigation. I can see you've become obsessed with this, Marcus."

"Chief Lansdane, I understand that you don't put very much stock in such things. There's a reason why you don't want to handle this case internally, and I need to know what it is. If you don't tell me, I'm going to the press."

Lansdane sighed deeply. "You know how Perry always described you,

Marcus? A pain in the ass—a nice guy, but a pain in the ass. I have to agree with him. I don't want news of this letter getting around because, at this point, I want to avoid complications and pointless rumors. If there's new evidence, that means we have to reopen the investigation into Alaska Sanders's murder. And before I do that, I need to identify the author of that letter—discreetly. And you're the man for the job."

"So you're going to leave me to deal with this shitshow by myself, Lansdane?"

"I'm the chief of police; I have plenty to keep me busy."

"Exactly, you're the chief, which means you're not obligated to explain yourself to anyone. So, let's get to work!"

To locate the address, Lansdane and I had no other option but to identify all those that began with "10 Nor." The beauty of modern technology is that, after searching online for a while, we were easily able to prepare a list. Unfortunately, the list was interminable. The huge number of streets, roads, avenues, and boulevards in the country that began with "Nor" would keep us busy for months.

We needed to limit the scope of our search, and Lansdane suggested a method that turned out to be useful. We knew that Helen was at Fanny's, near the westward exit off I-393, at around ten p.m. Meanwhile, I was convinced that she had driven to the mystery address that same evening. If we could determine when she left the office, the time it took her to get from there to the restaurant would help us to define our search area.

Mads Bergsen, Helen's boss, was the only person who could ask the head of security at his office to provide us with a record of Helen's arrivals and departures. As is often the case in office buildings, every employee had a badge they used to pass through the security gate providing access to the elevators. Their comings and goings were easily traceable.

Still, it took a lot of work to persuade him. "Why do you need this information?" he asked me suspiciously.

"All I can tell you is that it's important."

"I don't really approve of what you're doing. And behind her husband's back, no less. I thought you were friends."

"It's because we're friends that I'm trying to protect him. Please, Mr. Bergsen, I promise to get out of your life after this."

The argument seemed to persuade him. He left me alone for a moment and then returned with a record of Helen's entrances and exits over the previous few weeks. On the day she died, she had left the office at six p.m.

In Lansdane's living room we reconstructed Helen's final hours. He had spread out a map of New Hampshire on the coffee table. I repeated what we already knew. "At six, Helen leaves her office, at 9:05 she phones Perry, at ten, she reaches Fanny's near the westbound exit off I-393."

"That's the most logical exit for returning home," Lansdane remarked.

"So, she's on her way home. But she's very upset. She's just discovered something that deeply disturbs her. Perry isn't picking up the phone. She's having trouble breathing and starts to feel sick to her stomach. She sees Fanny's and decides to stop there to calm down and collect her thoughts. She doesn't know what to do with the information she has and so she calls you."

"If she found out something important that evening, she most likely wanted to warn Perry right away."

"She called him at 9:05, meaning she was at most an hour's drive away from Fanny's."

"Right," Lansdane agreed. "And she left the office at six. So it takes her three hours to get to wherever she's going. But at that moment, she's still floundering. She's probably looking at a whole list of addresses, just like we're going to do. She may not have driven right there; she would have had to check a bunch of different streets that might match the fragment on the letter. Until her discovery. But if she called right away, at 9:05, it has to be within an hour of Fanny's."

Based on this assumption, Lansdane drew a circle on the map. It was within that area that our search would begin.

*       *       *

I spent nearly every one of the next ten days driving around New Hampshire alone after dropping Lisa off at school. Town after town, village after village. I visited 10 North Street, 10 Norton Street, 10 Nordham Boulevard, 10 Norfolk Avenue.

I stopped in front of each of the addresses and inconspicuously waited around, in the hope of finding an occupant or some clue, without knowing exactly what I was looking for. Each day, my sleuthing came to an end when Lisa finished school. Then I resumed my existence as a substitute father. Perry soon began to wonder about my absences. Obviously, I had a few alibis—doing the shopping, taking a walk in the countryside, going to the mall. As proof, I even brought back a completely useless shoe cabinet that I had bought out of desperation. But Perry was no fool. He suspected that I was up to something. When he asked questions, I was evasive, which is never a good strategy to adopt with a determined cop.

One morning—a Thursday—after ten days of fruitless searching, I drove to Barrington, a small, quiet town, about fifty minutes from Concord. There I found Norris Street.

As I had done at the previous addresses, I parked not too far from number 10. It was a pretty little house of red brick, like the others along the street, all separated by well-maintained strips of lawn. I had a pair of binoculars and could see inside the living room. What I saw shocked me. I was about to call Lansdane, but at that moment, something struck my window. It was a police officer. He made a sign for me to lower the window. "Can I help you, sir?" he asked.

The officer had parked behind me with his roof lights on. Preoccupied by what I had discovered, I hadn't noticed the patrol car pull up.

I couldn't explain the real reason for my presence on Norris Street, and in light of my confused reply, the officer suspected that I might be a thief casing a residence. I was taken to the Barrington police station for more detailed questioning.

I was interviewed by the chief of police, Captain Martin Grove, a cheerful, heavyset man whose small mustache danced whenever he spoke.

"I'm taking over because you're a celebrity, it seems," Grove said. "We checked you out—you've got quite a reputation. So what brings you to Barrington? We don't appreciate trouble around here."

"Nor do I, Captain," I reassured him. "I didn't come to your town to cause a problem."

"I'm told you were checking out some houses. Are you like one of those Hollywood nuts who steals things because it turns them on?"

"I'm here conducting a confidential investigation."

He laughed. "You're joking."

"If by 'joking' you mean *lying*, I suggest you call Chief Lansdane of the New Hampshire State Police at once."

"We're first going to take a blood sample to make sure you haven't taken any drugs."

"Captain Grove, I strongly suggest that you refrain from putting a needle in my arm. Pick up your phone and call Chief Lansdane."

Lansdane had to come in person to Barrington to straighten things out. Once he had collected me, he took me to Norris Street. He parked behind my car.

"Look at the living-room window, Chief. You remember I had a theory about someone who might be locked up in some way?"

He looked and then said, "I owe you an apology, Marcus."

In the living room, a man in a wheelchair was reading a newspaper. A man who couldn't leave his house, or not without a great deal of difficulty, at least, judging by the stairs that led from the front door down to the sidewalk. He had his back to us, so Lansdane couldn't see his face.

Once again, someone was knocking on the car window. This time it was an elderly woman. I lowered my window. "Get away from here or I'm calling the police," she said.

"We are the police," Lansdane, who was in uniform, replied amiably.

She seemed horrified by her mistake. "I'm terribly sorry, I didn't realize. Are you here because of what happened the other day?"

"What happened the other day?" I asked.

"A Black woman turned up at the neighbors' place; it was a little before nine. I saw her in her car, a Toyota Camry, a gray one, staring at the house. I have nothing against Black people, but I found it strange. So I took a good look. And the Black lady finally knocked on the door. And that created a ruckus. She started shouting. The woman next door started shouting as well. I was about to call the police, but she had already left."

"And when was that?"

"About a month ago."

I stared at the old woman. "Weren't you being a bit racist?"

"No, I keep my eyes open, that's all," she replied primly. "I want my neighborhood to stay peaceful. There have been so many robberies lately. Besides, you're white, and I still called the police earlier. I have nothing against Blacks, but I don't want any trouble, that's all."

The nosy neighbor kept talking, but I raised my window so I wouldn't have to listen to her. As she continued her soliloquy, I turned to Lansdane. "It was Helen in her Camry. Helen was here the day she died."

Once the neighbor had left us, Lansdane got out of the car and approached the house. He looked at the name on the mailbox and returned. He got into the passenger seat, white as a sheet.

"What is it, Chief Lansdane?"

"The name on the mailbox . . . it's Kazinsky."

"Kazinsky?" I repeated without understanding what he was implying.

"He's the only person alive who was present in the interrogation room the night that Matt Vance and Walter Carrey died."

# 8

## *Disagreements*

*Concord, New Hampshire*
*Monday, June 14, 2010*
Having discovered that Nicholas Kazinsky was almost certainly the author of the anonymous message, I returned to Concord at once to inform Gahalowood. But just as I arrived home, Perry got a call from Mads Bergsen.

When I entered the house, Gahalowood was standing in the hallway glowering, as if he had been waiting for me. The words *Joie de Vivre* that I'd passed on my way in had never seemed so inappropriate.

"Everything okay, Sergeant?"

"So, just like that, you decided to poke your nose into Helen's life? Is that what you've been doing all day long?"

I bitterly regretted my secretiveness. I felt the force of Gahalowood's anger and tried to calm him down. "Sergeant, it's more complicated than you think."

He threw a sheaf of papers in my face: my articles on the Alaska Sanders case. He had found them. "For God's sake, Marcus, tell me you have a good reason . . ."

That Gahalowood was calling me by my first name wasn't a good sign.

"Helen wasn't cheating on you, Sergeant. If her behavior was unusual these last few weeks, it was because she was trying to protect you. She found an anonymous note intended for you and she didn't want to talk to you about it before she knew what was going on. The night she died, the night she tried to reach you, she had discovered something. And I know what it was."

From my back pocket I retrieved the envelope and offered it to Gahalowood. When he saw the message, I could see the astonishment on his face.

"Nicholas Kazinsky sent you that message, the cop who—"

"I know who Kazinsky is," Gahalowood cut me off.

"And I guess Helen knew him as well. He's the one who wrote the letter, I'm almost certain."

"Almost?"

"There are several pieces of convincing evidence, Sergeant. The start of his address on a piece of newspaper used to compose the message, for one thing. That can't be a coincidence. We just have to question him. *You* have to question him."

Gahalowood was speechless. He stared at me with contempt. I felt I had to say something to fill the silence.

"Sergeant, I didn't talk to you about it before, but that was for your sake. With all that you've been through, I didn't want to add to your worries."

After another long, uncomfortable silence, Gahalowood said to me in a hollow voice, "Get out, Marcus. Get out before the girls come home from school."

There was no arguing with him. I went to the guest room and gathered my things, stuffing them helter-skelter into my small suitcase. Five minutes later, I was in my car. Gahalowood watched me from the front porch as if making sure I had really left. Before shutting the car door, I yelled, "Keep going! Keep going, Sarge! You have to find out why Kazinsky sent you that message."

"Who says Kazinsky sent it? Anyone could have picked up a paper and composed that ridiculous letter. And you, you fell for it, just like the amateur you are. Your book has gone to your head. Do you think you're some big-shot detective now? You're nothing but a clown, Marcus!"

But I was stubborn too. "Obviously Kazinsky wrote the letter. Your theory doesn't make sense, Sergeant."

"It makes even less sense that he would suddenly think Walter Carrey was innocent. Carrey admitted it: there's a video recording of his confession. Why would Kazinsky stir it all up again eleven years later?"

"Because it's been haunting him all this time. Maybe he wants to clear his conscience."

"Marcus, it's time for you to leave."

He turned his back on me and went inside. And I cried out, "Helen would be ashamed of you!"

Gahalowood stormed back out, furious. In his anger he ripped the *Joie de Vivre* plaque off the wall and threw it as hard as he could in my direction. It struck the hood of my Range Rover, denting it.

Before leaving Concord, I stopped to say goodbye to Lansdane.

"Don't leave like this, Marcus," he pleaded, after I told him what had happened.

"I can't wrap my head around it. And Perry's right, what business do I have getting involved?"

"You have to get to the bottom of this!"

"Why don't you do it? *You're* the cop!"

"I can't."

"What do you mean, *you can't*?"

"I can't simply reopen an investigation like that. Can you imagine the chaos within the department? I can't act without concrete proof."

I was taken aback by his last sentence. "Wait, is that why you encouraged me to look into this? So I would be the one to do the grunt work without anyone finding out? So that you wouldn't get your hands dirty? Terrific! You get the Nobel Prize for cowardice!"

"You didn't need much encouragement, Marcus."

As I was turning to go, Lansdane added, "You know what Helen would've said?"

"Don't bring Helen into this . . ."

"She would've said that the Marcus Goldman who wrote *The Truth About the Harry Quebert Affair* never would've let this drop."

"Novelists have a habit of embellishing the truth. I should know."

Five hours later I arrived in Manhattan to be greeted by traffic jams, streetlights, and the noise of early evening. I returned to my apartment three weeks after having left it. I took a shower, ordered something to eat, then stood by the window contemplating the city's wild energy on that summer night. I thought about Perry. I stared at my phone, hoping in vain for a call from him. I wondered whether we would be able to pick up the pieces or if I had lost my last friend once and for all.

*　　*　　*

Several days went by and I had no news from Gahalowood. I tried to call him several times, without success. The chill between us was unbearable, and in the end, I got into my car with the idea of returning to Concord and talking it out. But as I was crossing Massachusetts, I lost my nerve. And without really knowing how or why, I ended up at Burrows University, my alma mater, where I had met Harry Quebert.

It was with a sense of wistfulness that I entered the campus. I made a pilgrimage to the boxing ring, the large auditorium where I had distinguished myself in front of Harry one day in 1998, and the hallways I had walked so often with my roommate, Jared—I wondered what had become of him.

The semester was over and the place was deserted. I walked to the English department and stopped in front of Harry's office. The plaque bearing his name had been removed. Almost without thinking, I opened the door: the room appeared to be unoccupied. It smelled musty. Nothing but a few of the standard furnishings—shelving and a cheap plywood desk. No-one had replaced Harry since his dismissal in June 2008. I opened the desk drawers. The first two were empty. In the third I found an old newspaper and a statuette of a seagull. I shivered—what was that doing here? I was about to grab it when a voice made me jump.

"This could be your office, Marcus."

It was Dustin Pergal, chair of the English department.

"I . . . I came to pay a visit," I stuttered.

Pergal smiled. "I see that."

"How are you?"

"I'm no longer the chair. I'm now president of the university. I've been promoted, but not as much as you. To think that I nearly threw you out in '98 and you're now the star of American letters and the pride of this university."

Pergal invited me to have dinner with him. I accepted and found myself in his comfortable little house on campus. I met his charming wife, and I have to acknowledge that my evening was delightful.

"Thanks to your writers' residence, Burrows University has gained considerable prestige," Pergal confided during dinner. "A number of students have applied to the English department in the hope of taking advantage of a retreat in Somerset."

"I'm delighted."

"And Ernie Pinkas has been terrific."

"That he is."

"Did you come to see Ernie?"

"No."

"You didn't tell me what brought you here. Are you looking for someone in particular?"

"Yes—me."

Pergal couldn't help but smile. "You know, Marcus, my proposal before was serious. Harry's office could be yours. Why don't you teach a writing course? I have a spot for the fall semester."

"I'll have to think about it."

"We could try it for six months. To see if you like teaching. Obviously, this isn't Columbia, but it has its charms. Well, you know that."

Then, just like that, I decided to take him up on his offer. "That works, you can count on me. I'm in."

Pergal was delighted and we shook hands. As I was leaving, he walked me to my car. I was finally able to ask him the question that I had been burning to ask all evening. "Heard anything from Harry?"

"Harry Quebert? No. Why would I?"

"I don't know. Just asking."

"I'll send you a draft contract by mail. In the meantime, can I announce the good news inside the department?"

"Of course."

It was already late; I didn't feel like driving back to New York. Rather than stopping at some gloomy motel on the edge of the highway, I drove into Boston. I took a room at the Boston Plaza, where, thinking they were doing me a favor, they put me in a very large suite where I felt lost. I stayed in the dark for a while, looking out at the Charles River and the city of Cambridge outlined on the horizon.

Boston reminded me of Emma Mathews. The city brought back memories of our affair, which, in spite of its intensity, had ended after a few months. As my mother would have said, "Emma could have been 'the one.'" We had met shortly before my breakthrough success, as I was writing the book I hoped would bring me fame.

\*      \*      \*

*Burrows University, Massachusetts*
*March 2005*

"How's your book going?" Harry asked as he offered me a cup of coffee in his office.

"I've never written so much in my life."

"Do you have a title yet?"

"*G, Like Goldstein.*"

"Sounds good. I'd be interested in reading it."

"Soon, I promise."

Harry suggested that we attend a play being given in the school auditorium, a modern adaptation of Chekhov's *The Cherry Orchard*. There I sat, in the first row, during that awful performance. The actors were terrible, the staging catastrophic. The intermission was my chance to escape, and I joined Harry at the bar. When it was time to return to the auditorium, I let him go ahead. The audience all returned to their seats, and soon there were only two people in the lobby: myself and the girl with green eyes who was looking at me. The attraction was irresistible.

"It's a very bad production," she said.

"Chekhov would turn his gun on himself!"

She laughed and extended her hand. "I'm Emma."

"Marcus. Marcus Goldman."

She looked surprised. "You're Marcus Goldman?"

"Have we met before?" I asked.

"No. But Professor Quebert has been talking about you all semester."

"Oh?"

For a moment I thought that Harry had been singing my praises, but Emma clarified things by simply saying, "So you're Mr. Blow Job."

I was mortified. Seven years earlier, when I was a first-year student, I had managed to scandalize Harry Quebert's class by stating that I was a fervent admirer of fellatio. This was during the sordid business of President Clinton's blow job from Monica Lewinsky in the Oval Office. My outburst nearly cost me my place at Burrows and had followed me ever since.

Emma noticed my crestfallen look, leaned over, and whispered into my ear, "I never said I didn't like blow jobs."

I offered her a drink. Emma was a senior, studying literature. That's about all I recall of our discussion—I was too busy admiring her face, her lips, imagining them pressed to my own. She interrupted my reverie by asking, "And what about you, what do you think?"

Not knowing what she was alluding to, I simply said, "I feel the same way as you," sounding very sure of myself.

"Finally, someone agrees with me! Professor Baxter gave a biased overview of the chronology. You have to take the context into account. That's pretty obvious, isn't it?"

"Very obvious. Chronology is fundamental!"

"It's like Professor Quebert's class. Sure, it was interesting. Last semester we visited Edith Wharton's home in Lenox. I'm not saying she was a great novelist. But, still, an amazing body of work. Yet once again we were reading only dead authors. I wish Professor Quebert had brought in some living writers, I mean, aside from himself, of course. So we could talk to them, understand them . . ."

"Well, this is your lucky day. I'm a writer."

Emma crinkled her eyes and smiled. And the smile made her even more beautiful.

"You're a writer?"

"Working on my first novel. My agent thinks it has potential."

It was only half a lie. I had sent the first chapters of *G, Like Goldstein* to an agent in New York, Douglas Claren. But I was still waiting for him to finish reading them. But the mere mention of my so-called agent had worked. Emma now looked at me with an intensity that had nothing unpleasant about it. "Can I read it?"

"No."

"Please?"

"I'd prefer it if you didn't."

"I'd love to read it," she said again.

"We'll see . . ."

She smiled triumphantly. "That's wild—you're the first writer I've met! Besides Professor Quebert, of course. I find that so fascinating."

She bombarded me with questions. How did I write? Where did I get my ideas? Did I use events from my own life? How often did I have to rewrite a chapter and how many words did I write a day? Were the mornings better for writing than the evenings?

Just then one of Emma's girlfriends appeared in the lobby. "Emma, what are you doing here? We should go, the play has started."

Emma sighed and stood up. Since I stayed at the bar, she said to me, "You're not going to make me watch the rest of that horrible play alone, are you?"

I followed compliantly. The seat next to hers was free. We sat down side by side. She placed her hand on mine. The contact made me shiver. The second half of the play was even more dismal than the first. But I had something to compensate for it: Emma fell asleep and rested her head on my shoulder.

*    *    *

That night in June 2010, as I looked out over Boston, I felt the urge to contact Emma again. Find out what she was doing, what she had become. The internet helped me locate her—she was running an interior design store in Cambridge. I went there the following morning. When she saw me walk through the door, she just stood there.

"Marcus?"

"Emma! I was passing by and saw you through the window. It's crazy, I know."

She asked me what I was doing in Boston. I told her that I'd come to visit friends. When she suggested we go out for a coffee, I looked at my watch, pretending I had a full schedule. "Yes, of course," I finally agreed. "I have some time." She left an employee in charge, and we strolled over to a nearby restaurant.

The last time I had seen Emma was on August 30, 2005, the day of our breakup. She had since gotten married and had a young daughter.

"All that in five years?" I asked.

"Well, in the same time, you've become a star."

"I'm not really sure what I've become."

She burst out laughing.

"And your store?" I asked. "Back then you were finishing up your studies."

"I went to school to make my parents happy. You know I've always adored contemporary design. My dream was to have my own store."

"You never talked about that."

"I realized afterward that we . . . well, you inspired me."

"Me?"

"Yes, the way you shaped your life around your dreams so you wouldn't get trapped in the everyday grind. You wanted to live faster and harder than everyone else."

Looking at Emma, I thought about the months we had been together. Those were happy times, spent for the most part in Boston.

*    *    *

*Boston, Massachusetts*
*June 2005*
Whenever I met up with Emma, we had a ritual. We would relax in the sun on the grass in Boston Common, the emblematic park at the center of the city. Stretched out on my stomach, I would write, using a book as a support. Emma read, her head resting on my back. Invariably, she ended up rolling on top of me until I yielded, and we embraced on the soft grass, kissing, like the carefree young lovers we were. We had been together for three months.

The evening we met, after the play, Emma suggested getting a drink in Boston, where she was living, which was only thirty minutes from Burrows. Obviously, I accepted, and after we hit a few bars, she invited me to her place. Emma came from a very wealthy family and had an apartment on Beacon Hill. We talked, we laughed, we drank tequila, and we ended the night in her bed without getting much sleep.

My life then had taken the form of a three-act play. In Act 1, I was writing my book *G, Like Goldstein*, in Montclair, at my parents' place, in what used to be the guest room, which they had converted into an office. In Act 2, with every significant advance—about every ten days—I sent my text by email to Harry and my agent. In Act 3, once my pages were sent, I jumped into my old Ford and got on the road in the direction of Somerset, to talk about my work with Harry. I stopped in Boston on the way there and on the way back to see Emma.

That day in June 2005, Emma and I were lying stretched out on the grass in the park as usual. Suddenly, slightly drawing back her head, she looked deep into my eyes and tenderly passed her fingers through my hair.

"What's bothering you?" she asked.

"Nothing."

"I can tell something's bothering you."

She already knew me well.

"Roy Barnaski called."

She opened her eyes wide. "Roy Barnaski? The head of Schmid & Hanson?"

"The same."

"And . . . ? Tell me! Tell me!"

"He read the first chapters of the manuscript; my agent sent them to him. He loved them. I have a meeting with him next Tuesday. In New York."

"Oh, Marcus, that's fantastic!"

She pressed herself against me before lifting her head with a somewhat guarded expression on her face. "When did you talk to him?"

"Day before yesterday."

"Day before yesterday? Why didn't you say anything?"

"I don't know. Superstition, I suppose. By then he'll have had the chance to read the rest of the finished chapters; maybe he'll change his mind and tell me my book is terrible."

"Are you afraid of failing or succeeding, Marcus?"

"That's a good question."

She took my face in her hands. "Everything is going to be alright. Be confident."

That evening, as she did every Sunday, Emma dined with her parents. And lately I had been going with her.

Michael and Linda Mathews, Emma's parents, lived in Chelsea, the chic suburb outside Boston, on a large property with a manicured garden, a pool, a tennis court, sculpted shrubbery, gravel pathways, and a small dog that smelled bad. On Sunday, they organized family dinners with their three daughters, Emma, Donna, and Anna, and their respective partners. Donna, twenty-eight, planned to get married in September to the epitome of boredom, a computer programmer by the name of Theodore, who insisted that I call him Teddy. Anna, who was thirty-one, had married a lawyer called Chad, who, by his own admission, was talented and destined for great things. Teddy and Chad, like good sons-in-law, fought to outshine each other before Michael and Linda. They took advantage of these dinners to politely wage war, laying their successes out before us. My arrival in the family provided comic relief—a penniless writer, they couldn't have dreamed of a better foil.

The duel between the future brothers-in-law began as soon as we arrived at the Mathewses' home. Each of them parked in front of the house, Chad in his convertible sports car, Theodore in his luxury off-road vehicle. The paint shone, the rims gleamed. Then Emma and I stepped out of my beat-up old Ford, dusty from all the miles we had clocked on the highway. Teddy and Chad elbowed each other complicitly, pleased with themselves, fidgeting in their designer shirts.

I remember that Sunday evening in June; Chad and Teddy were eagerly one-upping each other. Chad boasted of a new case he had landed, which was going to be *the big one*, while Teddy congratulated himself on *the incredible opportunities available in an emerging and highly lucrative field*. And as they continued raising the stakes this way, desperate to impress, Mr. Mathews, who had until that point simply nodded along, turned to me. "And you, Marcus, what's new?"

"I'm moving ahead with my book," I replied, laconically.

I intentionally omitted the meeting with Roy Barnaski. Emma, always ready to come to my defense, wanted to let them know, but I discreetly squeezed her hand to dissuade her.

"So do you have a plan B?" Mr. Mathews asked.

"A *plan B*? What do you mean?" I asked, though perfectly aware of what he was driving at.

"Most writers don't live off their writing. They teach or something like that. You could become a high-school teacher, even aim a bit higher, a university professor. A little ambition, you know."

There was an uncomfortable silence. Then Emma flew to my aid: "Marcus is too modest to tell you, but he has a meeting with Roy Barnaski next Tuesday."

The name didn't appear to mean anything to those assembled around the table. "Barnaski is one of the most powerful editors in the country," she continued. "He loves Marcus's book. If he's asking to meet him, it's because he wants to make him an offer."

Mr. Mathews then assumed an air of condescension. "I don't want to criticize you, Marcus, but just how much is this going to bring you? Peanuts. It's admirable that you aspire to become an artist, but books take a great deal of time to write and they don't pay anything! You're an ambitious young man. I can find you a position in the office of one of my companies, with a good salary and reasonable hours. It will give you security. Think of your future, at least a little. You need stability. Build something for Emma and yourself. You're not going to be satisfied just being some kind of writer all your life."

Emma was crestfallen. Compared with her, I took the blow quite well. But then Chad felt it was a propitious moment to add his two cents to the conversation: "It's true, Marcus, after all, you're not going to drive around in that old Ford all your life, are you?"

*     *     *

In that coffee shop in Boston, five years after our separation, I wondered what my life would have been if Emma and I had stayed together. Would I have settled in Boston? Would I now be the head of a family, living the American dream in some quaint suburban home? Reflecting on this brought me back to the eternal question: Would I have been at peace?

Emma tore me from my thoughts by finally asking the question that must have been eating at her ever since I walked through the door of her store. "What's going on, Marcus? What are you doing here? I have a hard time believing that you just happened to be passing through."

"I was wondering why it didn't work out between us."

Emma nearly choked. "Are you serious, Marcus?" she replied, amused. "You're still worried about that?"

"I'm just trying to figure out what I did with my life."

In a solemn, almost sad, voice she said to me, "You became successful, Marcus. That's the reason we broke up."

Leaving the coffee shop, we walked for a while together. When we reached my car, she saw it was a Range Rover and made a face.

"I liked the Marcus who drove that old Ford. You know why? Because your old rattletrap was a sign that, in spite of your talent and all the success I knew you would have, you were different. I left you because the book was already taking up too much space in your life. You were going to be famous, I knew that. You had the makings of success. I left because I knew you were going to slip away from me."

I didn't say anything. She looked at the hood, dented by the wrought-iron plaque from the Gahalowood home.

"Better get that fixed," she ordered, mockingly. "It doesn't look so good."

"It's staying. It's a scar." I opened the door.

"Do you have a piece of paper and something to write with?" Emma asked.

I gave her my notebook and a hotel pen from the glove compartment. She wrote down a few lines. "Here's my address. The next time you want to see me, don't bother making up some story and showing up at the store. Come to the house."

Leaving Cambridge, I saw myself for a moment as Marcus in his old

Ford, the man she had loved. I would have become a teacher at a high school in Boston, following the path laid out for me by her father. Emma would have been happy in her store. A comfortable family life. A life without the success, yes, but perhaps more serene.

I got on the highway headed for New York. Then I decided to continue on Route 95 south to Florida. Because Miami was too far to drive without stopping, I spent the night in Richmond, Virginia. I reached my uncle Saul's place the following day in the late afternoon. He was happy to see me suddenly show up on his doorstep.

I took advantage of my stay to jot down a few memories of the Baltimore Goldmans. Uncle Saul wanted to know what I was working on. I didn't tell him, but he must have understood that it had something to do with his family. A few days later, he showed me a photo he had found while going through some of his things. It was a picture from 1995. I was in it, as a child in Baltimore, flanked by my cousins Woody and Hillel, along with Alexandra, a woman who had meant a great deal to me. Back then I thought she would be the love of my life, but I lost her when I lost my cousins.

After studying the photo, I wanted to give it back to Uncle Saul, but he suggested I keep it. He never knew just how deeply it was going to affect the rest of my life.

That same day, an unexpected call upset my summer plans. It was Gahalowood. In a voice that again sounded firm and confident, he said to me, "I'm just a poor slob who owes you an apology. You were right after all—it's been eleven years, and the murderer is still walking free."

# Part Two

## *The Consequences of Murder*

# 9

## *Reconciliation*

I drove up the entire East Coast in two and a half days to reach New Hampshire: fifteen hundred miles covered, twenty-six hours at the wheel, twelve states crossed, seven stops to fill the gas tank, three quarts of coffee, a dozen donuts, four packets of M&Ms, and three bags of cheese-flavored chips.

It was five p.m. when I arrived at the Gahalowood home. The sergeant was waiting for me on the porch. He looked like he hadn't moved since our argument. As I got out of the car, his daughters ran from the house and threw themselves into my arms. "Uncle Marcus," they shouted together, "you came back!" Then Lisa said to me, "So, that problem with your movie? Did you take care of it?"

I assumed their father had made something up to justify my sudden departure.

"Everything's settled," I replied tersely.

The girls went back inside. Gahalowood and I sat down on the steps of the porch. He pulled two beers from a cooler and opened them. "Writer . . ." he began, somewhat sheepishly, as he offered me a bottle.

"You don't have to explain, Sergeant."

He nodded toward the Range Rover. "Sorry about the dent."

"No need to apologize; I think I hate that thing."

"Oh?"

"Long story."

After a slug of beer, Gahalowood went on. "About eleven years ago, on an April evening, I was sitting on these same steps with my partner, Matt Vance. I had just moved here, Lisa was about to be born. It was the day Alaska Sanders died. Vance told me it would be his last case. He wanted to call it quits. Three days later, I found him dead in the interrogation room. What really happened?"

The sergeant didn't expect an answer to his question. At least, not yet. But it was his way of telling me that he was ready to open the door to the past.

So I asked him, "What finally convinced you that the events of April sixth, 1999, didn't happen the way you thought they did all these years?"

"You were the one who convinced me. You and your goddamn altruism. Your unbearable sense of justice. Your incredible, ball-busting stubbornness. I ended up looking through the case file again."

"And?"

"I noticed something no-one had seen at the time. Come on." He led me inside and sat me down at the table, spreading out photocopies of the documents.

"Is it legal to copy a case file?" I asked.

"No. Are you going to report me to internal affairs?"

"I simply wanted to evaluate your state of mind, Sergeant," I replied with an amused smile.

"Determined," he assured me.

"Well now, that's the old sergeant I knew! 'The Alaska Sanders Affair,' the new investigation by Perry Gahalowood and Marcus Goldman!"

"You're not going to write about this, are you?"

"I'm not making any promises."

Gahalowood then went over the elements of the case: the experts' conclusions confirmed Nicholas Kazinsky's story. The number of bullets in Matt Vance's gun, the three shell casings found in the room, the shot at the one-way glass, the traces of powder on Walter Carrey's hand.

Powder was also found on Vance's hands, but these were explained by the struggle between the two men, which led to the first shot being fired.

"So nothing unusual?" I asked him, cutting short his explanations.

"Don't interrupt me, Writer. This is where it gets interesting."

He summarized the statement in which Kazinsky explained that Vance had forgotten to remove his weapon when he took water to Carrey.

"Look," he said, holding the photos taken that night in front of my eyes. "You see what I see? Or, rather, what I don't see . . ."

I looked closely at the photographs, surveying the same scene from various angles. Lying on the ground, in a pool of blood, the two bodies, each shot in the head. Even without seeing their faces, it was easy to make out who was who: Vance had his police badge on his belt and an empty holster. Walter Carrey had Vance's weapon in his hand. I couldn't make out anything unusual. Gahalowood had a gleam in his eye.

"There's no water. No bottle, no glass. Nothing. But it's a crime scene. No-one touched anything while waiting for forensics to take the photos. Somewhere in that room, there should have been a glass or a bottle of water that Vance took to Carrey."

"Which means . . ."

"That Kazinsky probably lied."

I wasn't totally convinced by his argument. "That's not much by way of proof, is it?"

"You're right, it's not much. But it's what got me thinking. Now, look at the photos again." I stared at the photographs once more.

"Look carefully at the two bodies. What comes to mind?"

"Disgust."

"Look harder!"

"Enough with the guessing games! Tell me what I'm supposed to be looking for."

"Walter Carrey shot himself in the left temple."

"Yes, and he's holding the gun in his left hand. That's perfectly logical."

"Except that Carrey was right-handed. I checked. He was right-handed and we missed that detail completely. As for the rest of it, since Kazinsky's statement was corroborated by the forensic department's analysis, there was no reason to doubt the sequence of events. I then remembered something that Vance had told me in private the evening after we found Alaska's body. He wanted to make this his last investigation. He had compared it to an unsolved crime that he never forgot when he was a detective with the Bangor police, back in Maine. That case involved the murder of a seventeen-year-old girl by the name of Gaby Robinson. Well, I went up to Bangor and found one of his former colleagues. He told me that Gaby Robinson's unsolved murder had really taken a toll on Vance. The investigation had been wound up because there wasn't enough evidence, but Vance had continued on his own. He ended up arresting a guy and he got a confession by shoving his gun in his mouth. He told him, 'I'm finally going to be able to look Gaby's parents in the eye and tell them that justice has been served.' But the guy had nothing to do with it. Vance's superiors got wind of this and quietly let him go. The brass don't like bad press. That's how Vance ended up in New Hampshire."

I was stunned. "But if Walter Carrey didn't shoot himself in the head, that means . . ."

"He was executed."

Only one person could clear things up for us—Nicholas Kazinsky. Obviously, he had lied. Perry and I went to find him the following day in his home at 10 Norris Street in Barrington. When he opened the door, sitting in his wheelchair, and saw Perry before him, he simply said, "I've been waiting for you for a long time."

*　　*　　*

Kazinsky insisted on making us tea. It was a strange ceremony. Without exchanging a word, all three of us sat in the kitchen watching the kettle boil. Its whistle came as a relief. He led us into the living room and served us in porcelain cups. He then said, in a horrified tone of voice,

"I forgot the cookies! My wife makes delicious cookies." He rolled into the kitchen and returned with a tin box. Then he said to Perry without any further commentary, "You got my letter?"

"What the hell is going on, Nicholas?"

"I can't take it anymore, Perry. I can't stand it. It's been years I've been thinking about this."

"Thinking about what?"

"Killing myself."

Kazinsky told us that in early 2000, less than a year after the events in the interrogation room, he quit the police to join his brother-in-law's security company: "That case was the pretext I was looking for to quit. You're right to think that selling alarm systems wasn't exactly my passion. But my brother-in-law claimed there was no-one better than a cop to convince people to get their checkbooks out. It's true. I would say, 'With this system, you can sleep without a care in the world.' We sold a ton of them and made pretty good money. That lasted two years, until my accident."

"What happened?" Gahalowood asked, hoping to encourage Kazinsky to go on, since it was obvious that this digression was merely a prelude to the main event.

"On January thirtieth, 2002, about six in the morning, I left the house to go running. It was still dark and had started to snow. Miserable weather. The irony in all this is that I've always hated running. But my idiot brother-in-law had signed us up for a half-marathon. I had no interest in competing, but I felt obligated. And my wife kept telling me that a bit of exercise would do me good. So, I trained for the damn race, which is why, that morning, like every morning for the previous few weeks, I went for a run around the neighborhood. It was garbage day, and to avoid the trash cans that my stupid neighbors had dragged onto the sidewalk for pickup, I ran in the street. Like I said, it was still dark out. A car didn't see me and ran into me at full speed. After that, nothing. I woke up in an ambulance, and I couldn't feel my legs. I still can't. Can't get a hard-on, can't even control when I take a leak. A damn paraplegic. You know, I don't believe in God, but I keep wondering if he's punishing me."

Gahalowood asked him, "Punishing you for what?"

Kazinsky shrugged. "For what I did. It's been eating at me all these years. If I hadn't been such a coward, I would've contacted you sooner."

"What finally made you do it?" I asked.

Kazinsky gave me a look that sent shivers up and down my spine. "Your damn *Harry Quebert* book. My wife bought a copy. She couldn't stop reading it, so I thought I'd give it a try. And because I knew you were in it, Perry. You know, reading that book, I had the impression we were working another case together. I admired how hard you worked trying to find out who killed that Kellergan girl. Obviously, I couldn't help thinking about Alaska Sanders. After Vance's death, you were never the same, Perry. You wrapped yourself up in your solitude. You told us you wanted to work alone. I would see you leave the morning briefing alone, conduct your investigations alone, drive alone, eat lunch alone. And all that solitude was right there in the book. And it broke my heart. You shut yourself off from everyone because, for all those years, you felt guilty for something you were never responsible for."

Here, Kazinsky turned to me. "You know what I liked about your book? The idea that it's never too late for redemption. I wanted to take that weight off your back, Perry. So, I wrote to you. First, I wrote a letter in which I told the whole story. But I ended up burning it. Because I didn't have the balls! Then, I prepared that message, with letters cut out of the paper. I wanted you to figure it out without my getting involved. I was a coward, I know, it feels good to admit it. I wrote that message several times: it had to be short but clear, I didn't want to make a mess of it. When it was done, I gave the cleaning lady a hundred bucks to drop the envelope off at your home. But then Helen showed up one evening. I don't know how she found me. I wondered if the cleaning lady hadn't snitched. Maybe she just rang your doorbell, your wife answered, and she said to her, 'I have a letter from Nicholas Kazinsky.'"

"Part of your address appeared on the back of one of the pieces of newspaper you used," Gahalowood told him.

Kazinsky slapped himself on the forehead. "I'm such a jerk! So *that's* how Helen found me. She showed up here, furious. My wife answered the door. Me, I was in the living room. I could hear Helen yelling, 'Is Nicholas here? I'm Perry's wife; why did your husband send him an anonymous letter?' My wife thought she was nuts, and I was careful not to show my face. They argued on the doorstep, and finally, Helen left. After that, I played dumb with my wife, obviously. I told her I didn't know anything about any letter. Perry, please apologize to Helen for me."

"Helen's dead," Gahalowood said.

"What? When?"

"The night she came here. She had a heart attack on her way home."

Kazinsky appeared to be deeply upset by the news. "Shit, Sergeant, I'm really sorry."

Gahalowood quickly changed the subject. "Nicholas, what happened that night, back in 1999?"

"This is strictly off the record," Kazinsky warned. "No recording. Nothing."

"Deal. So, start talking. I know that Walter Carrey couldn't have shot himself in the head. So, for the love of God, what happened?"

Kazinsky took his time before answering. He sipped his tea and delicately nibbled on a cookie. Then he rolled his chair to the window. He stared out at the street, no doubt to avoid having to look at us. And then he began to talk.

*     *     *

*April 6, 1999*
It was 8:40 in the evening.

Kazinsky and Vance were alone in the crime squad offices. Gahalowood had just left headquarters to join Helen, who was about to give birth. The two detectives were in the observation room watching

Walter Carrey through the one-way glass. He was alone in the interrogation room.

"I hope that lawyer isn't going to take all night getting here," Kazinsky grumbled.

"Don't worry about it; there's no lawyer," Vance informed him.

"What? What do you mean, *no lawyer*? You said he was on the way."

"I didn't call the office. There's no need to have some small-town lawyer getting in the way during my interrogation. It's time Carrey lays his cards on the table."

"What are you planning to do?"

"I'm going to use our time alone to make our little friend here talk. The stage is set, there's no-one around to hear him squeal. You know, I like Perry, but he follows too many rules to suit me. Sometimes you need to use other methods."

"What methods?" Kazinsky asked him.

In reply, Vance tapped the grip of his pistol. Kazinsky, close to panic, muttered, "Hold on a minute, what are you planning to do? You're not going to threaten him with a gun?"

"What? You scared? You going to turn me in?"

Kazinsky, fundamentally a coward, didn't like having problems with anyone. "I'm not against it, but I don't want to get in trouble."

"Don't worry about it, you won't be involved. And you'll get the praise, along with Perry. Just sit tight and watch the show. And while you're here, hold this for me, will you?"

Vance drew his semiautomatic pistol and removed the clip, which he handed to Kazinsky. He then holstered the weapon and, seeing the terrified look on his colleague's face, told him, "Don't worry! I'm just going to give him the fright of his life."

"And if he accuses you of making him confess under duress?"

"You'll say he's lying. That's all you have to do."

"I don't like it, Vance."

186

"If you don't like it, you shouldn't be in the crime squad, my friend. Watch and learn."

Vance stepped out. Through the glass, Kazinsky saw him enter the interrogation room.

"Can you take the cuffs off?" Carrey asked. "My wrists hurt."

"No."

Walter was surprised at the detective's harsh tone. "Did you call a lawyer?"

"No," Vance replied, glaring at him.

"What do you mean, *no*?" Walter huffed. "I have the right to an attorney. This isn't legal."

Vance remained calm and silent. He just kept staring at Carrey, who was starting to get nervous. He approached slowly until he was quite close and, then, with a quick movement, grabbed him and pushed him against the wall. While maintaining his grip, he unholstered his gun and drove it into Carrey's groin. "Here's your rights, right here!"

"Stop!" Walter screamed. "You're out of your mind!"

"So, confess it. Admit it and it'll all be over."

"Admit what?" Walter implored, terrified.

"Admit you killed Alaska Sanders, you dumb shit."

"I didn't kill anyone! How many times do I have to tell you? I was at the National Anthem until they closed."

"Don't give me that crap. No-one can confirm you were there. I know you were in the forest by the lake. We have proof—your car, your DNA. You're fucked, Walter. You'd do yourself a favor by telling us the truth."

Now desperate, Walter began to cry. Not knowing what to do, he tried to threaten Vance. "I'll tell my lawyer everything—you'll be fired! You have no right to treat me like this!"

"Oh? I have no right? But you had the right to kill that girl? Trust me, if you say anything about me, you're going to live to regret it. With or without a confession, you'll be found guilty and you're going to need a friend like me in prison. I can arrange it so you rot in solitary, or would you rather find yourself in a cell with six other guys who use you as their little bitch all day long? You'll be under my protection."

Then Vance pressed his gun to Walter's temple. The man cried out in terror. Vance felt he was finally getting somewhere. "Confess! And do it now! Because pretty soon I won't be able to help you."

"I . . . I . . ."

"Confess to the murder!" Vance repeated, as if possessed. "Say it and it'll all be over."

Kazinsky watched, petrified. From the observation room, he could see Carrey, who was now crying like a baby, Vance's gun at his head.

"I want my parents," he begged.

"No-one can save you," Vance replied, keeping the barrel of his gun pressed to Walter's head. "Not after what you did. This all has to stop."

"Yes, it all has to stop," Walter begged, in tears.

"So tell me you killed her, and it will."

Walter appeared to hesitate. Vance forced his mouth open and stuck the barrel of the gun into it. Walter, traumatized, tried to cry out.

"You trying to tell me something?" Vance asked.

He removed the gun and Walter screamed, "Yes, okay! Okay! I killed her! There, are you happy?"

A victorious smile spread across Vance's face. He turned to the glass to address his colleague. "Kazinsky! Get in here and record this."

Behind the glass, Kazinsky stood stock-still. Vance told him he wouldn't be involved. Why did he want him in there now? And why use his name? When Kazinsky didn't open the door, Vance grew impatient. He didn't want to let go of Carrey, but the camera was on a tripod next to the table and he had to move to turn it on. Kazinsky's voice resonated through the interrogation room.

"You've gone too far, Vance."

"What the fuck are you talking about, Kazinsky? Get in here now and turn on the goddamn camera."

"No, Vance, you've gone too far."

Vance swore. Keeping his gun pointed at Walter, he stepped back to the camera and turned it on, taking care to remain outside the frame. In a perfectly calm and well-modulated voice, he said, "Walter, I'm going to state that you agreed to have this conversation recorded. Can you repeat what you just told me, Walter?"

Walter burst into tears again. "I killed her. I killed Alaska . . . *We* killed her. I wasn't alone. Eric Donovan was with me."

Vance was stunned by this revelation. He repeated Walter's words, to make sure that he'd heard him correctly. "Eric Donovan took part in the murder?"

"Yes, I didn't kill her all by myself. We did it together. That sweater you found—it's his. The initials, *MU*, that's for Monarch University, where he went to school. Check it out, you'll see I'm telling the truth."

With those words, Walter broke down again.

"You see, it's good to get it off your chest," Vance said, trying to console him, before turning off the camera.

Walter stood against the wall, terrified. Vance approached him and said, satisfied with himself, "You're not so clever when you've got a gun to your head, are you? You thought I was going to kill you, right? Now you know what Alaska felt that night when you strangled her. Well, no, you don't really."

Vance grabbed Carrey again and put the barrel of the gun to his temple.

"Stop, fuck!" the man screamed, terrified. "I did everything you asked!"

"Just bluffing," Vance whispered, triumphantly. "There's no clip in the gun, you dumb shit. If you had looked closely instead of closing your eyes like a little pussy, you would've known that. You work in a hunting store: you should know something about guns."

To frighten his victim one more time, Vance glanced at his harmless weapon and pressed the trigger. But instead of the metallic click he expected, a loud detonation exploded in his ears. A few moments of shock followed. Kazinsky rushed into the interrogation room and found

Vance, stunned, covered with blood and brains, and Walter Carrey on the ground, part of his head missing.

"Vance, what the fuck did you do?" Kazinsky shouted hysterically.

"There was no clip in it," Vance muttered, incredulous. He was in a state of shock. "There was no damn clip. You know because I gave it to you."

"There was still a bullet in the chamber. Why didn't you completely unload your goddamn gun?"

"What the hell do I know?" Vance yelled, coming back to his senses. "Why didn't you tell me to?"

"Do you think I expected you to pretend to execute him to get him to talk?"

The two detectives stared at one another in fear as they stood over Walter's body.

"For God's sake! For God's sake!" Vance shouted. "We killed the guy."

"*You* killed the guy," Kazinsky clarified. He had no plans to share in the blame for his colleague's rash stunt.

"If I go down, you go down," Vance said to him. "This is no time to get cold feet—we have to act."

"Act? Just what do you think you're going to do? How do you plan to discreetly get rid of a body here?"

"We're not going to get rid of it. We're going to say that Walter took my gun and killed himself."

"We'll still get busted," Kazinsky whined. "You know the rules, you can't take a gun into an interrogation room."

"Trust me, a dressing-down from the people upstairs is better than a murder trial. We'll say that Carrey pretended to be sick, we ran in to help him, and he grabbed my gun."

"No-one's going to believe us."

Suddenly, Vance thought of the confession he had just obtained. "His confession is going to save us. Carrey is guilty, we have the recording to prove it. A murderer, all things considered, doesn't matter all that much. Now, we have to act fast. Someone might've heard the shot and they're liable to show up here at any moment. Give me my clip and take off the cuffs."

Kazinsky gave Vance the magazine from his gun. Then, with disgust, he bent over the body. He removed the handcuffs and freed Carrey's hands. "What am I doing?" he asked himself, like a lost child, shaking the bloodstained cuffs.

"Get them out of here, for Chrissake," Vance ordered, now fully recovered. "Put them in your pocket for now, you can clean them in the bathroom later. We need to fix this mess."

"*Your* mess, Vance! This was your idea."

Vance reloaded his gun and put it in Walter's left hand, given that there was a gaping hole in his left temple. He bent the dead man's fingers over the grip, careful to place the index finger on the trigger. Then he swore. "Shit!"

"Now what?" Kazinsky whined.

"If we say that Carrey shot himself, forensics is going to get involved. The medical examiner is going to do an autopsy and all the usual analyses. And since he's a nosy son of a bitch, he's going to see that the so-called suicide doesn't have any traces of gunpowder on his fingers. And he'll conclude that he didn't have the weapon in his hand when it was fired. Damn it. We're fucked."

Vance, a tough cop, fast on his feet and ordinarily coolheaded, looked like he was about to crack. Kazinsky saw that Vance wasn't going to get them out of this mess. He would have to do it alone. He was overcome with despair. He had always counted on others to avoid making decisions. The other evening, he'd had dinner with his wife at an Indian restaurant on Lincoln Boulevard and she had ordered for him. "Go on, dear, you can order for the two of us." His little wife, his "dear," he thought about her now. He wanted to go home to her. Collapse into her arms. He was tired of being a cop. His mind was made up. If he got out of this mess, he would quit the force. Too much stress. And he didn't like the responsibilities that came with the job. He didn't like writing reports or conducting interrogations. He liked working with his partner, Johnson, who was as craven as he was. They took long lunch breaks and always called for reinforcements if things got hot. Why did he ever accept that fool Lansdane's proposal to join Gahalowood and Vance in this murder investigation? Why didn't he stay with Johnson, doing nothing all day, and stare at his shoes whenever they asked for volunteers? He was done with the police. His brother-in-law had been bugging him about joining his security systems business, and that's what he would do. Selling alarms to terrified homeowners, that was the job for him. Yes, a small, comfy life, just him and the wife. She would choose his clothes in the morning and decide what they would eat at the restaurant at night.

"Kazinsky, are you there?"

Vance's voice brought him back to reality. He gathered his wits. Now was the moment for him to take his fate in his hands and find a way out of this.

"I know!" he shouted, suddenly consumed by an idea. "We'll fire it. We'll fire your gun. That way he'll have powder on his hands."

"We'll have to explain the impact of the bullet," Vance replied. "Why would he have pulled the trigger twice?"

"Change the story," Kazinsky suggested. "Here's the new version. Walter confesses to the crime. You turn off the camera and he pretends to be sick. You go over to him and he grabs your gun. You grab his hands, you struggle, and a shot is fired, but it doesn't hit anyone. Then Carrey pushes you away and shoots himself."

"Why does he kill himself?" Vance asked.

"Remorse. Classic."

Vance was a bag of nerves. "No-one's going to believe it. And when he felt sick, why didn't you come into the room with me? It's kind of strange that I would go in alone, right?"

"I can be in here too, but the story makes more sense if you're alone in the room when you struggle. If we were both there, we could've easily subdued him. Come on, we can't dawdle, it's a miracle no-one has come up here yet."

Kazinsky took Walter's hand, the one with the gun. He pointed it at the ceiling and pressed Walter's finger on the trigger. A shot rang out. His aim was clumsy, however, and the bullet struck the one-way glass, which shattered noisily.

"Oh, shit," Kazinsky said.

"Fuck!" Vance yelled. "Now we're really in deep shit."

"Don't worry about it, that doesn't change anything," Kazinsky said in a vain attempt to reassure Vance. "That'll make our story more believable. Go ahead, now you can call for backup."

Kazinsky bent over the corpse to return it to a more plausible position. Suddenly, he felt a hand slip in under his jacket. He didn't have time to react. Vance had grabbed his weapon and was holding it against his own temple.

"Vance!" Kazinsky screamed, terrified. "What the hell are you doing?"

"It's over, Kazinsky! Open your eyes, for Chrissake!"

"Put the gun down. We'll be okay, I'm telling you."

"We're fucked. Your story makes no sense. Why would I be covered in blood and brains? If he'd fired at me, I would've taken cover. If I was far enough away to avoid being shot, how could I have gotten his brains splattered on my face?"

"We'll say you tried to save him. Give me my gun, Vance."

"No, nobody is going to believe that."

"Put the gun down! I'm telling you, we'll be alright."

"And I'm telling you we're fucked," Vance screamed, driving the gun into his temple. "We're going to spend the rest of our lives in jail. You know what happens to cops in jail?"

With those words, Vance closed his eyes and pulled the trigger.

*     *     *

"I just stood there, in shock, staring at his head," Kazinsky said to the living-room window, eleven years later. "Suddenly, it looked like he was still moving. I don't know if I was hallucinating or if it was a reflex movement, but I grabbed him as if I could still do something to help. My face came close to his—at least, what was left of it—and I retched. I couldn't move, then my survival instinct kicked in—I wasn't going down for that fool. I took my gun from his hand, cleaned it off, and put it back in my belt. I left the handcuffs in my pocket and went to get help. But then I started to panic again—the number of bullets left in Vance's gun didn't match the number of shots fired. I had to remove one. I hurried back to the interrogation room and pulled the clip from the weapon in Carrey's hand. I removed a bullet, then replaced the clip in the grip. Just in time, before the others showed up. Then I made up some story to explain what had happened. And everybody believed it. No-one ever doubts a cop's word. They didn't even ask to see my gun to check if it had been fired. If they had searched me that night, they would've found in my pocket the cuffs and the bullet I had removed from the clip."

"Why not tell them the truth?" I asked.

Kazinsky, who had remained glued to the window while he spoke, turned his wheelchair and looked at me. "I would have paid the price no matter what. I would have been reprimanded for letting Vance do what he did and not stopping him, and for not immediately calling for backup when I had a chance."

"So you preferred to lie," Gahalowood spat out.

"Yeah, I'm a coward, Perry. We can't all be like you. We do what we can to survive in this shitty world."

There was a lengthy silence. Then Kazinsky continued: "Leave me, please. Go before my wife gets back; I don't want her to find you here, Perry."

Gahalowood rose without a word. I did the same. As we left 10 Norris Street, I asked him, "Okay, Sarge?"

"I have no idea."

# 10

## *Start of the Investigation*

*Concord, New Hampshire*
*Friday, July 2, 2010*

The morning after our visit to Kazinsky, we went to see Chief Lansdane. Gahalowood didn't tell him the reason for the meeting to maintain the element of surprise. Unfortunately, we were the ones to be surprised.

"You're here too?" Lansdane said, when I showed up with Gahalowood.

"Don't look so shocked; you were the one who got me involved in this investigation."

"Investigation? What are you talking about? I thought Perry was here to ask to rejoin the department," Lansdane responded.

"Well, that's true," Gahalowood confirmed. "And I want to be put in charge of the Sanders case."

"Alaska Sanders? There's no way we can officially reopen the investigation. I already explained that to Marcus."

"Except that things have changed," I told him. "We have new information. Carrey's confession was false. Kazinsky admitted yesterday that Walter Carrey was coerced into confessing and killed by Matt Vance during the interrogation. And then Vance killed himself."

"You have to reopen the case, Chief," Gahalowood insisted. "And we need a wiretap authorization on Kazinsky from the public prosecutor. He's not going to want to testify on the record, but nothing prevents us from paying him another visit and recording a statement without his knowledge. But we have to act fast. Yesterday, he was feeling talkative, but I'm afraid that won't last."

Lansdane stared at us. "So, you didn't hear the news?"

"What news?" I asked.

"Kazinsky's dead. He killed himself last night, at home, a bullet to the head. Not long after he got it all off his chest, I suppose."

Gahalowood banged his fist on the table. "So he died the way he lived—like a coward."

"Either way, the sergeant and I can testify under oath about what he told us," I said.

"I can do better than that," Gahalowood said, pulling his phone from his pocket.

He had saved our conversation on the voice recorder. He turned it on. The sound was a bit muffled, but the voices were clear.

SERGEANT GAHALOWOOD: Nicholas, what happened that night, back in 1999?

NICHOLAS KAZINSKY: This is strictly off the record. No recording. Nothing.

SERGEANT GAHALOWOOD: Deal. So, start talking. I know that Walter Carrey couldn't have shot himself in the head. So, for the love of God, what happened?

Lansdane listened to Kazinsky's confession, horrified.

"I knew Vance was a hothead. He'd had some serious problems with the Bangor police department. But he was a good cop, and working with Perry helped him control his impulses. That's why I put Kazinsky on the investigation. That stuff about workload was just a pretext. I knew Helen was about to deliver, and I didn't want Vance handling the case by himself. Assigning you some spineless fool like Kazinsky would provide balance."

"What do we do with the recording?" Gahalowood asked.

"Nothing," Lansdane said.

"*Nothing?*" I gasped.

"You both know that statement can't be used as evidence. It was recorded illegally."

"I don't see it as police work," Gahalowood added. "I did it as a citizen."

"Yeah, but Kazinsky knew you were a cop, whether you like it or not."

"We could say the writer recorded it," Gahalowood suggested.

"Writer or no writer, you're a cop, Perry! You can't make a recording without prior authorization or a warrant from a judge."

My frustration was boiling over. "It's easy to wave the flag of official procedure when it's convenient," I said.

"Marcus, there's no point in insisting. The prosecutor's office will throw your recording back in your face. And besides, the distressing circumstances of Walter Carrey's confession don't prove his innocence."

"*Distressing circumstances?* Chief Lansdane, you can't be serious. Vance stuck the barrel of his gun in his mouth. The confession was clearly made under duress."

"Even without a confession, he was clearly the culprit. You know the case file—all the evidence points to him. His car. His DNA. He had a motive and no alibi. The same goes for Eric Donovan, who also pleaded guilty. What more do you need?"

"There's reasonable doubt about their guilt, Chief," Gahalowood insisted.

Lansdane was categorical. "We cannot reopen this investigation without disclosing what Vance and Kazinsky did to him. Can you imagine the consequences? The press will have a field day."

"On the contrary, the police would be commended for setting things straight."

I felt something was holding Lansdane back, and he finally admitted it. "Listen, gentlemen, I won't hide the fact that the governor and I are going through a rough patch right now . . ."

"What's that got to do with the case?"

"There's a rumor that he wants a new chief of police. He can't fire me without a valid reason because I'm popular in the department. But he'd burn the place down to get rid of me. And this scandal affects me directly—remember, I was head of the crime squad at the time. It would be the perfect opportunity for him to replace me."

"So, that's it?" I said. "All this nonsense is to save your career?"

"That's the reality of politics, Marcus. And Walter Carrey is dead."

"But Eric Donovan has been rotting in a state prison for eleven years! We would be freeing one innocent man and restoring the reputation of two!"

"And what if they really are guilty?" Lansdane asked.

"You're not going to find that out by playing golf with the governor."

"Do you think this doesn't bother me? Tell me, why do you think I asked you to investigate that anonymous letter?"

"Because you're a coward. You needed to find out but didn't want to risk going through official channels; you didn't want to make any waves. You manipulated me. You made it about Perry and Helen, but you did it for your own benefit. You're a nice guy, Lansdane, but you sure know how to look out for number one."

"And you, Marcus, you're a nice guy but you can be a real pain in the ass. I seem to recall I've said that before, by the way. Here's what I propose. If you can find me irrefutable proof—irrefutable, do you hear me?—of Carrey and Donovan's innocence, then I'll reopen the investigation officially. And I'll deal with the fallout."

"If you reopen the case, I'm working on it with the writer," Gahalowood insisted.

"I can't authorize a civilian to conduct an investigation . . ."

"That didn't prevent you from using me to track down the source of that anonymous letter!" I objected.

"Then finish the job, Marcus. Show me why I should let you work this case. Show me why I should risk my career for you when the union is still demanding to know why I allowed some literary star to get involved in a criminal investigation. Bring me back some proof. I don't want you anywhere near this, Perry. I don't want you flashing your badge all over Mount Pleasant asking questions. The whole town is going to start talking. People aren't stupid. If word gets back to me, if the Mount Pleasant police call to complain that one of my officers is poking around in their business, I'm burying this case for good!"

"And what reason do I give for showing up in Mount Pleasant?" I asked. "Do I just happen to be passing through?"

Lansdane thought about it for a moment before replying. "There's got to be a decent bookstore in Mount Pleasant. Organize a signing. And who knows, maybe you'll even feel like spending a couple of days in town."

"And . . . ?" I didn't fully comprehend what he was implying.

"Well, eventually someone is bound to mention a terrible thing that happened there in 1999. And, suddenly, you have material for your next book. No-one will suspect a thing."

# 11

## *Dedications*

*Mount Pleasant, New Hampshire*
*Thursday, July 8, 2010*

About a week later, following Lansdane's advice, I arrived in Mount Pleasant for a book signing at Lockart's Bookstore. I had arranged to spend several days in town.

Gahalowood had prepared me for my visit as if it were a commando operation. He briefed me in detail, going over every facet of the original investigation. And he was fully on board with Lansdane's plan of using Cinzia Lockart's bookstore as a way to meet the locals.

"All you have to do, Writer, is to get them to bring up Alaska Sanders. Make out you're surprised, and then dig deeper."

"And how do I do that?" I asked, sarcastically. "Do I interrogate the owner about the existence of some dark criminal past so that I can base a novel on it?"

"Make friends with the locals. Tell them Mount Pleasant reminds you of Somerset. Mention Nola Kellergan's name, and the subject of Alaska is bound to come up. Then you can start to dig a bit more openly."

"Anyone you have in mind?"

"Try the gas station where she worked. Lewis Jacob, the owner, is bound to remember her."

"So what do I do? I just show up and say, 'Hi, I'd like a tank of gas, a coffee, and some info about Alaska Sanders'?"

"Be creative, Writer. That's your job, isn't it?"

Easy to say.

On the road to Mount Pleasant, I asked myself how I was going to manage to find this irrefutable evidence proving Walter Carrey and Eric Donovan's innocence. I had almost reached my destination when I received a call from Roy Barnaski.

"Hello, Roy."

"Goldman, I heard a rumor that you'll be at a bookstore in New Hampshire tomorrow signing books."

"That's correct."

"What's gotten into you that you decide to go off signing books at the height of summer in some town in the middle of nowhere? If you want to do this properly, we can organize something appropriate, nationwide. Not a tour of America's worst ratholes."

I had to be cautious with Roy. If he suspected anything at all, he would spread the news in the press to drum up publicity. "It's a charming bookstore," I said.

"There are thousands of charming bookstores, Goldman!"

"True, but this one is in trouble."

"Goldman, a bookstore is in trouble by definition! I sense there's something else going on here. What are you hiding from me?"

"Nothing. Really."

At that moment, a siren sounded. In my rearview mirror, a police car was coming up behind me, its roof lights flashing. "I have to leave you, Roy."

"What's going on?"

"Police."

"Goldman, you're a disaster."

Should you travel to Mount Pleasant one day, you'll find that the last section of Route 21, at the edge of town, is a straight line that encourages you to ignore the speed limit. Following the officer's orders, I pulled over to the side of the road. The police car stopped behind me and a young woman got out. I watched her approach in the rearview mirror. She was cinched into her black uniform, with sunglasses covering her eyes. She must have been about my age. She was beautiful.

"License and registration, please."

I handed them over. She was both charming and authoritative.

"Marcus Goldman," she read off my license.

"That's me," I replied, smiling.

"You coming from New York?"

"Yes, with a stop in Concord."

"What do you do in New York?"

"I live there."

"I assumed as much. I'm asking you what you do there, your job."

"My job?"

"Yes, your line of work. Your profession. What do you do to earn money?"

"I'm a writer."

She didn't blink. "Writer of what?"

"I'm a novelist."

She shrugged. "You can't be very well known . . ."

"A little."

"Whatever, I've never heard anyone mention you. You bought this fancy car with the money from your books?"

I smiled. "No, drug trafficking."

I felt her relax a bit. She pulled out her notebook and wrote something down.

"What brings you to Mount Pleasant, Mr. Goldman-the-writer?"

"I'm doing a signing at the bookstore tomorrow. You should come along."

"Who knows?" she replied, handing me a piece of paper.

"Is that your phone number?"

"It's a ticket for 150 dollars for speeding. Drive carefully!"

She got back in her vehicle and took off. Our interaction, in spite of the money it had cost me, left me with a good feeling. I quickly read the name at the bottom of the ticket, next to her number: Officer L. Donovan.

At the time, no doubt too occupied with my flirtatious banter, I failed to make the connection. It hit me an hour later in my hotel room. Comfortable and spacious, it had a desk that faced the window, over-looking a small public garden. I sat down to study the Alaska Sanders case file, which Gahalowood had entrusted to me. While reading through it, I recalled the name of the officer who had stopped me: L. Donovan. Was she connected with Eric Donovan?

Eager to check it out at once, I turned on my laptop and searched for a website titled "Freedom for Eric Donovan," which I had come across a few weeks earlier during my initial research on the Sanders case. Now, I took the time to look through it. There were several photos on the home page. In one of them I recognized the police officer who had stopped me: Lauren Donovan, Eric's sister. The photo was recent, taken during a demonstration in support of Eric, outside New Hampshire State Prison for Men. It was a place I knew well, unfortunately. Harry Quebert had been held there in the summer of 2008.

"Freedom for Eric Donovan" was fighting to have his case retried, claiming he was the victim of judicial error. It had been established in 2000 (shortly after Eric was condemned to life in prison) by Lauren Donovan and Patricia Widsmith, an activist criminal lawyer. Once a month, the association organized a demonstration outside the prison. Lauren, for her part, did what she could to further her brother's cause. I could very well imagine it—she had expressed herself clearly and sharply. There was no denying I had a bit of a thing for her, and I began to examine the photographs on the site, not knowing whether I was doing it to advance my investigation or to see more of her.

One section of the site, called "Life Before," was filled with pictures of Eric taken while he was fishing, in the family store, training with Lauren for the Boston marathon, and celebrating his twenty-ninth birthday, which fell a few months before his arrest.

When it was time for lunch, I walked over to Main Street. Mount Pleasant was a picturesque little town. The storefronts were carefully maintained and the streetlamps were still decorated with ribbons and banners from the Fourth of July. I ate in a small coffee shop, which just happened to be located next to the offices of the *Mount Pleasant Star,* the local paper. It was hard to imagine a better source for information on the events of 1999. I stopped by after lunch. At the front desk, a young man studied me attentively, and asked, "Are you Marcus Goldman?"

"Yes," I replied, flattered to be recognized.

"You're wearing the same shirt as in the photo. Be careful, people will think you never change."

He gestured with his chin to a poster by the entrance announcing my signing at Lockart's Bookstore. "My mother works at the store. She loves your work. Personally, I've never read any of it."

"It's never too late to discover a good book," I replied.

"My mother says they're kind of like crime novels. I don't really read that crap."

"Thanks, it's always nice to get a compliment."

"Watch out for that shirt, all the same. I mean, change it by tomorrow."

I nodded approvingly to end our absurd conversation. The young man asked how he could help me.

"I'd like to look through the paper's archives."

"Subscriber?"

"No."

"You have to be a subscriber."

"Okay, then I'd like to subscribe, please."

"It's four hundred dollars a year."

I took out my credit card and paid him. "Here you go. Can I access the archives?"

"I'll need your subscriber card, which will be sent to you in two days."

"But I just took out a subscription."

"Without your subscriber card, I can't help you. That is, unless you want to hand over that hundred-dollar bill I saw in your wallet."

I was about to argue with him but let it go. I gave him the bill, and a minute or so later, I was sitting in the archive room. The collection was digitized, with a search function, so I could easily find any articles that mentioned Alaska Sanders, Walter Carrey, or Eric Donovan. I printed them out and took them back to the hotel to read.

When I left, I made one mistake that would quickly come to work against me—I didn't erase my search history. After I left, the young man at the reception desk—although I'm not entirely certain it was him—went back to the archives and had no trouble finding out what I had been looking for. The reason for my presence in Mount Pleasant didn't take long to get around.

The next day, following Gahalowood's advice, I went to the gas station on Route 21 on the pretext of getting some gas. In the store, I was greeted by a man in his sixties, whom I soon learned was the owner, Lewis Jacob.

"Afternoon, sir," he said, pleasantly.

"Pump number 2, please."

Showing up at a gas station to ask about a young woman who died eleven years earlier required a certain amount of tact.

"Anything else?"

I wanted to say, "Everything you know about Alaska Sanders," but instead, I grabbed a handful of chocolate bars from the display on the counter. Jacob put them into a plastic bag and said, "Eighty-five dollars and twenty cents."

I gave him my credit card. His face lit up when he read my name. "You're the writer! Thought I recognized you. I was planning to go to the bookstore tomorrow to have you sign my copies."

This was the opportunity I was waiting for. "If you have them here, I can do it now."

"Well, if it's not too much trouble. They're in the back room."

He led me through to a narrow space he used as an office. "You see, there they are," he said, pointing to my books arranged on a table. "I wanted to make sure I didn't forget them."

I wrote a friendly dedication in each of the books. Then, looking around the room, I noticed a photo of Jacob, younger, together with a young blond woman: Alaska Sanders. Bingo!

"Your daughter?" I asked, innocently, pointing to the picture.

"No, I don't have kids. She worked here in the store. She was a great gal."

"*Was?*"

"She died years ago."

"That's terrible. I'm sorry to hear that. Car accident?"

"Murdered. By two young guys who lived around here. One of them's dead; the other one's in jail for life. I shouldn't say it, but if he were to get out, that would make my day. Alaska—that was her name—was a wonderful person. Just the nicest girl you'd ever want to meet. Look how beautiful she was! They strangled her by a lake in the middle of the night. When a jogger found her, a bear was eating the body. Well, I don't want to bother you with these unpleasant old stories. I'm sure you have better things to do."

"I have plenty of time. I'm not due at the bookstore until four this afternoon."

"Coffee?"

"Yes, please."

*    *    *

*October 9, 1998*

The first time he saw her was a day of torrential rain. It was still early morning, yet a screen of heavy clouds had plunged the region into shadow. She pushed the door open but hesitated before entering.

"Good day, young lady," Jacob said, assuming it was a customer.

"I came for the position . . . Eric Donovan—he's a friend—he said you

206

were looking for someone. And here I am!" She punctuated her sentence with a disarming smile.

"I'm the owner, Lewis Jacob."

"Alaska Sanders, your future employee."

Jacob was immediately charmed by the young woman. The interview took the form of a brief conversation: she was originally from Salem, Massachusetts, and had just settled in Mount Pleasant with her boyfriend.

"Who's your boyfriend?" Jacob asked. "It's a small town, I'm sure to know him."

"Walter Carrey. He runs the hunting and fishing store with his parents."

"The Carreys, yes of course. Have you worked in a gas station before?"

"Well, I'm very motivated, Mr. Jacob. Ready, willing, and able!"

"So, you have no experience."

She pouted appealingly. "I worked in an ice-cream store for the summer when I was sixteen."

Jacob decided to give her a chance. He really did need help, and the few applicants who had showed up hadn't impressed him. He could sense that she'd be good with customers. And in fact, the young woman soon became the town sweetheart. For the regulars, standing at the cash register was an opportunity to talk with Alaska, who asked about their families, their children—remembering their names—even their household plumbing problems. She was always in a good mood. And that smile . . . Lewis Jacob thought about it often. At night, in bed beside his sleeping wife, he would stare at the ceiling for a long time. And in the darkness, he could see the smiling face that delighted him so much.

But Lewis Jacob would soon discover that her luminous smile was a veil that hid profound distress.

*       *       *

"Something weighed on her," Jacob confided as he finished his coffee.

"What?"

"A secret, something that was bothering her. She never told me what it was, but one evening, when I mentioned that she looked sad, she said to me, 'It's because of what happened in Salem.' I never found out what she was talking about. But you know, there's enough there for you to write a book about."

An electronic chime interrupted us. A customer had just entered the store. Jacob got up from his chair.

"I'm alone in the store now," he said, leaving the small office to get back to the counter. "I only have help on Saturdays. These are tough times."

That was the end of our exchange. But as I was getting ready to get back in my car, Jacob caught up with me. "Mr. Goldman!"

At first I thought he had remembered some detail about Alaska. But he was holding a plastic bag. "You forgot your chocolate."

*     *     *

There were a large number of people at the bookstore, and for the three hours I sat signing books, a long line snaked down the sidewalk of the main thoroughfare.

It was seven when I finished. I left the store slightly dazed. The air was soft, a pleasant summer's evening. I was getting ready to walk to the hotel when a voice called out to me, a woman's voice: "Can you sign a couple more books?"

I turned around. It was Lauren Donovan. In one hand she held a copy of *G, Like Goldstein*, and in the other *The Truth About the Harry Quebert Affair*.

"I couldn't get here earlier, I was finishing my shift."

"I thought you didn't know who I was."

"I bought them yesterday, after I saw you. I started the first one; it's not bad."

"Only 'not bad'?"

"Not bad is already pretty good."

"You're not bad yourself."

She burst out laughing. "You really are pathetic, Mr. Goldman, but I like you all the same."

I sat on a nearby bench and took a pen from my pocket. "What's your first name?" I asked, to avoid revealing that I already knew.

"Lauren."

I wrote a dedication in each of the books. When I returned them to her, she glanced with amusement at the cover page of *G, Like Goldstein*, where I had written:

> *For Lauren,*
> *From a pathetic guy.*
> *M.G.*

She smiled, although I felt she was holding back. Her eyes shone brilliantly.

"Could you recommend a place to eat? I'm famished."

"Luini's," she replied without hesitation. "Outstanding Italian food. My favorite."

"Thank you, Lauren. See you around."

I hurried off as if I were heading for the restaurant, though I had no idea where it was.

"It's in the other direction," she said, laughing.

I turned around. She added, "Anyway, they're full, you'll never get a table. But I can."

"The benefits of being a cop?"

"No, I have a reservation."

"If you're okay with it, I can share your table. I promise you won't have to talk to me."

She looked at me mischievously. "Sounds like a fair proposal."

During the course of my travels and business trips, I've had the pleasure of eating in a number of Italian restaurants. As far as I'm concerned, Luini's in Mount Pleasant is one of the best, along with Il Salumaio di Montenapoleone in Milan. The setting alone makes it worth a detour through New Hampshire. Located on a quiet street, it filled the ground floor of a large building once occupied by a printer. There's an extraordinary interior courtyard, decorated with hortensias and a large lime tree, whose flowers scent the whole space. A fountain completes the décor. Candles add a romantic touch to the scene.

"Who were you planning to eat with?" I asked Lauren when the hostess sat us at a table near the fountain.

"Not with you. Well, yes, with you. We can be honest with each other, can't we? There was a time when I came here often with my brother."

"He's not around this evening?" I asked, feigning ignorance.

"My brother is . . . it's complicated with my brother. So, every Friday evening, if I'm not working, I eat here."

"Alone?"

"With myself. It's not the same thing."

I hesitated to ask about Eric: she didn't look like she was ready to confide in me, and I didn't want to rush her. We ordered wine and quickly moved on to less serious topics: books, movies, television. It was a pleasant evening, somewhat playful. We flirted, just not in so many words. When dinner was over, we continued our conversation. The night was warm. A few additional drinks inspired boldness.

"What made you become a writer?"

"My cousins."

"Why?"

"Because of what happened to them," I replied laconically. "What made you become a cop?"

"My brother."

"What happened?"

"Long story."

210

She took a sip of wine, and I suddenly noticed the watch on her wrist. It was expensive, Swiss, with a gold housing and a green alligator-skin strap.

"Nice watch."

"It was my brother's. Well, it's still his."

"Is your brother dead?"

"In prison. For the past eleven years. I don't really want to talk about it. You want an ice cream?"

She was clearly upset. I had to gain her confidence. I liked her, respected her, and it bothered me that I couldn't be entirely honest. But how would I explain it? How could I tell her about the unlikely chain of coincidences? Helen Gahalowood, the anonymous letter, Nicholas Kazinsky, the unofficial investigation I had undertaken, the proof required to persuade Lansdane to reopen the investigation into the murder of Alaska Sanders—and maybe even set her brother free.

I decided to say nothing. We went to get dessert at Deer Cup Ice Cream on Main Street. We separated at one in the morning, after exchanging phone numbers, and a brief but more than merely friendly embrace.

I returned to my hotel, which was only a short walk away. Pushing open the door to my room, I saw, on the desk, a small box. It had my name on it. Seeing the writing, my heart began to beat wildly. It was impossible.

I opened the package and, inside, found a small sculpture of a seagull, similar to the one I had seen in the drawer in Harry Quebert's old office at Burrows University. It was accompanied by a note:

*Whatever you do, don't teach at Burrows.*

I was stunned—Harry had been here. How did he know? I stood by the window. I thought I could make out a figure on the street. I ran out of the room and down the stairs to try to catch up with him.

# 12

## *With Harry Quebert*

*Somerset, New Hampshire*
*February 29, 2008*

During the winter of 2008, a few months before the Harry Quebert affair and roughly two years before the events described in this book, I went through a terrifying period when I was unable to write. In the hope of finding inspiration, I spent a few weeks with Harry.

I had been at Harry's for nineteen days, in his large house by the ocean. Nineteen days during which I tried in vain to sketch out the framework for my next book, but it was impossible to write even the first line. I was contractually bound to turn in my manuscript at the end of June; my editor, Roy Barnaski, threatened to sue me if I didn't meet the deadline.

I spent most of my time in Harry's office on the ground floor of the house. That morning, I stared desperately at the blank page before me. The atmosphere couldn't have been more propitious for writing: Maria Callas was singing "Casta Diva" in the background, and snow was falling lightly outside.

Careful not to make any noise, Harry entered on tiptoe and placed a cup of steaming coffee and a muffin before me.

"Don't worry," I said to him, looking defeated, "I've done absolutely nothing today."

"Then try these muffins," he shouted happily. "They just came out of the oven. They're to die for."

"I'm already dead," I noted.

"Oh, Marcus, for the love of God, don't be so dramatic! Today is a day of hope."

"Really?"

"It's February twenty-ninth. A day so rare we don't really know where to put it on the calendar. It's a day that doesn't exist. Take advantage of it to clear your head. What if we went skiing? It would do you good."

"No thanks."

"Okay, so what if we watched some old movies? That's good for finding inspiration. We'll make a fire and have a couple of cups of black coffee with whiskey."

"And then what? Do we kiss?"

Harry burst out laughing. "Marcus, you really are in a foul mood. Come on, let's at least go for a walk on the beach; it'll clear your head."

Bundled up in our coats, we left to walk along the shore. The air was very cold but not unpleasant. The snowfall was heavier now. It was low tide, and where the ocean had withdrawn, clouds of noisy gulls had colonized the shore. Harry had brought along his tin box, marked *Souvenir of Rockland, Maine*, in which he kept some dry bread for the birds, which he distributed as we walked along the wet sand.

"Why do you insist on feeding the gulls?" I asked him.

"It's a promise I made one day. You have to keep your promises. To tell the truth, I don't really like gulls. They're noisy, lazy birds. They go through the garbage, wander around the dump, follow the fishing boats to steal their fish. Gulls are birds that refuse to confront difficulty. That reminds me of someone."

"Are you referring to me?" I asked, slightly annoyed.

"No, to me. But you wouldn't understand. Not yet."

At that moment I didn't grasp the meaning of his words. And I couldn't begin to imagine what I would discover a few months later.

We walked in silence for a while. Suddenly, Harry said to me, "You know, Marcus, I'm very happy to have you at the house for a while. But why did you come to Somerset?"

"I was hoping to find inspiration," I replied as if it were obvious.

"You think there's some kind of box of miracles here?"

"I thought the change of scenery would do me good."

"But you've never really done any writing in Somerset before this trip. Why not return to where you wrote *G, Like Goldstein*?"

"At my parents'? I tried, but it was impossible. My mother was a pain in the ass."

"Marcus, I think you came here hoping that something would simply fall into your lap. You've been behaving like a gull when you should be a migratory bird."

"What does that mean?"

"Migratory birds follow their instincts. They don't submit, they anticipate."

"I'm not sure I follow you."

"Find your own world, Marcus. Find a writing space that's yours. It can't be at your parents' home: you're a big boy now. It can't be here with me; you're a writer. You're no longer the young Marcus, you're Goldman, an established name. If you want to cure your writer's block, accept your success by accepting who you are."

A few days after this conversation, Harry placed a small gift box on my desk.

"What's this?" I asked.

"Open it. There were a few stands in the supermarket parking lot. I saw this one and thought of you. For when you have doubts."

Inside the box I found a sculpture of a seagull.

"We all have a gull inside us—the temptation to take the easy way out or just do nothing. You have to keep fighting that, Marcus. Most people in this world are conformists, but you're different. Because you're a writer. And writers aren't like other people. Don't forget that."

# 13

## *First Clues*

*Mount Pleasant, New Hampshire*
*July 10, 2010*

My hotel had an obsolete video surveillance system, but the camera installed behind the reservation desk allowed me to identify, with near certainty, the person who had dropped off the package for me: Harry Quebert.

I called Gahalowood at once to let him know.

"Harry? Impossible!"

I was surprised by his categorical reaction. "Why?" I asked.

He hesitated before replying, "I was sure he killed himself."

"Killed himself? Never. You don't know him very well."

"Apparently not. You're sure it was him?"

I looked at the screen capture that the concierge had printed for me. The image was poor quality and he was wearing a hat, but I would have recognized his face anywhere.

"I'm sure. He was here around four thirty, while I was at my book signing. It can't be a coincidence."

"Guess not. If he knew you were in Mount Pleasant, he knew when you'd be at the bookstore. What was in the package?"

"A small statue of a seagull."

"Again with these stupid gulls? What is this, some sort of code between you two?"

"Harry once told me not to behave like a gull. Clearly, he's sending me a signal. A warning."

"A warning about what?"

I hesitated. I hadn't told Gahalowood about my recent agreement with Burrows University, and I had no desire to broach the subject now.

"I couldn't say, Sergeant. Maybe you could do a bit of research on him?"

"You already asked me that last year, and you know the results: he doesn't show up anywhere. I couldn't find an address, a credit card, a telephone number. He didn't show up on any passenger list at any airport in the country. A real ghost."

A ghost. That was exactly it. There was a moment of silence. Gahalowood, sensing my confusion, added, "Monday, at headquarters, I'll check again. Maybe there's something new."

"Thanks, Sergeant."

"So, tell me what you've got, after forty-eight hours in Mount Pleasant."

"I talked to the gas station attendant, Lewis Jacob. It seems like something happened to Alaska in Salem, but I don't know what."

"It's a start. We'll have to visit Salem to question her parents in any event. Anything else?"

"I met Lauren Donovan, Eric's sister. She's a cop in Mount Pleasant."

"She became a cop? Back then, she wanted to study biology."

"Her brother's sentence changed her life. She set up an association to try to get the conviction overturned. The group seems to be pretty active. I don't know much more though: she was a little cagey about it all."

"You have to find a way to get her to talk. She'll surely have information that could prove helpful."

"And how do I do that without revealing what we're up to?"

"Sweet-talk her the way you usually do."

"The way I *usually do*? I'm not exactly a smooth talker, Sergeant."

"You're a writer, it's the same thing. Just tell her you were searching online for information about her brother and you found out about her association. That you're interested and you want to help."

Two hours after my conversation with Gahalowood, I sat down with

Lauren for lunch. We had agreed to meet at the Season. No sooner had we settled into our seats on the terrace than I went straight to the matter at hand: "I was searching online for information about your brother." She looked stunned, staring at me over the menu she was browsing.

"You did what?"

"Don't take it the wrong way, but I was curious last night when you told me you had become a cop because of your brother. I found your association's website. I didn't really look through it, but I saw your photo on the home page."

Her face grew dark. "You shouldn't have done that."

"I'm sorry. I did it because I wanted to find out more about you."

She shrugged. "Anyway, it's public information. And everyone here knows about it. My brother was accused of being involved in the murder of a young woman—she was twenty-two. That was back in 1999. He's been in prison ever since. But he's innocent, I know he is. Eric wouldn't hurt a fly. Anyone who knows him is sure there was some sort of mistake."

"Why was he arrested then?"

"Alaska—the victim—was going out with a good friend of his, a guy named Walter Carrey, who confessed to the murder and implicated my brother. After that, Walter managed to grab a policeman's gun and kill himself. My brother was arrested shortly afterward. He was unlucky. The police found a sweater at the crime scene, one he had lent to Walter, stained with Alaska's blood."

"But if your brother's innocent, why did he plead guilty?"

Lauren looked at me suspiciously. "How do you know that? It's not mentioned on our website."

"I read it online," I lied with an assurance that swept away her doubts.

"He was coerced," she replied. "Sorry if I seem a bit sensitive, but it's a difficult subject."

I had covered up my blunder, but only just. I knew that sooner or later I was going to make a mess of this. The situation was untenable.

"We don't have to talk about it."

"No, it's okay. Anyway, it does me good to discuss it."

"So, why did you say your brother was coerced into pleading guilty?"

\*     \*     \*

*Concord, New Hampshire*
*January 2002*

The sinister silhouette of the New Hampshire State Prison for Men was being hammered by a cold rain. It was a dark afternoon, as if the world had been extinguished.

In a dank, poorly heated visiting room, Lauren Donovan sat in on a tense conversation between her brother and his attorney, Patricia Widsmith, a young but determined criminal lawyer. She was only in her thirties, but Lauren felt that she'd go all the way for Eric. She was a woman of conviction, who took the case without pay, aware that the Donovan family was in no sense wealthy.

Eric's trial was scheduled to begin in two days, and Widsmith was visibly upset. Until then, she had supported Eric in his decision to plead not guilty to the murder, but now she was on the point of changing her mind. The stakes were high. By pleading not guilty, Eric exposed himself to a trial whose outcome was uncertain and could result in the death penalty. If he pleaded guilty, he would likely avoid it if they could come to an agreement with the prosecutor's office.

"What do you mean, *if we go to trial*?" Eric asked in an uncertain voice. "All of a sudden you want me to plead guilty? What's gotten into you?"

"I don't want anything," Widsmith replied softly. "We're two days away from the trial and I need to be sure that you're aware of what might happen. That's why I asked Lauren to be here. We still have time to think this through. When the trial starts, it'll be too late to change course. As you know, the judge for the case is Mike Peters. I did some digging, and he's in favor of the death penalty. If the jury finds you guilty, that's how he's going to rule, I'm sure of it."

"But I'm innocent, for God's sake!" Eric shouted, exasperated. "Do you think I did it now too?"

"Not for a second, Eric. But what kind of lawyer would I be if I didn't share my doubts with you? Your life is on the line! In two days, I'm going to stand in front of a jury and the prosecutor is going to explain to them that your DNA was found on a sweater stained with the victim's blood, that a threatening message was printed with your printer, and that you have no alibi for the night of the murder. I'm going to do all I can to defend you, Eric. For the past three years, I've been trying to get this evidence thrown out, and two days before the trial, I have nothing that would allow me to look you in the eye and tell you I'm going to get you off. If you're not acquitted, that means you'll be found guilty of the murder of Alaska Sanders. You won't escape the death penalty."

"We'll appeal!" Eric protested.

"Of course we'll appeal. But the law in the state of New Hampshire is clear: the execution must take place within a year of the verdict. There's not much we can do to change that. And there's one thing you should know. The law requires that anyone condemned to death be executed by lethal injection, unless it's deemed 'impractical.' But New Hampshire doesn't have an injection room or even the necessary drugs."

"Are you saying it would be the electric chair?" Lauren cried, terrified.

Widsmith waited a few moments before responding: "New Hampshire doesn't have an electric chair. They would hang him. Eric would be hanged in this prison."

"What?" Lauren cried out. "That's impossible. We don't hang people anymore."

"We do much worse," Widsmith said.

Eric just sat there. Lauren started crying.

There was a lengthy silence. In the background, they could hear the daily sounds of the prison. In a muted voice, Eric asked, "And if we accept the prosecutor's deal?"

"New Hampshire law requires that, for a capital crime, if the verdict isn't the death penalty, the defendant will be condemned to life in prison without parole. That's what the prosecutor is asking for in this case."

"What do you think?" he asked Widsmith.

"Eric," Lauren interjected, "you can't plead guilty. You're innocent, you can't do that to yourself."

"Lauren, will you be here when they hang me? Will you have the courage to watch me die at the end of a rope?"

Eric had turned cold and hard. Lauren put her face in her hands.

"Eric," Widsmith resumed, "whatever you decide, I'll be there with you. I'll defend you body and soul. I know you're innocent, I'm convinced of that. I wouldn't be here at your side if I weren't. But part of me feels that by pleading guilty, you give us the time to find the proof of your innocence. I'm hopeful I can do that. But what good does it do to prove you're innocent if you've been executed? You'll just be one more name to add to the debate about the death penalty. All I need is a little time. And you're the only one who can give it to me."

\*       \*       \*

"That's why Eric pleaded guilty," Lauren explained. "It was his only chance to escape the death penalty and try to prove his innocence. So, he accepted the prosecutor's offer and there was no trial. But he got life without parole. Ever since, Patricia and I have been fighting to get him out. We set up 'Freedom for Eric Donovan' to stir up public opinion. But most of all, we conducted our own investigation."

"And how far have you gotten?"

"We have some new information. A few leads—but after eleven years of research, nothing really concrete, not enough to reopen the case. It's infuriating. There are days when it just seems hopeless."

"So it was after your brother went to jail that you became a cop?"

"Yes, to try to reform the system from the inside. To provide real justice and not some parody that lets innocent people spend their lives in prison. But mostly, I said to myself, who better than a cop, in the town where the murder occurred, to understand what happened that night in April 1999?"

Sunshine reflected off the face of her watch, and a beam of light shot out. It was as if the watch were suddenly manifesting its presence. She looked at it nostalgically. "After Eric went to jail, I swore I'd never resign myself. Never let it go. One day, when I was visiting him in prison, he said he was worried about our parents. He knew that the case had been bad for the store, that customers were reluctant to shop there. I tried to reassure him, saying, 'It'll pass, Eric, don't worry about it.' But he said, 'And what about Patricia? How are they going to pay her?' I explained to him that she had been working pro bono, that it was something her law firm did. I told him not to worry about it. He talked to me about this watch, which he had hidden under a loose board in the floor of his bedroom. It was valuable, and he'd kept it hidden just in case. He'd bought it three months before he was arrested—he got a great price—and was planning to resell it and make a nice profit. That day, Eric told me to get the watch, which he would never need again, sell it, and give the money to our parents. He doesn't know it, but I didn't do that. It would have meant accepting the fact that he'll never get out of prison. Instead, I started wearing it. I wear it so I can give it back to him the day he gets out. It reminds me what I'm fighting for."

"It chains you down," I noted.

Lauren winced at my remark, no doubt because I was right. "Why are you interested in all this, Marcus?"

"Two years ago, I started my own investigation. One of my closest friends was arrested for murder. Everyone said he was guilty. I managed to show that he was innocent and get him out of jail."

"I didn't know that."

"It's the subject of *The Truth About the Harry Quebert Affair*."

"I still haven't read it."

She immediately picked up her phone to search the web for details on the Quebert case. She appeared to be impressed by what she found.

"That's wild. I must have followed Quebert's arrest at the time, like everyone else. I know the name, but I never read the book. I had no idea you were behind that investigation. So, from one day to the next, you just decided to leave for New Hampshire to try to prove his innocence?"

"That's exactly what happened. One morning in June, when I heard the news, I left New York by car, come what may. My editor, my agent, my family—everyone tried to talk me out of it."

"But you insisted."

"I knew Harry was innocent. I was absolutely certain. He couldn't have killed that girl. When you know, you know. You of all people should understand what I'm talking about."

"I do. I've been going through it for eleven years."

I hoped that my role in the Harry Quebert affair would finally convince Lauren that I could help her. After lunch, she suggested I come to her place for coffee; she wanted to share the information she had gathered about her brother's case.

*       *       *

Lauren lived in a charming redbrick house. Classic architecture, with a porch that provided the perfect place for spending summer evenings sitting in a chair and watching the quiet street. The house was surrounded by a small but very well-kept garden.

I sat down in the kitchen while she made two espressos with a shiny Italian machine and sat at the marble counter opposite me. From a drawer, she removed a cardboard file box—this held the documents concerning the Alaska Sanders case. I pictured her, morning and night, tirelessly rereading those pages.

"There isn't a day goes by that I don't look through this file. I don't know why. After all this time, I couldn't even say what I'm looking for. I'm starting to give up hope."

"Could I take a look?"

"Of course."

I spread the pages out before me. I began with the question of the pullover.

"The pullover belonged to my brother, yes. But, as I said earlier, he lent it to Walter Carrey when they went fly-fishing."

"They were good friends, then?"

"From childhood."

She went through the documents, which included a picture of a printer. "And that?" I asked. "Is that the printer you were talking about earlier?"

"Yes. Alaska Sanders had gotten some threatening messages, one of which was found on her corpse. The messages all showed a printing defect, which the police experts used to identify my brother's printer as the one that produced them."

"What did your brother say?"

"My brother was living with my parents. He had just come back to Mount Pleasant after several years in Salem. Anyone who had access to my parents' house had access to my brother's bedroom and his printer. And shortly before Alaska was killed, Walter had stopped by to use it because his wasn't working."

"So Walter killed Alaska and then framed your brother?"

Lauren made a face. "That's what Eric's lawyer believes."

"You don't look convinced."

In response, Lauren pulled a picture from the folder—a group of young women at a bar, who appeared to be celebrating. Within the frame, I saw a man I recognized immediately from Gahalowood's case file: it was Walter Carrey.

"Who is this?" I asked, pretending not to know.

"Walter Carrey. The photo was taken the evening of the murder in a local bar, the National Anthem."

"And?"

"It proves Carrey's innocent."

"How?"

"That evening, Eric, Walter, and I were together at the bar. Eric and I left at eleven. Walter stayed. Alaska was killed between one and two in the morning. Walter always claimed that he was still there at the time of the murder, something no-one has been able to confirm. This photo is his alibi. Look at the screen behind the bar."

She grabbed a magnifying glass from a drawer and handed it to me. In the foreground, the group of girls had their backs to the bar, and in the background, above a row of bottles, was a giant TV screen. With the magnifying glass I could see that it was showing the weekend weather forecast. At the bottom of the image, a news ticker showed the time of the broadcast: *10:43 PT.*

"The photo was taken at 10:43, long before the murder," I noted.

"10:43 *PT*," Lauren corrected. "Pacific time. Over here it was three hours later."

"1:43 in the morning," I exclaimed.

"Right. When Alaska was killed, Walter Carrey was still in that bar."

I was stunned. "How did you get this picture?"

"I got it shortly after my brother's arrest, when I was trying to help his lawyer gather proof of his innocence. The owner of the National Anthem liked to take pictures and post them online for publicity. And it was busy that night, so a perfect time for it. I wanted to run through the evening's events and asked him if I could see the photos he'd taken. There were a lot of them. I looked through the pile and came across this one."

I had to make an effort to control my excitement. This was the evidence Gahalowood and I had been looking for. It could be enough to persuade Lansdane to officially reopen the investigation.

"Have you shown this picture to anyone?"

"Aside from Patricia Widsmith, no."

"Why not? It shows that Walter Carrey was telling the truth."

"Because it would make my brother look even worse."

I was doubtful. Lauren noted my skepticism and asked, "What are you thinking, Marcus?"

"That you're going about this the wrong way."

"How so?"

"You're trying to prove your brother's innocence, and clearly, you're not getting anywhere. If you want to get Eric off, you have to reexamine the entire case. You need to find the real killer. And it looks like it's neither your brother nor Walter Carrey. So who could it be?"

Lauren just looked at me for a long time, her eyes staring deep into mine.

"Marcus, I don't know you, but for some reason I feel I can trust you. For the first time in eleven years, I feel less alone. Do you think you can help me?"

# 14

## *Lauren*

*Mount Pleasant, New Hampshire*
*Sunday, July 11, 2010*

Late Sunday morning Gahalowood came to meet me at the hotel. To avoid being overheard, we stayed in my room. He looked worried. I asked whether it had something to do with the investigation; he replied that it mostly had to do with life. As always, he refused to elaborate.

Gahalowood poured himself some coffee and sat in an armchair. I followed suit and perched on the edge of the bed.

"In my office at headquarters there's a cabinet I almost never open. It was mostly Vance who used it. He stuffed all his crap in there. And God knows he accumulated a lot of crap. You know me, I'm a neat freak. He was the opposite. He collected all sorts of old things. Absolutely useless stuff he hated getting rid of. 'You never know,' he would say. And I would tell him, 'Long as I don't see it, it doesn't bother me.' I haven't opened that cabinet in eleven years."

\*     \*     \*

*April 16, 1999*

Gahalowood sat in his office, staring at Vance's desk, which was cluttered with the usual mess: papers, notes, and pens, most of which didn't work. Vance had been dead for ten days now, and Gahalowood missed him like hell. Every morning was like another funeral; he couldn't wrap his head around it. He spent his days staring at Vance's desk. He could see him, grabbing a pen, then realizing it had no ink, putting it down and trying another. And another. Gahalowood called it "the cemetery of pens." He knew he should clean up, get rid of Vance's things. Lansdane had asked him to see to it. But he couldn't work up the courage.

A knock on the door interrupted his reverie. Kazinsky entered the room holding a thick envelope. "This came for Vance."

Gahalowood opened the envelope. It was the report from the fire inspector on the fire in Walter Carrey's apartment. He had concluded that it was intentional, with three different points of origin. An accelerant was used, probably gasoline. In the photographs accompanying the report, one could see the damage done by the flames, with the bedroom the worst affected, and on the walls, the words UNFAITHFUL WHORE in capital letters.

"That guy was really nuts," Kazinsky remarked. "You want me to add this to the Sanders file?"

"There's not much point," Gahalowood replied. "The case is closed."

"So, should I pass it on to the Mount Pleasant police? They handled the fire. If you want to draft a short note, I can send it."

Gahalowood, who had no desire to think or do any paperwork, said, "You know what, Kazinsky, do me a favor. Empty Vance's desk. Put everything in a box with that envelope and all his other crap and put it in his cabinet. I'm tired of looking at it."

*       *       *

"Vance had no immediate family," Gahalowood explained, "but I thought someone would come to get his belongings. A brother, a cousin, a nephew. But no-one ever showed up, and the cabinet remained just as it was. Once in a while I'd get it into my head to clean it out. But then I'd change my mind, afraid of what I might find—memories, that sort of thing. I don't like memories, Writer. They make us nostalgic. And you know how little time I have for nostalgia. You're not the only one who has a problem with ghosts."

"Why are you telling me all this, Sergeant?"

"Because yesterday's conversation has been bothering me. I spent the day asking myself what happened in Salem. And the more I think about it, the more I realize that Vance and I focused our investigation only on Mount Pleasant and ignored that angle. It bothered me so much that I went over to headquarters and opened Vance's cabinet. I found the box Kazinsky had shoved in there along with his other stuff. I found the pens, a restaurant bill, a ticket from the dry cleaner, the fire department report, but—most of all—this."

From his pocket he removed two sheets of paper. Photocopies. One of a handwritten note by Vance, the other a newspaper article. On the note, in the midst of various observations, Vance had written in capital letters:

WHY DID ALASKA COME TO MOUNT PLEASANT?

The newspaper article was dated September 1998. It had appeared in the *Salem News*, which covered the town and the surrounding region. The headline said it all: "Alaska Sanders Elected Miss New England."

"You're telling me you didn't know that Alaska had competed in a beauty pageant?"

"Of course we knew. Besides, Donna Sanders, her mother, gave us that article. But look at the date: September 1998. Alaska wins an important beauty contest, and right after that she shows up in Mount Pleasant. Strange, don't you think? You see, at the time, we had the question backward. We shouldn't have been asking why Alaska came to Mount Pleasant, but why she left Salem."

It was a very good question. "We have to go to Salem, then," I said.

"That's what I intend to do. And you? Any news from Donovan's sister?"

"Yes, I think we finally have concrete evidence that will force Lansdane to reopen the investigation. Lauren Donovan has a photograph that proves Walter Carrey's innocence."

Gahalowood's face lit up. "And you wait until now to mention this? Tell me you have a copy, Writer."

I held up my phone. "I took a picture when she wasn't looking. The quality isn't great."

I showed my screen to Gahalowood. He instantly recognized Carrey at the edge of the frame.

"The picture was taken at the National Anthem at the time Alaska was killed," I explained. "You can see the time on the television in the background: that's 1:43 on the East Coast."

"Well, damn! That's it, that's our proof! Send it to me: I'm going to show it to Lansdane tomorrow morning. You know how I hate giving you compliments, but you did well!"

"Promise me you'll handle this delicately, Sergeant. I don't want to jeopardize my relationship with Lauren. She can't find out why the investigation has been reopened. She'd lose all confidence in me."

"You like her that much?"

"Maybe."

Just then someone rapped on the door. The knocks were followed by a woman's voice: "Marcus, it's Lauren."

I froze. So did the sergeant.

"What's she doing here?" Gahalowood whispered.

"I have no idea."

"I'm not sure she'll be happy to see me here. I doubt her memory of our first meeting is a pleasant one."

"So go, get lost, then!"

He ran into the bathroom.

"Not the bathroom," I whispered.

"Why not?"

"What if she has to go?"

He looked at me quizzically. "Writer, you're completely nuts. This girl likes you, she's telling you about her life. Believe me, she did not come up to your hotel room to use the toilet."

More knocks. And Lauren's voice again through the door. "Marcus?"

"Be right there."

When I opened the door, I found Lauren standing there holding a copy of *The Truth About the Harry Quebert Affair*. She skipped any pleasantries.

"You know Perry Gahalowood?"

From her tone, I felt that a "yes" would not be a good response. So I chose the second option. "No."

"What do you mean, *no*? You spent a whole summer working on a case with him. I read your book. I started it yesterday when you left and finished it last night."

I tried making a joke. "You didn't like it and want your money back, is that it?"

"I'm serious, Marcus. What's your connection with Gahalowood?"

"Tenuous at best. I met him briefly during the investigation, but it's not as if I went to his house to have dinner with his wife and kids."

"That's not what you write in the book."

"It's a novel, Lauren. And it's a writer's job to spice things up for the sake of the readers."

"Fine. Tell me you're not writing a book about my brother."

"No, of course not. That's crazy! I knew nothing of this case until this weekend."

She seemed relieved, and changed the subject.

"So, what are you doing now?"

"Nothing special."

"Care to go for a drive? I want to see the ocean."

"I'd love to."

I left Perry in the bathroom and went with Lauren. We got into my car and headed for the coast. We crossed the border into Maine and, an hour and a half later, reached Kennebunkport. We walked around the historic downtown area before lunch. Then Lauren led me to the beach, which she loved. It was low tide and we strolled, barefoot, among the rockpools of water, in which crabs, large shrimp, and starfish made their homes. She marveled at every discovery. At first I thought that the biologist in her was coming back to the surface, but in reality, she was reliving a large part of her childhood.

"You come here often?" I asked as she proudly brandished a large crab.

She put it back in the water before answering. "I used to come with my parents and my brother. Almost every weekend. This is where I caught the biology bug. Who would have imagined I'd end up a cop?"

There was a silence. She looked out at the horizon for a moment. "Marcus, I'd like to set the investigation aside for today. I'd like to take advantage of this moment alone with you. Without ghosts."

"I'd like that too."

It was late afternoon by the time we left Kennebunkport to return to Mount Pleasant. The July sun shone brightly, lighting up the sublime landscapes of the New Hampshire countryside. As we approached town, Lauren suggested, "Let's say hi to my parents." I agreed, as if it were the most natural thing to do.

Janet and Mark Donovan lived in a quaint house that resembled them in many ways: simple, modest, solid. When we arrived, Mark was working in the garage and Janet was busy in the garden. When she looked up from the flower beds, her gaze was at first circumspect. Then, recognizing me, she smiled. "You're better-looking in person than on television, Mr. Goldman."

The Donovans were charming people. We had tea on the porch. Then, when Lauren and her father left us alone for a moment—Mark wanted his daughter's help with some paperwork—Janet began to confide in me.

"Thank you for coming, Mr. Goldman. Lauren doesn't bring many people over."

"Please call me Marcus, Mrs. Donovan."

"Call me Janet."

I smiled.

"Are you and Lauren seeing one another?"

"No, but I like your daughter very much. She's fantastic. She has character."

"She is fantastic! But I'd like her to think more about herself and less about her brother. Sometimes, it's as if she feels guilty for something. I guess she told you about Eric."

"Yes."

"Lauren is his younger sister, but she always felt she had to protect him. He was a kind boy, easygoing, while she was the opposite. One day, in high school, Eric was pulled aside by a bunch of bullies. Lauren got mixed up in it and broke someone's nose. She was suspended for two weeks. Can I be frank with you, Marcus? I don't think Eric is ever going to get out of prison. Lauren should live her own life. She should settle down somewhere far away from New Hampshire, so she can pick up her life where she left off eleven years ago."

I felt sufficiently at ease to ask her, "Do you think Eric is guilty?"

"Do you have children, Marcus?"

"No."

"For a parent, a child remains a child. We never ask ourselves that kind of question. Our brain isn't capable of contemplating it. It's a love that lasts forever, the kind you feel for a child, and it outweighs anything else."

After our visit I accompanied Lauren back home. She asked me to stay for dinner, and I gladly accepted.

We prepared supper together while sipping California cabernet. We chatted casually, about nothing in particular. Our conversation was lighthearted. Lauren had let her guard down. She had a luminous smile, and her laugh was irresistible.

With the second bottle of wine, the evening took a romantic turn. We ate without conviction, too busy holding hands. Lauren made the first move. She got up, seemingly to collect the dishes, but left them where they were. She came over and placed her lips on mine. I returned her kiss.

"You can sleep here if you want."

"It's kind of you not to throw me out at this hour."

She laughed. "I start work early tomorrow. I would have preferred a more romantic morning . . . but I'd like it if you stayed."

"Then I'll stay. Besides, I wouldn't miss an opportunity to see you in uniform again."

She smiled.

*     *     *

The following morning, a Monday, Lauren woke up at dawn. I heard her showering and got out of bed. When I joined her in the kitchen, she was in her uniform, drinking coffee. She poured me a cup and kissed me. "I'm going outside to get the paper," she said before leaving the room. I took a sip of coffee. I felt good.

A few moments later, Lauren reappeared in the doorway. I could tell she was livid. Her eyes drilled holes in me.

"You pathetic shit," she screamed. "Get out of my house!"

I was utterly taken aback. "Lauren, what's going on?"

"Get out, Marcus. I never want to see you again."

With a determined gesture, she led me to the kitchen door, opened it, and pushed me out, throwing the paper in my face. Realizing that the explanation would be there, I unfolded the *Mount Pleasant Star* to discover the following headline, right on the front page:

### MARCUS GOLDMAN REOPENS THE
### ALASKA SANDERS INVESTIGATION

The celebrated writer, known for having proven the innocence of Harry Quebert, is in Mount Pleasant to investigate the murder of Alaska Sanders. At least, that's what his recent visit to the archives of the *Mount Pleasant Star* suggests . . .

# 15

## A Careless Mistake

*Mount Pleasant, New Hampshire*
*Monday, July 12, 2010*

Gahalowood was the first person I told about the leak in the newspaper. He was aghast. "Writer, you're not exactly a rookie. How could you make a mistake like that?" I had forgotten to delete my search history and the receptionist had gone snooping around behind my back and hurried to tell the editors. I was beside myself. It was early, so the information hadn't yet had time to circulate; we had to warn Lansdane at once.

On Gahalowood's advice, I returned to Concord. In any event, my only desire was to get out of Mount Pleasant. I felt awful for Lauren and her parents. Especially her mother, who had confided in me.

The sun was rising gently on the horizon as I headed for the state capital. I drove quickly, and since there was no traffic at that hour, I reached Concord earlier than expected.

As America woke up, the news spread among the media, hungry for something sensational in this ordinarily quiet season of the year. It was quickly picked up by all the morning news broadcasts.

My editor, Roy Barnaski, wasn't slow to get in touch. "Damn, Goldman!" he crowed on the phone. "Another book on the way already! And a criminal case as well. That's terrific; it's what we've all been waiting for. And we already have a title: *The Alaska Sanders Affair*. When can we anticipate its release?"

"I told you, Roy. There's no book."

"Yeah, yeah, you can't keep secrets from me. So that's what you've been up to under the pretext of a book signing."

"Roy, I got exposed by some nosy little asshole who works for the local paper."

"You allowed yourself to be exposed," Roy corrected. "For the publicity. Because you love it, you narcissist! And so much the better. I'm going to get the marketing team together for a conference call, okay? Wonderful!"

I hung up on him.


Chief Lansdane was somewhat less enthusiastic than Barnaski. As Gahalowood and I entered his office, he exploded: "Marcus, you're either a careless son of a bitch or a complete idiot."

"Maybe a bit of both?" Gahalowood suggested.

"I'm not in the mood, Perry. I already had the governor on the phone and I'm going to have to explain myself to the press in a little while."

"I was negligent, but it wasn't intentional."

"Oh, don't worry, Marcus, I know you didn't do it intentionally, just out of stupidity."

"The good news," Gahalowood cut in, "is that we have proof that Walter Carrey is innocent." He showed Lansdane the photo taken at the National Anthem at the time of the murder.

"You call that good news?" Lansdane grumbled. "I call that a serious complication, all things considered."

I tried to win Lansdane over to my point of view. "It's the proof you wanted to reopen the case, isn't it?"

"That's for me to decide!"

"You've been contradicting yourself since the very beginning!" I shouted. "You asked me to investigate under the pretext of writing a book, and now when you have what you wanted—"

"Calm down," Gahalowood interjected. "There's no point in getting hot under the collar. But we have to do *something*. Chief, no matter how it looks, the situation works to your benefit: we release no information at this point, you let the Writer take the heat. You say that after today's news, you're forced, for professional reasons, to assign a detective to make sure proper procedures are followed."

"And that detective would be you, I imagine."

"Yes. Marcus and I will continue our investigation, discreetly. We won't make waves, I promise. We'll ask questions only in connection with Marcus's book; people will open up if that's the way we play it. Once we have all the answers, I'm sure we'll find what we're looking for. And it'll be a lot easier for you to manage."

Lansdane stared at us. We knew he wasn't happy, but he had no choice. "The governor is threatening to replace me if this isn't dealt with before the end of the month."

"We'll do our best," Gahalowood assured him.

"It'll be your neck too, Perry. If I go, you go."

"You know, Chief, I already lost my wife," Gahalowood shot back. "So, losing my job . . ."

Leaving state police headquarters, I was morose. Gahalowood noticed it at once. As we got into my car, I put my hands on the wheel, a little dazed.

"We've had worse, Writer," Gahalowood said, trying to console me.

"I know."

"It's the situation with Lauren that's bothering you, isn't it?"

"Yes."

"I'm sorry about that, Writer. But look at the bright side: you're the key to the investigation she's been conducting for eleven years. She'll have to get in touch with you."

"We'll see."

"Come on. Let's get moving. We're not going to spend the day in the parking lot."

"Where are we going?"

"It's the first day of our second investigation together. That calls for a celebration. We're going to grab some donuts and coffee."

I smiled. "I didn't think I'd ever hear you say that, Sergeant."

"What?"

"That you were looking forward to working on a new investigation together. After all, we know how the beginning of the Quebert case went . . ."

"Don't congratulate yourself too much, Writer. Since I lost Helen, I no longer like being alone. Nobody likes it when it's forced on them."

"And for a second there, I thought you wanted to be friends."

"In your dreams. Come on, drive."

"Aside from stuffing yourself with donuts, do you have a plan of attack?"

"Obviously. Remember what I told you at the beginning of the Nola Kellergan investigation?"

I recalled Gahalowood's advice very clearly. "Concentrate on the victim, not on the murderer," I said.

"Exactly. We're going to pay a visit to the *Salem News*. It's time to dig into Alaska's past. And find out what happened in Salem."

*       *       *

Contrary to what its name led one to assume, the offices of the *Salem News* weren't in Salem but in Beverly, a neighboring town. Fifteen years earlier, the paper had merged with the *Beverly Times*, whose offices it shared. Its current address was 32 Dunham Road, in the industrial zone.

An apathetic receptionist greeted us lethargically. When we asked to see the archives for the late 1990s, she assumed an expression of mild terror. "Impossible to search before 2000," she told us. "There was a project to digitize the archives, but they never finished it."

Gahalowood showed her the copy of the article found in Vance's files. "We're looking for information about Alaska Sanders."

The receptionist narrowed her eyes as she scanned the page. "I don't know anything about that; I can call Goldie if you like. She's here today."

"Goldie?"

"Goldie Hawk, she's the one who wrote the article. She still works for the paper."

A short while later, an elegant woman in her fifties introduced herself. She recognized me at once. "Marcus Goldman?"

I nodded. "Pleased to meet you, ma'am. And this is Sergeant Perry Gahalowood."

"Like the book?"

"Like the book" Gahalowood sighed.

Alaska had appeared in the paper on several occasions. Goldie Hawk was able to find the relevant articles, as they all bore her byline. She led us to her disorderly office and pulled out a thick binder containing everything she had written since she started working for the paper.

"My mother religiously saved everything I wrote. When I turned fifty, she presented me with this file. At least it will have been good for something. The articles are arranged chronologically. The ones about Alaska start somewhere in the middle."

The early articles were about Mini Miss beauty pageants for children and teens.

"I was very young at the time," Hawk explained. "It was my first job. The editor in chief was a bit old-fashioned: he thought the *Salem News* was a local paper and nothing more. He had no illusions about being the *New York Times*, he wanted regional content—fairs, sports events, even beauty pageants, which were very popular. Obviously, none of the other reporters were interested, so I grabbed it. The result: twenty-five years later, I'm still here. But who knows if it was for the best or not." She smiled as she considered this. "Well, there was also a financial incentive for covering the pageants, because several families whose daughters were in the competitions took out ads in the paper."

By now we had found the articles about Alaska, starting in 1993. By the time she was seventeen, she had won a number of beauty contests. I looked at the photos, taken over the years. She was radiant.

"And Alaska?" I asked.

"Alaska showed up late, kind of by accident. Since it worked out, she just kept going. She wasn't like other girls."

"How's that?"

"She was superior in every respect: smarter, more mature, more beautiful. And she wasn't looking for glory. She really didn't have an ego—she just didn't care. She entered the contests for two reasons: to get into the movie business and to earn some money. The prize money was pretty good, and she put together a sizable nest egg. I remember her talking about it once; I was surprised by her maturity. She said she gave the money to her parents. They put 10 percent into an account for her and the rest into an account she couldn't access. She told me, 'That way I'll have some savings when I settle in New York or Los Angeles.' I was impressed by this determined adolescent who had already mapped out her career. I was sure I'd see her on a movie poster one day. I never imagined she'd end up dead in some New Hampshire backwater. Whatever was she doing there?"

"That's a good question," I replied.

"You'll notice I didn't write about her death. I let a colleague take care of it. I felt I would be dishonoring her, writing about the murder, it was so sordid."

The last article Goldie Hawk had devoted to Alaska was the one found in Vance's file. It was a portrait of the Sanders family, published on Monday, September 21, 1998. The previous Saturday, Alaska had just won the Miss New England competition.

"That was an important step in her career, her first adult competition. Everyone was very excited for her. I wanted to do a whole article on her, not just about the competition. To talk to her parents and get an insight into their day-to-day lives and how focused they were on her career. For the photo, we had them all pose together."

I took a closer look at the picture. Alaska was there in a white chiffon dress, flanked by her parents, in the living room of their house in Mack Park.

Twelve years later, Robbie and Donna Sanders's living room hadn't changed a bit. That's what struck Gahalowood when we went to see them after leaving the offices of the *Salem News*. Same imitation-leather sofa, same thick carpet, same bric-a-brac on the shelves. According to Gahalowood, they hadn't changed either.

When she opened the door, Donna Sanders just said, "So, it's true, you're reopening the investigation."

Before we got down to business, there was a brief ceremony to navigate. We sat in the living room; Donna brought us coffee and insisted we try her homemade muffins. Then she reviewed the contents of a cardboard box containing mementos of her daughter—a hodgepodge of pictures, a hairbrush, concert tickets, a plastic bracelet, and several cheap tiaras from her beauty pageants.

Donna was leaning over a low table, sorting through her treasures; Robbie sat at one end of the couch, his arms crossed.

"None of this is going to bring her back," he said, irritated by the display. "And reopening the investigation even less so. Why can't you leave us alone?"

"Robbie, don't you want to know?" his wife protested. "Sergeant Gahalowood says the murderer is still walking free."

"That's just an assumption," Gahalowood insisted. "I'm sorry for making you go through this again, but if we have a hunch, we have to look into it."

"How will that make any difference to us?" Robbie interjected bitterly.

"It won't. We can't erase the pain of losing your daughter. But I believe it's important to find out what really happened. Especially since an innocent man has been locked up for eleven years."

"Right, an 'innocent man' who was confronted with irrefutable proof and pled guilty!" Robbie exclaimed. "What do you want, Sergeant? Have you come to ask for our blessing to open our wounds again?"

"I've come to look for answers to a few questions, Mr. Sanders. Questions I probably should have asked you at the time."

"Such as?"

"Who was Alaska, really?"

"What?"

"What were her dreams, her aspirations, her regrets, her doubts? I'm thinking that I may have missed something back in 1999. I recently discovered that Alaska confided in her employer in Mount Pleasant. She told him that something had happened back in Salem. So, I'm asking you, Mr. and Mrs. Sanders, what happened that could have affected your daughter so deeply?"

Donna and Robbie stared at one another, speechless. Finally, Donna spoke. "Nothing we know about. Alaska was a radiant child. She loved life. Of course, she had her worries, like everyone else, but there's nothing in particular that comes to mind. Did something happen at school? You'd have to ask her friends; I can give you their names if you like. You know, she was very secretive."

Donna went on to describe a young woman who was admired by everyone around her. Alaska, their only daughter, their shining light. Cheerful, intelligent, witty, kind. Always pleasant, praised by her teachers, loved by her friends. Perfect, and a perfectionist.

As a child, Alaska liked to make people laugh. No-one could resist her clowning, which soon developed into imitations that were even more compelling. From family gatherings to Christmas parties, her popularity only continued to grow.

"She was a born actress," Donna told us. "She had so much talent. When she was twelve, we spent a weekend in New York City. She used to dream of going to see a Broadway play, so we took her to see *The Merchant of Venice*. I thought she'd find it terribly boring, but she loved it so much she decided to study theater. She joined a local company that she stayed with until the end of high school. She had found her vocation—to become an actress. Alaska was always very flirtatious, and she loved shopping. To make a little pocket money, she started babysitting. The children adored her, the parents as well. She created her own little network. But when she turned fifteen, sixteen, she changed—I mean physically. Within a few months, she became a different person. This rather ordinary looking child was transformed into an adolescent who looked like a grown woman and grew more beautiful with each passing day."

*     *     *

*Salem, Massachusetts June 1993*

"I understand, Mrs. Myers, no problem. See you soon."

Alaska hung up the wall phone in the kitchen. She sat down cross-legged on the bench and put her head in her hands, disappointed. It was a Friday, late afternoon.

Donna Sanders entered the kitchen. She was concerned to see her daughter looking so distraught. "What's going on, dear?"

"Mrs. Myers just called. She canceled my babysitting job for tonight. Her husband isn't well so they're staying home."

"Well, it happens. What's bothering you?"

"Mrs. Myers sounded strange on the phone. And that's the third cancellation in two weeks. I have to earn a living!"

Donna burst out laughing. "You know what, dear, how about the two of us go out tonight? Let's go to the mall, do a little shopping, have supper, and then see a movie."

"What about Dad? I heard him get angry the other day because of the credit card bill."

"Your father isn't home tonight. It'll be just us girls. And no-one will be any the wiser." Donna smiled, grabbing a terra-cotta pot from the shelf, from which she retrieved a handful of bills. "I have my secret savings account. If it doesn't show up on the credit card, it never happened."

Alaska's face brightened. The idea of going out with her mother delighted her. Half an hour later, Donna and her daughter were at the large nearby mall. They walked around, did some shopping, then had a pizza before going to the cinema. They wanted to see *Jurassic Park*, which everybody was talking about. As they were waiting in line to buy their tickets, they came face-to-face with Mr. and Mrs. Myers.

"Mrs. Myers?" Alaska said, astonished. "You ended up going out?"

Mrs. Myers was visibly annoyed by this, but her husband didn't seem to know what was going on. "Why wouldn't we?" he asked.

Alaska, nobody's fool, explained: "Your wife told me you were sick. You look like you're doing much better; I'm glad you got back on your feet so fast."

Mrs. Myers turned beet red. The ticket window was now free, and Donna took the opportunity to put an end to the embarrassing situation.

"We're up, Alaska. Good evening!" She grabbed her daughter by the arm.

"Mom, she lied!" Alaska huffed.

"I know, dear."

"But why did she do that? I take good care of their children."

"I'm sure you do, darling."

Donna knew perfectly well why Mrs. Myers no longer wanted to use her daughter's services. She was all too aware of Alaska's appeal. Everywhere she went, her daughter turned heads. Alaska was probably the only one who didn't know the effect she had on people, men in particular, even though she was still only sixteen. And neither Mrs. Myers nor any of the other local mothers wanted her anywhere near their husbands.

*       *       *

"Poor Alaska, that really hurt her morale. Mrs. Myers wiped out her entire list of clients. It's a small community, people talk. Mrs. Myers told her friends that her husband had already cheated on her once, so she certainly wasn't going to put Alaska in his lap. And now all those other fools believed their own husbands were uncontrollable predators—so long neighborhood harmony. 'Watch out for Alaska' was the message they were sending one another, as if my daughter was some kind of temptress. I was disgusted by the whole thing. But Alaska wasn't the type to give up. That summer, to replace the babysitting, she found a job at an ice-cream parlor. Once again, she had money coming in, large tips. One day, a customer suggested she enter a local Mini Miss he was organizing. He told her she had a good chance of winning. That she could even become a model. She decided to try it out, and you know what, she won. And it put a thousand dollars in her pocket.

"For Alaska, something just clicked then. She became aware of her body. She began to enter as many contests as she could, and she was successful. Then she was asked to appear in ads. Regional stuff—an automobile dealer, a restaurant, a hardware store. But soon we were seeing her all over Salem. She was a local celebrity. People would stop her in the street—'Hey, aren't you the girl in the ad for the pizzeria?' After high school, she didn't want to go to college. She wanted to give herself a chance to make it as an actress. She earned a living from the ads and beauty contests while she went on casting calls. She even had an agent in New York. It was serious. She tried out for roles by filming herself in the kitchen with my husband's video recorder. That girl had everything it took to make her dreams come true . . ."

Donna suddenly fell silent, as if she had run out of words. She rose and grabbed a thick bound book sitting on the chimney mantel.

"It's not worth the bother," Robbie told her, failing to conceal his annoyance.

"That way they'll see for themselves," his wife said to him. "They'll *see* how beautiful she was."

She placed the book on the table and opened it. It was an album she had put together for her daughter. Everything was there: family photos, ads for a store selling outdoor furniture, a pizzeria, a discount tire store. We saw Alaska, beautiful and full of life.

Among the collages and loose sheets of glossy paper, there was a professional photo book, put together, according to the logo on the cover, by the DM Agency in New York.

"She was so proud," her mother told us. "Just look at her . . ."

"What's the DM Agency?" Gahalowood asked.

"It's the Dolores Marcado Agency. She's the one who repped Alaska. She said she was very promising. She really believed in her. Dolores told us our daughter would be a star. Alaska went to quite a few casting calls. She locked herself up in her bedroom with the video recorder. Look . . ."

"Not the videos!" Robbie objected. "These gentlemen didn't come here for that!"

Donna pretended not to hear her husband's protests as she fiddled with an ancient video player. We marveled at the fact that it still worked. On the old tube television, probably kept just for this purpose, a poor-quality image flickered into life. And soon Alaska's face appeared in the foreground, lit up by the camera. She smiled brightly, rearranged her hair, and stepped back a few feet until her whole body fit in the frame. And suddenly there was her voice. "Hello, I'm Alaska Sanders, from Salem, Massachusetts. I'm twenty-one years old and I'm trying out for the role of Anna."

We watched, rapt, as she recited her lines. It was hard to resist her magnetism. The recording came to an end and the screen dissolved into a cloud of white pixels. Donna turned the TV off. Robbie wiped away his tears. For a few precious moments, it was as if Alaska had come back to life.

"It's eleven years since she left us," Donna said. "Eleven years, and I still can't accept that she's dead. I've never been able to come to terms with the idea that she's no longer around. How can I resign myself to the fact that one horrible night in April 1999, someone took my daughter's life? Her bedroom is still the way it was, I didn't touch a thing. It's waiting for her."

"Not the bedroom!" Robbie begged.

But Donna was already walking toward the stairs, encouraging us to follow her. Gahalowood and I did as she asked, ill at ease. She wanted us to visit her ghost museum, the same teenager's bedroom we had seen a moment earlier on the audition tape. In the middle of the room was a round bed covered with pink pillows. Opposite the window was a dressing table in lacquered wood. Her closet was still filled with her clothes. The walls were covered with posters of bands from the time— Goo Goo Dolls, Smashing Pumpkins, Blink-182—faded over the years from the sunlight. As with the rest of the Sanders home, everything remained as it had been in 1999.

I asked Mrs. Sanders the question I most wanted to ask. "How did Alaska end up in Mount Pleasant? What happened? Excuse me if I seem a bit direct, but listening to you, the next stage of her life should have taken her to New York or Los Angeles."

"Well, you're perfectly correct, Mr. Goldman," she said, smiling sadly.

"So what was it?"

"She met Walter Carrey. That two-bit loser. He turned her head. He was a good-looking guy, rough around the edges, seductive. He had a wild side to him. He was well built, rugged, but there was something shady about him. Everything a girl her age would be attracted to."

"When did she meet him?"

"The summer of 1998. In a popular bar in Salem. When she turned twenty-one, she started going out all the time."

"Could you tell us exactly when that summer they met?" Gahalowood asked.

Donna Sanders thought for a moment. "Oh, I don't know. Maybe June or July. In any case, it was before the big Miss New England pageant at the end of September."

"What happened at the contest?"

"It was one of the most popular in the region. There were girls from Massachusetts, Vermont, New Hampshire, and Maine. A professional competition, with a first prize of fifteen thousand dollars."

"And she won," I said, recalling the article in the *Salem News*.

"Yes, indeed. It caused a big stir—everybody was talking about it. Alaska's agent even said that a Hollywood director had taken an interest."

"What happened then?" I asked.

"About a week after the contest, Alaska had a terrible argument with her father."

"Why?"

A voice sounded from the bedroom doorway. Robbie Sanders had silently joined us.

"I found marijuana in her bag."

*        *        *

*Salem, Massachusetts*
*Friday, October 2, 1998*

Donna Sanders would never forget that day. She was returning home from a brief trip to Providence, where her family was from. She and her sisters had arranged the sale of the house, following her mother's death a few months earlier. It was late afternoon when she pulled into the driveway. A black Ford Taurus was straddling the sidewalk; Walter Carrey was sitting inside it. He gave her a friendly wave.

"Hi, Mrs. Sanders," he said through the open window.

"Hello, Walter. You're not coming in?"

"No, thanks. I'm about to leave. Your husband and Alaska are really getting into it."

"What's going on?"

"I don't know," he replied as he backed the car up. "I was supposed to come get Alaska. We were going to spend the weekend together, but when I showed up, she was arguing with your husband. She told me to leave and said she'd meet me in Mount Pleasant."

Donna hurried into the house. Inside she could hear shouting from the floor above. She climbed the stairs. In Alaska's room, Robbie and her daughter were screaming at one another. Alaska hurriedly threw some clothes into a travel bag.

"What's going on?" Donna cried.

Her presence imposed an immediate silence in the room. Alaska looked defeated. Donna had never seen her daughter like that before.

"You really want to know?" Alaska asked, in tears, a note of defiance in her voice.

"Of course I want to know."

Her husband said, "I found marijuana in Alaska's things!"

"Dad!" Alaska yelled.

"Alaska, tell me you didn't," Donna pleaded.

"She sure did!" her husband burst out. "She betrayed our trust. I can't believe it."

"Alaska, you promised me you would never touch that stuff. Do you realize the consequences? If this gets out, you could lose your Miss New England title. And you can say goodbye to your dreams of becoming an actress."

Glowering at her father, Alaska grabbed her bag and ran out of the room, her eyes filled with tears. She tore down the stairs, grabbed her car keys, and slammed the door, before jumping into her blue convertible and speeding off.

Donna Sanders bolted out of the house, begging her daughter not to go. "Wait, dear, wait!"

She ran behind her daughter's car for a hundred yards before resigning herself to the fact that she wasn't going to stop.

*     *     *

"We could have worked it out!" Donna assured us. "Obviously, at the time, we overreacted a little. Alaska signed an ethics statement for the Miss New England contest. She had agreed not to smoke, take drugs, or pose naked. Quite a few jealous mothers would have been delighted to drag her name through the mud if they'd known she'd smoked a joint."

"It was only a little grass," I objected.

"It might seem stupid today, Mr. Goldman, but my husband and I were brought up very strictly. For us, smoking marijuana was always seen as drug use, period. Besides, legally, it was a controlled substance, the same as heroin. And don't forget that the policy back then was 'smoke a joint, lose your license.' If you were caught, the penalty automatically included a six-month suspension of your driver's license."

"Are you saying you didn't smooth things over with Alaska?"

"No, she was too angry with us. As if the argument brought up some hidden rage she'd kept bottled up inside her. I think that fool Walter Carrey put ideas in her head. I don't know what he told her or what he promised her, but she left to go live with him in Mount Pleasant. Clinging to a guy who was living above his parents' store! She was completely under his sway, if you must know. But she was an adult by then, so what could I do? Force her to come back to Salem? All that promise—just to go work at a gas station and get herself killed."

"You didn't try to reach out to her?" I asked.

"I tried everything. It was hopeless. I thought it would work itself out in time, but time doesn't fix anything, it makes it worse, everything bubbling up inside, all the resentment. I went to Mount Pleasant a few times to have lunch or coffee with her. But something had snapped. She didn't even bother coming home for Thanksgiving or Christmas. I spent Christmas Day in tears."

# 16

## *Marcus in His Ford*

*Boston, Massachusetts*
*Monday, July 12, 2010*
When we left the Sanders home, it was still early in the day. As we were in Massachusetts, we traveled to Boston—about a half hour on the highway—to visit Patricia Widsmith, Eric Donovan's lawyer.

Cooper & Associates was located in a redbrick townhouse directly behind the state capitol building in the center of the Beacon Hill neighborhood, where Emma Mathews had lived when we were together. The firm specialized in criminal law, and it was known to take on challenging cases involving high-profile individuals, but also for championing certain worthy causes pro bono. It had recently represented a man who was proved innocent after thirty-two years in prison.

Gahalowood and I sat in a waiting room surrounded by framed newspaper articles covering the many cases the firm had won over the years. A receptionist came over to get us.

"Ms. Widsmith will see you now." We were led to an elegantly furnished office, where a woman of around forty was waiting for us. She and Gahalowood hadn't been in contact since the case was resolved.

"Finally," she said to him. "About time you reopened the investigation! I've been waiting eleven years for this."

We sat down around a glass table, where we were served espressos in porcelain cups. Patricia Widsmith was casually dressed, but her designer T-shirt and sneakers must have cost at least four hundred dollars. Her jewelry made it clear that she made a good living doing what she did. I couldn't help but say, "I didn't really imagine you in a place like this."

She smiled. "Because I'm defending Eric Donovan pro bono? Did you think I worked in an office in the basement?"

"Well, just not quite this stylish, perhaps," I stuttered.

"That's always been Sean Cooper's philosophy—he was the man who founded the firm. Principles are expensive: you have to be willing to pay the price. It's precisely because we're a well-known law firm with wealthy clients that we can defend those who need it most."

"What made you want to defend Eric Donovan?" I asked. "The evidence is pretty damning. It's hard at first glance to identify any legal error there."

"Well, that's your opinion. I know Eric personally. When you know him, you know he didn't kill that young woman."

"How did you meet?"

"In Salem. We hung out at the same places and we got to talking. He was a nice guy, always in a good mood. When a relationship I was in fell apart and I needed to change my outlook, I made the rounds of the bars with him. Then he went back to live in Mount Pleasant. When he was arrested, he called me. I knew at once he was innocent."

"How do you explain the mountain of evidence against him?"

"He was trapped," Widsmith said.

"Trapped by whom?"

"That's what I never managed to find out. I don't have any proof—and unfortunately, I never will—but I think it was Walter Carrey."

"Why?"

"Because Walter was always jealous of Eric. And he thought Eric was having an affair with Alaska. He planned Alaska's murder so it looked like Eric was responsible. It probably would have worked if he hadn't banged up his car in the woods, allowing the police to trace the accident back to him."

"Sorry to contradict you," Gahalowood intervened, "but there are two reasons your argument doesn't hold together. First, Alaska left Walter only a few hours before she was murdered, which didn't give him much time to orchestrate a setup like that. We also know, and I imagine you do as well, that Walter had a solid alibi at the time of the murder."

"Are you referring to the photo Lauren found that places him at the National Anthem at 1:43 in the morning?"

"Yes."

"That wouldn't stand up for five minutes in front of a judge. As you know, Alaska Sanders's death was estimated to have taken place between one and two in the morning. Walter Carrey could easily have killed her around one in the morning and been back at the bar to be photographed at 1:43."

I hadn't thought of that possibility. I shot a withering glance at Gahalowood.

"That doesn't change the fact that Alaska had only just told Walter she was leaving him," Gahalowood objected. "He would've needed a certain amount of time to set Eric up."

"I know Walter suspected they were having an affair before she actually left him."

"If you're referring to the suspicions raised by Sally Carrey, she only opened up to her son when he told her that Alaska was gone. Your theory doesn't stack up."

"Walter knew long before that."

"How do you know?"

Widsmith pulled a thick folder from a cabinet, her own investigation into the death of Alaska Sanders. "Don't take this the wrong way, Sergeant, but at the time, I quickly understood that the investigation wouldn't get very far: you had your killers, the case was closed. So, I had to figure things out for myself; I went door-to-door with Lauren. That's when we learned we were able to work together, and over time, we formed the idea of setting up an association. I spoke to half the town. Including Regina Speck, the owner of the Season, the coffee shop on Main Street. You know it?"

"Yes," I said.

Widsmith flipped through the file until she found what she was looking for. "Sally Carrey, Walter's mother, confided in Regina Speck. It's here, look."

She [Sally Carrey] comes to the coffee shop every day. About a week before Alaska's death, she told me that Alaska and Eric were having an affair. She had seen them together when her son wasn't around. She said that her son was too naïve, that he must have suspected something but preferred being cheated on to finding himself alone.

"If Walter Carrey's mother was publicly spreading the news of an affair between Alaska and Eric," Patricia reasoned, "surely she would have shared her suspicions with her son before Alaska left him."

"Could I borrow that folder, just to have a look?" Gahalowood asked.

"I'll ask my assistant to make you a copy. You can verify it all; it's very clear."

"If you were having doubts about the police investigation, why didn't you tell us about these new witnesses at the time?"

Widsmith hesitated a moment before responding. "The notion of an affair between Eric and Alaska wasn't really beneficial to my client."

"And so your theory would be that Walter Carrey acted out of jealousy. He killed Alaska and set a trap for Eric?"

"Absolutely."

"I'd very much like to see some evidence."

The attorney spread out before us various pages from her investigation. This was, for the most part, information from the police file.

"Walter thinks Alaska and Eric are seeing one another. He wants to take revenge on them both: kill her, and make him suffer for it. So, he uses the excuse of going fishing to get hold of one of Eric's sweaters. He now has the first piece of proof against him. Then he writes anonymous

253

messages to Eric and Alaska to frighten them: 'I know what you did.' He goes so far as to print the messages at Eric's place, which is very easy because he's always over there. He knows that when Alaska is found dead, the police will eventually get to Eric. I'm surprised you never considered this possibility. There was both motive and opportunity, the two key elements investigators look for in a murder case, as you know."

Gahalowood didn't react, but the look on his face was one I knew well: he was taken aback. Patricia Widsmith had made her point. She went on: "Now that Walter Carrey is dead, my theory is, unfortunately, impossible to prove. But even when he eventually confessed to the crime, he still tried to drag Eric down with him. Not only because of Alaska. Walter was jealous of Eric all his life."

"Yet Eric and Walter were friends, weren't they?"

"Sergeant, have you never been jealous of your friends? Eric and Walter grew up together in Mount Pleasant. For a while, they were insep-arable. But when they reached adulthood, the first signs of bitterness began to appear. Eric went to a good university, while Walter vegetated. Eric moved to Salem, a good place to live, while Walter lived above his parents' store and worked for them. His mother yelled at him all day long. Ask around Mount Pleasant what he was like at the time—you'll see. And I know what I'm talking about because I saw them together."

"Eric and Walter?"

"Yes, in Salem once. At a bar. Walter was visiting Eric. Even then, their relationship was beginning to fray. But Eric always agreed to let him spend the weekend on his couch. I don't want to sound cruel, but Walter was a bit dull. He was desperate to find a girlfriend. In fact, that's how he met Alaska."

"Did you know Alaska back in Salem?"

"No, she was much younger than I was. At that age, it makes a big difference. Have you spoken to Eric Donovan?"

"Not yet," Gahalowood answered.

"We can go see him together if you want."

"That would be helpful."

"Is tomorrow morning convenient? I'll be at the prison anyway for a demonstration."

"A *demonstration*?" Gahalowood said. "What demonstration?"

"Every second Tuesday of the month, our association meets outside the state prison where Eric is being held. I made the suggestion to Lauren two years ago, and it's been working quite well. We need to mobilize public opinion to shine a light on his situation and help get his case reviewed. Unfortunately, it's a classic example of judicial error, and without real pressure, the authorities won't lift a finger. Whoever makes the most noise has a chance of being released; the others will rot in silence. Come, it'll be an opportunity for you to join our cause."

"We're conducting an official police investigation," Gahalowood replied. "We can't take sides."

"Do you know how many innocent people are rotting in jail in the United States, Sergeant?"

"You can't hold up just a few dramatic errors to discredit the entire legal system."

"*A few dramatic errors?*" she huffed. "What would you say if your children were behind bars for a crime they didn't commit? I have to wonder which side you're on, Sergeant."

"The side of justice."

"Do as you wish. I'll be at the prison at ten a.m. Stop by if you want me to introduce you to Eric."

Leaving Patricia Widsmith's office, I struggled to persuade Gahalowood to join her at the prison the following morning.

"Because your girlfriend Lauren will be there?" he said, sarcastically.

"Because we need to talk to Eric Donovan."

"I'm a cop. We can see him whenever we want; we don't need to ask anyone's permission."

"Yes, but if his lawyer and his sister introduce us, he'll feel more comfortable. The goal isn't to see him but to get him to talk!"

"You're not wrong there."

"Sergeant, why didn't you tell Widsmith that Carrey's confession was coerced?"

"Because I first need to know if she's ready to accept her client's guilt at the end of our investigation. Can we trust her? Or will she jump on what I tell her to accuse us of making a procedural error and bring us before a judge as witnesses?"

When we reached my Range Rover, I asked Gahalowood, "Sergeant, would it bother you to take my car and return to Concord without me? I'll join you later."

He looked at me suspiciously. "What's going on with you?"

"Nothing, I have an errand to run."

"We can do it together. Or I can wait for you. How are you going to get back to Concord?"

"I'll figure it out. Don't worry. I'll see you later."

I left him the keys. He didn't insist. I walked to a car-rental office I had seen earlier. When I got to the counter, I said to the clerk, "I need a Ford, the oldest you've got."

The only Ford available was a low-end model, which was exactly what I was looking for. Once behind the wheel, I took from my pocket the piece of paper on which Emma Mathews had written her address during my previous visit to Boston two weeks earlier.

Following the directions on the GPS, I reached Emma's home in Cambridge. On either side of the street, the houses were pretty, perfectly aligned and separated by gardens, with no hedges or fences between them. I parked discreetly near number 24 and positioned myself so I could see without being seen. After a while, I saw Emma emerge, accompanied by a little girl who began running around on the grass.

They played together outside for a while. Then a car parked in the driveway and a man wearing a suit and tie got out. The child ran to him, crying, "Daddy!" He kissed the girl, then Emma. I observed the little tribe, nurturing my soul with that joyful image. I wondered whether one day I would be the father of a happy family. Suddenly, the passenger door opened. I jumped. It was Gahalowood.

"Sergeant, what are you doing here? You scared the hell out of me!"

"Allow me to ask you the same thing," he said, as he settled into the passenger seat. "I imagine you have a good reason for sitting in this shitty old rental car spying on that family."

I tried to smile. "I'm trying to remember the Marcus who used to drive an old Ford. A young writer, with no reputation, but full of hopes and dreams."

*    *    *

*New York*
*Early August 2005 (three weeks before the breakup with Emma)*
In his office on the top floor of the tower on Lexington Avenue that served as the Schmid & Hanson headquarters, Roy Barnaski had laid out a lavish spread: champagne, petit fours, and other delicacies. My agent, Douglas Claren, and I were seated opposite him at a large ebony table. Before me lay the contract and a pen. All I had to do was sign. My first contract as an author. Barnaski loved the first chapters of my book, and he had offered to publish it.

"You know what this contract means, Marcus?" Barnaski asked me. "More money than you'll know what to do with. Because you have an exceptional gift. Your book is marvelous, and I have a feeling that the others will be even better."

"I appreciate your enthusiasm, Roy."

"It's not my enthusiasm that counts, but what you put down on the page. This is only the beginning of a long adventure, Marcus. You'll need to work hard."

"That's my greatest wish."

Barnaski pointed to the contract and summarized the terms. "A million-dollar advance for your first book, which will be paid upon submission of the fully revised manuscript in September. You also agree to write two additional books. The next will have to be completed and delivered by the end of June 2008."

"I won't let you down." With those words, I signed the contract with a lighthearted gesture. Barnaski smiled triumphantly. He grabbed a bottle of champagne, popped the cork, and filled three glasses.

"To Marcus Goldman, the next star of American letters!"

Three weeks later, on August 29, 2005, I completed my second draft of *G, Like Goldstein*. I had worked into the night. After a few hours' sleep, I jumped into my Ford and drove directly to Somerset to show my manuscript to Harry.

"This is a great day," he said to me, looking at the manuscript I had placed on the table on his terrace. We were outside, taking advantage of the summer morning. The ocean was majestically calm. On the beach below, the gulls came and went.

"All this is your doing, Harry."

Harry swept away my compliment with a dismissive gesture. "Marcus, there's only one person you need to thank for what you've achieved— yourself."

He rose, opened his *Souvenir of Rockland, Maine* tin box and took out a few pieces of bread, which he threw to the gulls.

That afternoon I had arranged to join Emma in Boston to celebrate with her. As I was leaving and Harry was accompanying me to the door, I looked at my beat-up Ford parked next to his red Corvette. "Harry, could you lend me your car for a few days?" I asked.

"Of course," he said without hesitation.

I left him my Ford and took off at the wheel of his 'Vette. On the highway leading to Massachusetts, I experienced a feeling of lightness. It was as if I were leaving the old Marcus behind.

Emma, however, was far less impressed when she saw the red Corvette. "What's with the car?"

"It's to go to your parents' for dinner," I replied, only half joking.

"Marcus, stop. You're not serious, are you? What happened to your car?"

"The Ford is the old Marcus."

"*The old Marcus?* What on earth are you talking about? Now that you've written a book, you want to change who you are?"

"It's not me I want to change; it's the way people see me." I was unaware just how accurate my prophecy would turn out to be.

"Promise me you'll give it back."

"Promise. I have to go back to Harry's place in a few days, after he's read my manuscript."

"I love the Marcus who drives the Ford."

"I know."

Harry had promised to let me know about my book as soon as possible. I didn't suspect he was going to call me twenty-four hours later, at an unsociable hour. It was the evening of August 30, 2005, around ten thirty at night. I was stretched out against Emma, caressing her in the darkness of her bedroom. Light from the streets of Boston filtered through the window. We were lying down but still dressed; she was wearing a short skirt that I had slowly slipped up her thighs. Suddenly, my phone, forgotten in my pants pocket, began to ring. I grabbed it to silence it but then saw the call was from Harry.

"Who is it?" Emma asked, seeing the expression on my face.

"Harry."

"Call him back tomorrow."

"If he's trying to reach me at this hour, it's important."

The phone continued to ring. I answered. "Hello? Harry?" Emma sighed and adjusted her skirt.

"Marcus . . ." His voice was sepulchral.

"Harry, is everything alright?"

"It's about your book, Marcus. It's serious. I found something that worries me. I have to talk to you. You have to come to Somerset."

"Now?"

"Yes, now." He sounded strange, not in his normal state of mind, and I told him I'd leave at once.

"I'll be there in forty-five minutes."

I hung up. Emma stared at me uneasily. "What's going on, Marcus?"

"Harry wants to talk to me about the book."

"What? *Now?* You're going to drive to New Hampshire in the middle of the night to talk about your book?"

"He said it was serious."

"*Serious?* What's serious is to run out of here like a thief. Your book can wait until tomorrow morning. Why do you have to go right this minute?"

"I'm sorry, Emma. Harry's a friend, he sounded like he needed me."

"You're not going for Harry, you're going for your damn book!"

I put on my T-shirt and shoes.

"If you go out that door . . ." Emma threatened, beside herself with anger.

"What if I go out that door?"

"If you go out that door, it means you're no longer the Marcus I once knew."

"You've known me barely five months."

"If you leave, Marcus, it's over."

"Why? Because I'm leaving to help a friend?"

"You're not going for Harry. It's your ambition that's calling. Ambition will be your worst enemy. It's going to consume you. If you can't control it, I'm going to leave you."

I left.

It would be five years before I saw Emma again, when I met her in her store in Cambridge, in late June 2010.

That night, on August 30, 2005, it was almost midnight when I arrived in Somerset. I followed Shore Road, plunged in total darkness, until I reached Goose Cove. The house looked dark, but my Ford was parked out front. He had to be there. I knocked on the door but there was no response. I decided to go inside. No-one in the living room. I called out. No sign of life. I went out to the terrace and it was then that I saw a silhouette on the beach, staring into a small fire. It was Harry. I walked down to join him.

"Harry?"

He stared at me curiously. "Oh, Marcus, you came!"

I could tell by the way he was speaking that he was very drunk. A bottle of whiskey lay on the sand. He grabbed it and held it out to me. I took a slug, not wanting to offend him. I felt my heart beating in my chest. I had never seen him like this.

"What is it, Harry?"

He looked at me with his glassy eyes, then said, "You're not just a writer, Marcus, you know how to love. I know it, I read it in your book. It's a rare quality."

I repeated my question. "What is it, Harry?"

"This is the evening of August thirtieth, 2005, Marcus. That makes it thirty years exactly."

"Thirty years of what?"

"Thirty years I've been waiting."

"Waiting for what?"

He avoided my question. "You can't imagine what it means when someone suddenly disappears from your life and you don't know what happened to them. Is she dead? Or alive somewhere? Does she think about you the way you think about her?"

"I'm not sure I understand, Harry."

"That's to be expected. Can you keep a secret, Marcus? The difficulty with a secret is not so much keeping it to yourself but living with it."

"What secret?"

"I can't tell you. You would be horrified."

"You can't know how I'll react."

"I found the book, Marcus."

"What book? What the hell are you talking about?"

"The one in your glove compartment."

He pulled from his back pocket a copy of *The Origin of Evil*, his seminal novel, published in 1976. I couldn't help asking myself whether Harry's strange mood, and his mutterings about the year 1975, had anything to do with it. I immediately recognized the copy he was holding as the one I'd carried with me for years and annotated extensively. It had been sitting on the passenger seat of my Ford when I arrived in Somerset and I'd shoved it into the glove compartment without thinking when I changed cars. I was mystified. Even more so when Harry threw his own book into the flames.

"What are you doing?" I protested.

I wanted to rescue my copy, but it was impossible. The fire burned my hands. I could only look on, powerless, as the book was consumed. Harry's face on the back cover slowly curled before turning black and disappearing. Raising my head, I watched Harry watch his image burn.

"What am I doing? I'm doing what I should have done thirty years ago with the manuscript of this damn book. I wish it had never existed. You'll be very successful, Marcus. You'll be the writer I never was."

A few months after that strange evening, I used some of Barnaski's advance to dump my Ford and buy a black Range Rover. Harry was the first person I wanted to see my new acquisition. So for my initial trip, I drove to meet him at Goose Cove. He examined the new vehicle for a long time. But instead of congratulating me, he said, "All that for this, Marcus? All those hours, all those years, that fury to live bent over a piece of paper, all that to swap your Ford, which was in good shape—I know because I drove it around a few times—for some luxury car? I don't blame you, Marcus, it's not you, it's society: the only thing that impresses people is money. And you know, that's a problem all artists have. We admire them as long as they're misunderstood, but once they succeed, we shun them because we realize they're just like everyone else. When traders, who make money with money, spend money, no-one is surprised, though we might have contempt for their greed. But we expect artists to raise the bar a little, to remain above all that. Then again, isn't it normal that an artist who makes money might want to spend it? You're going to discover, Marcus, that success is a disease. It changes your behavior. Public recognition, celebrity, the way people look at you—it all has an effect. It prevents you from living a normal life. But don't worry, because success is a disease like any other: it generates its own antibodies. It will do battle with itself within you. So you see, success is a kind of programmed failure."

*    *    *

When I had finished, Gahalowood stared at me strangely. "So, the Marcus with the Ford is what you would've been without all the success, is that it?" he asked.

"Precisely."

"And you would've been happier?"

"I have no idea."

"But you still love this girl?"

"No, I love the ideal she represents. A little like my aunt Anita, or even Helen."

"Stop idealizing and try being practical. A couple's happiest days last no more than a few months. Then, it's work, compromise, frustration, tears. But it's worth the effort because the result is a bond that's not made by chemistry or magic—it's something you built. Love doesn't appear by itself: it's made."

I nodded. Gahalowood patted me on the shoulder with a fraternal gesture. "Come on, return this rust heap and let's go home."

"First I have to tell you why I'm here."

"Why you're here spying on people? You just told me."

"No, Sergeant. You need to know why I got involved in this investigation. I have to be honest with you. I don't know whether I'm doing it because of Helen, or to ease your conscience, or, simply and very selfishly, for myself. Because for as long as I stay focused on this case, I don't need to think about my own life."

There was a lengthy silence before Gahalowood replied: "You know why I came to your hotel yesterday morning?"

"To talk about our progress, I imagine."

"On a Sunday morning? You think I don't have better things to do on a Sunday morning than drive to Mount Pleasant to go over an ongoing investigation?"

"Yes," I answered, not sure what he was driving at. "You probably do have better things to do."

"Well, no. And that's the reality. I don't have much left in my life. Aside from this investigation . . . and you."

"You have your daughters."

"They left Saturday morning for three weeks at a camp in Maine. Malia's a counselor, Lisa's a boarder. We've been planning it for almost a year; they insisted on going. And it'll do them good to get a change of scenery after everything that's happened. So now it's my turn to be frank, Writer. Without this case, I'd be alone at home dying of boredom, stewing in solitude. I'm going to say one nice thing that I'll probably never say again: thanks."

I smiled. He smiled back.

"Come on, turn this car in and let's go back to New Hampshire. On the way, you can tell me more about that good old Marcus in his Ford."

"Nothing good about him, Sergeant."

Gahalowood burst out laughing and rolled his eyes. "If you didn't exist, Writer, someone would have to invent you."

# 17

## *Trout Paradise*

*Mount Pleasant, New Hampshire*
*Tuesday, July 13, 2010*

I was familiar with the New Hampshire State Prison for Men because I had visited Harry there several times while he was incarcerated in the summer of 2008. So that morning, when I arrived at the visitors' parking lot, I had an unpleasant feeling of déjà vu.

The demonstration was being held before the entrance to the prison, without interfering with access. About a dozen protesters stood quietly on the sidewalk, penned in between two barriers. They waved signs calling for the release of Eric Donovan under the placid gaze of two visibly bored police officers, who were drinking coffee in their car.

Over the course of the changing seasons, the tireless supporters materialized every second Tuesday of the month and stayed for an hour, indifferent to rain, snow, cold, heat, or wind. It was always the same crowd: Lauren Donovan; her parents, Janet and Mark; Eric's lawyer, Patricia Widsmith; and a few family friends, mostly retired. But this time, journalists were also present. When they saw Gahalowood and me arrive, they rushed toward us, brandishing microphones and cameras.

"Have you come to demonstrate for Eric Donovan's release?" a journalist asked.

"We're only here to speak with Donovan," Gahalowood told them. "Our presence is not associated with any particular event."

"How's the investigation going?" another journalist asked.

"It's an official police investigation," Gahalowood replied. "As you can imagine, I can't reveal any details."

Gahalowood had determined in advance the procedure to follow to avoid having conflicts with Patricia Widsmith and the Donovan family or putting himself in an awkward situation with respect to his superiors and his sense of professional responsibility. He immediately went through the visitors' entrance gate and disappeared inside the brick building, while I joined Patricia Widsmith. She wore a T-shirt that read "Free Eric."

"You brought the media with you," she said. "We've never seen so many journalists, though we send notifications out the night before each demonstration. Thanks to you, general interest in Eric's case is growing."

"I'm only here to try to discover the truth."

Lauren, who had remained at Widsmith's side until then, walked away.

"She'll get over it. The truth is, she likes you a lot."

"I'm not so sure."

"Trust me, Marcus. I know her well."

My gaze crossed that of Janet and Mark Donovan. I approached them. "I'm very sorry," I said.

"Sorry for what?" Janet asked in a soft voice. "Defending my son? It's been years since we gave up hope, and now you arrive."

She shook my hand. Mark Donovan gave me a friendly pat on the shoulder and whispered, "Thanks, son."

"Come see us, Marcus," Janet said. "At the house or the store. Whenever you like. We'd be happy to talk through all this with you."

I agreed, and then asked, "Do you think Eric will open up a little?"

"It could be tricky," Janet warned. "Eleven years locked up with murderers and rapists has hardened him."

"Why should I speak to you? It's your fault I'm rotting away in here." Those were the first words Eric Donovan said when he saw Gahalowood in the visiting room. He was about forty but looked considerably older. Although he was solidly built, his features were drawn, his face marked by years behind bars. He stood up as if he wanted the guard to return him to his cell, but Patricia Widsmith quickly calmed him down.

"Sit down, Eric, and don't be an idiot. Sergeant Gahalowood and Marcus Goldman are your one chance of finally getting out of here. It was my idea that they come talk to you."

"Talk about what?" Eric asked sarcastically. "When I tried to talk to Gahalowood eleven years ago, he wasn't very eager to listen."

Gahalowood simply said, "I want to know why Walter Carrey set you up for Alaska's murder."

The question hit a nerve. Eric sought Lauren's eyes; she was standing in a corner of the room. She didn't say a word, but her presence spoke volumes: if she didn't have at least some confidence in us, she would never have allowed us near him. Gahalowood continued: "I'm convinced Walter didn't kill Alaska Sanders. Mostly because I know now that his confession has no value. Walter lied. About himself and about you. I know why Walter incriminated himself. What I don't know is why he implicated you. What reason could he have had to want to destroy you?"

"Maybe he thought I was having an affair with Alaska. You already told me that at the time."

"That's what Sally Carrey thought," Gahalowood said.

"She was the one who got him worked up."

"Something's not right here," Gahalowood objected. "I questioned Walter in the presence of his parents the day after Alaska's murder. His mother brought up the idea of an affair, but Walter strongly rejected the possibility."

"Exactly," Widsmith interjected. "It was the day after the murder. Walter had a good reason for hiding his anger at being cheated on. To reveal it would give him a motive."

Gahalowood looked unconvinced. "I see what you're saying, but still, something's not right. That's what's been bothering me, and it's the reason I dragged Marcus down to headquarters last night, where we spent the evening. You know what we were doing? We pulled out files on crimes of passion. Because if Walter killed Alaska because she was cheating on him, well, that would be a crime of passion. It's the moment when anger pushes us to do something that can't be undone. In all the cases we looked at, the decision to act was almost immediate. It's a sudden impulse. A husband surprises his wife in bed with another man or he discovers some compromising letters, and he acts under the sway of uncontrollable emotion. But that's not the case with Walter."

"Yes, it was," Widsmith objected. "You seem to be forgetting that Walter Carrey killed Alaska a few hours after she left him."

"Walter didn't kill Alaska," Gahalowood repeated. "You know as well as I do that the photo proves he was at the National Anthem at the time of the murder."

"And you know that the photo won't hold up before a jury," Widsmith reminded him. "Walter could have killed Alaska and been back at the bar in time for the picture. I'm going to be honest with you, Sergeant, I'm having trouble following you. It's been eleven years; you closed your investigation in three days. You obtained a filmed confession from the murderer. And yet you show up yesterday in my office suddenly convinced that Walter Carrey was innocent. You have something more than that photograph, right? You found something that calls his confession into question. And I'd like to know what that is."

"Unfortunately, I can't tell you anything more at this point. I'm obligated to maintain professional discretion."

"It's easy to hide behind the badge."

Gahalowood made a movement with his lips that I was very familiar with: he was playing his role to perfection, positioning the lawyer where he wanted her, cornering her with cold analysis.

"Okay, let's examine your theory. Walter Carrey framed Eric and arranged it so several pieces of damaging evidence pointed to him. Okay. That Friday night, April second, 1999, when Alaska leaves Walter, he doesn't act out of anger: he follows a carefully prepared plan. He doesn't act on sudden impulse: he's been planning the murder for a long time, down to the smallest detail."

"That's exactly what I think," Widsmith replied. "Walter planned to murder Alaska and have Eric take the blame. He did everything he could to make sure his plan worked: the sweater Eric lent him and the messages he printed from Eric's printer. And, Sergeant, you seem to be forgetting that debris from his car was found near the crime scene, a car he hurried to have repaired within twenty-four hours. If that's not a sign of guilt, I don't know what is! It would have been the perfect crime if Walter hadn't been betrayed by his car."

"The perfect crime?" Gahalowood repeated.

"Yes. The perfect crime isn't one that leaves no trace. It's one that gives the police something to go on and leads them to suspect the wrong individual."

Gahalowood placed the pictures from the fire department report on the table in front of Eric.

"What's this?" Eric asked.

"On the night of Monday, April fifth, to Tuesday, April sixth, 1999, Walter set fire to his apartment after painting the words 'Unfaithful Whore' on the walls."

"Obviously I knew there was a fire at Walter's," Eric said, surprised. "The cops said that he was the one who started it. But I didn't know about the writing on the wall."

"Neither did I," Widsmith said, surprised. "Why weren't those photographs in the case file?"

"Because we received them after the case was closed. And to be frank, at the time, they seemed to me to be nothing more than a footnote. But what a footnote! The fact is, Walter was losing it. That Monday night, he fell apart. He defaced the walls of his apartment and then set it on fire. The guy was completely out of his mind. He had obviously just discovered something that made him lose control."

"That Alaska really was cheating on him?" Widsmith suggested.

"It's possible," Gahalowood acknowledged. "But this suggests that until Monday night—in other words, *after* the murder—he didn't suspect his girlfriend of having an affair. Not in the least. So he had no reason to kill her two days before or to frame Eric, as you seem to think. Of course, you could find some psychiatrist who'll say something like, 'Well, he was in denial when he killed her and wasn't fully aware of the situation until afterward.' You still have to admit that something doesn't sit right with this theory. And that's what I've been trying to tell you since I got here."

"I never had an affair with Alaska!" Eric shouted. "I swear to you! And if Walter suspected something, believe me, I would've known. Walter was impulsive. He wasn't the type of guy to hide his feelings and dream up some complicated plan. If he thought I was seeing Alaska, he would've slugged me without hesitation. He would've regretted it after, but that's the way he was."

"You're saying he wouldn't have gone to the National Anthem with you that Friday night to eat hamburgers and then leave to kill his girl-friend and accuse you of the crime."

"Never!" Eric assured us.

"I believe you," Gahalowood said. "So you yourself reject your lawyer's line of defense. I go back to what I said earlier: Walter didn't set a trap for Eric. Walter didn't plot anything. Walter didn't kill anyone. Walter wound up not only admitting to a murder he didn't commit, but dragging his childhood friend down with him. I call that revenge. So, to get back to my initial question, Eric, what happened between you and Walter that made him do that to you?"

Lauren and Patricia Widsmith remained silent, hypnotized, as I was, by Gahalowood's performance. Eric looked at him like a lost sheep searching for its shepherd. He said, in a hollow voice: "Walter and I knew each other from when we were kids. We went to school together. Our parents' stores were practically next door to one another. We grew up in each other's homes. We spent a huge part of our lives together. I'm not sure I see the connection with Alaska's death."

"It's my job to make connections, Eric. But to do that I need you to tell me everything."

The story Eric Donovan told was of a happy childhood in Mount Pleasant. A comfortable life in a small town sheltered from the outside world. It was in 1980, when he was ten years old, that he became friends with a boy from his class: Walter Carrey.

*     *     *

*Mount Pleasant, New Hampshire*
*Summer 1980*

For the first four years of elementary school in Mount Pleasant, Eric Donovan spent the majority of his time with three other boys in his class. When not in school, they would ride around Mount Pleasant on their bicycles; in town they were known as the Bike Gang.

In the fourth year, when classes were over, the Bike Gang, looking for something exciting to do, made it their mission to commit a few minor transgressions of no great consequence, such as making anonymous phone calls from the telephone booth on Main Street, or carving their initials into public benches. One afternoon, when Eric hadn't heard from the rest of the group all day, he set off to find them. His three friends were in the town square sharing some candy. Intrigued, Eric joined them.

"What are you doing? Why didn't you tell me you were here? I was at home waiting around like an idiot."

"You should've stayed home," one of his friends said, offering no further explanation.

"Where'd you get the candy?"

"Don't worry about it; we took it," another said.

"Can I have some?" Eric asked.

"You won't like it," the third one snickered.

Eric understood at once. "Where'd you steal it? My parents' store?"

"What do you care? You going to tell on us? Besides, they have a ton of it; they won't even notice it's gone."

Eric turned red and threw himself at his friends. But, three to one, he didn't have much of a chance and got a beating for his troubles. The three boys left him on the ground, his nose bleeding. "If you talk, you're dead! Don't even look at us, you jerk!"

Eric cleaned himself up at the fountain. Then he went to his parents' store. When they asked about the blood on his shirt, he told them he had fallen off his bike.

"You looking for your friends?" his mother asked him. "They were just here."

"I know," he grumbled.

"You okay, dear?"

"I'm fed up with those jerks. I need to find new friends. Real friends."

"Why not go see Walter? I ran into his mother a little while ago. She's desperate. He spends his days hanging around their store and she doesn't know how to get rid of him. She says he has no friends."

Eric, for lack of anything better to do, went to the hunting and fishing store a few yards away. He was met by Walter's mother, Sally.

"You looking for Walter?" she asked, delighted. "He's in the back room. He'll be happy to see you."

Eric passed through a small door and entered a poorly lit room, filled with store inventory. In one corner, Walter was seated at a workbench.

"Hi, Walter."

"Hi," Walter replied, without taking his eyes off his work. He was using a small pair of pliers to wrap a length of colored thread around itself.

"What are you doing?" Eric asked.

"Flies. For fishing."

"Flies with thread?" Eric asked, intrigued.

"For fly-fishing."

"Can I help?"

"You can watch if you want."

Eric watched, fascinated, as Walter wrapped the thread around a hook until it gave the illusion of being a fly. No sooner had he finished than he started on another. After a few days of watching him make flies, Eric, under the watchful eyes of his new friend, began to do the same. And when he succeeded in making his first fly, Walter said to him, "We have to try it!"

"We're going fishing?"

"Sure."

"I've never been fly-fishing."

"I'll teach you."

The two boys gathered the equipment they needed from the store and then got on their bikes and headed for Lake Skotam. In their backpacks they carried folding fishing rods and waders. Walter led the way. He knew better than anyone where to find fish. They rode to the parking lot at Grey Beach, where they left their bicycles. At first, Eric thought they were going fishing on the beach, but Walter explained that they were heading for the river. They took off through the woods, Walter striding ahead with purpose; he knew exactly where he was going. After fifteen minutes, they reached the mouth of a river. They walked upstream, through the lush bracken, until they came to a small waterfall.

"Welcome to Trout Paradise!" Walter exclaimed.

The two boys prepared their rods and waded into the water until it reached their waists. Walter taught Eric to cast. His initial attempts were awkward. A good cast required an expert snap of the wrist to imitate the flight of an insect as it settles on the surface of the water. It would take several days for Eric to finally make his first correct cast: at first the trout sensed the deceit before swallowing the fly. Walter, however, possessed extraordinary dexterity. He pulled several trout from the water, one after the other, immediately releasing them each time.

Walter and Eric spent the summer together at Trout Paradise. It was there that they forged a friendship that would last almost twenty years. Until death and prison separated them.

*    *    *

In the visiting room, Eric Donovan was visibly moved by his memories of childhood. It was as if that river and its fish allowed him to forget his confinement, at least for a moment.

"We were inseparable until the end of high school. We did everything together. We even joined the high school track team and won the regional relay race. That victory was miraculous. Nobody would've bet two cents on us, and we took the title."

"And after that?"

"After high school, our paths were radically different. I left for school in Massachusetts. Walter joined the army. In 1990, while I was wandering around campus, he was sent to Saudi Arabia with his unit during the Gulf War. And when I got my diploma, he was fighting in Somalia. You can see the difference. But for all those years, in spite of everything that happened—especially to him—fly-fishing remained our connection. Whenever he was on leave, we met in Mount Pleasant and returned to Trout Paradise. Everything had changed around us, except for that small corner of the world, which had remained untouched. When we were done fishing, we took the two fish we'd kept and went to make a campfire on Grey Beach, where we spent the night, eating, drinking, and putting the world to rights. On those nights we felt like nothing could ever touch us."

"Did Walter stay long in the army?" Gahalowood asked.

"A few years. I remember that he returned to civilian life the year the World Cup was held in the United States . . . that was 1994. We watched a game together in Foxborough. I had gotten the tickets, I don't remember how."

There was a silence, then Gahalowood continued his questioning. "What happened between the time Walter got out of the army and 1998?"

"After the army, Walter came back to Mount Pleasant. At first, he said it was only temporary. He moved into the apartment above the store, which his parents had been renting out until then. He was comfortable there. The store was his thing. He liked hunting and fishing. He was in his element. And the store never did so well as when Walter was there running things. People came from all over the region for advice. He was *the* specialist. And when you like the outdoors, there's no better place than Mount Pleasant. I'd say Walter was happy."

"And you?"

"After college, I got a job in Salem, working for a chain of super-markets. I was satisfied. I wanted to create a regional brand in New Hampshire modeled on my parents' store. I knew it could work, especially in the northeastern part of the state."

"And Walter came to visit you in Salem, right?"

"Yes, he came often."

"So, it's through you that Walter met Alaska?"

"Yeah. I'd made a lot of friends in Salem—I went out a lot. Walter always looked forward to those visits; it gave him a chance to chase girls a little. He hit a few rough spots back in Mount Pleasant with his ex-girlfriend, Deborah Miles. I guess you heard about her."

"We did."

"So Walter had sort of burned his bridges in Mount Pleasant, and Salem was his outlet. In the spring of 1998, I began to hang out regularly with a group of girls that included Alaska. They had just turned twenty-one and they wanted to take advantage of it to go out and party. When Walter met them for the first time, he immediately took a liking to Alaska. I have to say, she was really something. He chatted her up like the ex-GI that he was, a fan of the great outdoors and a part-time photographer. Photographer, my eye. He went around with my camera to look important. He stole it from me and slung it over his shoulder as if he was an artist, when half the time there wasn't even any film in it."

With that, Eric laughed—as if, in the space of a moment, he was back in some noisy bar in Salem, drinking and smoking, while Walter, at his side, waved his camera around to impress the girls.

"Alaska and Walter finally started going out together. He must've had to talk her into it. But I think his rough side appealed to her. He traveled back and forth for a while until she moved in with him in Mount Pleasant. At the time, it seemed strange to me."

"Why strange?" Gahalowood asked.

Eric smiled. "Sergeant, if you had known Alaska, you would understand. She had class, like some sort of princess. She was amazing. Not just because of the way she looked. She was magnetic. I still remember the day she showed up in Mount Pleasant. I had just left Salem and moved back in with my parents."

"Why did you leave Salem?"

"I got fired after a disagreement with my boss. We had different ideas about strategy. I felt that working in my parents' store would be an opportunity to test the concepts I wanted to introduce when I started my own business. And besides, my parents weren't doing that well; I was happy to help them out. My father had cancer, nothing too serious, and fortunately, he's since recovered, but he was very tired. I was glad to be there with them. So, I'd been back in Mount Pleasant for a few weeks when one fine day Alaska shows up."

\*       \*       \*

*October 2, 1998*

The afternoon was drawing to an end. Eric Donovan was helping a customer load his shopping into the trunk of his car when he noticed a blue convertible parked in front of Carrey Hunting & Fishing. The driver's side door opened, and to his great surprise, he saw Alaska step out. It was the first time he'd seen her in Mount Pleasant; she looked up and down Main Street. It was a gray autumn day; dark clouds indicated it would rain soon. Then the first drops began to fall. Alaska ran her hand through her wavy hair, which cascaded over her leather jacket, and started to walk away from her car.

"Alaska?"

She turned and saw Eric, wearing an apron embroidered with the words "Donovan's General Store." Her smile was brilliant. "Hi, Eric."

"What brings you to Mount Pleasant?"

"If there's one thing you do in life, see Mount Pleasant before you die," she replied in a burst of laughter.

"Are you here for the weekend?"

"A few days at least. Maybe a little more. I need a change of scenery, and the country air will do me good."

A week later, the morning of Friday, October 9, Eric ran into Alaska at the Season, drinking a cup of coffee. "Still here, then?" he asked, good-humoredly.

Her smile was sad. "New York's loss is Mount Pleasant's gain."

"How's that?"

"I decided to move here, at least for a while. I moved in with Walter."

"You're staying in Mount Pleasant? What are you going to do here?"

"I have no idea. I had a fight with my parents; I had to get out of there."

"Oh, I'm sorry. If I can be of any help . . ."

"You can. I need a job, I'm broke. You think your parents would hire me?"

"Unfortunately, this is a tough time for us. And I've just come back to help them out, so we don't need anyone else at the moment."

She looked disappointed. "Walter asked his parents; they'd be happy to have me help out, but they don't want to pay me. Such cheapskates. If you hear of something, let me know."

She put some money on the counter and left. Eric caught up with her on the sidewalk. "Hold on. I know Mr. Jacob at the gas station is looking for someone. There's been an ad on the door for months. It's on Route 21, right before Grey Beach. You can't miss it."

"I'll check it out. Thanks." With that, Alaska hurried away. It was starting to rain.

"You're not really going to work at a gas station, are you?" Eric shouted after her.

She turned to face him. She had a fatalistic air about her. "When you're in the shit, you can't afford to be picky," she said before running off to get out of the rain.

\* \* \*

"'When you're in the shit, you can't afford to be picky,'" Eric repeated. "Those were her exact words. For a long time, I wondered what had happened in Salem."

"Alaska's mother mentioned an argument," Gahalowood said. "Apparently, she and her husband found out that Alaska was smoking marijuana."

Eric seemed to find that amusing. "Alaska smoked grass like everyone else her age. But to leave Salem and bury herself in Mount Pleasant for that? No. There had to be something a lot more serious going on."

"Walter never said anything to you about it?"

"No. And not because I didn't ask. But he avoided the question. He pretended that it was some great love affair and I ended up convincing myself that Alaska was happy in Mount Pleasant. It's a good place to live. Nothing like the excitement of New York or the glitz of Los Angeles, but it has a quietness and simplicity that's worth all the money in the world. Sergeant, I've been talking for a while now about my life and my memories with Walter, and not only the good times. I don't see what you're driving at with your revenge theory. I think about Walter all the time. That's how I can forget about being here. In this dark prison, I stretch out on my bed, I close my eyes, and everything around me dissolves— the noise, the smells, the cries. Then I'm able to hear the laughter of children. I see us, me and Walter, together, running down Main Street. We meet in front of our parents' stores and challenge one another—see who can get to the bookstore first before the next car passes. And we take off like a couple of rockets. We often challenged each other like that. We got hooked on running after a while. By the time we were in high school, we were fast as hell. That got us onto the track team and got me a college scholarship. Every day I'm stuck in here, I can leave my cell and find myself in Mount Pleasant with Walter. So, when I think about him, Sergeant, I'm not thinking about revenge: I'm thinking about going fishing, about the trout we cooked over the open fire on Grey Beach, about our nights talking on the shore. And when I think back on all that, I tell myself it was all so easy . . ."

"What was easy?"

"Freedom, Sergeant."

*     *     *

Leaving the prison, Patricia Widsmith asked Gahalowood what he thought about all they had just heard. "I have to admit, I'm a bit confused," he said. "If we believe Eric, Walter had no reason to want to hurt him. And yet, he did. Walter deliberately accused Eric. Why?"

She stared at Gahalowood. "Does that mean you think Eric's innocent?"

"We have to start with some assumption if we're to move forward."

Lauren and I walked side by side in silence. Hearing Gahalowood's words, she gave me a hopeful smile. I had a strong desire to take her hand but held back. I simply said, "I'm very sorry."

"Not as sorry as I am."

We separated in the prison parking lot. Once back in the car with Gahalowood, I asked him, "Do you really think that Eric is innocent?"

"No. I told Widsmith what she wanted to hear. What I am certain of is that Eric isn't telling us the whole truth. I'd really like to know why Walter Carrey accused him of Alaska's murder. Something must've happened between them. I've heard Eric's version; now I'd like to hear Walter's."

"Sergeant, do I have to remind you that Walter is dead?"

"I know, thanks for your insight. We're going to talk to his parents."

# 18

## Sally and George Carrey

*Mount Pleasant, New Hampshire*
*Tuesday, July 13, 2010*

After the fire in April 1999, Sally and George Carrey had the building restored just as it had been: the hunting and fishing store occupied the ground floor, and the apartment upstairs was now rented to a city employee. As Gahalowood and I entered the store, an electronic chime alerted a woman who came out from the back room. Seeing Perry, her face froze.

"Oh, so it's true. You've reopened the investigation."

"We have new information, Mrs. Carrey."

She stared at me. "You're that writer, is that it?"

"Yes, ma'am. Marcus Goldman."

She stuck her head through the doorway to the back room to call her husband. "George, come out here, it's about Walter."

Sally and George Carrey insisted that we continue our discussion at the Season, on the other side of the street. Gahalowood had suggested staying in the store, out of consideration for them, but Sally Carrey said, "I want everyone to see us talking to the cops. It's been eleven years we've been hiding ourselves away, eleven years that people have been looking at us like we're dirt. It's time to set the record straight about our boy." The terrace was full, so we sat down indoors. We had barely taken our seats when Sally said, "Walter didn't kill himself, is that it? And he didn't kill that detective either."

Gahalowood remained impassive. "Who told you that?"

"A mother knows her son. Walter was a soldier, a man of honor. He was no murderer. Nor a coward. If you're here, you know that."

"We're here because we have to verify certain elements of the investigation."

"What is it that you want, exactly?" asked George Carrey, who seemed less inclined than his wife to reopen old wounds.

"To learn more about your son. We'd like to get to know him a little better through you."

"Eleven years later, you finally wake up?"

"I understand how difficult this must be," Gahalowood said.

"Difficult? Unbearable you mean!"

"George," his wife admonished. "Calm down."

He remained silent, his face hard. Sally then began to describe, in a calm voice, their son Walter, an introverted boy who loved the outdoors: "He was a loner. As a boy, he kept to himself. He made his own flies and spent his days fishing. When he was ten, he already knew all the best spots. At the store, he helped the customers, and many of them, even experienced anglers, sought his advice. 'Is the little guy here?' they would ask. 'Oh, no,' I told them, 'he's at school. You have to come on Saturday. But come in the morning. He goes fishing in the afternoon.' If he wasn't at school or out fishing, Walter was in the store. I thought maybe it was too much. I wanted him to have friends, to have fun. I even spoke to Janet Donovan about it. Eric had a group of friends, and I would have liked my son to join them.

"One day, Eric showed up at the store. I guess his mother had asked him to try to make friends with Walter. They soon grew close; the two of them were always together. In fact, they were inseparable. If Walter wasn't at home with us, he was with the Donovans, and vice versa. I remember how, to get from one house to the other, they would always run. Like a shot. As if life was too short to walk. Always running around like two little devils. When they were around fifteen, the coach of the

Mount Pleasant track team, who was a customer, came to the store one day and said to me, 'Is that your son I just saw take off like a rocket?' I said yes, and he asked me, 'Why doesn't he join the track team?' That's how Walter joined the team. And Eric too."

"Eric was a good athlete," George interjected. "But he wouldn't have thought to join the team if Walter hadn't taken him along. And Walter told the coach that he wouldn't join without Eric."

"It sounds like they were great friends," Gahalowood said.

"They were until they got older," George replied.

"Are you referring to anything specific?" Gahalowood asked.

"Yes," George said. "Eric Donovan set a trap for Walter at a track meet."

\*       \*       \*

*February 1988*

Walter and Eric were in their senior year of high school. It was time to think about the future. Both of them wanted to go to college to study business, and they spent hours examining brochures from various schools. They ruled out those that were too far away, because they wanted to be able to return to Mount Pleasant without too much difficulty. Then they set aside those that were too expensive. They finally settled on Monarch University in Massachusetts, which had a solid business program. Their parents didn't have the money to pay the tuition, and so the two boys had considered taking out a loan. But Mark Donovan and George Carrey dissuaded them, saying, "A school loan is a burden right from the start. It would be better to get a scholarship." Although their grades were good, they weren't good enough for academic scholarships. Their only chance was a hail mary: to try the athletic route as last-minute recruits. The previous year, they had surprised everyone by winning the regional relay championship. They were hoping to attract the attention of university recruiters.

Mark Donovan and George Carrey asked the track team coach to sponsor their sons. "I can't hide the fact that Mount Pleasant doesn't attract many recruiters," he warned them. "In my entire career, I've never been able to win a scholarship for any of my boys. But Eric and Walter did beat several favorites for the relay. We should be able to do something. Maybe at the next indoor competition in early March. It's still pretty local, but I'll try to get some recruiters to show up."

The coach kept his word and worked his network of contacts. But none of them seemed convinced. "If your kids were as good as you say, we would have heard about them," they said. Now desperate, he traveled to Massachusetts to meet the coach at Monarch University. "These two boys are excellent athletes," he pleaded. "They've been dreaming of coming to Monarch and they're working their asses off." One spot on the team had opened up, and the coach was looking for that rare pearl. Nor could he be too picky, as several of the athletes he had wanted to recruit had answered the siren call of more prestigious schools. "I'll make it down for the meet," he promised. "But I can take only one of them. It's up to them to show me what they can do on the track."

"There's only one spot," the coach explained to George Carrey a few days before the competition. "I told the boys a recruiter from Monarch would be there, but I didn't tell them only one could be chosen; I don't want to stress them out needlessly. I told the guy from Monarch that Walter's the best. Your boy's fast, very fast. I think he'll get the nod. I wanted to let you know."

"Thanks, coach, thanks for everything. What do I tell Walter?"

"Don't tell him anything. Just make sure he gets some rest and he's in good shape for the meet."

On the day of the race, the Donovan and Carrey families traveled together to the track to support their sons. Everyone was in a good mood. Eric and Walter were running the hundred meters and, later that day, the 1,600-meter race.

The participants took their places on the starting line for the first race. Eric was very focused. Walter looked uneasy and had difficulty getting on his marks. Then, when the starter was getting ready to give the signal, Walter left the track and hurried to the locker room.

*    *    *

"Walter had terrible diarrhea," George Carrey explained. "He couldn't compete. The coach thought it was nerves, but I think he was poisoned. I think someone put a laxative in his drink."

"And you think that someone was Eric?" Gahalowood asked.

"With Walter out of the competition, Eric had a chance of winning the scholarship. He must've found out there was only one spot on the team, and he knew Walter was the favorite. So he got rid of him. Eric was always jealous of Walter. That continued with Alaska. He couldn't stand the fact that my son was going out with a girl like her. So he killed her and made it look like Walter did it. He set a trap for him just as he set a trap at the meet."

"Do you have any proof to back this up?" Gahalowood asked.

"For the race, no. As for Alaska, Eric was definitely interested. My wife noticed it. But you already know that because she told you at the time."

"True. But I also remember that Walter dismissed any connection between them out of hand. Did he ever talk to you about Eric and the race?"

"No. But you know, sometimes friendship blinds people to the truth."

"After the race, how did Walter react?"

"Very philosophically, as always. He repeated what the coach had put in his head—that it was 'nerves.'"

"So Eric went to college and Walter . . ."

"He still wanted to go to college, but since I had convinced him not to take out a student loan and get himself into debt, he had no choice but to join the army to finance his studies. Three years in the service of Uncle Sam. On the other hand, his university training would be paid for by the government. He enjoyed his experience in the military. The first two years went smoothly. He was based in Virginia and came home on leave on a pretty regular basis. Everything was going well. And then, in 1990, the US went to war.

"Operation Desert Shield started in early August, deploying troops to the Saudi desert. Walter spent several months protecting oil wells there. Several months waiting for an enemy that would never show up. He spent his days exercising, doing guard duty, and hanging out with his pals. When he got back from the Gulf, Walter hadn't fired a single shot. The only soldiers he met were those in his own company, and he hardly left his base in the middle of the dunes. He enjoyed the experience, and it helped swell his patriotic convictions. He decided to reenlist for three years, and soon he was sent to Somalia. That was a real war, dirty and violent. Not at all like his tour in Saudi Arabia. The games of flipper and darts that had filled his days during Desert Shield were replaced with dangerous patrols in the streets of Mogadishu, where snipers tried to pick US soldiers off from the rooftops.

"Somalia was hell. During our rare phone calls with Walter, he told us about his fear. He had one horrific night supporting a team of Rangers who were charged with capturing a rebel chief. Their unit was caught in an ambush. He saw several of his buddies killed. I think that's when it all changed, that night. After that, he started to lose his nerve.

"Shortly after Walter returned to the States in early 1994, his military career ended prematurely after an incident at his base in Virginia."

"What sort of incident?" Gahalowood asked.

"I'm not going lie to you, Sergeant. It would be easy enough for you to find out. Walter had a violent argument with a superior officer. They got into a fight."

"What happened?"

"The lieutenant in charge of his unit was a mean SOB. He wanted to punish one of the soldiers, whom he considered undisciplined, and he ordered Walter and a small team to take care of it. Walter refused. They started arguing and things quickly degenerated. The matter was hushed up: the army preferred to suppress the superior officer's behavior by not punishing Walter. So he was released from his military duties. In any case, I think he'd had enough by then.

"Walter returned to civilian life tired and worn out by his experiences. He had only one wish: to lead a quiet life in Mount Pleasant. Return to the family store, spend his weekends fishing. He wanted to stay hidden from the world.

"He gave up his studies. He had no interest in them whatsoever. 'I don't want to chase after life, I want to live, that's all,' he said. The apartment over the store was vacant, and he settled in. He joined us back at the store and devoted himself to it, body and soul. My wife and I were thinking of retiring and selling the business, but the potential buyers we met weren't offering us a good price. And we liked the idea of turning it over to our son. We had a number of good years after Walter's return to Mount Pleasant. That is, until the autumn of 1998."

"What happened then?" Gahalowood asked.

"One day, Eric Donovan showed up. He had just decided to settle in Mount Pleasant. After that, everything changed. Especially when Alaska got here. As I told you earlier, I think Eric had eyes for her. He couldn't bear the idea that she was going out with Walter and not with him. So he killed her."

"That's what you truly believe?"

"Absolutely. He killed her and made it look like Walter did it. We were on vacation in Maine when we heard the news. We came back at once. I remember that when we arrived, Eric was walking back and forth outside of the store. He was nervous. I suspected him at once."

"And Walter?" Gahalowood asked. "How was he after the murder?"

"Defeated. Worried," Sally replied. "You saw that for yourself."

"Seems to me that when faced with difficult situations, Walter had a tendency to lose control," Gahalowood remarked. "With his superior in the army, for example. Or with his girlfriend back then, Deborah Miles. Or when he set fire to his apartment. Why did Walter break down that night?"

"I have no idea," Sally replied.

"He covered the walls with graffiti, writing 'Unfaithful Whore.' Did he find out Alaska was having an affair?"

"I don't know," she repeated.

"But you yourself had suspected Eric and Alaska for a while, isn't that right?"

"Yes, for about two weeks before she was killed."

"And when did you tell Walter?"

"When he called to tell me that Alaska had left him. It was Friday afternoon, the day before the murder."

*　　*　　*

*Friday, April 2, 1999*
"Mom? She left me!"

"What? Who?"

"Alaska. I went up to the apartment. I was cold and wanted to grab a sweater. I found her in the living room, dressed as if she was going on a date, high-heel boots and all. She didn't look happy to see me. She quickly changed and told me she'd stopped by to get her things and that she was leaving me."

"Oh my God, Walt! But why?"

"I have no idea. No idea at all."

"Should we come back, Walter? We can leave early tomorrow morning; we can be there before noon."

"No, don't bother. Besides, it won't change anything. Enjoy your vacation. I don't really know what to do."

"Talk to her," Sally Carrey suggested. "Go see her at the gas station, ask for an explanation."

"Knowing her, that'll make her want to leave even more. She told me she was going to her parents'; maybe I should give her a little breathing room."

"Well, whatever you do, don't stay home alone tonight. Go out, keep yourself busy."

"Don't worry. Eric suggested we watch the hockey game at the National Anthem."

There was a brief silence. Then Sally said, "I have to tell you something. Last week, when you were at that fishing convention in Quebec, I saw Eric and Alaska. They were getting out of your car."

"Alaska's car had an oil leak so I told her to use mine while I was gone. She must've met Eric while she was out and given him a lift home."

"No, Walter, that's what I'd like to believe, but there was something strange about it."

Walter made a sound resembling a stifled laugh. "Eric and Alaska? No, not possible."

"I hate hurting you, Walter, but if she's leaving, it's probably because she's met someone else."

"Well, I've suspected something like that for a while now. She's changed. And she's been getting gifts. The other day, she had a new pair of shoes. She told me she bought them in Wolfeboro. But I checked, and that brand is only sold in a store in Salem. Alaska isn't seeing Eric, Mom, it's probably someone who lives in Salem. Besides, I wonder if she really is going to her parents' place; she doesn't get along with them that well. If she's going to Salem, it's probably to be with him."

*      *      *

Eleven years later, Gahalowood said to Sally Carrey: "There's something I don't understand. You say that Walter suspected Alaska was cheating on him for a while. You also admit that he's impulsive, someone who reacts unexpectedly when he's upset. Like the night he set fire to the apartment. I keep coming back to that night. Why was Walter so distraught? He's not a slow fuse: he's impulsive. He explodes when he gets worked up. So, what got him so worked up? Did you see him that night?"

"He came over for dinner," George acknowledged. "I couldn't stay, I was playing cards with my club. But I was there when he arrived; he seemed perfectly normal."

"And then?" Gahalowood asked, addressing Sally.

"We had dinner together. I remember that evening very well . . . how could I forget? It was the last time I saw my son alive."

*    *    *

*Monday, April 5, 1999, eight p.m.*
"How are you feeling, Walt?" his mother asked.

"As well as can be expected," he replied, shrugging. "I can't believe she's gone."

"I know, dear. It's terrible."

Sally had made veal stew, Walter's favorite dish. He barely touched his plate.

"You have to eat something, dear."

"Not hungry. Sorry."

"I made carrot cake for dessert."

"Mom, I have to talk to you about something."

"I'm listening. You can tell me anything, you know."

"I did something stupid."

"What do you mean, *stupid*? Does it have anything to do with Alaska?"

"Yes and no. Saturday afternoon, in town, everybody was talking about what happened at Grey Beach. I ran into Tim Jenkins—you know, he was in high school with me and now he's a cop in Mount Pleasant."

"Yes, I know him."

"Tim told me what happened at Grey Beach. He said they found pieces of a taillight and some black paint on a tree trunk."

"So?" his mother asked, her heart beating rapidly.

"Saturday, I discovered that one of my taillights was broken. The bumper was damaged too. But I didn't hit anything: I would've known about it. I think someone did it deliberately."

"Someone took your car the night of the murder? Did anyone else have keys?"

"No-one. No-one had the keys to my car."

"But you always leave your car unlocked, your apartment too; it's so careless. Dear, this is all very strange. You have to tell the police. We can go now, or you can call Chief Mitchell if you prefer. He can put us in touch with the state police investigators who came to see you."

"Mom, the last people I want to see are the police. That's where I did something stupid. When Tim was telling me about the taillight, I made the connection with my car and I panicked. I was afraid the cops would trace it back to me. That they'd find out about my fight in the army and the incident with Deborah and accuse me of freaking out after breaking up with Alaska. So I got in touch with Dave Burke at the Ford dealership. He came over here last night. I put my car in the garage so we could work on it without being seen."

Sally was horrified. "Walter, what have you done? It'll look like you're guilty! If the police question your friend Dave, he's going to tell them what happened."

"Don't worry. It'll be alright. The cops have no reason to question Dave. Besides, he won't tell them anything. He's a friend."

"You shouldn't put so much trust in your friends, Walter."

"What do you mean?" he asked, realizing that his mother was alluding to something else.

"Be careful around Eric, dear. I can't help but wonder if he's the one who killed Alaska."

*    *    *

"I had no idea that you'd warned Walter about Eric," George Carrey said to his wife.

290

"I had to! I just felt he didn't know what was going on around him."

Gahalowood cut in. "This simply proves, once again, that Walter acts on impulse and makes poor decisions. He panicked when he found the broken taillight on his car and reacted by getting it fixed immediately. And when you warned him about Eric, did he get upset?"

"No, not at all. He was very calm. He told me he trusted his friend. After that, he left. He was tired; he said he needed to rest."

"So, he was calm when he left your house?"

"Yes."

"What time was that?"

"About nine."

"Then why would he set fire to his apartment a few hours later?"

"I have no idea," Sally said. "Maybe he had a breakdown when he got home."

"No," Gahalowood insisted. "I think he discovered something. I'd like to know what. Mrs. Carrey, one thing has been bothering me. Why did you never mention this conversation before? Why did you wait until today to mention the broken taillight he had repaired?"

Suddenly, Sally exploded. "Because the next day he was dead, Sergeant! He walked out the door and that was the last time I saw my son alive. So what difference would it have made for me to tell you? Would it have given me back the handsome face that bullet destroyed? Have you ever seen someone who's been shot at close range, Sergeant? Because I have, and it was my son. So tell me something: What would it have changed in my broken life to talk to you about these things? All I knew was that Walter would never have killed that officer, and he would never have taken his own life. He's a victim, a victim of Eric Donovan, and a victim of the police! When are you going to rehabilitate my son, Sergeant Gahalowood?"

Sally Carrey's voice resonated throughout the coffee shop, drawing the waitress's attention. Sally rose, followed by her husband, and they left.

Gahalowood and I remained at the table. Aside from the staff, the place was empty.

"Sergeant, why didn't Eric mention the track meet?"

"Maybe because he really did arrange to get Walter out of the way, just as his parents believe."

"By giving him a laxative?"

"It's possible. Still, even if you cheat during a race in high school, that doesn't mean you're going to murder someone eleven years later. To tell the truth, I don't know what to think. The only thing I'm sure of is that if Walter Carrey did set fire to the apartment on that Monday night, he did it because something upset him. I need to know what it was."

A short distance away, behind the counter, a woman was half-heartedly consulting the cash register. She seemed to be watching us.

"Are you Regina Speck?" Gahalowood asked her.

She looked at us in surprise. "Yes, how did you know?"

"Patricia Widsmith, Eric Donovan's lawyer, mentioned you."

She approached the table. "And you're that cop and the writer every-one's talking about."

"Yes. Mind if we ask you a few questions?"

"Go ahead."

Gahalowood invited her to join us. She sat down on the other side of the table. Regina Speck was in her midforties, much younger than I had imagined when Patricia Widsmith spoke of her. Gahalowood must have felt the same way because he asked her, "Mrs. Speck, how old were you in 1999?"

"I was thirty-four."

"And you were already the owner of the coffee shop?"

"Yes. My father was officially, but he couldn't stand up straight past ten in the morning."

"Why's that?"

"He drank. He died a few years ago."

"I'm very sorry."

"You couldn't have known. Anyway, by 1999, it was me running the restaurant. My parents were divorced—my mother took off when I was seven to make a new life for herself. She didn't want to have to take care of a kid. I grew up behind this counter. I had a decent education, though. I got good grades at school and I won a scholarship to Princeton, where I studied economics. After I graduated, I worked for five years for a large New York auditing company. What a bore! I ended up returning to Mount Pleasant. That was a kind of revelation for me—why live somewhere else when I can live so well right here? That was the early nineties. My father's drinking had gotten worse and the restaurant was in trouble. Coming back here was the best decision of my life. I took over management of the place and used all my savings to renovate it, make it look like one of those hip restaurants in Manhattan. Comfy interior, high-quality food, a wide selection of Italian coffee: ristretto, espresso, macchiato, cappuccino. I have to admit, it came as something of a shock to the regulars. With my father, they were used to French fries cooked in day-old oil. But it didn't take long to win them over, and it's been going strong ever since."

Clearly, Regina Speck liked to talk, so Gahalowood tried to bring her back to the topic. "Tell us about 1999, if you don't mind."

"Not much to say. The place was doing very well. What do you want to know?"

"Were Eric Donovan and Walter Carrey customers here?"

"Yeah, regulars. Especially Walter. He lived across the street above the store. He'd come over for breakfast before he started work."

"And Walter's mother, was she also a customer?"

"Since I took over the Season, Sally came over nearly every day for her espresso. She said it was a nice change from the dishwater they used to serve, and it reminded her of a trip to Rimini before she got married. Sally went to Italy once, years ago when she was much younger, and every day she drinks a ristretto in memory of that trip."

"So, you know her well . . ."

"I've seen her every day for twenty years. You get to know people that way."

"Did she ever mention an affair Alaska was having while she was with Walter?"

"Yes. Shortly before Alaska died, in fact. If I'm not mistaken, I spoke about it with Eric Donovan's lawyer."

"Do you remember what Mrs. Carrey told you?"

"There wasn't much to it, like all our conversations. She sat at the counter, I served her her ristretto, we chatted for a few minutes. But she did look worried. I asked her if something was wrong. She told me that the day before, she had seen Alaska and Eric together outside her store. As far as she was concerned, they were behaving like a couple. I asked her why she said that. And she said they were arguing and it seemed very emotional between them. I was doubtful. I told her that if they were having an affair, they wouldn't be making eyes at each other in front of her store window."

"Why didn't you say anything back then?" Gahalowood asked her. "After all, we put out a call for witnesses."

"What would I have told the cops? It was just a conversation in a coffee shop: it didn't amount to much. Besides, two or three days after the murder, you arrested Walter, then Eric, so what was there to add? I only ended up talking to that lawyer because she was sniffing around asking questions."

"I see. And Eric? Did he come here?"

"From time to time. Usually at the end of the day, to relax and have a drink. To tell the truth, he was mostly trying to flirt with me, but I wasn't interested."

"If you don't mind my asking, what was it about him you didn't like? He was a handsome guy, generally easygoing."

"He wasn't even thirty; I was almost thirty-five. I was thinking of having kids, and he had just moved back in with his parents. Not exactly the kind of guy I was looking for. And crybabies are not really my thing."

"Crybaby? Why's that?"

"Eric was always ill at ease. He wasn't happy."

"What makes you say that?"

"He opened up to me. One night, we were alone at the bar. This was the fall of 1998—I remember because it was right before I met my husband. We'd had a few drinks and we were slightly drunk. At one point he pulled me in like he wanted to kiss me, so I pushed him away. He excused himself, then played the victim. He said something like 'You're just like all the others; they push me away too.' We talked a bit and he mentioned his girlfriend in Salem who had dumped him from one day to the next. She was seeing another man. He felt so depressed he decided to cut Salem out of his life. He left his job and returned to Mount Pleasant."

"He was fired, wasn't he?" Gahalowood asked. "I heard about the breakup, but I wasn't under the impression that he quit. He was fired after a disagreement with his boss."

Regina Speck smiled. "That's the official version. For his parents. The truth is he quit. Well, that's what he told me. You can check with his employer at the time."

We had just left the Season and were walking down the street when a police car pulled up alongside us. An officer, a man with an athletic build belted into his uniform, got out and approached us. "You could've dropped by the station, at least," he said to us.

"Chief Mitchell," Gahalowood said. "It's good to see you again."

"Sergeant Gahalowood, I don't know if I should be delighted to see you or concerned about your reason for being here."

According to Gahalowood, and it was something I was able to confirm from pictures of him in various newspapers, Chief Francis Mitchell had hardly changed since 1999. He was slightly thinner and a little paler, but he had kept his crew cut, his general physique, and his air of determination. Even his sunglasses, large aviators with smoky lenses, seemed to have traveled through time with him. "Have you really got enough to reopen the Sanders investigation?" he asked.

"We wouldn't be here if we didn't," Gahalowood replied.

"What have you got?"

"Certain concrete facts . . . but it's sensitive. I promise to fill you in as soon as possible."

"Why not now?" Mitchell suggested.

The Mount Pleasant chief of police had shown up fishing for information. Gahalowood wasn't about to give him that satisfaction, but he didn't want to anger him either. "It's possible the evidence was poorly interpreted," he explained simply.

"You're referring to the evidence against Eric Donovan?"

"Among others."

"Among others? Walter Carrey confessed, didn't he?"

Gahalowood avoided the question. "When you reopen an investigation, you need to be ready to challenge everything. But you already know that."

"Listen, Sergeant, I appreciate what you're doing. But this is a quiet town; the less commotion the better. It's taken a while for folks to get over that murder. It was the first in more than thirty years, and fortunately, there hasn't been one since. It's a peaceful place; there's no need to stir things up again."

"I understand your concern, Chief Mitchell. We'll be careful, don't you worry."

"I'm not going to lie to you—I am a little worried. If you don't mind, I'd like one of my officers to join you as long as you're within the jurisdiction of the Mount Pleasant police. Out of concern for local folks."

Gahalowood smiled ironically. "The eternal mistrust of the state police."

"I'm doing you a service, Sergeant. Mount Pleasant is a small community with its own rules. You'll have an easier time of it if you take someone from the area with you. You're here as part of a state police investigation, and it's my job to make it as easy for you as possible. But this is my home. You need to respect the master of the house."

"Couldn't agree more," Gahalowood assured him. "Can we meet tomorrow at the station to go over our strategy?"

"Sounds like a good idea. I'll see you in the morning." He strutted down the street, visibly satisfied with his attempt at intimidation.

"Why is Chief Mitchell acting like that?" I asked.

"He's defending his territory. And he's a few months from retirement. I know, because I inquired. He's been running the police in this town for fifteen years, and he has no desire to end his career on a bad note. And he's right to worry. If Eric Donovan is innocent and there's a murderer running free, it's going to cause one helluva scandal. C'mon, let's go to your hotel; I need to book a room."

"You're staying here? So *that's* why you were carrying that suitcase this morning."

"I'm not leaving you all alone."

"You worried about me?"

"If there is a murderer out there, you're next on the list."

"Don't you think you're making this into something bigger than it is, Sergeant?"

"If anyone's making a big deal of it, it's you."

I smiled. "You'll like the hotel, Sergeant."

"I'm not on vacation: I'm trying to conduct an investigation."

"Oh, I know. But I can't help wonder what you would do differently if you could go back to 1999."

"Meaning what?"

"Eleven years have passed, and a lot has come to light."

"At the time," Gahalowood said, "I didn't ask enough questions around town. That's something I got from you and the way you handled the Quebert case."

"Sergeant, are you admitting that I taught you how to do your job?"

"That's not what I'm saying!"

"I'm very touched, Sergeant. Dinner's on me."

"I don't want your dinner."

"Come on, don't be stubborn. Book your room at the hotel and then I'll take you to an Italian place I know."

That evening, Gahalowood and I ate at Luini's. On the way back, as we approached the hotel, I noticed, on a bench, a small statue of a gull, identical to the one I had found in my room. I walked over to it. It was resting on a brochure from Burrows University. On the cover, someone had written with a red marker:

> *Marcus,*
> *My one piece of advice: don't go to Burrows.*

"What's that supposed to mean?" Gahalowood asked, reading over my shoulder.

"It's a message from Harry. Like the one I had a few days ago."

"What's this about Burrows?"

"I agreed to teach a class next autumn."

"*Now* you tell me? Good work, Writer! University professor—that's a nice promotion."

"Harry doesn't seem to agree with you. He wants me to back out, but I still don't know why."

# 19

# *The Gulls*

*Mount Pleasant, New Hampshire*
*Wednesday, July 14, 2010*

At the breakfast table of the hotel, I was reading *The Seagulls of Somerset*. I had bought a copy at Lockart's Bookstore and dug into it at once. I already knew it well, but I was eager to find something I'd missed about Harry—something that could tell me why his life had turned out the way it had.

Gahalowood joined me. I quickly put away my book but not before he could register what I was reading. I'd forgotten that nothing escapes him.

"Still with your Harry Quebert," he said.

"It worries me, I can't help it. I want to know what's become of him." A waiter came over and filled our coffee cups.

"I made a couple of phone calls," Gahalowood said. "I promised you I would. But I found nothing. Not a trace of him anywhere—no address, no credit card, no traffic tickets, no phone number. Nothing. He's completely off the radar. I'd even say he could be dead if he wasn't playing this mysterious game of hide and seek."

"If he knows I'm here, why doesn't he come see me directly?"

"If he wanted to see you, he would've gone to New York. I think he's running away from you."

"Buy why? I fought to prove he was innocent."

"Innocent of murder, yes, but you also revealed a disturbing truth about him. I think he's having trouble dealing with that."

Gahalowood swallowed a mouthful of coffee and looked at his watch. "Let's go. The Donovans are waiting for us."

We had agreed to meet Janet and Mark Donovan at their home. They were waiting on their porch, where I'd had tea with Lauren the previous Sunday.

"Eric was a good boy, a hard worker, ambitious," Mark told us. "His teachers in high school liked him. We were very proud when he won that college scholarship. He worked hard at Monarch and he left with good grades. It didn't take him long to find a management position with a supermarket chain in Salem. He was happy."

"Sally and George Carrey told us that Eric won the Monarch scholarship because Walter quit that race in 1988."

Janet Donovan shrugged. "They like to dwell on the past. I recently heard that George Carrey accused Eric of poisoning Walter to stop him competing. Those are serious accusations. If they'd suspected as much, why didn't they say something back then? It's easy to rewrite history twenty years later."

"You have to admit that it's a strange coincidence," Gahalowood insisted.

Janet regarded him darkly, a look that reminded me of Lauren. "Are you investigating a murder or a track meet from 1988?"

Gahalowood quietly returned to the topic at hand. "You told us that Eric was happy in Salem."

"Very," Janet said.

Mark had a photograph album in his hands. He opened it and passed it around. It was full of pictures of the Donovan family when they were together and happy.

"Eric was a very quiet boy," Mark insisted. "The type of kid you never have to worry about, always ready to help out. He had a heart of gold. And he was gifted. Look at these—he took most of them. When he was seventeen, we gave him a camera. He had been wanting one for a long time. He took all sorts of photographs; that's how he spent his time.

When Eric got into something, he went all out. Back then, there was a professional photographer on Main Street. His business was doing well. That was a different time, of course. He sold equipment and developed film. Everybody in town went there. He was fond of Eric. He took him under his wing and showed him how to develop film in the darkroom."

"What was his name, this photographer?" Gahalowood asked.

"Morgan. Jo Morgan. But you'll have trouble finding him—he died years ago."

"So, after college, Eric settled in Salem and was doing well there. Why did he come back to Mount Pleasant?"

"Because I had cancer," Mark replied. "It shook him up. He moved in with us. It was only supposed to be temporary, but he stayed. He wanted to make sure I was getting enough rest and followed my treatment plan. A good kid, I'm telling you."

"Do you think his return to Mount Pleasant might also have something to do with getting fired?" Gahalowood asked.

"It's possible," Janet answered. "Maybe that was the push he needed to come back to us."

"So, he was fired . . . he didn't quit."

"Yes, Eric always said he had been fired. Why do you ask?"

"I just want to make sure," Gahalowood said, avoiding saying more, aware that anything he told them could get back to Eric. "Could you say exactly when he returned to Mount Pleasant?"

"Right before Labor Day, the first weekend of September 1998. I remember because we had that terrible storm that tore up part of the East Coast. When I saw Eric arrive, I thought it was just a surprise visit for the holiday. But he looked at me and said, 'No, Mom, I'm back for good.'"

Leaving the Donovan home, Gahalowood looked worried. "We have to find out whether Eric got fired or quit. If he quit, that means he lied about it. But why? There's nothing wrong with quitting your job. Especially if you're going to take care of your father. Pretending to be fired makes it look like it wasn't his choice to come back. That makes me think it was a way to get out of Salem without drawing attention."

I immediately knew where Gahalowood was going with this. "Which brings us back to the central question," I said. "What happened in Salem in the fall of 1998?"

"That's where we have a connection linking Eric and Alaska. They both left Salem, a few weeks apart. Why? What happened there? That's where we'll find the answers."

We had walked to my car as we were speaking. It was then that we were stopped by a middle-aged woman. She held a longhaired dog on a leash, which seemed to be suffocating from the heat. "You're the writer who's been asking questions, right?" she asked me.

"Yes, ma'am."

"I recognize you, I saw you on TV. My husband said you were over at the Donovans'; he saw you arrive. Was it alright?"

I was a little disconcerted by the question. "I don't know if it was *alright*, but it was interesting."

"Interesting for the investigation?"

"Yes. That's all I can tell you; it's a police investigation, you understand."

She fixed me with a stare. "I'm not really out walking my dog; I wanted to talk to you."

"That's very kind of you. Well, here we are, mission accomplished."

"You've misunderstood me. I wanted to speak to you about what happened with the Carreys in 1999."

Seeing that I was intrigued, she pointed to a house along the street. "You see that little house with the green shutters? That's me. The Carreys are my neighbors. That Monday night, just before the fire above their store, something happened. I'll never forget those days. Little Alaska murdered, the fire in Walter's apartment, then his arrest and his death. It was all so tragic!"

"What happened that night at the Carreys'?" Gahalowood asked her.

"A terrible argument. I remember it clearly. My husband came home about nine. He told me he had overheard the neighbors fighting. Naturally, I was curious: I wanted to know what was going on. So I went out to the porch, yes to have a smoke, but mostly to listen in. And I heard a man screaming. I couldn't make out what he was saying, but it sounded serious. I thought it was George Carrey yelling at his wife. That surprised me because he's not the type to get carried away like that. And then, all of a sudden, the front door flew open. I flattened myself against the bench so I wouldn't be seen. Walter Carrey rushed out of the house, mad as could be. His mother went after him, begging him to stay. But he got in his car and roared away. After that, all was quiet."

"Why didn't you tell the police?" Gahalowood asked. "Especially since that was the night Walter's apartment was set on fire."

"I did," she assured him. "I told Chief Mitchell about it the next day."

*        *        *

The Mount Pleasant police station was located in a two-story brick building. Judging by its general appearance and the well-kept parking lot, the local police force enjoyed substantial financial resources. Chief Mitchell met us in his spacious office, which was tastefully decorated, probably at considerable cost.

"It's a shame I had to run after you, Sergeant," Mitchell reproached Gahalowood. "I would have preferred for you to have taken the initiative."

"You didn't really give us a chance," Gahalowood said.

"You had time to visit Sally and George Carrey."

"Let's get straight to the point, Chief Mitchell. What exactly do you want from us?"

"Like I said yesterday, I'd like the Mount Pleasant police to be a part of the investigation."

"The state police have responsibility for the case."

"What happens in Mount Pleasant directly concerns the local police," Mitchell replied. "Given the high-profile nature of the case, I'd like to assign my deputy to join you."

"I was thinking of Lauren Donovan," Gahalowood said to him.

Chief Mitchell seemed surprised. "Why Lauren?"

"She's directly involved in this story. No-one has the credibility she does."

"That's exactly the problem. She has opinions; I always told her that they shouldn't get in the way of her job as a cop."

"Her opinions make her a valuable asset. She's been brooding over this investigation for years. Having her on the team would be a big advantage. And the faster we finish our work, the faster we can get out of your hair," Gahalowood explained.

"I'd prefer if it were my deputy," Mitchell insisted.

"Chief," Gahalowood said in a voice that was both firm and conciliatory, "I understand your concerns. You don't want this to get out of hand, and it won't. But nothing says I have to work with somebody local. You seem to forget that the state police doesn't report to the local police. So let's do this the smart way. You want one of your own people on the investigation? Fine. Then it's going to be Lauren Donovan. That's it."

Mitchell made a face. "Okay, but she goes with you everywhere, even outside our jurisdiction."

"Okay," said Gahalowood.

Mitchell grabbed his phone and asked for Lauren. A few minutes later, she pushed open the office door and strode briskly into the room before stopping short when she caught sight of me and Perry.

"You asked for me, Chief?"

"Lauren, I assume you remember Sergeant Gahalowood. And this is Marcus Goldman."

"I know him too," she replied in a dull voice.

"Lauren," the chief explained, "as you know, the state police has reopened the investigation into the murder of Alaska Sanders. Their work will be conducted with the help of the Mount Pleasant police. I'm assigning you to the investigation."

Lauren was obviously surprised, but she hid it well. "Yes, sir. But if you don't mind my asking, why me?"

"It was a specific request from these gentlemen."

"We think you're well placed to help us," Gahalowood explained.

As little as I knew Lauren, I knew she would have liked to refuse, out of pride. But she had been waiting for this opportunity for eleven years—a chance to shed some light on the case. She limited herself to a brief, "Yes, sir, Chief."

"Lauren," Mitchell added. "I'd like you to a submit a detailed report every day."

"Yes, sir."

"Good," Gahalowood said with a forced smile. "Now that the investigation has officially gotten underway, allow me one question, Chief Mitchell."

"I'm listening, Sergeant."

"A neighbor of the Carreys was witness to a violent argument between Walter and his mother the night of Monday, April fifth, a few hours before Walter set fire to his apartment. She claims she spoke to you about it. So my question is, why didn't this information ever get back to us?"

"Well, I have a vague recollection of something like that. Don't forget, it all happened very quickly. Walter turned himself in after a few hours of running around, and then there was all that commotion in the state police building. Once he was dead, and especially given that he'd confessed, I didn't see the point in burdening you with a minor detail."

When our interview with Mitchell was over, Lauren led Gahalowood and me to the station's break room. No-one else was there, so we could speak freely.

"Mitchell's a moron and he's leaving at the end of the year," Lauren told us as she slipped a quarter into the coffee dispenser. "We'll all be happy to see him go."

"I can see there's no love lost between you," Gahalowood added.

"It's not so much that, but he's stuck in the past."

She handed me one of the coffees from the machine. I interpreted it as a peace offering and said, "Once again, I'm sorry, Lauren."

"Don't think I'm forgiving you just because we're going to be working together, Marcus."

"He didn't have a choice," Gahalowood interjected, trying to defend me. "He was told not to reveal his reason for being here. Express orders from the head of the state police."

"Did someone ask you, Sergeant?"

He smiled. "Well, your girlfriend has quite a temper."

"I'm not his girlfriend!"

"I'm delighted to be working with you, Lauren. We're going to get along famously."

*    *    *

That afternoon, at Lauren's invitation, we set up operations at her place to pick up where we had left off. She put us in her living room and offered us drinks and snacks. She was both forbidding and welcoming at the same time. The woman was a walking paradox. Gahalowood had brought the case file from 1999, along with the more recent additions. Placing several items from the file on the floor, he began to summarize what had happened so far. Lauren interrupted him and brought out some pushpins and a roll of adhesive tape and suggested that he put anything relevant on the wall. She also gave him some markers. "Write down anything you want," she said. "I'll repaint it when we're done. I never invite anyone over anyway."

Gahalowood balked at the idea of transforming her living-room wall into an evidence board, but Lauren insisted, and finally, he set to work.

Watching Gahalowood as he carefully stuck pieces of paper to the wall and scribbled down annotations, I had the impression I was witnessing his thought process in action. As he placed each item on the wall, he

306

added various notes with the marker, then explained what he had done. His thought process was taking form before our eyes.

"What new information do you have?" Lauren asked.

"This," he said, placing on the wall the article from the *Salem News* found in Vance's cabinet:

### ALASKA SANDERS ELECTED MISS NEW ENGLAND

"Shortly before moving to Mount Pleasant," I explained, "Alaska won an important beauty pageant. And her acting career was starting to take off. She even had an agent in New York. Logically, her next step would have been to move there. But instead, she settled in Mount Pleasant, and quite suddenly. Why?"

"We can't explain that decision," Gahalowood added. "Even if we take into account her relationship with Walter. And in an investigation, anything that can't be explained is suspicious. We interviewed her parents at length, and we've established a timeline: September nineteenth, 1998, Alaska was named Miss New England. On October second, she leaves the family home after an argument. She takes off with her boyfriend, Walter Carrey, and moves in with him."

"She was still pretty young," Lauren noted. "She got angry at her parents and ran off with her boyfriend: she was being rebellious. Nothing out of the ordinary at that age."

"If it were just for a weekend, I could understand," Gahalowood said. "But she had apparently settled in Mount Pleasant for good. Why throw it all over from one day to the next?"

"Hold on, Sergeant," I said, grabbing my notes. "Yesterday, Eric said that when Alaska got to Mount Pleasant, she told him she really needed a job, any job. She said something like, 'When you're in the shit, you can't afford to be picky.' Sounds like she had no choice."

"Didn't you say she slammed the door behind her when she left her parents' house?" Lauren asked. "She must have been upset about something. Maybe she felt she had to take responsibility for her life and for that she needed money."

"Except she *had* money!" Gahalowood shouted. "She'd just won fifteen thousand dollars in the Miss New England competition. It wasn't the first one she'd entered either, and they all offered prize money. And the reporter for the *Salem News* told us that Alaska was frugal and saved her winnings to finance her move to New York. Why this sudden need to work at a gas station when she had all these savings?"

"Maybe she didn't want to dip into them?" Lauren suggested.

"There's something else, I'm sure of it," Gahalowood replied. "Why tell Eric that she was 'in the shit'?"

"You're right, Sergeant," I told him.

"Thanks, Writer."

Lauren stared at us in shock. "Excuse me, but can't you use your actual names?"

Gahalowood smiled. "That's what my wife said."

"Your wife is right. You can tell her I said so."

"She died a few months ago."

"Oh, I'm so sorry."

"No way you could have known."

After a brief silence, Gahalowood continued. "In addition to Alaska's reasons for moving, there's something else that bothers me—Eric Donovan." He was careful to use his full name to help Lauren keep the necessary distance. "On Friday, September fourth, 1998, he left Salem to return to Mount Pleasant. Was he fired? Did he quit? I'd like to get in touch with his employer and ask him; it could be important."

"I can find out," Lauren said, trying to appear detached.

"Thanks. Your brother knew Alaska back in Salem. He leaves Salem and comes back to Mount Pleasant. I don't know if we could say he left in a hurry, but the move was certainly unexpected, because his parents, when they saw him arrive, thought he had come just for a visit."

"I have to say, I was surprised as well," Lauren acknowledged.

"So what happened between September fourth and October second to prompt Donovan, then Alaska, to leave Salem for Mount Pleasant? Did they have an affair? We know that Donovan had a bad breakup with his girlfriend just before he left. Who was she? Was it Alaska? Did she follow him to Mount Pleasant because she felt bad about leaving him?"

"No," Lauren said. "Having seen Alaska and Eric together, I doubt there was anything between them."

"Then who was he dating in Salem?"

"I have no idea. He never mentioned anyone."

Gahalowood then moved on to the threats Alaska had received.

### I KNOW WHAT YOU DID

"Did Alaska come to Mount Pleasant to hide? Did she receive similar threats back in Salem? Or did they start in Mount Pleasant? Donovan, Alaska, the messages—they all have to be connected. But how? What are we missing?"

As he spoke, Gahalowood held up a document with the words "DM Agency" on the letterhead.

"What's the DM Agency?" Lauren asked.

"Dolores Marcado Agency. Dolores Marcado was Alaska's agent. I checked. The agency still exists; I even have a phone number. I tried calling twice but there was no response."

"Try again," I suggested.

This time, Dolores Marcado answered. She told Gahalowood: "It shook me up when I heard the investigation into Alaska's murder had been reopened. What a waste: that girl had so much talent!"

"According to her parents," Gahalowood said, "Alaska left for New Hampshire just when her career was starting to take off."

"That's right. Her Miss New England title was opening doors. The very next day, I got a call from a director who wanted her for a short screen test."

"And Alaska was looking forward to it?"

"Very much so. She already had her heart set on New York; she could see herself on the red carpet. The director gave her a scene to work on. She filmed herself reading the script, and I passed the video on to the director."

"And you can confirm that this all happened after she won the pageant?"

"Absolutely. The director was very keen. He wanted her for a second test, a longer one, but when I called her, she refused."

"Why?"

"Because she had just moved to New Hampshire and she was giving up her career, at least for a while."

"Did that surprise you?"

"Obviously! Three weeks earlier she was ready to pick up and leave for New York."

"Ms. Marcado, could I have a copy of Alaska's last audition tape, if you still have it?"

"If I find it, I'll send it to you. We make digital archives just in case our clients make it big. The first casting calls, their first roles—that all has value. So I'm confident we can dig it up."

After he hung up, Gahalowood said to us: "Between September nineteenth, when Alaska won the Miss New England competition, and October second, when she left Salem, something happened to prompt her to leave town and give up her acting career. And it was serious enough for her to bury herself in Mount Pleasant and take a job behind the cash register at a gas station. Serious enough to generate those threatening notes. Serious enough for her to be murdered."

"And where's Walter Carrey in all this?" I asked. "We've talked about Eric, about Alaska, about Salem. But not him. As if he played no role in what happened."

"I agree there's something odd there," Gahalowood said, holding up the pictures of the fire in Walter's apartment. "Walter was impulsive:

he was known to lose his temper. Could he have killed Alaska in a fit of anger? The murder was too well planned for that. And why set fire to his apartment two days after she was killed? There's nothing impulsive about that."

I risked a contrary argument. "Maybe he was covering his tracks. Maybe he wanted everyone to believe that the rumors about Alaska cheating on him caused him to blow his top."

"Then why run?" Gahalowood objected. "If it was all staged, wouldn't he wait for help to arrive, play the heartbroken lover, tell everyone that he was going to throw himself into the flames because he couldn't go on living without her? But instead, he flees the scene. What better way to mark yourself as a suspect?"

I saw that Lauren looked troubled by his remarks, but Gahalowood continued regardless: "And how do you explain this? Sally Carrey told us that she'd had a quiet supper with her son just a few hours before the fire, while the neighbor claimed to have witnessed a violent argument. I'm inclined to believe the neighbor because we know Walter was impulsive. But we also know that his mother had already told him she thought Eric and Alaska were having an affair. What could she have said that night to put him in such a state? I think he learned something that led him to accuse Eric of Alaska's murder. It was an act of revenge. But what for? Why did Walter want to get back at Eric Donovan?"

Lauren had turned white. And in a barely audible voice she said, "I have to show you something. Even Patricia doesn't know about this."

She left the room for a moment and returned with an envelope. "I never mentioned this because I didn't see a connection with the case. And when I discovered it, I already had doubts about Walter Carrey's guilt after getting hold of the photo that shows him at the National Anthem at the time of the murder . . . I didn't want to make Walter's parents feel any worse, not after what they've been through. I didn't see the point of destroying them."

"What are you talking about, Lauren?" Gahalowood asked.

"When Eric was found guilty, a photographer came to see me. He had a store in town, everybody knew him."

"Jo Morgan," Gahalowood said, referring to his notes.

"How did you know?"

"Your mother mentioned him. She said that Eric used his darkroom to develop his pictures."

"And that's just it. After the trial, Jo came over to give me the equipment Eric had left at his studio—lens, tripod, flash, that sort of thing. Then he handed me an envelope. He told me that he had never intended to go through Eric's things, but he had found some negatives. Assuming they were family photographs, he developed them to give to us. He said, 'It wasn't just family photos, Lauren. I'm sorry, I can't keep this to myself. I'm leaving you the prints along with the negatives. Do what you want with them. I'll never mention this again. In fact, I've already forgotten it.'"

Lauren took a photograph from the envelope. Gahalowood and I were rendered speechless by what we saw.

It was a picture of Sally Carrey, naked, kissing Eric Donovan on the mouth.

# 20

## *Unfaithful*

*Mount Pleasant, New Hampshire*
*Thursday, July 15, 2010*

Along Route 21, as you leave Mount Pleasant, there's a small rest area a few miles past the gas station, always deserted. It consists of a parking lot and a strip of grass with a few picnic tables here and there. That's where we arranged to meet Sally Carrey.

Gahalowood and I were early. I paced up and down on the asphalt while he waited in the passenger seat with the door open. He stared at the photo of Eric Donovan kissing Sally Carrey. When she had first gotten hold of the picture, Lauren had asked her brother about it. He spoke of a passing flirtation with Walter's mother and asked her to keep it a secret to avoid needless suffering. Lauren did as she was asked, not realizing at the time the significance it would hold for the investigation.

A car arrived. It was Sally Carrey. She parked a few yards away from us. It took her a while to emerge from the driver's seat, and then she walked toward us hesitantly, her gait betraying her nerves. I don't know whether she already knew that we had discovered her secret, but she must have realized that it was something important, if only because we had asked to meet her here.

Gahalowood didn't prolong her torment: "We know about you and Eric Donovan."

She stared at us uneasily. Maybe she was wondering whether it was still worth denying it. But then Gahalowood showed her the photograph. Tears of panic welled up in her eyes. "Who gave you that?" she asked.

"No-one knows," he reassured her. "And I'm planning for it to stay that way. The photo was found by Jo Morgan, the photographer, who gave it to Lauren Donovan. But since he's dead and Lauren has kept it to herself for more than ten years, you can rest easy. We're not here to destroy you."

"You already did that when you took my son, Sergeant."

Gahalowood pointed to a picnic table and suggested that we sit down to discuss the matter calmly. Once seated, Sally asked, "Why didn't Lauren say anything if she's known about it all this time?"

"After her brother's arrest, she found evidence that could prove Walter's innocence. She never made it public because, with Walter out of the picture, the investigation would focus on Eric. So when she received this photograph, she chose to spare you any additional grief."

"Lauren is a kind young woman," Sally murmured.

"She is," Gahalowood agreed. "Mrs. Carrey, I have to ask you to fill me in on your relationship with Eric. It may have a direct connection with our investigation. I can promise you that everything you say will remain confidential."

Sally burst into tears. "What a nightmare."

"When was this picture taken?" Gahalowood asked her calmly.

"In 1987. The boys were seventeen. I was forty-three. My life was quiet. The store was doing well, I was happy with my husband and with Walter: we were a happy family. I had known Eric for a long time, since he was ten. He and Walter were inseparable. He was always at our house. And then, one summer day, they went to paint the wooden fence in the garden. It was unbearably hot that year. I went out to take them something to drink. Eric had taken his shirt off. He was a very good-looking boy, like a god. I offered him a glass of lemonade and our hands briefly touched. I felt a shiver. I realized that I wanted that muscular body, that tanned skin. It bothered me so much that I had to take a cold shower to calm myself down. For a week they were out there painting that goddamn fence. For a week I watched Eric from the house. And when my fantasies got the upper hand, I ended up in the shower. I was ashamed of my desires. At the time I didn't foresee it actually becoming a reality."

She hesitated. Gahalowood encouraged her to continue. "But it happened," he said.

"Yes, when I least expected it. It was a Saturday, toward the end of August."

*       *       *

*Saturday, August 29, 1987*

Sally was alone in the house. Her husband was at the store and Walter was out for the day. She wanted to bake a cake, but she discovered she was out of eggs. She could have asked her neighbors or made a trip to the grocery store, but she was feeling lazy. For once she had the house to herself, and she wanted to take advantage of it. So she decided to call Donovan's General Store. Janet Donovan answered the phone. Sally asked if they might drop the eggs off at the Carreys' store, so George could bring them back home with him.

But ten minutes later, her doorbell rang. It was Eric. He took care of the deliveries for his parents' grocery. "Your order," he said to Sally.

"Thank you, Eric, that's very kind of you. You could have left them with George; you didn't have to come all the way over."

"I know, but I was happy to stop by."

"Walter isn't here."

"I know."

He looked at her intently. She asked him to come in for a moment. "Can I offer you something to drink, Eric?"

"Yes, thanks."

They went into the kitchen. She opened the fridge, nervous and excited. She had no idea what she was doing. But she knew what she wanted.

315

"You want a beer?" she asked.

"You bet."

The pact was sealed. By offering alcohol to a minor, Sally showed Eric she was prepared to do something she knew was wrong.

She opened a beer and gave it to him. He took a swig in silence. He was nervous as well. Then she took a chance. She took the bottle from his hand and brought it to her lips. No longer able to restrain herself, she bent toward him and pressed her mouth against his. He grabbed her and returned her kiss. The bottle fell to the floor and broke, but lost in their embrace, they barely noticed.

\* \* \*

"It was the start of a burning passion," Sally told us. "When we returned to our senses, we felt good. I didn't feel guilty or uncomfortable. I felt serene. When Eric had to leave to make his deliveries, I said to him, 'I want to see you again.' And he said, 'So do I.'

"After that, it was all I could think about. But where? I couldn't take any risks. There was a motel on the road to Conway, but I felt that an isolated location might draw even more attention. Someone would inevitably question the presence of a boy who arrived on a bicycle. Then I had a crazy idea. At the time, my husband and I were in the process of renovating the apartment above the store so we could rent it out. I was the only one who went there during the week. George only stopped by on Sundays to work on the place. The entrance, via the stairs at the back of the building, wasn't visible from the street. That's where I decided to meet Eric. After school, he would stop by his parents' store. Then, he'd disappear and slip into the apartment, where I was waiting. Once inside, I filled the entrance with bags, tools, and boards to warn us if anyone showed up unexpectedly. But I knew no-one would. In the midst of everyone, we had found sanctuary. There was something powerful between us. He made me feel like no-one has ever made me feel. Not my husband, not anyone. That seventeen-year-old boy was my sexual education. I was wildly in love.

"I realize, in telling you all this, that it must sound ridiculous, or insane. But that was my reality for several months, months when I felt happier, freer, more alive. As Christmas approached, Eric even spent the night with me. I was starting to take serious risks with him."

*    *    *

*Saturday, December 12, 1987*
George Carrey's father, who lived in a retirement home in Minneapolis, had had a bad fall, so George and Walter went to visit him for the weekend.

The moment her husband had told her the news, Sally was already picturing herself alone with Eric. She was tired of hiding away in the unfinished apartment above the store. But she had to tread lightly. First, suggest that the entire family travel to Minneapolis. Then, before calling the airline to reserve the tickets, claim that she regretted having to close the store and miss out on sales on one of the last weekends before Christmas. Then, suggest that she make the sacrifice and stay behind in Mount Pleasant. And then, the trap would be sprung: her husband was certain to reply, "You don't mind?"

That Saturday morning, George and Walter left early for Minneapolis. She opened the store alone. The day felt interminable. Eric stopped by, pretending to ask about Walter.

"Is it okay for tonight?" she asked him.

"I told them I'm staying at a friend's house. They'll never check."

"I left the back door open. Come whenever you like, make yourself at home."

At seven thirty, after she closed the store, Sally hurried home. She found Eric reading comic books in Walter's bedroom. At first, she was hesitant. She was tempted to call the whole thing off. Tell him to go back home. She felt foolish in her new underwear: she wanted to put her dowdy old mom panties back on and step into her jogging pants. But Eric kissed her and passion got the upper hand. Momentarily. The next morning, finding him beside her in her bed, she felt ill at ease. Suddenly, she regretted everything. And for the first time, she felt guilty—as if a spell had been cast over her and it was now beginning to wear off. At breakfast, he ate Walter's chocolate-flavored cereal. Eric had two helpings, noisily slurping the milk from the bowl. Now she examined him with a clear head. She had slept with a child. She had to break it off.

"Eric, we can't keep doing this. Someone will find out, and it would hurt everyone involved."

"Okay" was all he said. "I understand."

*     *     *

"Our story ended the way it had begun: in my kitchen. He disappeared from my life just as he had arrived. After that, he continued to come to the house with Walter, and everything was like it was before. As if nothing had happened. But great passions never pass without sorrow. And that was the case with us. About two months after we broke up, Eric came to the store. I was alone. It was February. At the time, Walter and Eric were both desperately trying to get a college scholarship. That was right before the track meet we spoke about the other day, when a recruiter from Monarch came to see the boys race and Walter suddenly fell ill."

*     *     *

*February 1988*
"Hello, Eric," Sally said as he entered the store. Eric didn't return her greeting. His expression was hard. She understood at once that something wasn't right.

"You alone?"

"Yes, why?"

"It's about the track meet the day after tomorrow. It's a very important race; a recruiter from Monarch University will be there."

"Yes, Walter told me."

"I don't want Walter to compete in the race."

318

"What are you talking about?"

"I need to win that scholarship. I chose Monarch first; Walter only picked it because I did. It would be unfair if he won the scholarship ahead of me. But he will, because he's faster than me."

Sally was afraid. She sensed danger. Then Eric added, "I want you to keep Walter from competing. It's the only way I can win."

"Eric, you're crazy. What do you expect me to tell Walter?"

"You don't have to tell him anything. I want you to make sure he can't run the race. Otherwise, I'll send this picture to your husband."

Eric pulled a photograph from his coat. It showed them naked in the apartment upstairs, kissing. She clearly remembered that moment. Eric had interrupted their lovemaking to grab his camera, which he took with him everywhere. At the time, she had asked, half worried, half amused, "What are you doing?" He replied, "I'm pretending we're free. It's what I'd do if we could love one another openly: I'd take pictures of you all day long. Don't worry, there's no film in the camera." He put his arms around her and kissed her, holding the camera at arm's length and pointing the lens in their direction.

Now she knew he had lied. How could she have been so stupid? She hated him at that moment. Then he said, menacingly, "Just so we're clear. If Walter wins the race, the whole town is going to see this photo, and everyone will know you're just a dirty whore."

*     *     *

"So you're the one who got Walter sick the day of the race?" Gahalowood asked.

"Yes," she said, crying. "That morning, I put a laxative in his thermos and encouraged him to drink. I told him, 'Make sure to stay hydrated, dear. That's what your coach said.' I saw him drink the whole thing in a few gulps. I'd put enough in there for a horse, and I was hoping for an immediate reaction, so he couldn't even leave the house. But at first, nothing happened. We got in the car and drove to the stadium.

I waited for him to tell his father to stop by the side of the road, but he seemed fine. During the warm-up, I watched him frolic like a baby goat. I couldn't understand. Eric was glowering at me. I tried to hide my confusion by shouting encouragement; I knew that Eric was capable of carrying out his threat and that all Mount Pleasant would see me naked, in bed with a teenager. When they were about to start, I thought I was going to faint. It was then that Walter left the starting line at a run, heading for the locker room. I knew he wouldn't be back."

"And after that?" I asked.

"After that, I avoided Eric like the plague until he left for Monarch. It was a big relief when he went away."

"And when he came back?"

"When he returned in the fall of 1998, ten years had gone by. I had managed to bury those terrible memories in a corner of my mind and I hoped he'd done the same. When I saw him with Alaska, I grew suspicious. I knew he could be dangerous. And then, on the Monday after she was killed, my world turned upside down . . ."

"When Walter had dinner with you? A neighbor told us that you had a terrible argument that night. Why didn't you tell us about it on Tuesday?"

"Because it's connected to my affair with Eric. I couldn't tell you about it without revealing what happened. Now that you know, I have nothing more to hide. You remember I told you how Walter came to the house that evening and told me he'd done something 'stupid.'"

"Yes, when he rushed to have his car repaired."

"Right. But there's something else that I deliberately failed to mention. Walter told me about Eric's sweater. His police friend, who told him that pieces of a broken taillight had been found near Grey Beach, also mentioned a gray sweater stained with blood."

\*　　　\*　　　\*

*Monday, April 5, 1999*

During dinner, Walter confided in his mother that he had hurried to have his taillight repaired out of fear of getting caught up in Alaska's murder.

"And there's something else, Mom. More serious . . ."

"What is it?"

"The cops found a gray pullover stained with blood. A gray pullover with the letters *MU* on it."

"And?" his mother asked, her heart pounding.

"*MU* stands for Monarch University. The sweater belongs to Eric. Two weeks ago, we went fishing and got caught in the rain and he lent it to me."

"The sweater was at your apartment?"

"It was on the back seat of my car. As I was leaving for the convention in Quebec, I grabbed a folder from the glove compartment. It smelled bad inside the car—from the wet sweater. I didn't have time to go back up to the apartment, so I threw it in the trunk. The day after I left, Eric called me. He said he needed his sweater back urgently. I told him it was in the trunk and said he should ask Alaska for it. But when I got back from Quebec, it seemed to have disappeared. Eric kept asking me for it, but now you say you saw him getting out of my car when I was away, I'm wondering if he didn't take it back after all."

Sally looked terrified. "Are you saying Eric's mixed up in the murder?"

"I don't know, Mom."

*     *     *

Sally told us that she had started to panic. "Between the sweater and the car repair, I was afraid he would be a suspect. I even wondered if he'd been set up by Eric. I knew what that man was capable of! So I begged Walter to be careful. He was very surprised to hear me say that: he wanted to know why I was so suspicious of his friend. Then he got angry, telling me, 'You're always criticizing him, you even accused him of sleeping with Alaska. I'm tired of it!' All I wanted was for him to keep his distance from Eric. But Walter didn't want to know. He kept saying that he was his boyhood friend and he trusted him completely. So I decided to tell him what had happened between us. To hell with the consequences. My son had to know who Eric Donovan really was. So I told him everything: our affair in the apartment over the store, the blackmail, the laxatives. I had never seen Walter so angry: I thought he was going to break everything in the house. You know the rest. He went back home. On the walls of the apartment where Eric and I had sex, he wrote a message intended for me: 'Unfaithful Whore'. Then he set fire to that miserable place and fled."

Sally burst into tears. Gahalowood asked her, "So, Eric did lend Walter his sweater, and you knew that?"

"Yes."

"What happened to the sweater? Do you know? Mrs. Carrey, you have to tell us everything now."

She hesitated for a moment. "I don't know if you recall, but at the time, I told you I'd seen Alaska and Eric arguing while Walter was away at the convention."

"I remember," Gahalowood acknowledged.

"They were arguing about that sweater. When Walter came for dinner, it helped me make sense of what I'd seen. The first time, Eric said he was looking for a sweater he'd lent to Walter. He thought it might be in the apartment. Alaska told him to get lost and said that he should call his friend. Eric came back the next day. He cornered Alaska as she was leaving the apartment, asking to look in the trunk of Walter's car. I was watching them from the door to the store, wondering what they were up to. Like the day before, Alaska appeared to be very irritated by Eric's insistence. But in the end, she opened the trunk and Eric saw that the sweater wasn't there. That was around two weeks before the murder."

"For eleven years, you've been sitting on information that corroborates Eric's story!" Gahalowood shouted. "He insisted he'd lent his sweater to Walter and had never gotten it back. Why didn't you say anything? It could have changed the course of the investigation!"

"I know! I know!" Sally said, tearfully. "I think about it every day. At the beginning, I just felt empty inside—my son was dead. When I learned that the sweater directly incriminated Eric, I knew I should contact the police. Then I had second thoughts—Eric was the manipulative type. I thought there was a good chance he was guilty, and I didn't want to be the one to prove him innocent. Time passed, and when I realized I had crucial information, it was too late. I was afraid I'd be accused of withholding evidence. So I just kept quiet, and then kept on keeping quiet. Sergeant, if you only knew how much I regret what I've done."

When she had finished her confession, Sally Carrey collapsed, lying slumped over the table. "Am I in trouble for hiding the truth?" she asked, choking back tears.

"No, ma'am," Gahalowood promised. "You've already been through enough."

He rose and headed for one of the barbecue pits on the grass. He placed the photograph and the negative on the grill and set them on fire.

*     *     *

The interview with Sally Carrey marked a turning point in the investigation. Although it revealed a dark side to Eric's personality, it also proved that Walter Carrey's accusations had been purely vindictive.

For obvious reasons, Lauren hadn't accompanied us to the meeting. We met up with her at her place, where she was waiting. When we told her what we'd learned, the scales fell from her eyes.

"Eric blackmailed Sally?"

"That's how he was able to get his college scholarship," I explained.

"Why didn't Eric mention this when we were there?" Lauren asked, visibly troubled.

"Perhaps he never made the connection with Walter's accusations," I suggested. "Or maybe he was afraid it would cast him in a bad light."

"Lauren," Gahalowood said, "to be honest with you, after the visit with your brother, I had no real reason to believe in his innocence. It may seem counterintuitive, but Sally Carrey's revelations support the idea that neither Walter nor Eric killed Alaska. I think there's someone else behind all this, someone who's been manipulating the police from the start. The other day, Patricia Widsmith mentioned the perfect crime, carefully orchestrated to mislead investigators. I'm beginning to think she's right. It would have had to be meticulously planned, with prior knowledge of your brother's secret. An ideal culprit has shameful secrets that bury him deeper in the trap. Which leads to my next question, Lauren: Did anyone else know about the affair? Or about Eric's blackmail?"

"I have no idea, Sergeant. You'd have to ask Eric. But I should tell Patricia about this immediately."

While Lauren made her phone call, Gahalowood turned to the wall. He added a sheet of paper on which he had written: *blackmail.*

I studied the pictures surrounding it. The telescoping baton found in the lake, the sweater stained with blood, the threatening messages.

"What are you thinking?" Gahalowood asked me.

"That this is one strange puzzle. There must be something that ties it all together. Something right in front of our eyes that we're not seeing."

"Such as?" asked Gahalowood, who was taking my musings seriously.

"You asked the right question: Who knew about Eric's blackmail? And I'll add two more. Eric's sweater was in Walter's car. Who might have had access to it? And to the Donovan home and Eric's printer? At this point, I can think of only one person who checks all the boxes: Sally Carrey."

"Damn it, you're right! She's getting back at Eric. But she never imagined that her plan would explode in her son's face. It makes sense. But why kill Alaska?"

"Because she thinks she's cheating on her son."

Gahalowood looked through his notes. "At the time of the murder, Sally was hundreds of miles away, on vacation in Maine with her husband. That's a pretty solid alibi."

"Sergeant, we both know an alibi can be faked."

He didn't look convinced. "That would mean George Carrey was in on it. Both parents get together to punish Eric and kill the unfaithful girlfriend? That's a lot to swallow."

I had gotten in the habit of using my phone to record—with the other party's agreement, of course—any conversations about the investigation. It had served me well during the Harry Quebert case. At Gahalowood's request, I replayed parts of our exchange with Sally and George Carrey from the day before yesterday, focusing on the moment when she told us about the call from her son informing her that Alaska had just left him:

Walter insisted that there was absolutely nothing between Eric and Alaska. So I ended up telling him that if Alaska had left, it was probably because there was someone else. He told me he had suspected as much for a while. That he had found her changed recently. And that she had been getting gifts. He mentioned a pair of shoes, which had arrived a few days earlier and which Alaska had claimed to have bought in a store in Wolfeboro. But he had checked: that brand is sold only in a store in Salem. He then assured me, "Alaska isn't seeing Eric, Mom, it's probably someone who lives in Salem. Besides, I wonder if she really is going to her parents' place: she doesn't get along with them that well. If she's going to Salem, it's probably to be with him."

"The romantic dinner!" Gahalowood exclaimed.

"What are you talking about?" I asked.

"The day before she was killed, Alaska told her boss, Lewis Jacob, that she was meeting someone for a 'romantic dinner.' At the time, we thought she was seeing her lover, before discarding the idea. But Alaska did have a lover, and it's unlikely to have been Eric because he was with Walter and Lauren at the time."

I took advantage of the fact that Lauren was still on the phone to add: "Or perhaps it *was* Eric. He agrees to meet Alaska somewhere for that so-called romantic dinner, but he stands her up and heads to the National Anthem to give himself an alibi. She tries all night to reach him, but he ignores her. Until that midnight meeting."

"Writer, you're making me dizzy. Your theory would make sense . . . but for one small detail: those shoes, which came from a store in Salem."

"Eric lived there for five years. He must have known the store."

"Except that everything points to him having fled Salem. If that's the case, he had no reason to return just to buy a girl a pair of shoes. On the contrary, he would've kept away from the place. By the way, we still need to find out whether he was fired or quit."

"Eric quit," Lauren suddenly announced behind us. "You asked me to find out and I did. I called his old boss, a nice guy who runs a small retail empire. He liked Eric very much. In fact, he had high hopes for him within the company. But he just quit, from one day to the next, to everyone's surprise, even though things were going well for him."

"He's hiding something. Why would he just up and leave?" Gahalowood asked.

"I agree with you, Sergeant. I don't think Eric is telling us the whole story."

"It's time he told us the truth. The lies are only making things worse for him."

"I know," Lauren said. "If Patricia can persuade him to trust you, he'll talk. He swears by her. Why were you discussing Eric quitting?"

"Because it looks like he was running from something," I explained. "It would actually work in his defense. Alaska had a lover who sent her gifts, including a pair of shoes that were sold only in Salem. But with Eric leaving Salem the way he did, he was hardly going to go back there just to buy a pair of shoes; so I doubt he's the lover."

"What are you driving at?" Lauren asked.

"I think the lover is the murderer," Gahalowood interjected. "We overlooked this angle at the time. We have to find him. And quickly."

326

"And where are we supposed to start?" I asked. "It was eleven years ago, and we don't have a single lead."

"Not true," Gahalowood replied. "We know he knew Eric and Walter because he ensnared them. And he was familiar with Salem. That's a start."

"Speaking of Salem," Lauren said, "I've been through the list of Alaska's friends we got from her parents. I was able to track most of them down, but they didn't have much to tell us. None of them mentioned any threats Alaska might have received."

"Maybe we should pay them a visit," Gahalowood mused. "When there's a cop in the kitchen asking the questions, you'd be surprised what people can remember, believe me."

Just then, Gahalowood got a call. It was Dolores Marcado's assistant, asking him for an email address so she could send him a file—the video of Alaska's audition right after she won the Miss New England title.

A few minutes later, we were gathered around Lauren's computer. Alaska was delivering a lengthy monologue. It was a convincing performance. We tried to determine where it had been filmed. There was a large painting behind her showing a sunset over the ocean, but it didn't look like anything we'd seen in the Sanderses' home.

"Do you recognize it?" I asked Lauren.

"No, not at all."

We replayed the video. It was impossible to identify the painting. No signature. Nothing distinctive about the composition.

"It could've been filmed at a friend's place," Gahalowood said. "Maybe it's not important."

But we all knew that nothing was without significance in an investigation like this. We spent a long time going over the evidence, reviewing the leads we already had and the photos and notes stuck up on the wall. Finally, Gahalowood, after yawning noisily, said, "Let's pick it up again tomorrow morning. I'm beat."

As I gathered my things, Lauren said, "Marcus, I was thinking maybe we could have dinner together."

I was dying to accept, but decided against it. "Unfortunately, I'm not free tonight. The sergeant wants me to take a look at something . . . concerning the case."

"He's as free as air," Gahalowood blurted out. "The sergeant wants some peace and quiet. I'm going to order a hamburger and read my book on the hotel terrace without any writers around to talk my ear off."

Lauren offered me a timid smile. "Looks like you're free."

But our plans hit a snag. A moment later, the doorbell rang. It was Patricia Widsmith, who had just arrived from Boston.

"Patricia! What are you doing here?" Lauren asked, surprised.

"What am I doing here? Did you think I was going to stay at home with my feet up after everything you told me? I've been waiting eleven years to see some action on this case. We can't let Eric rot in prison another minute. I'm going to file a request for his release tomorrow."

Lauren's face lit up. "Do we have a chance?"

"Absolutely! Not only has Sally Carrey confirmed that Eric lent his sweater to Walter, but we now know that Walter accused Eric to get back at him when he learned he'd been having an affair with his mother. I have to congratulate you, Sergeant: your retaliation theory was on the money. Walter killed Alaska and blamed it on Eric."

"But Walter didn't kill Alaska," Gahalowood said.

"But he implicated Eric," Widsmith remarked. "I'm going to take the photo of Sally and Eric to the judge, and believe me, this is going to be settled quickly. Lauren, I don't understand why you didn't tell me about it before."

"The photo doesn't prove anything," Gahalowood said. "If anything, it reveals a dark side to Eric. After all, he blackmailed a woman and forced her to poison her own son. That's not going to work in his favor."

"Let's let the judge decide. Where's the photograph?"

"I burned it," Gahalowood told her. "The negative as well."

"You did what?!" Widsmith screamed.

"I burned the photo. It wouldn't have gotten Eric out of prison, but it would've done serious harm to Sally Carrey, who deserves some consideration."

"You destroyed evidentiary material! I could have you brought up on charges for that, Sergeant."

A bitter argument followed. While Widsmith and Gahalowood were feuding in the living room, Lauren led me to the kitchen and opened a bottle of wine.

"You did well to destroy it. It's pointless making that woman suffer, and my parents as well. I'm with Perry on this: the photo alone won't save Eric. You know, Marcus, for eleven years I remained hopeful. But since the investigation was reopened, I've been wondering about him. When it comes right down to it, we never really know the people we love."

"We don't even know ourselves," I remarked.

She clinked her glass against mine. "Cheers, Mr. Philosopher."

"Lauren, I . . ."

She placed a finger on my lips. "Shhh, Marcus. I'm doing the talking. Thanks. Thanks for being here."

She removed her finger and brought her lips to mine.

Our kiss was interrupted by Gahalowood clearing his throat. He stood in the doorway with Widsmith beside him.

"The sergeant's right," she admitted. "He told me about the lead regarding Alaska's lover. We risk compromising that approach if we file a request for release now: it would force us to tell the court where we are with our investigation. If they refuse to release him, Eric stays in prison, but we risk alerting the lover, who probably has no idea we're on to him."

"I want to bring Patricia up to date on what we know so far," Gahalowood added.

Before getting back to work, we had supper together. It gave us a chance to relax and get to know each other. I realized that Gahalowood was warming up to Patricia when, after a couple of glasses of wine, he asked, "How does your husband manage to get along with you?"

She burst out laughing. "He didn't. It didn't last that long. I married a shrink, which is never simple. And you, Sergeant, how does your wife manage to keep you in line?"

"She didn't."

"So, you're divorced as well? But you're still wearing a ring."

"She died. Two months ago."

"Oh my God, I'm so sorry."

Gahalowood changed the subject.

Seeing them together, I felt they might be a good match—the irascible detective and the tenacious attorney. Sparks were guaranteed. Gahalowood certainly wasn't thinking of remarrying yet, but his daughters would leave home before too long, and he would find himself alone with his thoughts. I didn't have time to dwell on any of this, however, because the others had gotten up to discuss the investigation in the living room.

Patricia wanted to make sure she hadn't missed anything. She compared the information she already had with what was displayed on the wall. "You mentioned an incident report that wasn't included in the original case file."

"Yes, the photos here on the wall," Gahalowood said, pointing to the images of the burned-out apartment. "I have a copy of the fire inspector's report; you can hang on to it if you like."

He rummaged through the papers scattered on the low table and offered a few pages to Patricia. "And there's something else; it wasn't in the file because it wasn't very conclusive. I found it in my former partner's notes. A witness claims to have seen a blue car with Massachusetts plates go down Main Street at 1:40 in the morning."

"How's that relevant?"

"Alaska Sanders drove a blue car with Massachusetts plates. What was she doing there? Did she come to get her things from Walter's apartment? Or was this connected to her meeting with Eric? At the time, the presence of the car raised a number of questions. But ultimately, the statement was a little too circumstantial to include in the case file. The prosecutor's office would've dismissed it."

"But it's a key piece of evidence for us," Patricia noted. "If Alaska was still alive at 1:40 in the morning, it supports the theory that Walter Carrey, though still at the National Anthem at 1:43, could be the murderer. Are we sure about the time of death?"

"There's no reason to doubt it," Gahalowood said. "Besides, the car left in the direction of Grey Beach. Ten minutes later it was by the shore of the lake. That would make it 1:50. That holds up. And as far as I'm concerned, it confirms that the murderer was waiting for her and killed her the moment she got there. First, he bashes her on the head, then he strangles her. Walter wouldn't have arrived until later. You have to abandon that assumption, Patricia: you're going around in circles."

"It's hard to let go of an idea that's been haunting you for eleven years. What else do you have that's not in the case file?"

"Walter Carrey and Alaska had a violent argument outside a supermarket in Conway on March twenty-second."

"What constitutes 'violent'?" Patricia asked.

"It was enough for the manager of the supermarket to call the cops. They came out to investigate. They reported it in their notes as 'Couple in a car, no visible signs of violence. No intervention necessary.'"

Lauren glanced at the document that Gahalowood was pointing to. "Alaska and Walter aren't named here," she noted.

"The report is incomplete," Gahalowood admitted. "That's the reason it wasn't included in the case file. Besides, it doesn't do much to advance the investigation."

"But how do you know it was Alaska and Walter?" Lauren insisted.

"The manager recognized Alaska when her picture was released to the papers."

"And Walter?"

"It was his car," Gahalowood said.

"But was he identified?"

Gahalowood had no answer to that.

"Writer," he said to me, "that argument between Eric and Alaska that Sally Carrey mentioned. She said that Eric got out of Walter's car." Gahalowood looked through his notes. Then his face suddenly lit up.

"Walter wasn't in Mount Pleasant that day! He was at the convention in Quebec."

"Yes, and . . . ?" I said.

Gahalowood checked his notes once more. "Sally Carrey told us that the argument happened two weeks before the murder. Which means that the fishing convention took place in the week beginning March twenty-second!"

Lauren quickly interjected: "So when the police were called for the argument in the parking lot, Walter was probably already in Quebec."

"Exactly," Gahalowood said.

"So who was in the car with Alaska?" Patricia asked.

"Well, if we're to believe Sally Carrey, it was Eric," Gahalowood concluded. "It seems to me that we need to have another little talk with him."

# 21

# *Panic*

*Concord, New Hampshire*
*Friday, July 16, 2010*

At the state prison, Eric greeted us warmly. But when Gahalowood told him we were aware of the blackmail, his smile quickly vanished. "How did you find out?" he stammered. "Sally must've told you."

We were in the small room set aside for attorney visits. Gahalowood and Patricia were seated opposite Eric at the table, while Lauren and I stood in a corner, observing.

"I showed the photo to Perry and Marcus," Lauren told him, barely able to contain her anger. "Why did you ask me to keep it secret, Eric? So we wouldn't find out what you did to Sally Carrey? You manipulated me, while I've been fighting for you for eleven years!"

"Fuck," Eric whined. "I'm still disgusted by what I did. I was a wreck. I was in love with Sally, and when she dumped me, I wanted to get back at her."

"Is that what you do when someone breaks up with you?" Gahalowood thundered.

"Of course not!"

"Or are you just the vindictive type? I hope you understand this won't work in your favor."

"Sergeant, it's been more than twenty years! I was a kid. A stupid kid!"

"What else?" Patricia asked dryly. "Is there anything else from that time you forgot to mention? Something that could affect the investigation?"

"I don't know," Eric said, uneasily. "I guess just about anything could be important."

"That's true," Gahalowood interjected. "So let me refresh your memory. Were you and Alaska questioned by the police in Walter Carrey's car, on Monday, March twenty-second, 1999, in the parking lot of Conway's supermarket?"

Once again, Eric glowered, as if he had been caught in the act. He couldn't help asking, "How do you know that?"

Patricia made a gesture of annoyance. Gahalowood exploded. "Because, in the end, everything comes out, Eric! That's how it is. So tell us now and in detail. And if you continue with the lies or your memory lapses, I'm closing the case and I'm going to let you rot in here."

"What was I supposed to do, Sergeant, when you interrogated me for twenty hours straight, eleven years ago? Shouting at me, telling me I was fucked, that I would end up being executed, waving my sweater, covered with Alaska's blood, in front of my face, or those threatening messages printed from my printer! You have any idea what was going through my head? I was trapped. No sleep, nothing to eat. It was a nightmare, everyone was saying I was guilty. I didn't know how to defend myself. I screamed that I was innocent, but you didn't want to hear it. Everything I said was turned against me. You had your culprit, Sergeant, and you dragged me down to hell. So don't come around now preaching at me and telling me what I should've done. Don't complain because I didn't tell you about something I did when I was young, something I was ashamed of, especially when I didn't see any connection with the case other than the fact that it made me look like a madman. Or because I forgot to tell you that I was questioned by the police while having an argument with Alaska!"

There was a long silence. Eric and Gahalowood stared at one another like two lions ready to leap. Finally, Patricia spoke: "Eric, tell us about the argument now. What happened between you and Alaska outside the supermarket?"

334

"It was a Monday. I don't remember the exact date, but if you say it was March twenty-second, then that's when it was. I remember the day of the week because I was off on Mondays. I didn't go to the supermarket, exactly. There was a photography store in the same shopping center that sold used equipment at good prices. There were a lot of stores there; the supermarket was just one of them."

*　　*　　*

*Conway, New Hampshire*
*Monday, March 22, 1999*
Eric was leaving the photography store when he noticed Walter's car pulling into the parking lot. The car was backing up so Eric couldn't see the driver, but he could easily read the license plate, which he would have recognized anywhere. He smiled at the way the driver tried to maneuver the Ford Taurus between a panel truck and a minivan. He was preparing to chide Walter for his lack of skill when, to his surprise, Alaska stepped out of the car. She was alone. No sign of Walter. She headed toward the supermarket, and he stopped her before the entrance.

"Alaska?"

"Hi, Eric."

"Is Walter with you?"

"He left yesterday for Quebec, for a fishing convention."

"How's he getting there without his car?"

"In his father's pickup. He wants to bring back some equipment. My car has an oil leak, so I took his. Any other questions?"

She seemed defensive.

"Sorry, I didn't mean to be nosy. I'll leave you to your shopping. Have a good day."

She gave a heavy sigh. "Sorry, Eric, I'm not in a great mood and I guess maybe I'm feeling a little guilty for shopping here instead of in your parents' store. I didn't expect to run into you."

"You can shop where you want."

"You know what I don't like about Mount Pleasant? The sense that everyone's spying on everyone else. Even when I'm shopping for groceries, I feel they're checking out my cart and judging me on what I'm buying. I've always dreamed of being famous, but if being famous means feeling like I do in Mount Pleasant, frankly, no thanks."

Eric burst out laughing. "I'm not judging you, Alaska. You can do your shopping in peace. Have a good day."

He turned to go, but she held him back. "Eric, I'm going to leave Walter."

"What?"

"I'm leaving him. I want out of Mount Pleasant. Keep it to yourself, please. I just wanted you to know."

Her secret revealed, Alaska quickly ducked into the supermarket. Eric turned to go, but he decided against it. He wanted to know more. He couldn't be party to that kind of admission without doing something to help his friend. So he decided to wait. When she came out with her shopping, he stopped her. "Why are you leaving him?"

"It's none of your business, Eric."

"Is there someone else?"

"Leave me alone, please."

"You can't say that and expect me to do nothing."

"I'm sorry I said anything."

"It's too late. What's happened with Walter?"

Eric's insistence was beginning to annoy Alaska. They began shouting, which attracted the suspicious glances of other shoppers. Suddenly, she burst into tears. "Leave me alone, Eric!"

"Walter's going to be heartbroken. At least tell me why you're leaving him. You can't just ask me to keep it to myself. You're putting me in an impossible situation here."

A man came up to them. It was the manager of the supermarket.

"Everything okay, miss?"

"Yes, everything's okay," Eric replied for her.

"I'm not asking you," the manager said to him.

"It's private!" Eric shouted. "Mind your own business."

"Well, if that's the way you want it, I'm calling the cops."

*　　*　　*

"The manger went back inside," Eric told us. "And suddenly, Alaska just lost it. She began to panic. 'He's going to call the cops, fuck! He's going to call the cops!' And then she took off for her car, leaving her groceries. I couldn't understand what had gotten into her. I grabbed her bags to take them to her. She was already in the driver's seat, ready to take off. I opened the trunk to put the groceries in, and she began shouting, 'What are you doing, Eric? I have to get out of here!' She was panicking, but she couldn't drive off because I was standing behind the car. She got out and yelled, 'Get lost, Eric!'"

*　　*　　*

*Conway, New Hampshire*
*Monday, March 22, 1999*

"Get lost, Eric!"

"Alaska, what's up with you?"

She wanted to push him away, but he grabbed her hands.

"You don't understand!" she screamed, crying.

"What don't I understand?"

"Let me go!"

"I'll take you back," Eric told her. "You can't drive like this. I'll come back later to get my car."

Without waiting for her approval, Eric got into the driver's seat. She ran over to the passenger side. "Go! Go!" she ordered. But Eric had barely fastened his seatbelt when a patrol car blocked their exit, its lights flashing. Alaska was struggling to remain calm. As if she had something to hide. She wiped her eyes. An officer approached the car and stuck his head in the window Eric had lowered for him.

"What's going on here?" he asked.

"Nothing," Alaska assured him.

"Nothing? We were called about a fight."

Alaska smiled. "Don't you ever yell at your wife, officer? If we can't have an argument without the police showing up . . ."

The policeman gave Eric's license and the vehicle's registration a quick once-over. When he saw that everything was in order, he left. Alaska started crying again, but this time they were tears of relief. Eric placed a hand on her shoulder to comfort her. "Alaska, what's got you so worked up?"

"The police," she said quietly.

*       *       *

"It was as if she was terrified of the police," Eric said.

"Did she explain why?" Gahalowood asked.

"No. I took her back to Mount Pleasant. We didn't speak the whole time we were in the car. It was upsetting to see her like that. I parked on Main Street, near the Carreys' store, and I handed the keys back to Alaska."

"And Sally Carrey saw you," Gahalowood told him.

"It's very possible. We were in front of her store. I had nothing to hide."

"Sally Carrey mentioned another argument."

Eric frowned as if he were trying hard to remember. "Oh yeah, because of my sweater."

"The sweater that was found near the crime scene?"

"The sweater I had lent to Walter two days earlier, on the Saturday, when we were caught in the rain while out fishing. I already told you about that the other day. I also told you eleven years ago . . . So, that Monday, when I dropped Alaska off, I didn't find the sweater on the back seat. I assumed it was at their place. When we were standing on the sidewalk, I asked her for it. She said she didn't know what I was talking

338

about. I told her it was a gray pullover with *MU* on it. She said she hadn't seen it, but I asked if I could come up and take a look around because I liked the sweater and wanted it back. Then Alaska got annoyed and said, 'Is that all you're worried about after what we've just been through? Why don't you ask Walter?' So I shot back at her, 'You really want me to call Walter and tell him what just happened?' She left, really angry, and went up to her apartment."

"And the sweater?" Gahalowood asked.

"Alaska said I should call Walter, and that's what I did. He told me it was in the trunk of his car. So the next day, when I saw, from my parents' store, Alaska parking Walter's Ford on the street, I caught up with her and asked her to open the trunk so I could get my sweater. She told me I was starting to get on her nerves. But she opened the trunk, reluctantly, and it wasn't there. I couldn't figure it out. I asked Walter about it when he got back from Quebec. He said Alaska might've washed it and put it away with his things by mistake, that he'd ask her, but I told him I'd already asked her and she had no idea where the damn thing was. A total misunderstanding. Then Walter told me he'd check his apartment. I assumed it would show up eventually. But by the end of the next week, Alaska was dead.

"Then everything happened really fast: three days later, I found myself in a police interrogation room with that bloodstained sweater now the key piece of evidence against me. Walter and Alaska, the only two people who could confirm my version of events, were dead. Whenever I think about that sweater, I remember the moment, back in the parking lot outside the Conway supermarket, when I put Alaska's groceries in the trunk. Was the sweater there? I have no idea. I keep replaying it in my head. I can see myself opening the trunk, but I can't remember if it was in there. Did Walter lie about it? Was it stolen from his car? People in Mount Pleasant aren't like that—at least, not back then. Everybody left their car unlocked; we only bothered with the front door if we were going to be gone awhile."

Eric's explanation matched Sally Carrey's version to a T. Gahalowood didn't tell him that, but instead asked him about his job in Salem. "Something else has been bothering us, Eric. In September 1998, you left Salem—just packed up and left. You told your family you'd been fired. But that's not true: you quit. You ran away from Salem. Why?"

"'Ran away' is pretty strong, Sergeant. I couldn't stand living there any longer. My girlfriend had left me for another guy, I was distraught, my father was sick. I needed to get back to my roots. That doesn't seem so strange to me. And yes, I lied to my parents, told them I'd been fired. But you don't know them like I do. You can't imagine the scene if I'd told them I'd left a good job that paid well when they often had trouble making ends meet."

Eric's reasons for leaving Salem tallied with what we'd heard from Regina Speck at the Season.

We now knew that Alaska was scared of the police for some reason. But why? We could only imagine it had something to do with her sudden departure from Salem and the messages she had received: I KNOW WHAT YOU DID. What was Alaska running from?

Leaving the prison, Lauren, Gahalowood, and I decided to drive to Salem. Patricia would return to Boston.

It was late morning when we arrived in Salem, Massachusetts. We first went to see some of Alaska's old friends, whom Lauren had been able to locate. Many had known her from childhood or school, and their stories, mostly about the years before she turned eighteen, weren't much help. But the friends Alaska had made through the beauty competitions, that is, in the last few years of her life, did have useful information. Brooke Rizzo, Andrea Brown, Stephanie Lahan, and Michelle Spitzer—we interviewed them in succession. They all agreed on one thing: Walter Carrey was definitely not the love of her life.

BROOKE RIZZO: We never knew what she saw in Walter. I thought it was just a passing fling. Besides, he only showed up from time to time. I thought she was just playing around. I could never see her sharing her life with him in some New Hampshire backwater.

ANDREA BROWN: I think Alaska got a kick out of going with an older guy. At the same time, it seemed like this was her first serious relationship. Well, if you can call it that.

STEPHANIE LAHAN: We couldn't understand what had happened or her reason for taking off with Walter. She had just been named Miss New England, she was working hard to break into the movies, and it seemed like she was off to a good start. Why give it all up?

[. . .]

Threats? No. Well, Alaska never mentioned anything to me.


Neither Brooke nor Andrea nor Stephanie was able to make a connection between any particular event in Alaska's life and her departure for Mount Pleasant. It was Michelle Spitzer, whom we visited last, who gave us a possible reason and, crucially, a name we hadn't heard until then.


MICHELLE SPITZER: What happened in Salem? I don't know. She must have been shaken up by Eleanor's suicide, as we all were. You said that Alaska received threatening messages? What kind?

[. . .]

No-one ever mentioned Eleanor Lowell? She was one of our friends. A beautiful girl, but very troubled. Just the opposite of Alaska.

Eleanor was always worried, always anxious. She was even seeing a shrink.

[. . .]

She drowned herself. We found her car and clothes on the beach at Marblehead.

The appearance of Eleanor's ghost intrigued us. That same day we paid another visit to the editorial offices of the *Salem News* to question Goldie Hawk, the journalist. She would surely be able to fill us in.

"A sad story," Hawk said. "I met Eleanor on several occasions. The typical young model: a diaphanous beauty, with an angelic face. She had already appeared in ad campaigns for a few leading brands. She was a whole other caliber."

"And her death?" Gahalowood asked.

"Very sad. She sent her mother a text message in the middle of the night telling her she no longer wanted to live. She saw it when she woke up. Eleanor's bed was empty, so she notified the police at once. Her car was found at Marblehead, in the parking lot of Chandler Hovey Park. They found her clothing and personal effects on the beach near the big lighthouse on the cape. The police ruled it a suicide, probably by drowning."

"*Probably?*"

"Her body was never found."

Gahalowood was perplexed. Leaving the newspaper's offices, he said to me and Lauren: "In August 1998, a model disappears near a beach. Eight months later, one of her friends, also a model, is murdered by a lake. In her pocket, there's a message: 'I know what you did.'"

"You think there's a connection between the two deaths, Sergeant?" I asked.

"It seems more of a reach to believe it's just a coincidence. Especially when Alaska fled Salem shortly after Eleanor's death. That could be the reason she left in such a hurry."

"You think Alaska killed Eleanor?" Lauren asked.

"I have no idea," admitted Gahalowood, who didn't like hasty conclusions. "But we have to look deeper."

Lauren couldn't help voicing the question she'd been itching to ask: "Sergeant, how did you manage to overlook Eleanor Lowell back then?"

"We neglected Salem. We believed the murder was firmly rooted in Mount Pleasant. And nothing connected our investigation to Alaska's hometown. I can't help coming back to the idea of the perfect crime. I think we were deliberately misled."

Gahalowood proposed we make a detour to the offices of the Salem crime squad, which would have overseen the investigation into Eleanor Lowell's disappearance. We could also take advantage of our presence in town to question Alaska's parents about their daughter's finances. We wanted to understand why, in spite of her savings, she needed to find a job the moment she arrived in Mount Pleasant. For the sake of efficiency, we decided to split up. Lauren went with Gahalowood to the Salem police station, while I took a taxi to the Sanderses' home.

Donna Sanders was alone when I arrived. "Robbie went to play golf with his friends. He needs to clear his head from time to time. I have to say, this is really stirring up painful memories. Would you like a coffee, Mr. Goldman?"

We sat down together in the living room. I got the impression that Donna felt more alone than ever. She was eager to talk about her daughter, while her husband wanted to avoid the subject. "We all deal with grief in our own way," she explained. It seemed like a good time to play her the audition video sent by Alaska's agent. We had also showed it to Alaska's friends—I'd brought along my laptop for that purpose—but none of them was able to identify where it was filmed. Nor was Donna Sanders.

"I've never seen this video," she said after watching it.

"Alaska filmed it right after she won the Miss New England competition. Do you recognize the background?"

I played it again, but Donna was categorical: "No, I have no idea where this might be. Is it important?"

"It could be. Do you recognize the painting?"

"Absolutely not. Did you come all the way to Salem to show me this video, Mr. Goldman?"

"No. I'm also interested in the money Alaska had around the time she left Salem. She had savings, didn't she? The money she was putting aside from the competitions?"

"Yes, she was very thrifty. She had an account with the Bank of New England. That's all I know. Robbie took care of everything else. You'll have to ask him. You could call his cell phone, but he'll be in a bad mood: he hates it when anyone bothers him while he's playing golf."

"I understand, don't worry. Would you have any of Alaska's old bank statements?"

"If there's anything, it would be in her bedroom; I kept a lot of paperwork. Robbie still complains about it. He says we should clear out the room. Come, I'll show you."

A few moments later, I found myself seated at a small pressboard desk that Alaska had used as a teenager to do her homework and write letters. Donna Sanders pulled out several binders that contained, in no particular order, correspondence, a few more or less official documents, and photographs of her daughter. I skimmed through them until I found a statement from the Bank of New England. It was dated 1997, which wasn't much help, but it did give the address of the Salem branch and, intriguingly, the name of an employee: Gary Stenson. The bank was still open. I called without much hope of reaching Mr. Stenson, who had likely retired, but the receptionist transferred me at once.

"Hello?"

"Mr. Stenson? This is Marcus Goldman. I'm investigating the murder of Alaska Sanders; she was a client at your bank."

As far as introductions go, this one certainly made an impression. When I explained to Stenson how I had obtained his name, he suggested that I come to the bank. "I'll wait for you. But hurry, we're closing soon."

Twenty minutes later, I found myself standing in front of Gary Stenson at the Salem branch of the Bank of New England. He was a few months from retirement, after more than forty years with the bank. He had silver hair and a thick mustache that made him look like a very friendly walrus. He was wearing a short-sleeve shirt and a striped tie.

"I've heard of you. But I'm sure you know that I have to maintain professional secrecy with regard to my clients."

"I can well imagine."

"Of course, Alaska is no longer a client, her account was closed after her death. I don't have many details to give you, which makes answering your questions a little simpler. What is it you want to know?"

"Did you know Alaska personally?"

"Yes, of course. Her father still has an account with the bank. I've known him since forever. She was a delightful young woman. If you knew how I cried when she died. I was beside myself. I didn't know her all that well, but there was such a strong sense of something wasted. Why are you interested in her bank account?"

"I was told Alaska was a very thrifty young woman, who set money aside to finance her dream of going to live in New York City. In October 1999, about two weeks after she won a fifteen-thousand-dollar prize, she moved to Mount Pleasant. When she got there, she took a job at a gas station. She didn't waste any time either. She was in such a hurry to find something that I can't help but wonder whether she was broke. Could you shed any light?"

The little man stared at me in confusion: "Son of a . . ." I could tell he was holding something back.

"Mr. Stenson," I urged him, "you may have information that's crucial to the investigation."

"The check you speak of . . . Alaska came to deposit it at the bank with her father. The parents had power of attorney, as is always the case when we open an account for a minor. But that day I told Alaska that because she was now an adult, she didn't need her father to approve her banking activity. She was very proud. Independent. The next day, her father came to ask me to transfer his daughter's assets to another bank.

345

Altogether there was about fifty thousand dollars. He told me he was going to put the money into an account with Alaska as the sole beneficiary. I had no reason to doubt him, but in any case, he had power of attorney; he could do what he wanted without my approval. So I did as he asked. But then, two weeks later, I don't recall the date, Alaska came to the bank to withdraw her money. When I told her that her father had closed the account, she turned white. I told her there must have been a misunderstanding. But she was in shock. And when she left, she was angry—very angry."

"Do you know how it all turned out?" I asked.

"I saw her father a few days later. Now it comes back to me. Robbie Sanders stopped by the bank, worried because his daughter had made such a fuss. He hadn't thought to warn her about the transfer. But he said everything was settled."

"And was that the truth?"

"I don't know. I never saw her again. She went off to live in New Hampshire."

I discovered that the incident that Gary Stenson was referring to had happened on October 2, 1998. That was the real reason for the fight between Alaska and her father that had led to her departure.

I needed to talk to the Sanderses at once, especially Robbie. But as I was heading back to their home, Gahalowood called me. "Writer, where are you? I have news."

"So do I, Sergeant. I was at the Sanderses' home. I just found out that the fight between Alaska and her father on October second was because he emptied her bank account. He lied to us! That story about the marijuana was bullshit. Robbie Sanders swindled his own daughter."

"Damn! Meet me at the Sanderses' place."

"And what did you find out from the Salem crime squad?"

"We asked to see Eleanor Lowell's file. Unfortunately, there wasn't much there. And we spoke to the investigator in charge at the time; he doesn't really see a connection between Eleanor's death and Alaska's. But we did have a chance to review the major criminal events in Salem in 1998. One of them caught my eye: on October eighth there was a break-in at the Sanderses' home. And a police officer was hit by a black Ford Taurus."

"A black Taurus?" I exclaimed.

"I knew you'd like that."

And there was more. I met Gahalowood and Lauren outside the Sanderses' home. We rang the bell together. Donna Sanders seemed to be in a good mood. "Oh, it's you again!" she said to me. "That's good, Robbie's back from golf."

Robbie joined his wife at the door. Gahalowood introduced them to Lauren, deliberately omitting her last name.

"Lauren's with the Mount Pleasant police," he told them. "She's working with us on the investigation." Lauren greeted the Sanderses with a handshake. She was wearing a lightweight shirt with rolled-up sleeves.

"Mr. and Mrs. Sanders," she said, "we'd like to ask you about the break-in that happened here in 1998."

Robbie Sanders looked at her strangely and replied, "Well, then, you've come at the perfect time. Why are you wearing my watch on your wrist?"

# The Night of the Break-In

*Thursday, October 8, 1998*

By nine thirty p.m. a profound darkness had settled over the Mack Park neighborhood in Salem. The street was deserted. A cold autumn wind was blowing.

No-one saw the black Ford Taurus, its headlights off, drive up to the Sanderses' house and reverse into the driveway, ready for a quick getaway. There were no plates on the car. The two people inside were wearing ski masks. They stepped out quietly and slipped into the Sanderses' backyard. Hidden by the bushes, they waited to make sure the house was empty, then approached the kitchen door. One of the figures lifted a doormat, then a small flowerpot, as if looking for a hidden key, but found nothing. The other broke one of the glass panes on the door with a gloved hand, stuck an arm though, and unlocked it. They entered the house.

The sound of breaking glass alerted Francisco Rodriguez, who lived nearby and was smoking a cigarette on his porch. Rodriguez was a police inspector, and the disturbance piqued his curiosity. When he had finished his cigarette, he walked down the street, listening carefully, but all appeared to be calm.

Inside the house, the two shadows went straight to Robbie Sanders's office. They opened the safe and emptied it. Nothing but documents, except for a gold watch with a green leather strap. They took it and left. Their work was done. The burglars left the house the way they had entered it—through the kitchen and the garden. They skirted past the last clump of bushes and ran to the car. At that moment, they saw a man

348

in the street—Inspector Rodriguez. He was approaching the driveway, intrigued by the sight of a car without license plates. All three of them remained motionless for a few seconds.

"Get in!" one of the figures said. Rodriguez shouted, "Stop! Police!" But the thieves were already in the car. Rodriguez placed himself in its path, using his body to prevent it from leaving the driveway, but the Ford was picking up speed. Realizing that the driver wasn't stopping, Rodriguez tried to jump out the way, but it was too late. He was struck and knocked to the ground. The car drove off into the night.

# 22

## *An Eye for an Eye*

*Salem, Massachusetts*
*Friday, July 16, 2010*

The weekend was proving to be trying but full of twists and turns, thanks to two new intersecting leads: on October 2, 1998, Robbie Sanders stole fifty thousand dollars from his daughter; on October 8, thieves stole a watch from him valued at thirty thousand. Mere coincidence?

Things picked up speed the moment Robbie Sanders recognized his watch on Lauren's wrist. It wasn't a unique model, but we were easily able to verify its provenance. Robbie had inherited it from his father, Christian Sanders, who'd had his initials engraved on it. There, on the back of the case, we found the letters *C.S.*, to which Lauren had never paid much attention.

"That's your watch, Rob," Donna Sanders said, stupefied.

"Where did you find this?" her husband asked.

"It was given to me," Lauren explained, "by my brother."

"And how did your brother get it?"

"I have no idea."

Lauren immediately removed the watch from her wrist as if it were burning her skin. Robbie Sanders thought he was going to get it back, but Gahalowood intercepted it. "I'm very sorry, Mr. Sanders, but the watch is now a piece of evidence for the investigation into the robbery."

"But that was twelve years ago," Robbie said.

"Yes, but the case was never closed. Your neighbor was badly injured when he tried to stop the thieves getting away."

350

In the Sanderses' living room, we began to put together the pieces of the large puzzle that lay before us. Robbie and Donna told us about the night of the burglary. It was their wedding anniversary, and as they did every year, they had gone for dinner at a steakhouse downtown. When they returned, they discovered the street lit up by police cars and neighbors assembled outside their house.

"Poor Mr. Rodriguez," Donna said. "He survived, but his life was never the same. He had to have a series of operations on his leg and he was never able to walk properly again. The police transferred him to a desk job. Since then, he's moved away; he couldn't stay in his old home because of the stairs."

"So according to the police report," Gahalowood interjected, "the only object taken during the robbery was this watch. Is that right?"

"Yes," Robbie replied. "They came in through the back door and went directly to my office."

"The report states that Officer Rodriguez was alerted by the sound of breaking glass—specifically a pane on the kitchen door. By the time he'd walked down the street to find the suspicious car in your driveway, the robbers were already outside. Seems like they were very well informed."

"Well, yeah, it seems that way," Robbie agreed.

"The safe wasn't forced open. You told the police that you might have forgotten to close it in your hurry to leave for the restaurant."

"That's true, we were running late that night. I didn't want to lose our reservation."

"You're always running late, Rob," Donna noted, oblivious to what was about to unfold in her living room.

"Was your watch insured?" Gahalowood asked.

"Yes."

"And you had no trouble getting reimbursed in spite of your absent-mindedness? Insurance companies aren't too fond of customers who forget to close their safes: in general they refuse to pay up."

"Yes, that's true," Robbie admitted. "I had to send a letter from my lawyer, but they settled. I don't see what you're getting at, Sergeant. Where are you going with this?"

"Mr. Sanders, when I got out of the police academy, I was assigned for a while to emergency response. It's standard procedure. I saw quite a lot of break-ins back then. And believe me, in almost all cases, the victims add things to their declarations, sometimes imaginary things. And they're careful not to reveal any failure on their part that might work against them—an open window, an unlocked door. They want to make sure the insurance company doesn't kick up a fuss . . ."

"Excuse me, Sergeant, but I still don't see where you're going with this," Robbie repeated.

The tension in the room was palpable. I watched as Gahalowood launched his first missile. "Well, Mr. Sanders, when someone has their thirty-thousand-dollar watch stolen from a safe and he thinks he's forgotten to lock it before going out, he usually tells the police something like: 'I don't understand what happened. It was locked, I checked twice before leaving.' Yet in your case, you admitted to the investigators that you were negligent. You're the victim in this case, not the guilty party. Is that right?"

"Of course I'm the victim! At the time, I was upset by what had just happened—the neighbor getting hit by a car, our house broken into. Maybe I didn't have the presence of mind. I'm an honest citizen, Sergeant!"

"Mr. Sanders," I interjected, "we're wondering whether the robbery is connected to another theft."

"Which one?"

"The fifty thousand dollars you withdrew from your daughter's bank account."

Robbie Sanders suddenly rose. "How dare you!" he shouted.

His wife uttered a cry. It was unclear whether it was one of shock or an attempt to calm her husband. For a second, I thought he was going to punch me in the face. But instead, he began to cry. Donna Sanders was completely beside herself. "Robbie, what are they talking about? What's going on?" He collapsed onto the couch and into his wife's embrace. He then told us about his demons from back then, which Donna knew nothing about.

"It all happened very quickly," he said. "I had never really gambled, until some clients insisted on taking me to a casino. That was in 1997. I couldn't refuse; I didn't want to upset them. Besides, I wanted to see what it was like. I sat down at the blackjack table and began to win, hand after hand. I had ten thousand dollars in chips in front of me. I was in a trance. The more I bet, the more I won. The intoxicating sensation of winning was strong—so strong! And then my luck changed. I started to lose, and lose bad. And the more I lost, the more I wanted to play. I only stopped when I'd lost everything. That night, when I got back home, I couldn't sleep. I was beside myself. How could I have thrown away all that money? Why didn't I stop sooner? And yet I had only one thing in mind: play again. And this time, I would win.

"I started going to casinos regularly, pretending I was out to dinner with clients. I avoided the one in Salem so I wouldn't be recognized. But whatever I won, I always ended up losing. At the start, I kept it under control. But in 1998, the losses began to pile up. I wasn't able to win the money back, but it was impossible to stop playing. I was up to my neck in debt; I needed cash. By the end of summer, the pressure from my lenders had cranked up. One of them threatened to tell my wife. To keep him quiet, I pawned my father's watch—the watch that meant so much to me. About two weeks later, when I went to the bank with Alaska to deposit her fifteen thousand dollars, I realized I had access to her money. Leaving the branch, that was all I could think about. She had enough money to get my watch back and pay off my debts. I wanted to turn the page on that dark part of my life. Then I would repay Alaska as soon as possible. And I wanted to get help—I had the name of a psychiatrist who specialized in gambling addiction. All I needed was a small push . . . all that money just sitting there in Alaska's account . . . So I went to the bank and cleaned it out. It was just a loan: I was planning to pay it back!"

"But Alaska found out," I said.

"Yes. It was a Friday, October second."

\*       \*       \*

*Salem, Massachusetts*
*Friday, October 2, 1998*

It was late afternoon. Hearing the front door open, Robbie thought at first it was his wife returning from Providence, where she had gone to settle some inheritance questions with her sisters.

"Is that you, Donna?" he asked from the living room, where he was reading the paper.

No reply. Then he saw Alaska. "Oh hello, dear. I thought you had already left for your weekend with Walter. Everything okay?"

His daughter simply stared at him.

"Alaska?"

"Where's my money?" she asked.

Robbie blanched. "Alaska, dear, let me explain . . ."

"Where's my money?" she screamed.

"Listen, it's complicated, I . . ."

"Gary Stenson at the bank told me you transferred it to another account. What's he talking about? I don't have any other account."

"I spent it. I've been having some problems . . ." Robbie had no choice but to tell her everything.

Alaska just stood there, shocked. "But you had no right!"

"I'll pay it all back, I promise!"

Their argument was briefly interrupted by Walter's voice. He had come to get Alaska as planned.

"Sorry," he said, "but I heard yelling, so I let myself in."

"Change of plan – I'll meet you in Mount Pleasant," Alaska told him.

Walter went back outside without any further questions.

"Alaska," her father muttered, "let me explain. I ran up some big debts, gambling debts, and I had to pawn my father's watch. You understand,

I had to get that watch back before it was sold and disappeared forever. It's a family heirloom, it'll be yours one day. It's one of a kind. Give me a week and I'll pay you back."

Alaska couldn't believe what she was hearing. "You stole my money so you could get back your stupid watch?! I hate you! I never want to speak to you again! I never want to *see* you again!"

She ran upstairs to pack some clothes. Her father tried to block her path, to reason with her. In her room, she grabbed a leather overnight bag and stuffed some clothes into it. Her father was pleading with her. "Alaska, listen to me, I beg you. It'll all work out."

"Liar! Thief!"

Suddenly, the front door opened. They could hear Donna's voice. "What's going on here?" she shouted.

"Please," Robbie whispered to his daughter, "don't tell your mother. I'll pay it all back. I swear. But, please, don't say a word to your mother."

"You had no right to do that to me!" Alaska yelled.

"If your mother finds out what happened, she'll divorce me. You don't want us to split up because of this, do you? I'm going to fix it, I promise."

Donna came upstairs. "What's going on?" she shouted again as she reached the door to her daughter's room.

There was a moment of silence. Alaska's face was twisted with rage and tears. She stared at her mother. "You really want to know?"

"Of course I want to know."

Robbie got there first. "I found marijuana in Alaska's things!"

"Dad!" Alaska screamed.

"Alaska." Donna sighed. "Tell me you didn't!"

"She sure did!" Robbie yelled. "She betrayed our trust. I can't believe it!"

"Alaska, you promised me you would never touch that stuff. Do you realize the consequences? If this gets out, you could lose your Miss New England title. And you can say goodbye to your dreams of becoming an actress."

Alaska stared hard at her father. She grabbed her bag, ran down the stairs, flew out the door, and jumped into her blue convertable.

*    *    *

Donna interrupted her husband's story. She was in shock. "You lied about the marijuana?"

"Yes, and Alaska didn't contradict me. She left rather than stand there and defend herself. To protect me. I indirectly caused my daughter's death. I'm no murderer, and yet, I was one of her killers!"

Donna collapsed in tears. In spite of the couple's emotional state, Gahalowood was obligated to pursue his line of questioning.

"It was Alaska who arranged the break-in on the evening of October eighth, 1998. She knew about the watch, she knew the code to the safe, and she knew you'd be away celebrating your wedding anniversary. So she stole the watch to get her money back. Or to get back at you. It was Alaska, and you understood that at once, which is why you told the police you had forgotten to lock the safe. You didn't want them to trace it back to your daughter."

"That's right," Robbie admitted. "I knew it was her right away. Not only because she knew the code to my safe but also because, for years, we'd left a spare key to the back door under the doormat, then under a flowerpot. I removed them because our neighbor—Rodriguez, the police officer—warned us about an uptick in robberies. And then there was that black Taurus the cops were talking about. I knew Walter drove one, something I was careful not to mention to them."

Gahalowood then turned to Donna Sanders. "And you, Mrs. Sanders, did you also suspect Alaska?"

She stared at Gahalowood, terrified. "Are you asking if I knew that my husband had stolen money from my daughter, and that she was getting back at him? Do you really think I had any idea about what kind of car Alaska's boyfriend drove? Or that I suspected my daughter, my darling daughter, of running over a cop?"

We didn't know whether Alaska had been at the wheel that night. But it's likely she was in the car, because Rodriguez stated he had seen a driver and passenger. Who was with her? Walter Carrey? Probably. Unfortunately, neither Alaska nor Walter was around to tell us. But at least we now knew—or so we believed—what had happened in Salem and what the messages Alaska had received were referring to. She had participated in the near murder of a police officer, and someone was threatening to expose her.

That helped us to understand Alaska's terror when the police stopped her in Conway, especially since she was in the car that had been used for the robbery. To confirm this, there was one final question we had to answer: Was it the black Ford Taurus that had belonged to Walter Carrey? According to Gahalowood, there was someone in Mount Pleasant who would be able to answer that question.

# 23

## *Side Business*

*Mount Pleasant, New Hampshire*
*Friday, July 16, 2010*
We knew that shortly after Alaska's death, Walter Carrey had his car secretly repaired by Dave Burke at the Ford dealership in Mount Pleasant. This was the man Gahalowood now wanted to question.

Gahalowood felt that if it had been Walter's car that struck Rodriguez outside the Sanderses' home, he would have had it repaired on the sly. "That kind of impact is going to leave a mark. I have a hard time believing that Walter would just make an appointment with a garage to have it repaired. However, I can see him getting in touch with his mechanic friend."

It was early evening when we arrived in Mount Pleasant. Dave Burke was having supper. The young mechanic of 1999 was now shop foreman at the Ford concession. He met us on his porch, still chewing on a mouthful of pasta from his family dinner. "Sorry, but my wife doesn't want us to talk about this in front of the kids," he said. "She says it'll scare them."

"We won't take up much of your time," Gahalowood assured him. "We only have one question: Did Walter Carrey ask you to repair his car in October 1998?"

"Hmmm," Burke replied, making an effort to think back. "I'm not going to lie: there was a time I did a lot of small repairs on the side, paid for in cash. I worked it out with customers from the dealership. It was mostly for scratches or light damage. The kids liked their cars to be perfect, and I worked fast and did a good job. I usually went round to their place with some materials I'd taken from the shop: paint, varnish, a few tools. I gave them a quality finish. It was a lot cheaper than the dealership, and I didn't add a bunch of other items they didn't need. Walter got in touch with me from time to time to retouch some small scratches. He took good care of his car; he wanted it to be perfect."

"These wouldn't have been superficial scratches," Gahalowood said, "but something bigger."

"Well, the day Alaska died, Walter asked me to fix his taillight and his bumper. After that, I put a stop to the side business."

"The event I'm referring to took place months before Alaska's death in October 1998. Did Walter come to see you after an accident? After he hit something or someone?"

"Yeah, yeah . . . now I know what you're talking about . . . I don't remember when it was, but he hit a deer on the road."

"A *deer*?"

"Well, that's what he told me. It was bigger than the usual repairs I did for him. I didn't want to do it, but Walter insisted. He didn't want to bring the car to the garage because if you hit a wild animal, you're supposed to tell the police, and he hadn't done that. He was at fault and didn't want to pick up a two-hundred-dollar fine. So I took care of it. It took me a few nights working in his parents' garage."

"Do you remember the date of the repair? That's very important to us."

Dave Burke closed his eyes as if he were trying to relive that time. I tried to help him focus.

"You said you were in Walter's parents' garage. Is there anything you can remember? Some detail? A story, a memory, anything that might help us identify when it happened?"

After a long moment of reflection, Burke said, "The papers . . . I laid newspaper on the floor. And I remember that at first, I was spending more time reading the articles than I was fixing that damn car. That annoyed Walter."

"What was so interesting in the papers?"

"President Clinton's impeachment!" Burke suddenly shouted. "That's what I remember. It was during the Lewinsky affair. I couldn't believe that the president would risk getting impeached for a blow job."

"When did Clinton's impeachment start?" Lauren asked me.

I looked it up online with my phone. "October eighth, 1998," I said.

"Bingo!" Gahalowood said. "The same day as the robbery. So it was Walter Carrey in the car with Alaska."

*       *       *

That night, in spite of the late hour, Patricia Widsmith met us at Lauren's, unwilling to be left out of the latest developments in the investigation. She was shocked by what we told her.

"If I understand correctly," she said, "Alaska's father emptied her account and she got back at him by showing up with Walter to steal his watch."

"Precisely," I replied. "And the idea of getting back at her father fits what we know of Walter's personality. A guy who can't stand injustice but, more importantly, also happens to be something of a hothead. Alaska must've told him about the watch, and he probably suggested they take it."

"So they steal the watch and then what?" Patricia asked. "How did it end up with Eric?"

"We'll have to ask him first thing tomorrow morning," Lauren suggested.

"Your brother never told you how he got it?" Patricia asked, surprised.

"Never."

"Lauren," I said, "you told me that Eric asked you to sell the watch when he went to jail. Was it really to help your parents pay the lawyer, or did he want to get rid of it because it connected him to Alaska and therefore the murder?"

"What are you getting at?" she asked.

"Maybe Eric knew what happened back in Salem and blackmailed Alaska. He demanded the watch in exchange for his silence."

"Marcus, I'm astonished that you would make such an accusation with nothing to substantiate it," Patricia said, raising her voice.

"Nothing? He blackmailed Sally Carrey, didn't he? It wouldn't be the first time for him. I'm not questioning Eric's innocence—he could have blackmailed Alaska without killing her."

"But didn't we establish that Alaska needed money?" Patricia reminded us. "Couldn't she have just sold the watch to Eric? What do you think, Sergeant?"

"I think that I'm wondering whether those threats Alaska received really were about the robbery."

"What else could they refer to?" Patricia asked.

"Eleanor Lowell's disappearance."

"Who?" Patricia asked, intrigued.

"Eleanor Lowell, a young model who knew Alaska and who disappeared under mysterious circumstances in August 1998."

"What's the specific connection between the two cases?" Patricia asked.

"I have no idea," Gahalowood admitted. "Maybe none. But I can't help but tie them together—call it cop's instinct. Two young women, from the same city, dead within seven months of one another, both under disturbing circumstances."

"Come on, Sergeant," Patricia chided. "Let's not let ourselves get carried away here; otherwise, we'll never get to the bottom of this. We could also bring in the assassination of JFK if you like, but I think it would be a step too far." She rose and grabbed her notes. "We're getting lost in conjecture. Let's wait to hear from Eric. A bit of rest will do us all some good. I have to get back to Boston, and it's a long drive. We can meet tomorrow morning at the prison."

"Would you mind dropping me off at the hotel?" Gahalowood asked her. "If I know Marcus, he's going to stick around, and I want to get some sleep."

I smiled at the remark. I didn't know whether Gahalowood wanted to offer Lauren and me a moment by ourselves or whether he was planning his own little heart-to-heart with Patricia. They left, and I found myself alone in Lauren's living room wondering whether I was disturbing her.

She disappeared into the kitchen for a moment and returned with a bottle of wine, two glasses, and a corkscrew. She opened the wine and offered me a glass. "Tell me about yourself, Marcus."

"What do you want to know?"

"When we had dinner at Luini's after your book signing, you asked me why I became a cop, and I told you that it was because of my brother. Then, I asked you why you became a writer, and you told me it was because of your cousins. We've talked a lot about my brother. Now tell me about your cousins."

That night I told her about Hillel and Woody, the heroes of my childhood. I had with me the photograph found by Uncle Saul, taken in Baltimore in 1995: me with my cousins and a young woman our age.

"Who is she?" Lauren asked.

"Alexandra, an old friend."

"A girlfriend?" Lauren teased.

"An ex-girlfriend. She meant a lot to me."

"What happened?"

"It was kind of dramatic. I don't really want to talk about it."

I placed the photograph on a table, where I would end up forgetting it. Lauren caressed my face. "Life is a succession of dramas, Marcus. You can't let yourself drown."

We kissed. For a long time. But I decided not to spend the night. I didn't want to rush things.

It was very late when I got back to the hotel. I was a bit dazed by the day's discoveries. On my way in, the night clerk called me over. He had an envelope for me. I opened it and found a ticket for a concert by a local orchestra and amateur choral group that were presenting the greatest arias from *Madame Butterfly*. Only one person could have sent me that ticket: Harry Quebert.

# 24

## *Security*

*Concord, New Hampshire*
*Saturday, July 17, 2010*

Eric Donovan must have been surprised to see us back at the prison. Unlike the last time, Gahalowood and Lauren sat at the table, while Patricia and I stood back, waiting in the corner. Eric immediately understood that the withdrawal of his lawyer didn't presage anything good for him.

Gahalowood wasted no time. "Eric, you remember our discussion yesterday? I told you that if you lied to me again, I'd drop your case."

Eric looked scared. "I didn't lie. What are you talking about?"

Lauren waved a plastic bag in front of him. It held her watch—or rather Robbie Sanders's watch. "You recognize this?" she asked him.

"Yes, it's my watch," Eric replied, ill at ease.

"No, it's not. It's a stolen watch. You know why it's in a plastic bag? Because it's connected to the attempted murder of a police officer in Salem."

"What? Hold on . . . I'm not following you at all now."

"On October eighth, 1998," Lauren said to him, "Alaska and Walter entered the home of Alaska's parents. They stole this watch and, in their haste to get away, ran over a cop who tried to stop them. Are you going to tell me you didn't know this?"

"Obviously not! How could I have known?"

"Eric, for once in your life, be honest. Did you blackmail Alaska?"

"No, of course not, what's gotten into you?"

"Did you send her the messages because you wanted something from her, like you did with Sally Carrey?"

"No, I swear!"

"Did you murder Alaska? Was it you who killed her?"

"No! I've been telling you I'm innocent for the past eleven years."

"Then speak! Spit it out. Where did you get the watch?"

"Alaska sold it to me. For ten thousand dollars. She was desperate for cash."

*　　*　　*

*Mount Pleasant, New Hampshire*
*January 1999*

Alaska had agreed to meet Eric at the Season. When he arrived, she was waiting at an isolated table at the back. She seemed nervous. "Want something to drink?" she asked.

"I asked Regina for a coffee. What's so urgent?"

"I have a problem, Eric. I need ten thousand dollars."

"That's a helluva lot of money. What do you need it for?"

"I owe Lewis Jacob. Well, that doesn't concern you. Can you help me or not?"

"What makes you think I have that much money?"

"You had a good job in Salem, you live with your parents, you have no fixed expenses. You wear new clothes all the time. And, besides, I can give you a guarantee."

Eric was amused by her comment. "What sort of guarantee?"

She showed him the gold watch. Eric whistled admiringly. "Wow! That's not just any old watch."

"I know. Gold case, alligator strap. It's worth at least thirty thousand dollars. I'll leave it with you as collateral. You can return it when I reimburse you."

"If you haven't paid me back in a year, it's mine."

"Deal," Alaska said. "I only ask one thing. Don't wear it out and about, and most of all, don't talk about our deal to Walter. He wouldn't understand. Can I count on you? This has to stay between us."

"I can keep a secret," he replied.

"When can you get the money?" Alaska asked.

"Right away, the bank's across the street."

*     *     *

"We went over to the bank," Eric explained to us. "I made a withdrawal and Alaska gave me the watch. After her death, I didn't know what to do with it."

"Why didn't you mention it to the police?" Lauren asked him.

"It would have been one more piece of evidence against me. I always suspected there was something suspicious about the watch. Especially since Alaska asked me not to mention it to Walter. If I'd told the cops about it, I would just be making things worse for myself. What's all this about a robbery?"

"Alaska's father emptied her bank account," Gahalowood explained. "She wanted to get back at him or, at least, help cover her losses. So Alaska told you the ten thousand was for Lewis Jacob?"

"Yes. I figured she'd been dipping into the cash register, but she didn't go into details. You'll have to ask Lewis."

"That's what we're planning to do."

Eric Donovan had been drawn into a plot that had cornered him into silence, slowing down the investigation. Anything he could have told the police eleven years ago to shed a different light on the affair would have made him look even worse. In a sense, Alaska's father had trapped himself in a similar way: both men had kept quiet out of fear of the consequences, but in doing so, they had protected Alaska's murderer. Their silence was a stain on their consciences. And Lewis Jacob was no different.

He was at home that day. We found him sitting outside his house, in one of those wooden Adirondack chairs typical of New England. He greeted us warmly. "Making progress with the investigation?" he asked.

"Yes," Lauren replied. "But we have a question about Alaska we were hoping you might be able to answer."

"I'd be happy to help. Let's go inside, we'll be more comfortable. And you can say hello to my wife; she likes it when people come round."

"Lewis," Lauren clarified, "this is private."

He found the comment amusing. "Fifty years of marriage, I have nothing to hide. Phyllis knows me inside out. I have no secrets from her."

And yet he did. The problem with secrets is that we often forget about them ourselves. And one fine day they come back to the surface, like overflowing sewage.

Phyllis Jacob was in the kitchen.

"Dear, it's about Alaska, the investigation," her husband announced.

His jubilant tone revealed his pleasure in having visitors. "You making progress?" she asked.

"Yes, ma'am," Gahalowood replied. "We've come to ask your husband why he asked Alaska to pay him ten thousand dollars in early 1999."

Mrs. Jacob remained motionless. Her husband's countenance darkened. He sat down and put his face in his hands. Gahalowood repeated the question.

"In January 1999, Alaska hocked an expensive watch in exchange for ten thousand dollars that she said she owed you, Mr. Jacob. What happened back then?"

"What happened, Lewis?" his wife repeated.

"Something happened at the gas station."

*     *     *

*Sunday, January 3, 1999*
It was early when Lewis Jacob arrived at the gas station. In general, he was off on Sundays, when Samantha Fraser, his employee, was working.

He liked Samantha, a pleasant young woman whom the customers were fond of. She was a hard worker as well. During the week she was in school, studying to be a nurse. In the evenings she worked at McDonald's and, on Sundays, at the gas station. Samantha and Alaska were very alike. They had everything going for them. According to Jacob, their only defect was their boyfriends. He felt that Alaska was being dragged down by Walter, who offered her nothing but a limited future in Mount Pleasant. But at least he was a nice guy. For years, Samantha had been seeing a man called Ricky, an ex-con who hit her whenever he felt she was getting out of line.

That Sunday, Samantha had called Lewis Jacob. "You have to come over, Mr. Jacob," she told him.

"What's going on?"

"You have a problem."

"What kind of problem?" He heard a voice shouting in the background.

"A big problem. You have to come over, Mr. Jacob!"

"Samantha, what's going on?" Jacob asked, thinking they'd been robbed.

"It's Ricky, Mr. Jacob. You have to talk to him. You have to come; if you don't, he says he's coming to you."

Lewis Jacob hung up and rushed over to the gas station. As he walked in, he found Samantha and Ricky behind the counter.

"You pig!" Ricky shouted in a voice that was both mocking and unpleasant.

Jacob had no idea what was going on. But his stomach, all twisted up in knots, told him it wasn't good.

"Why'd you do it, Mr. Jacob?" Samantha asked. "I thought you were respectful."

"Do what?"

Ricky showed him a small camcorder that he had just stomped on.

"What is it?" Lewis Jacob asked.

"Don't play dumb with me!" Ricky said, his tone increasingly aggressive. "This was hidden in the changing room. Have you been filming your employees while they get ready for work? You disgusting piece of shit. Does that turn you on? I would've loved to see the videos, but there's no cassette in the camera. Where are the tapes?"

Jacob was stunned. "Ricky, Samantha, I had nothing to do with this. You have to believe me. I have no idea where that camera came from."

"Shut up, you pathetic little shit," Ricky ordered him. "I don't want your excuses. I want money."

"Yes, Mr. Jacob," Samantha added politely. "We would like money."

"If you pay up, I'll leave you alone. But if you don't, I'll burn your gas station, I'll burn your house, I'll burn everything! Get it? I'll set fire to your balls as well."

Lewis Jacob realized there was no way he could convince Ricky that he hadn't placed the camera in the changing room. At that moment, he had only one thing in mind: get rid of them.

"How much do you want?"

"A hundred dollars," Samantha shouted.

"No, idiot, a lot more!" Ricky yelled.

"Five hundred," she announced.

"No, more!" Ricky screamed. "I want twenty thousand!"

"I don't have it," Jacob told him. "I don't have that kind of money. I could never pay you."

"How much do you have?" Ricky asked him, clearly no expert in the art of negotiation.

"I can get you ten thousand."

"And why should I believe you?" Ricky asked him. "I'm sure you have a lot more than that. I saw that safe in your office."

"It's empty," Jacob lamented. "I can show you."

He led them to his small office. He opened the safe in which there was three hundred dollars cash. Ricky put it in his pocket.

Jacob kept his business and personal bank statements in the safe. He

368

showed the latest statements to Ricky. "You see, I wasn't lying. There's money in our joint account—mine and Phyllis's. We have $10,039.40. That's what we set aside for emergencies."

"Well, that's convenient," Ricky told him. "Because this is a big emergency. I want my ten thousand within a week."

"You'll get it."

Ricky turned to leave, satisfied. "C'mon, Sam, let's go. Let's get out of here."

Samantha looked uncomfortably at her boss. "You want me to finish my shift, Mr. Jacob?"

"No, go on."

"One week, old man," Ricky reminded him. "If you don't have it by next Sunday . . . well, you heard what I said. Here, you can keep your shitty camera . . . or what's left of it."

They walked out, leaving Jacob alone with his despair. He had trouble understanding what had just happened. He phoned his wife to tell her that he'd sent Samantha home sick and he had to stay at the station. His mind was racing. Who could have placed the camera in the changing room? The only other people with a key were Samantha and Alaska. It was either a scam put together by Samantha and Ricky to squeeze money out of him, or it was Alaska. But why? Why film Samantha, the only other person to use the room? Jacob considered this. He had closed the store the night before. As always, he had checked the changing room before leaving. If there had been a camera there, he would have noticed. The room was tiny, and it was difficult to hide anything. So if Alaska had put it there, she must have come by in the morning, before the place opened. And if she had, she would have been filmed by the security cameras.

Jacob called his nephew, who had installed the security system and was the only person who knew how to navigate the hard drive. But his nephew couldn't come that day and the drive was automatically erased after twenty-four hours. Lewis Jacob had no choice but to call Alaska and ask her.

"So it was Alaska who put the camera in the changing room?" Gahalowood asked.

"Yes," Jacob replied. "I confronted her the same day. I asked her to come to the gas station and I showed her the camcorder. 'It's yours, isn't it?' I said to her. She broke down, which I understood to mean yes. I told her what had happened, and she asked me to forgive her."

*　　*　　*

*Sunday, January 3, 1999*

"I'm sorry, Mr. Jacob," Alaska said, sobbing. "I did something stupid."

"*Stupid?* You can say that again! I can't believe you'd put me in a situation like this. I'm very disappointed."

"I just wanted to have a laugh with Samantha," she explained. "That lunatic Ricky flipped out. I know Samantha tried to stop him, but he's out of control."

"What am I supposed to do now? Give Ricky ten thousand dollars? He said he'll burn this place to the ground if I don't, and I know he'd do it."

"I'll pay you back," she promised. "All of it. You can take it from my pay for as long as you have to. Oh Mr. Jacob, I'm so sorry to have gotten you into this mess."

"Ricky wants his money by Sunday. I have no way to pay it unless I empty the joint account I have with Phyllis. She'll notice right away. I have to talk to her."

"Don't!" Alaska begged. "She'll ask questions—she might even report me to the police. Word gets around quickly in this town. I'll get you the money. I'll take care of it, it's my fault."

"Where are you going to get that kind of money?"

"Don't worry about me, Mr. Jacob. I'll take care of it. I owe you that much. You've been good to me, and look how I thank you."

*　　*　　*

"A few days later she brought me the money," Lewis Jacob told us. "I immediately paid Ricky off and that was the end of it. We never spoke of it again."

"So you don't know why Alaska put the camera in the changing room?" I asked him.

"No."

"And Samantha? What happened to her?"

"She came to work the next Sunday as if nothing had happened. I asked her what she was up to and she just stared at me all innocent and asked, 'Am I fired?' I told her yes and she looked sad, even offended and said, 'I like you, Mr. Lewis.' 'And I like you, Samantha,' I told her, 'but you blackmailed me all the same.' She said, 'I had no choice. You saw how I tried to play dumb with Ricky.' But I told her she had to go.

"She didn't stay fired for long, though. A few days later she showed up, her face all puffy. She begged me to take her back, telling me the pay was so much better than at McDonald's. She said, 'Ricky said we need the money.' 'What about him, doesn't he work?' I asked. And she replied, 'No, he doesn't really like it.' Then Alaska got involved. She reproached me for punishing Samantha for something she herself had done. 'It's unfair,' she said to me. 'If you fire her, I'm quitting!' I didn't want to lose Alaska, so I took Samantha back. But then, a few weeks later, she quit, just like that. She'd given up her studies and was off on a road trip with Ricky. I never heard from her again."

"Lewis," Lauren asked, "why didn't you tell the police all this at the time of Alaska's murder?"

"I wasn't sure I should. I thought they'd think I was somehow mixed up in her death."

"Back then," Gahalowood noted, "you spoke about Alaska in glowing terms. You didn't even mention this business with the camera, but at one point, you insinuated that Alaska had a more devious side."

"*Devious?* Not at all. She was just a kid who did something stupid— which she took responsibility for, by the way. Ultimately, I was scared.

Ricky and Samantha had disappeared, yes, but I was afraid they might turn up again and start making accusations about that business with the camcorder. It was my word against theirs. The police would've taken me for some kind of pervert. I was the last person to see Alaska alive, and she was found dead less than a mile from my gas station. So I decided to say nothing. But I probably would have talked if Walter hadn't been arrested two days later. The investigation was over, and I felt it was better to keep it to myself."

"You were wrong," Gahalowood said.

Lewis Jacob, no doubt feeling the need to demonstrate his good faith, then said to us, "I put all this in my will. I didn't want to take the secret to my grave."

Phyllis Jacob, who until then had listened to her husband in shocked silence, finally found her voice. "You made a will?"

"Yes, I filed a copy with Brown, the lawyer. Along with the cassette."

"The *cassette*?" Gahalowood repeated. "What cassette?"

"Samantha came by at the end of February to tell me she was quitting. It was late. I was very surprised to see her. She explained that she was going away with Ricky. Then she handed me a small digital cassette and said, 'Give this to Alaska, please. It's hers. It's a souvenir.' I took the cassette, but I never gave it to Alaska. I wanted to see what was on it first, out of curiosity. But I didn't have the right equipment. A month went by and then Alaska was murdered. And I was left with the damn thing. Like I said, I was afraid of being named as a suspect. This is a small town: it doesn't take much to ruin a reputation. People would stop coming to the gas station; all my savings were plowed into that place. I was afraid the cassette might contain images of Alaska taken in the changing room at the gas station. I wanted to be sure I didn't have any further problems. I could've just gotten rid of it, but I felt bad doing that. So I put it in an envelope and left it with my lawyer, with instructions to open it after my death."

\*　　\*　　\*

Eddy Brown had been a lawyer in Mount Pleasant since 1955. He was the oldest, as well as the only, attorney in town. In spite of his age—he was over eighty—he continued to work in his office every day. That Saturday, when we showed up at his home, we had to gently persuade him to leave his chair, his book, and his lemonade and accompany us there. "It couldn't wait until Monday?" he grumbled as I helped him into my car.

Brown was still in good shape. And I believe that our interruption of his weekend routine secretly pleased him. "It's not every day you help the police with a criminal investigation," he told us. Then, turning to me, "I read your books, young man. Mention me in your next one, will you? I'd like that a great deal." Attorney Brown had a large safe in his office. "All the town's secrets are in here," he was happy to tell us. He quickly located the envelope left by Lewis Jacob. Inside was a digital cassette and a letter, dated April 11, 1999, signed by Jacob, in which he set down the events he had related to us an hour before.

"Do you think we can still play the cassette?" Lauren asked.

"I hope so," Gahalowood replied. "I'm going straight to Concord to hand it over to the forensics team. We'll find out soon enough."

This marked a new stage in the investigation. What if the threats Alaska received had nothing to do with the robbery at her parents' home but were instead related to the camcorder she had hidden in the changing room at the gas station?

### I KNOW WHAT YOU DID

Could the notes have been the work of Ricky or Samantha? Had they discovered that it was Alaska's camera? Having extorted Lewis Jacob, maybe they had tried to blackmail her as well? We had to find them, but we had very little to go on. We had Samantha's last name, but we knew almost nothing about Ricky.

After we dropped Brown off at his home, Gahalowood asked if I would accompany him to Concord. "I'm going to give forensics the cassette and start my search for Samantha and Ricky."

"I'm sorry, Sergeant. I have to go."

"Go? Go where?"

"I have an invitation that I can't refuse."

That afternoon I headed to Maine, alone. An hour later I arrived at the charming town of Bridgton. I was early. I walked around town, then, when it was time, I went to the auditorium of the local high school, where the concert was taking place. The seats were numbered. I sat down. Little by little the room began to fill, except for the seat next to me. When the lights went down, it remained empty. The show started with the first excerpt from *Madame Butterfly*, "America Forever." At that moment, a shadow slipped in and sat next to me.

It was Harry Quebert.

# 25

## Madame Butterfly

*Bridgton, Maine*
*Saturday, July 17, 2010*

When the performance was over, we joined the crowd as it left the auditorium, without exchanging a word. In the school parking lot, a cart was selling takeout food. Harry nodded at it and said, "I'll buy you dinner."

We ate burgers and fries on a bench facing the river. The silence betrayed our mutual discomfort. I wasn't hungry, but I still ate. I didn't know what to say to him; I didn't even know where to begin. I had been desperately trying to find him since we'd last seen each other, back in December 2008; I hadn't imagined it would happen like this though. Finally, I asked, "How did you know I was in Mount Pleasant?"

"The bookstore publicized your signing. And people are talking about you again, Marcus. The Alaska Sanders case, this new investigation the country is so caught up in. Your next book?"

"I don't know. Are you still living in New Hampshire? I thought you'd evaporated. I looked for you everywhere. It's been over a year. Every day I asked myself what happened to you."

"I became a ghost. It's the best thing that could've happened to me. The fame I didn't know how to handle, I'm finally rid of it. I'm a free man, Marcus."

"That's why you disappeared?"

"Let's just say I had to get away. It was better for all concerned."

"And now what? You suddenly felt the need to reappear with those seagull statues and mysterious notes?"

"There was nothing mysterious about my notes. I was telling you not to take the teaching position at Burrows. That would be a grave error. You'll never feel at home there."

"Why?" I replied, annoyed. "I'm not good enough to teach at Burrows?"

"On the contrary, you're better than that. Since I realized—rightly it turns out—that you hadn't understood what I was trying to tell you, I've been wanting to talk to you in person. That's why I arranged this meeting."

"And what are you trying to tell me, Harry?"

"That it's time for you to live up to your potential, Marcus. You're a wonderful man, tenacious, gifted. One of the finest writers our country will have ever known, you'll see. So when I found out you had this terrible notion of teaching at Burrows—"

I interrupted him. "How did you find out?"

An amused smile flitted across his face. "They didn't disconnect my university email when I was fired. I still have access to the system, and I receive, along with all the junk mail, the notices sent to the faculty. That's how I discovered, to my horror, at the end of June, a message from Dustin Pergal along the lines of: 'I'm pleased to announce that Marcus Goldman will be joining us as a teaching associate. He'll be teaching a writing course. Professor Goldman will be in room C-223, and I ask you to give him the warm welcome he deserves.' C-223 was my office—you knew that, of course."

"Yes."

"That's what bothered me. I get the impression you're trying to revive the past at all costs, Marcus. First with that two-bit writers' house in Somerset and now by taking my old office at Burrows. It's time to assert your own identity as a writer. And please stop trying to meddle in mine. Don't forget who I am, Marcus. Don't forget what I've done."

"Well, I certainly haven't forgotten what you did for me."

"You know what I'm talking about, Marcus."

"It doesn't matter, you're still my friend."

"And that's important to me. But we can't really be friends until you stop idealizing me and accept that I'm simply your friend and nothing more. When you finally let go of that stupid image of me as a mentor. An office at Burrows! Please, what a ridiculous idea. Your destiny lies far beyond Burrows—conducting your investigations, making people dream, feeding the excitement you create."

"I'm not sure I want all that, Harry. I think I'd like a normal life, a calmer life."

"That's impossible, Marcus. It's stronger than you! You've got the fire inside, and you can't do anything about it."

Night had fallen. The sky was filled with stars. Harry looked up. "I should go," he said. "I still have a long way to go."

"Are we going to see each other again?"

"Of course, what a question!"

"Well you know, it's been a year and a half since you showed any sign of life."

"That's roughly how long you stayed silent after your first success. You remember that? When you wanted to see me, I was there. Don't worry so much: we'll see each other again when you're ready, Marcus."

"I am ready."

"No, you're not. Not until you accept who you are."

"And who am I?"

"A great writer."

"You as well . . ."

"For the love of God, Marcus!" Harry shouted. "What's wrong with you? You won, you're better than me. Your name, your fame, your success. They far outweigh anything I could have achieved. Why do you insist on putting a crown on my head?"

"It was never a competition for me, Harry!"

"But for me it was! Since the very first day. And you never saw it."

I didn't know whether he was testing me or telling the truth.

"Go on," he said, "ask me the question . . ."

"Which one?"

"Why I disappeared. Why, when I left that day in December 2008, I swore I'd never see you again. Do you want to know? Because, for that whole year, when you were struggling to write your new book, a part of me was glad—glad you were having so much trouble. From the moment you showed up, in February, I hoped that you'd fail, Marcus! That you'd fail miserably. That you'd burn your wings. And you know why? So I could find you again. Your success had pulled us apart. We were so close and then, poof, you were gone. No more Marcus."

"I'm sorry, I . . ."

"But it's not your fault, Marcus. Don't you understand what I'm trying to tell you? You can't apologize for your success. It's part of you. You can't blame the caterpillar for becoming a butterfly. It's your destiny. It was written. And you know what? I always knew it. None of it was a surprise for me. And then, in early 2008, I found you again, feverish, in danger, riddled with doubt. You were a tortured writer unable to write, and Barnaski was making you feel like a puppet. You have a right to the truth. I liked seeing you vulnerable because I was jealous of your success. JEALOUS! You hear me? I wanted it to stop, to wither. Because it made me face my own failures, my own demons. So when you came to my place to write, every time I asked if you were making progress with your book, I rejoiced to hear that you weren't. And whenever I suggested we go out somewhere, whenever I took you away from the house, away from your work, to go running or walking on the beach, to go cross-country skiing, whatever, in reality I was trying to get you away from your writing. I was sabotaging your career. I wanted fame to pass you by."

There was a long silence before Harry spoke again. "You should hate me."

"How could I hate you?"

"Because people who like each other don't let jealousy get in the way."

378

"I like jealous people. They understand what's important in life."

Harry sighed. "How's your love life, Marcus? Have you found love?"

I was surprised by the question. "There's this girl I like a lot."

"I didn't ask if you had a girlfriend; I asked if you'd found love."

"No, you know I—"

"I know, Marcus, I do. I know there was a girl you were in love with once and deep down you're still in love with her. She's the love of your life."

"It's ancient history."

"Life is short, Marcus, especially from our perspective. No history is really ancient."

"I lost touch with her."

"I thought you would say that, so I allowed myself to find her for you." With those words, he handed me an envelope. I tore it open and . . . my heart began to beat wildly.

"Thinking back to 2008, I realize I wasn't worthy of your friendship," Harry said. "You want us to be friends? I'll start acting like one. I'm one of the only people who knows you well enough to know that your life is incomplete without her. Go see her. I'm sure she's waiting for you as well."

Before leaving, Harry embraced me. Then he disappeared into the night. I didn't follow him. I stayed there awhile, sitting on the bench. I let my mind wander until a message on my phone brought me back to reality. It was Lauren. She sent me a picture of the table in her living room on which could be seen the picture of my two Goldman cousins and Alexandra, which I had left there the previous night. Under the picture, she had written:

*Your little cousins are here. You're the only one who's missing. Stopping by?*

I got back on the highway and drove to her place. It was late. The night was warm. Lauren was waiting for me on her porch.

"Where were you?"

"I met an old friend."

"Was it okay?"

"It was strange."

I felt strange. Almost uneasy about being there. In my pocket, I fingered the envelope that Harry had given me. Inside was a ticket for an Alexandra Neville concert. When I thought about her, I was transported back to my childhood. With the Baltimore Goldmans. I had to close that chapter of my life.

# Part Three

## The Consequences of Life

# 26

# *Samantha*

*Rochester, New Hampshire*
*Tuesday, July 20, 2010*

Three days had gone by since the discovery of the videocassette. State police experts had been able to extract the footage, and what we discovered made it imperative we find Samantha Fraser as soon as possible.

That morning we crossed the city of Rochester, New Hampshire, accompanied by an impressive convoy of police vehicles. Gahalowood, Lauren, and I were in a SWAT team all-terrain vehicle. There was an officer at the wheel, with Gahalowood in the passenger seat and Lauren and me in the back. She discreetly touched my hand. We had spent Sunday on the beach in Kennebunkport, leaving the investigation and our worries behind, for a few hours at least. This respite allowed me to absorb my recent meeting with Harry. I had difficulty keeping my mind off the concert ticket and Alexandra Neville, and thinking about her gave me the unpleasant feeling that I was cheating on Lauren. I was unsure how to proceed. I liked Lauren a great deal, but was that enough?

The driver turned on the siren, bringing me back to reality. We had easily traced Samantha Fraser's whereabouts. The bad news for her was that the trail had led to prison. The good news for us was that she was in a conditional release program, assigned to a residence for several hours a day. She lived in a prefab house in a dangerous part of Rochester, where we were now arriving in force.

The vehicles stopped and the perimeter was quickly secured. Outside the house corresponding to the address, a woman sitting in a plastic chair watched as the police deployed. She was a shadow of what she must have been. Her hair, her skin, her body were all gray; her gaze, unfocused; her teeth, gone. She cursed at two children of about ten who were playing ball. According to our information, Samantha was thirty-six. This woman looked to be at least twenty years older. In the car, Gahalowood showed us a photograph.

"Not much of a resemblance, but it is Samantha Fraser."

"What happened to her?" Lauren asked.

"Crack. Let's go."

Lauren, Gahalowood, and I got out of the vehicle and approached the woman, all three of us wearing bulletproof vests.

"Samantha Fraser? I'm Sergeant Perry Gahalowood with the New Hampshire State Police."

"I've been a good girl, Sergeant," she said.

"I don't doubt it. We're here to ask you about Alaska Sanders."

"Don't know her. In any case, didn't see anything, didn't hear anything."

"She worked with you at Lewis Jacob's gas station in Mount Pleasant."

Samantha made a face as if she were searching her memory. She was forced to admit defeat. "Nope. Don't know her."

"She was your lover," Gahalowood said.

\*　　\*　　\*

The cassette kept by Lewis Jacob revealed a side to Alaska that took us entirely by surprise.

The first sequence was from September 21, 1998. We could see Alaska in the mysterious setting that no-one had been able to identify from the final audition video sent to Dolores Marcado, with that same painting of a sunset over the ocean in the background. It was clear that Alaska was conducting another screen test. Her face approaches the lens as she presses different buttons. The device must have been equipped with a small screen she could use to make sure everything was set up correctly. Suddenly, she raises her eyes to someone facing her and says, "Whooo, thanks for the camera. If this doesn't get me to Hollywood! You're a doll; you know I love you."

The sequence that followed—which turned out to be the audition we had already seen—was filmed at the same time. The camera was clearly a recent gift. But who was Alaska talking to when she said, "You know I love you"? Walter?

The next scene was recorded two months later, on a Sunday at the end of November, at Lewis Jacob's gas station. Alaska is filming a young woman behind the counter—Samantha Fraser. Samantha is smiling uncomfortably. "Why are you filming me?" she asks.

"Because I want to," Alaska tells her, as she approaches.

Samantha now appears in close up, and Alaska intones, "Ladies and gentlemen, I present Samantha Fraser!"

"Where'd the camera come from?" Samantha asks.

"A gift from my past. When I wanted to be an actress."

"You'd make a great actress!"

"That's nuts."

"Nuts? Wait, give me that."

Samantha takes the camera and now Alaska appears in the frame. Samantha comments: "Everyone take a look at Alaska Sanders, the future star." Then she points the lens at herself and says, "And here's her poor friend Samantha, who'll end up in the gutter."

Alaska bursts out laughing, approaches the camera, and turns it so both young women can be seen. Suddenly Alaska steals a kiss from Samantha.

"You're crazy. Not here!" Samantha exclaims, surprised. "Somebody might see us."

The next sequence takes place the following Sunday. Alaska is holding the camera at arm's length. The two women are naked in the changing room at the gas station. Alaska places the camera on a shelf, checks the angle, then she and Samantha kiss.

Sunday after Sunday, we see Alaska and Samantha at the gas station. They film each other imitating Lewis Jacob behind the counter. They laugh wildly. They make fun of him. "Mr. Jacob, if you see this one day, just know that we like you a lot!" Alaska says to the camera. "We wouldn't have met without you," Samantha adds. Then they raid the chips and candy displays, sharing out the spoils in the back room. They talk, they laugh, they kiss.

This intimate moment is disturbed by the arrival of a customer. We hear the electronic buzzer and understand that someone has entered the store. "Shit!" Samantha says as she releases her lover and quickly gets dressed while Alaska looks on, amused.

On another Sunday, Samantha is filmed in Lewis Jacob's office, reading from a magazine.

"*What animal are you?* Ready?"

"Go ahead."

"*In the morning, you ordinarily get up: (A) always briskly, (B) with difficulty, (C) you don't, you go to sleep because you've spent the night taking care of business.*"

The final sequence from the two-hour-long cassette is from January 3. Again they are kissing in the changing room. Suddenly, a voice can be heard: "Samantha?" Panic. "Shit, it's Ricky, go out the emergency exit." Alaska disappears and Samantha quickly stops filming.

That was the day Ricky discovered the camera and extorted ten thousand dollars from Lewis Jacob. Eleven years later, we finally found out what happened. Nothing remained of the pretty young woman seen on the video footage. The Samantha Fraser of 2010, with her thinning hair, mottled face, rough skin, and broken body, stared with fascination at the video we showed her in the pigsty she used as a living room. "That's me," she said, pointing at the laughing young beauty on the screen. Then, seeing Alaska, she murmured, "Alaska . . . Alaska . . . it's you . . ." We couldn't tell if she recognized her from the footage or if she was simply repeating what she heard in the video.

"Samantha," Gahalowood asked, "do you remember this woman?"

She stared at the sergeant with empty eyes. "Crack has stolen my memories," she whimpered.

She rose suddenly and dragged her frame over to a disorderly table. She rummaged among the muddle as if she were sorting through the pieces of a puzzle, then grabbed a school notebook. With a victorious smile, she crowed, "Alaska! Alaska!" She brought it over to us and handed it to Gahalowood. Someone had written *Alaska* on the cover in black magic marker.

Gahalowood opened it. "It's a journal."

"I wrote it," Samantha explained. "One day, I realized my brain was slowly disappearing. My memory was being erased. At first, I didn't think it was too serious, in fact, it might even be better if I could forget my life. But then I realized that I was going to forget her as well, and I didn't want that. She's the only beautiful thing in my life. So I wrote."

*The first time I saw Alaska, I made fun of her name. She said, "Samantha isn't much better," and we laughed. It was dumb but we found it funny. That was at the gas station. She had come for an interview. She said that we were now colleagues. I didn't give a shit if we were colleagues or not, but she seemed nice. And she was really beautiful. I'd never seen a woman as beautiful as her. Crazy beautiful! Pretty, smiling, well dressed, smart. Like my grandma would have said, "She checked all the boxes."*

*We got along right from the start. She came by the next Sunday to say hello. And the Sunday after that. And then every Sunday. She kept me company. There aren't a lot of customers on Sundays at the gas station. I don't know why Mr. Jacob insists on keeping the place open. Well, I'm not complaining, I was making twice what I was getting at McDonald's for working half as much. But I was still bored. So I was happy when Alaska came by. And she was different. She knew all sorts of things. Me, I was having a hard time in nursing school. Ricky told me I was useless. But Alaska told me right away, "You'll get there, you're beautiful, you're smart."*

*I remember because no-one had ever said anything like that to me before. First, that I would get somewhere, then that I was beautiful and that I was smart. When she said that, I almost started to cry. I told Ricky but he said I was a pretentious asshole with my nursing classes. She told me Ricky was the asshole. Then I told Ricky that Alaska had said he was an asshole. I didn't want to make trouble for her, but I wanted Ricky to know that she thought he was being shitty with me. That was a mistake. He was furious. He said he was going to teach her some respect.*

*Then Alaska met Ricky. He was waiting with me at the gas station. I was feeling really bad. I was crying and everything. Alaska arrived and, obviously, she was very surprised. Fortunately, Ricky didn't hit her, but they got into an argument. He grabbed her by the neck and told her the next time she insulted him, she'd find his big fist in her face. Then he let her go and left. Alaska was on the ground, crying. I understood because Ricky can scare you, I know that better than anyone. I got down beside her and I was so sorry that I started to cry too. I held her in my arms. And then she kissed me. I didn't expect that at all, but I liked it. I liked it when she slipped her tongue into my mouth. It was sweet, it was good. Tender, like she used to say.*

*I would never have thought of kissing a woman. That day, which had started out really bad, was a day I'll never forget because we became a couple after that, Alaska and me. She would spend her Sundays at the gas station, we hung out, laughed, kissed, did stuff in the changing room, read magazines, and ate potato chips. We could do what we wanted. There were hardly any customers and Mr. Jacob didn't know how to use the security cameras. He said only his nephew knew.*

*Alaska always brought her own little camera. She said it would make memories. She liked to film us when we kissed. I would have done anything for her. I even told her so, something I'd never told anyone: "I'd do anything for you."*

*I asked Alaska if I was officially a lesbian because of what we did. Alaska told me she couldn't care less, that we can love whoever we want. I agreed with her, but I still wanted to know. I told her I loved Ricky even though he hit me. She said, "Why do you stay with him if he hits you?" I told her, "I don't know, I'm attached to him. Sometimes you're attached to someone but don't know why." She said she understood, that she was attached to someone as well. But she knew why: she was madly in love. It hurt a little when she said that. I realized that I would have liked her to be madly in love with me. That's when I realized that Alaska wasn't going to stay in Mount Pleasant and I was just something for her to do on Sundays. I asked her, "Are you in love with Walter?" She said, "No, not Walter, I don't care about him. I'm stuck here because of something we did." She told me there was someone else. Someone who would get her out of this "rat hole." I asked her why he didn't come get her and what was he waiting for and Alaska said, "His divorce." Once the papers were signed, they would leave for New York. Alaska's dream was to go live in New York. She wanted to be an actress. At first, when I met her, she said her career was over. "Because of what happened in Salem," she said. It took her a while to tell me what had happened. Her father, who must be a real shit, had stolen her savings. She wanted to steal his watch in return, it would be quick and clean. She went with Walter, but they were seen and Walter ran over their neighbor, who was a cop. I told her it wasn't her fault if that asshole Walter hit someone with his car. And besides, the guy didn't even die. I knew she would live her dream, that she would become a famous actress, you could see it in her. While we waited for her to get famous, we made movies with her camera.*

*Like everything that starts off good in my life, it ended bad. The Sunday after New Year's, Alaska and I were in the changing room kissing. The camera was on. I had taken my top off and she was kissing my breasts. And suddenly, the door of the store opens and I can hear Ricky's voice. I panicked and told Alaska to go out the emergency door. I quickly turned off the camera. There was no place to hide it, but I put some bottles of cleaner in front of it and removed the cassette and put it in my pocket. I didn't want to think about what Ricky would do to Alaska if he found the video. By itself, the camera didn't prove anything.*

*Ricky pushed open the changing room door. He saw me half-dressed and made a funny face. He slapped me, hard, and yelled, "Is that how you serve the customers, you fucking whore?" I kept calm. "Ricky, it's the changing room, I'm changing. I spilled some coffee on myself." He laughed and said, "Strike first, ask questions later." I asked him what he was doing there and he said, "I've come to make sure you're not with someone." "You think I'm cheating on you?" "I don't know. You've been different lately." Then he grabbed my breasts and said, "At least I didn't stop by for nothing." He kissed me hard. Then he lifted his head and saw the camera pointing at us. He started shouting. He screamed, "What's this?" I had to find an explanation fast if I didn't want him to beat me with his belt to make me talk or do the same to Alaska. So I said, "Oh, shit, that pervert, Mr. Jacob is filming us when we change!" "And you didn't notice?" "Uhhh, no, Ricky, I don't look at the top shelves. I change my clothes and I go to work." He was red with rage. He grabbed the camera and opened it to take the cassette out but it was empty. He threw it on the floor and stomped on it. Then he screamed, "That fucking pervert! I'm going to take care of him. I'll kill him!" I was afraid he'd really hurt poor Mr. Jacob, so I said, "It's stupid to kill him. Better to ask him for money." He thought that was a good idea* *and he asked me to call him. Poor Mr. Jacob came over right away. Obviously, he knew nothing about this business with the camera. Ricky wanted to squeeze him. I tried to keep it small, $100, $200. But Ricky demanded $10,000 from Mr. Jacob if he wanted to avoid even bigger problems. I really felt bad for Mr. Jacob.*

*After that, I told Alaska. She said she'd fix it, she'd get the money and pay Mr. Jacob back. She told me not to worry about it. No-one had ever said that before. And then Mr. Jacob fired me. And when Ricky hit me because I'd lost a job that brought in good money—that's what he said—I cried like a baby, not because he hit me but because by leaving my job, I was losing those Sundays with Alaska.*

*Alaska got Mr. Jacob to hire me back. I don't know what she told him, but she took care of it. She looked out for me. She was the first and last person to do that. But after that, she never came back on Sundays. I waited for her, I was desperate. I hoped it was her every time the door opened. It felt like something had broken. Because of Ricky. Or maybe because of us. I always knew that Alaska loved me like a friend, or maybe more than a friend. A friend you could go really far with. But the truth is, she was in love with someone else.*

*Alaska Sanders was the most beautiful thing ever to happen to me. In my life, hers is the only memory I want to preserve.*

*   *   *

When Gahalowood had finished reading aloud, Samantha was crying. "Such a beautiful story," she said to us as if she were hearing it for the first time. "Is she alright?"

"Who?"

"Alaska. That's why you're here, isn't it? I hope nothing's happened to her."

Gahalowood remained silent for a moment. "She's good. She says hello."

Samantha Fraser smiled, revealing her few remaining teeth. "Tell her I send her a kiss. And that I miss her."

We took pictures of the notebook and left the original with Samantha. Then Gahalowood spoke into his police radio, indicating that we were ready to leave. Samantha accompanied us outside, where she again harangued the two boys playing ball.

But as we were getting ready to climb into the police car, she yelled, "That goddamn printer, I should have taken it back to Duty's!"

# 27

## *Strange Impressions*

*Rochester, New Hampshire*
*Tuesday, July 20, 2010*
*That goddamn printer, I should have taken it back to Duty's!* There had to be some connection with Alaska. Hearing Samantha, Lauren stared at us. "Did she just say Duty's? That was an electronics store in Mount Pleasant. It went bankrupt a few years ago."

Gahalowood signaled to his colleagues to wait and turned to Samantha. "What did you say?"

"I don't know," the specter replied.

The two children laughed. "She says that all the time, mister," one of them said. "Don't get angry with her; she didn't mean any harm."

"What does she say all the time?"

"'That goddamn printer, I should have taken it back to Duty's!' My father says it's an old story. We think it's funny."

"Are you Samantha's son?"

"Yeah. And that's my brother. You here because of my father?"

"No, I wanted to ask your mother some questions. What's your father's name?"

"Ricky. Ricky Positano."

"Where can we find him?"

"Where? I don't know."

Knowing his last name, we finally had a lead on Ricky. We were keen to question him and hear his side of what happened at the gas station. Gahalowood assigned a team to try to locate him.

Meanwhile, Gahalowood, Lauren, and I went to the state police head-quarters to review the situation with Chief Lansdane. Chief Mitchell, who wanted daily reports from Lauren, was invited to join the meeting, which no doubt made him feel very important. It allowed us to fill him in on the most recent developments in our investigation.

*October 2, 1998:* Alaska discovers that her father has stolen her savings. Furious, she leaves with her boyfriend, Walter, with whom she had plans to spend the weekend, and decides to stay a few days, probably without any intention of settling down.

*October 8, 1998:* Alaska steals the watch from her parents' house. This turns out badly. Walter, her accomplice, runs over a policeman when he tries to stop them. Alaska decides to stay in Mount Pleasant for a while. She can't sell her father's watch because it would risk implicating her. She then takes a job at the gas station.

*November–December 1998:* Alaska gets involved in an ambiguous relationship with a fellow employee at the gas station, Samantha Fraser. Alaska tells her she's involved with someone other than Walter. She's waiting for this person to come get her and take her out of Mount Pleasant. That person probably lives in Salem (they send her a pair of shoes sold only in a store in that city) and is about to get divorced.

→ Alaska was involved in relationships with both Walter and Samantha. She is clearly bisexual. Who is this third person she claims to be so in love with? Is it a man or a woman?

*January 1999:* Ricky Positano, Samantha's boyfriend, discovers the camera in the changing room. He thinks Lewis Jacob is filming his employees and blackmails him. Lewis Jacob discovers that the camera belongs to Alaska.

*February 1999:* Samantha suddenly quits her job at the gas station. Why? What happened?

*April 3, 1999:* Alaska is murdered. A note is found in her pocket:
I KNOW WHAT YOU DID.
→ What is the note about? The tragic robbery at her parents' home? Her relationship with Samantha? The blackmailing of Lewis Jacob?

"We're not out of the woods yet," Gahalowood remarked, "but we're beginning to get a picture of what really happened."

"Good work," Lansdane said to us. "And Eric Donovan?"

"Donovan had an affair with Walter Carrey's mother and used it to blackmail her. It could be the reason Walter accused him of being involved in the murder. And then there's Donovan's sweater, stained with Alaska's blood. Eric has always insisted that he lent it to Walter, which has now been confirmed by Walter's mother."

"Are you saying the evidence against Donovan is starting to crumble?" Mitchell asked.

"We still have questions about his printer, which was used to print those threatening messages," I clarified.

"About that," Lauren added. "Samantha Fraser said something strange when we went to see her: 'That goddamn printer, I should have taken it back to Duty's!'"

"Duty's?" Chief Mitchell echoed. "The old store in Mount Pleasant?"

"That's what we have to find out," Lauren replied.

"What's Duty's?" Lansdane asked.

"An electronics store in Mount Pleasant," Lauren told him. "The owner was an unusual guy, not mean exactly, but a bit of a swindler, who went out of business more than once. You know the type. The place closed four or five years ago. Since then, he's opened a new store selling used goods near Wolfeboro."

"Do you think there's a connection with Eric Donovan's printer?" Lansdane asked.

"Hard to say," I replied. "But in any case, we have to find out."

Gahalowood looked thoughtful. "Why is Samantha Fraser obsessed with a printer? She seemed to repeat the words like a mantra. 'That goddamn printer, I should have taken it back to Duty's!' What's she talking about?"

"Would Eric have purchased his printer there?" I asked.

"We'll ask him," Lauren replied, "but I'm pretty sure he did. Everyone in Mount Pleasant shopped at Duty's. He had the lowest prices. But there was always a problem with the merchandise. People figured it out pretty quickly and stopped going there. Which is why it went out of business."

*    *    *

That day, we did what Gahalowood and Kazinsky had failed to do in 1999: we got in touch with the manufacturer of Eric's printer, which had its headquarters in Seattle. After what felt like hours on the line, being passed from one department to another, we were finally able to speak to someone who could answer our questions.

"Well, that model was sold from 1997. Nothing special to report, except there was a defective lot, which shipped from the factory in April 1998. It was limited to around two hundred units, according to the wholesaler's report, all distributed in New Hampshire. But don't worry, almost all of them were returned to us."

"What do you mean by 'defective'?" Lauren asked.

There was silence on the line as the man went through his report to locate the information. "Looks like there was a problem with the print heads, which left small marks. They were almost invisible to the naked eye, but we recalled the printers anyway."

Lauren, Gahalowood, and I were shocked.

"How did I not realize it could have been a batch defect?" Gahalowood said.

The Seattle headquarters couldn't provide any further information: the regional wholesaler had taken care of the returns. The wholesaler's salesman, based in Manchester, New Hampshire, had been with them for more than fifteen years and he knew Neil Rogers, the owner of Duty's, quite well. On the phone, he told us, "He's a nice enough guy, but we no longer do business with him."

"Why?"

"He wasn't exactly honest. More than once, when there was a product recall, he didn't bother to tell his customers, to avoid the paperwork. That's not right."

"What do you mean, exactly?" Gahalowood asked him.

"When a defective product is shipped by the factory—and believe me, it happens—we have to recover it and replace it. It's not just a question of ethics: imagine if the defect caused a short-circuit and set your house on fire, then the manufacturer would be held responsible, there would be a lawsuit, and the damages would be enormous. So when there's a problem, manufacturers turn to wholesalers, who then turn to the retailers. Well, that's how it was done at the time. Today, with the internet, email, and so on, we can go directly to the customer, but in the past, the retailers had to track their sales."

"And I imagine Neil Rogers didn't always do that, right?" Lauren asked.

"Never. He wanted no part of it. He would say, 'When it's gone, it's gone,' and he didn't say a word to his customers."

"So if I understand correctly," Gahalowood said, "Duty's sold several printers with a similar defect in 1998."

"Definitely. You should get in touch with Rogers."

And that's just what we did. We found him at his used-goods store on the outskirts of Wolfeboro.

"They handle that kind of thing," Rogers said, referring to the wholesalers. "But they send you all sorts of paperwork with instructions you wouldn't believe. You have to replace the product at once or reimburse the customer, then fill out the forms, return the defective equipment at your expense, and wait for approval from the higher-ups, who take forever to settle. It's always the little guy who takes the hit!"

"So you didn't recall the printers you'd sold?" Lauren asked.

"Hell no! When I received the product-recall notices, I threw them right in the garbage. And if anyone asked, I told them I never got it. It's up to the sender to prove that I received it, right?"

"When Eric Donovan was arrested, why didn't you tell anyone you'd sold him a printer?" Gahalowood asked.

"What kind of a question is that? How was I supposed to know there was a connection between a printer and a police investigation? I sold electronics, that's all. I'm not Sherlock Holmes!"

"Did you sell other printers from that same lot? Would you remember who to?"

"Please, how am I going to remember? It's been eleven years! I have trouble remembering what I ate at noon."

"For example, Lewis Jacob?" Lauren suggested.

"Oh, well, now you mention it, if there's one guy I remember, it's him. He brought his printer in, claiming it wasn't working. Apparently, it kept printing the same page several times. I tested it and didn't find anything. But he kept pestering me about it. He said he had a warranty, but it wasn't valid because I hadn't followed through on the product recall. He was so insistent, I ended up going through the whole damn procedure of returning it to the factory, which took up a lot of my time. Since then we never got along. He never came back to my store, and I never bought another drop of gas from him."

"When was this?"

"Oh, I don't know. Was it even the model you're talking about or another one? Who knows?"

Since there had been a factory recall, we would surely be able to trace it. The manufacturer's legal department retained recall files for twenty years, primarily to demonstrate that they had followed proper procedure if they were ever sued.

It took most of the day, but we finally obtained two important pieces of information: the printer that Eric bought, whose serial number appeared in the police file, was part of the defective lot; and Lewis Jacob had indeed returned a unit from that same batch. The return was made on March 3, 1999. That meant that Jacob could have sent Alaska the anonymous notes and subsequently gotten rid of his printer. But what was Samantha Fraser referring to with her refrain, "That goddamn printer, I should have taken it back to Duty's!"?

It was near the end of the day when we informed Lansdane of these new developments. "If I understand correctly, several printers were sold in Mount Pleasant with the same defect," he said.

"Two hundred in New Hampshire," Gahalowood said. "And at least two in Mount Pleasant, but probably more."

"Is the gas station owner a suspect?"

"Maybe. He could be the one who sent the messages to Alaska."

Lansdane looked doubtful. "But that doesn't explain why we found one of them in Eric's bedroom."

"Because he received one as well," Lauren said. "Perhaps Eric wasn't the author but the recipient."

"So, you think Lewis Jacob sent similar threatening notes to Eric and Alaska?" I asked. "But why?"

"Maybe they had something to feel guilty about," Gahalowood speculated. "Which would explain why Eric never told us the truth about the note we found in his room. He didn't want to incriminate himself any further."

We were about to leave headquarters when an officer contacted us to report that Ricky Positano had been detained in a bar in Rochester. His interview that night would turn out to be significant.

Ricky hadn't fared as badly as Samantha. Comparing the police photos taken when he was arrested previously, which he had been several times, we saw that, although he had certainly aged and his body had grown softer, his hair was still black and he was still perfectly lucid.

"Of course I am," he boasted. "You've been talking to Samantha. I dumped her when she started smoking crack. Crack is the devil. It rots your brain."

"Even so, you had two children with her," Lauren noted.

"Those aren't my kids. Back then, she was sleeping around to get high. Now, no-one wants anything to do with her. She got it into her head that I was their father, can you imagine? I didn't recognize them as my own or anything, but I'm happy to buy them a meal from time to time. I'm good-hearted that way."

"Oh, is that so?" Lauren asked with considerable irony.

Ricky, obviously no stranger to being questioned, responded immediately. "Is that a Mount Pleasant police badge there on your belt? Seems to me you're a little outside your jurisdiction, young lady. Besides, no-one has read me my rights."

"You're not under arrest, Ricky," Gahalowood reminded him. "We'd just like to ask you a few questions."

"I'm listening. Always happy to help where I can."

"Why did Samantha start smoking crack? Because Alaska Sanders was killed?"

"No, we had already left for California when she died. We took a road trip along the Pacific coast. You know, the kind of thing couples do. Besides, I was spending the night in jail after a fight with some bikers."

"I know," Gahalowood said. "I checked. You were in Montecito jail the night of the murder."

"Yeah, for once I didn't go to jail for nothing. Otherwise, I'd have been a suspect."

Ricky immediately appeared to regret his words—he had said either too much or not enough.

"Why would you have been suspected of Alaska's murder?" I asked.

"I was just joking."

"We know you blackmailed Lewis Jacob for ten thousand dollars," Lauren said. "Maybe that's a reason?"

"Look, I know all about your games. You pretend you know everything so I lay all my cards on the table. I want a written guarantee: if I talk, I get immunity."

It was too late to make the request at the prosecutor's office, and we didn't want to delay Ricky's questioning until the following day. Besides, since he wasn't accused of anything, we could sign all the guarantees in the world, and they would commit us to nothing. So Lansdane quickly drafted an official letter that had no legal value but did have the merit of getting Ricky to talk.

"So one Sunday at the end of February, Samantha called me from the gas station. She was in shock. 'Come quick,' she said. 'Someone's trying to blackmail us.'"

*     *     *

*Sunday, February 28, 1999*

Ricky hurried over. Samantha was beside herself. She held up a page with the printed words: I KNOW WHAT YOU DID.

"I found it on the floor in the office."

"Shit," Ricky said. "Who would've done this? Old man Jacob?"

"He was out yesterday."

"So who was it?"

"Alaska," Samantha said. "That bitch is trying to blackmail me."

"Alaska? How does she know? Did you tell her about the ten thousand?"

Samantha didn't admit it, but from the look on her face, Ricky understood that she must have said something. "Shit, shit, Samantha! How can you be so stupid? I was let out on a suspended sentence: you know what that means? If I go down, I'm going to get five years for this. We have to get out of here."

"I don't want to leave," Samantha whimpered.

He took her by the shoulders and shook her. "Alaska might've told someone already. If she doesn't go to the cops, someone else will. I'm not leaving you here alone; you're going to blab and I'm going to get busted. Get your things and call Alaska. I'm going to tell her what'll happen if someone comes looking for me."

Samantha began to cry.

"Stop crying and call her! Damn it!"

"I don't want you to hurt her."

"If she doesn't do anything stupid, she'll be fine."

Hearing Samantha's panicked voice, Alaska rushed to the gas station. Finding Ricky inside the store, she understood what was going on, and it wasn't good. As she stepped through the door, he slapped her hard across the face, and she fell back into a shelf of chocolate bars.

"You bitch, were you planning to inform on me?"

"What are you talking about?" Alaska muttered in shock, rubbing her cheek.

He held up the message. "Did you write this crap?"

Alaska turned pale. "It's not what you think! I swear."

"You think I can't read? What were you hoping for? Money?"

Alaska, in tears, turned to her friend. "Samantha, that message wasn't for you. I swear!"

But all Samantha said in reply was "I left my key on Mr. Jacob's desk. You can give it to him. Tell him I quit."

Ricky and Samantha walked toward the door. "Samantha," Alaska cried out, "let me explain!"

Ricky held up a fist. "Shut the fuck up. Don't come near us again or try to contact us. Understand?"

"That message wasn't for you, Samantha!" Alaska repeated, desperate now. "I printed it yesterday and the printer must have printed it twice. It's not working right!"

"Don't listen to her," Ricky ordered Samantha. "Get your car, we'll meet at the house."

Alaska ran after them as far as the gas pumps, continuing to beg her friend. "When you shut it off, it sometimes prints another copy of the last page. You know that! We told Mr. Jacob about it. You remember, don't you, Samantha? Sam, Sam, wait!"

As Samantha was getting in her car, Alaska collapsed to her knees and cried out, "That goddamn printer, I should have taken it back to Duty's!"

Those were the last words Samantha heard from Alaska's mouth. They haunted her to the end of her life.

And that's how we found out Alaska wasn't being threatened. She was the one who was doing the threatening.

# 28

## *The Poison Pen*

*Concord, New Hampshire*
*Wednesday, July 21, 2010*

The investigation was about to take a significant turn. Bit by bit, we were gradually assembling the puzzle whose final piece we had missed up to that point. Gahalowood called it "the detonator": the spark that caused a chain reaction.

Lewis Jacob confirmed that Ricky Positano's story was accurate. The printer he had bought for the gas station wasn't working correctly and made unwanted additional copies. This led to an event that had been buried in his memory. Shortly after Samantha unexpectedly quit, Alaska got frustrated with the printer because it printed the same sheet twice. He had never seen her so angry, and because anger is contagious, he took it back to Duty's. After endless delays, "that crook, Neil Rogers," finally admitted it was part of a defective lot and replaced it free of charge.

We now knew that Alaska was the author of the anonymous notes. The messages found at the apartment and in her pocket had yet to be delivered to their recipients. Had she targeted several people? Or just one? And was that why she was murdered?

We also knew that Eric Donovan had received one of the messages. What was he concealing that was so important that he kept quiet about it for all those years?

"I can't talk about it," he said when we asked him at the state prison. "It would incriminate me by giving me a motive to murder Alaska."

"How many messages did Alaska give you?" I asked.

"Two. The first time, I found it on my car's windshield; the second, in my parents' mailbox."

"And when did you find out that Alaska had written those messages? Before or after your arrest?"

"You see" Eric sighed, not daring to reply. "I get the impression that the truth is only going to make things worse for me."

"Enough with the lies!" Patricia Widsmith said. "You have to tell us everything now!"

"I found out before her death."

"When?" Gahalowood asked.

"Two weeks earlier."

Patricia put her head in her hands.

"See?" Eric yelled. "It's just making it worse! All I want is to get out of this place."

"Then tell us the truth," Gahalowood ordered. "When exactly did you discover that Alaska was the author of those notes? I want to know everything, every little detail."

Eric lowered his eyes before responding. "That argument in the supermarket parking lot. It was Monday, March twenty-second; we talked about it the other day. When I told you what happened, I wasn't telling the truth exactly."

"You lied to us?" Patricia exploded. "You lied to us again?"

"I didn't lie, I just invented a few things. We never discussed the fact that Alaska was leaving Walter. She never mentioned it. I made up that story on the spot to avoid telling you the real reason for our argument."

"Everything on the table! Now!" Gahalowood cried. "I'm this far away from letting you rot in here for the rest of your life."

\*　　　\*　　　\*

*The truth about March 22, 1999*

It was early afternoon. Eric was enjoying his day off, alone at his parents' place. From the living room, he noticed a car stop briefly in front of the house. He heard the metallic creak of the mailbox as it opened and closed. Curious, he went over to the window just in time to see Walter's black Ford Taurus speeding away. He was surprised. Walter had left the day before in his father's pickup for a convention in Quebec. Eric stepped outside, opened the mailbox, and found a sheet of paper with the printed words:

I KNOW WHAT YOU DID

His heart began to beat faster. He had already received a similar message a week earlier, which he had found on his car's windshield. Suddenly, he understood: it was Sally Carrey! She was getting back at him for his blackmail. She must have borrowed her son's car to throw him off the scent.

Eric ran into the house to get his car keys, and then took off, determined to catch up with Sally. When he had moved back to Mount Pleasant the previous fall, he had feared that being so near her might cause problems. Turns out, he wasn't wrong. He had bitterly regretted his behavior at the time, but now, even more so. He had to find a way to nip this in the bud. With this second message, Sally was getting bolder. Placing it in the family mailbox meant she was willing to risk shaming him publicly, ensuring his parents would ask questions.

He drove like a madman through the residential neighborhood. At the first intersection, there was no Ford in sight, so he decided to go straight. It was the right decision: he saw the black Taurus as it headed for Route 21. He decided to follow it at a reasonable distance. When it stopped, he would confront her and demand she put a stop to it. But the car didn't stop; it passed the gas station, then the intersection leading to Grey Beach, before turning onto Route 28, heading north.

Eric kept right behind her, and twenty minutes later, he found himself in the parking lot of the Conway shopping center. He watched the Ford park, then did the same and jumped out of his car to confront the driver. To his amazement it wasn't Sally Carrey but Alaska.

His discovery left him weak in the knees. Alaska went into the supermarket. She hadn't seen him. Eric waited for her by the exit. When she came out with her groceries, he stepped into her path and said, "*I know what you did!*"

She shivered, making an effort to maintain her composure. "Oh, Eric, you scared me. What brings you out here?"

"*I know what you did,*" he repeated, waving the piece of paper.

She avoided his eyes and tried to slip past him, but Eric blocked her escape. "You think you can just walk away like that? You better explain yourself."

"I don't know what you're talking about, Eric."

"I know you're the one who's been delivering these messages. The other day I found one on my windshield, today in my parents' mailbox. If you have a problem with me, tell me to my face."

*    *    *

"The rest is just like I told you," Eric explained. "We argued about the messages. Then the manager showed up, and when he said he was going to call the police, Alaska panicked. She began to yell, 'Shit, he's going to call the cops! He's going to call the cops!' and ran to her car, leaving her groceries. I didn't know what was going on with her; I thought she just wanted to cut our conversation short. I grabbed her bags and caught up with her as she was getting into the car. I opened the trunk to load her groceries, which also meant she couldn't back up. She was crying and yelling, 'Let me leave, Eric!' She was clearly in no condition to drive: she was going to have an accident and I didn't want that. So I got behind the wheel to take her to Mount Pleasant. Then the policeman arrived. He talked to us for a while, and then I took her back home. Like I said the other day, when we got there, I asked her about the sweater I had lent Walter when we went fishing. Maybe it was from all the emotion, but she started yelling at me: 'Is that all you can think about after what just happened? Go ask Walter.' And I replied, 'Do you really want me to call Walter and tell him what just happened?' That's it. Now you know everything."

"Hold on," Gahalowood interjected. "You said Alaska gave you those messages, but you never told us what she was accusing you of."

"She accused me of killing one of her girlfriends."

A stunned silence descended on the visiting room.

"Killing who?" I asked.

"My girlfriend at the time. You know how I told you that I was dumped by my girlfriend and I took it so hard that I left Salem."

"Yeah," Gahalowood agreed. "Go on."

"She didn't really leave me . . . she killed herself. She had personal problems, serious problems. She was outwardly a very beautiful woman but in reality, she was deeply disturbed. Her suicide came as a terrible shock. Even if things weren't that serious between us, her death really shook me up. I kept asking myself if I could've prevented it. I had to leave Salem no matter what. But where would I go? So I went back to live with my parents. At the time, all I wanted was to forget. I had never told anyone about her, except Walter. To avoid my parents' questions, I pretended I'd gotten fired. And after Alaska's murder, when you began to question me about why I came back, I mentioned my father's cancer. I was afraid I would get mixed up in Alaska's death because of the messages she had given me. So I told myself it was better not to mention Eleanor's suicide."

Lauren, Gahalowood, and I looked at one another. "Eleanor Lowell?" Gahalowood asked.

"Yes," Eric said, "Eleanor Lowell."

"What's going on?" Patricia asked, who had noticed our reaction. "Have I missed something?"

"It came up last Friday night, at Lauren's place," Gahalowood replied. "The young woman who disappeared: the verdict was she drowned herself."

"Yes, I remember now you mention it."

"Eric," I asked, "when did Alaska leave that first note on your windshield?"

"A few weeks before the second. I'd say it was early March."

I turned to Gahalowood. "The dates match. That's when Samantha Fraser found the duplicate message at the gas station."

It was Lauren's turn to question her brother: "When you say Alaska accused you of killing Eleanor, did she suspect you of having murdered her, then making it look like a suicide?"

"No, she meant it figuratively. Eleanor was fragile. Alaska accused me of mistreating her psychologically. Obviously, she was wrong."

"There's something I'm not getting," I said. "If Eleanor committed suicide in late August 1998 and Alaska suspected you were responsible, why did she wait until the following March to start delivering the messages?"

"Alaska knew that Eleanor and I had dated because Eleanor told her. I found out around Christmas 1998, one night when I went out to grab a beer at the National Anthem with Walter and Alaska. I remember it was during the holidays because we were wearing stupid red Christmas hats. Alaska decided she had to find me a girlfriend, and she pointed out all the girls passing by, telling me, 'She's not bad, right?' I told her I wasn't into it. She said that everyone was into it once in a while. So I told her about my relationship with Eleanor and how deeply her suicide had affected me. That's when Alaska admitted she already knew about it. I was surprised to hear that Eleanor had spoken to her about us. About two months later, Eleanor's mother got in touch with Alaska. She'd found something and she wanted to talk to her about it."

*     *     *

*March 22, 1999*

After the argument at the supermarket, Alaska slowly calmed down on the way to Mount Pleasant. They drove in silence for a while, then Eric asked her, "You okay?"

"I'm okay."

"Why did you get so hysterical when the manager said he was going to call the cops?"

Alaska hesitated before replying. "I . . . I don't know. I panicked. I was afraid you'd tell them about the messages."

*     *     *

I interrupted Eric: "We now know that Alaska was really afraid of being linked with the robbery at her parents' house, when a cop was seriously injured."

"Yes, thanks, Writer!" Gahalowood groaned. "Eric, please go on."

Eric picked up where he had left off.

*     *     *

*March 22, 1999*

Alaska hesitated before replying. "I . . . I don't know. I panicked. I was afraid you'd tell them about the messages."

"Now that you've calmed down, maybe you can explain to me why you think I drove Eleanor to suicide."

"Her mother got in touch with me a month ago. She wanted to talk to me. She came to see me in Mount Pleasant."

*     *     *

*February 22, 1999*

Alaska had agreed to meet Maria Lowell, Eleanor's mother, at the Season.

"It's good to see you again, Alaska."

"Good to see you too, Mrs. Lowell. I think about you a lot—you and Eleanor."

Maria Lowell smiled sadly. "Life goes by quickly, you know. We think we can catch up with time, but time catches up with us. I spoke to your mother . . . she said you were having problems . . ."

"It's complicated."

"Sometimes it's less complicated than you think. That's what I tried to get Eleanor to understand. But nothing seemed to help; she couldn't shake those feelings."

"I know."

"She had her whole life ahead of her. Her father and I kept telling her that. But we were powerless to do anything. Alaska, just remember, you're not alone. Even if you feel like you are. Ask for help—promise me that if you're feeling depressed, you'll talk to someone about it. It's not an admission of weakness: it takes courage to find your way out of those feelings."

Maria Lowell appeared to be very emotional. Alaska, who didn't fully understand the reason for her getting in touch, said to her, "You know I'm happy to see you again, Mrs. Lowell, but did you come all the way here just to tell me that?"

"No, dear," she replied with a sad smile. "I came because I just found out that something was bothering Eleanor and she wouldn't tell me about it. She kept everything bottled up inside her, and I think that's what led her to kill herself. And now I want to try to fix it. Because it's never too late."

With those words, she took out a notebook.

"What's that?" Alaska asked.

"I finally decided to straighten up Eleanor's room. I found her journal. Some passages are very dark, others very beautiful. It took me a while to go through it. And I found this part, which I want to show you."

Alaska started to read.

*I thought he loved me but mostly he loves to make me suffer. On July 4, he promised we would go to dinner at a restaurant to celebrate. As I was getting ready, he said to me, "Don't get angry, Eleanor, but it's better we call it off. You understand, it's risky to be seen in public . . . the age difference and all that. People are going to talk." We stayed at his place. He ordered lobster. I barely ate anything. I wanted to show him I was sad. He looked at my plate and said, "Why are you behaving like this? You know perfectly well why I had to cancel our dinner reservation. Believe me, I'm just as disappointed. It's awful to have to watch you sulk over the slightest thing when I've worked so hard to satisfy your every wish." He thinks I'm sulking. He doesn't see how this affects me. That I desperately need him. That he's the only one who has the power to make me happy. Sometimes, I get the feeling he likes to play with my emotions and just drive me down. He feels he can control me that way.*

"I'd like to find this man, Alaska. I think it's because of him that Eleanor committed suicide. Do you know who he was? I've asked all of Eleanor's other friends, but they couldn't tell me anything. Eleanor told them she was seeing an older man, but she never mentioned his name. Do you know anything about him? You're my last hope."

"No, nothing at all," Alaska replied.

"You're sure? He drove a blue car—you remember anyone with a blue car? Look, she wrote it here, at the end of this poem. I'm sure she's talking about him."

Maria Lowell then showed Alaska a short excerpt that ended with the following lines:

*When I climb into his blue car, I wonder where my heart will lead.*
*When I see his blue car, I wonder if the day will be happy or sad.*

After a lengthy silence, Alaska shook her head. "I have no idea."

Maria Lowell looked desperate. "Does a gray house mean anything to you? In another entry, she talks about a gray house and red maples."

But Alaska wasn't listening. She was someplace else. She continued to shake her head.

"No idea, I'm sorry. I really have no idea what that's about."

A month after the meeting with Maria Lowell, Alaska said to Eric as he drove the black Taurus back to Mount Pleasant: "I told Mrs. Lowell I had no idea. I covered for you, I don't even know why. Afterward, it started to bother me. If you really did cause Eleanor's suicide, you have to pay for it. That's why I sent those messages."

"But I didn't!" Eric protested. "How can you think such a thing?"

"Come on, Eric. The blue car . . . I remember the blue Mustang you had in Salem. I thought it was strange when you got rid of it."

"I sold it when I moved back home. My neighbor kept asking to buy it and he offered me a great price. It came just in time too. I'd quit my job and wasn't about to turn down the money. I bought a used Pontiac for half the money and put the rest in the bank. That's how I was able to come up with the ten thousand dollars. It didn't just fall from the sky."

Alaska seemed troubled by his response. "I don't know if I should believe you."

"Wait. Eleanor mentioned July Fourth, right? The only July Fourth we could have spent together was last year, and I wasn't around. I was with Walter. I used the day off to go camping and fishing. Besides, Eleanor told me she was going out with her girlfriends. I remember because at first I suggested she go camping with me. I thought it would be nice. But she turned me down. You know, Alaska, if there's anyone who was suffering in that couple, it was me. I'm the one who was mistreated. I was attached to her, but she didn't care. I was just a part-time fling: she ignored me when she felt like it. You're mistaken if you think I could've pushed her over the edge. In any case, like I said, I wasn't with her on July Fourth."

Alaska, realizing she was getting nowhere with her questions, replied, "That means there was someone else in her life."

*       *       *

"I never found out who it was," Eric said. "After that, everything happened so fast. Two weeks later, Alaska was dead. I was arrested and ground up in the nightmarish whirlwind of evidence against me—my sweater, the printer, the message. They were already saying I killed Alaska. I didn't

413

want them to also accuse me of pushing Eleanor to commit suicide. Even worse, my only alibi for July Fourth was Walter, and he was dead. I felt that anything I said would only make things worse. So I kept quiet, and stayed that way for so long I couldn't break out."

Patricia was on the verge of tears. "If you'd told me, I could have helped you! I would have been able to get you out."

"Nobody could do anything for me! Things have only changed now because Lewis Jacob and Samantha Fraser spoke up. But they were around back then! You screwed up the investigation, Sergeant. How did you manage that?"

There was a profound silence in the room. Then Gahalowood spoke: "Patricia, you should submit the papers for his release to the judge. I'll contact the prosecutor's office and tell them we have new information. Eric should be out of here in the next forty-eight hours."

Within a few days, the entire case against Eric had collapsed. Sally Carrey confirmed that he had, in fact, lent his sweater to Walter; the printer used for the threatening messages was the one once owned by Lewis Jacob; and the messages hadn't been delivered to Alaska but by her.

Upon leaving the prison, Lauren wanted to celebrate the good news: "I'm inviting all of you to lunch." But Gahalowood declined. He was feeling pretty glum. He was angry with himself for the way he had handled the 1999 investigation. I suggested he and I go to a place he was very fond of—a small run-down shack by the side of the road that made the best hamburgers, which you ate in the open air, seated at wooden picnic tables. He refused that as well. "Thanks, but I need to see Helen." I accompanied him to the cemetery. He knelt by her gravestone and placed a hand on it. After a moment's thought, he said to me, "I think I'm going to resign."

"Lansdane will reject your request," I replied. "Besides, you can't quit. You're a great cop!"

"I'm not talking to you; I'm talking to Helen. It's my fault the guy was locked up for eleven years!"

"And thanks to your efforts, a legal error is going to be corrected," I replied. "Without you, Eric Donovan would've spent the rest of his life in prison."

"Why do you keep hanging around, Writer?"

I didn't let up. "It's not your fault, Sergeant. Donovan wound up in prison because Vance forced a confession from Walter Carrey and Kazinsky kept quiet and let it happen. Those two cowards preferred to take their own lives rather than assume responsibility!"

Suddenly Gahalowood looked at me strangely. "What the hell . . ."

"What's up with you?"

"Of course, it's obvious!"

Clearly, something was up. "For God's sake, what is it?"

"In 2002, shortly after Eric was convicted, Kazinsky was hit by that car, which left him paralyzed. At the time, Kazinsky was the only person alive who knew that Walter's confession had been coerced, right?"

"Right."

"Wrong! Someone else knew that Walter hadn't killed Alaska. The murderer. It was so close to being the perfect crime. The police thought they had the culprit. Walter Carrey was dead. Vance was dead. Eric Donovan, broken by the system, was forced to plead guilty to avoid the death penalty. But there was still someone out there who knew how Walter's confession was extracted: Kazinsky. He's the grain of sand that could've gummed up the wheels. So he had to be eliminated. Kazinsky didn't get run over by accident! Alaska's murderer tried to kill him. How could we have missed that?"

# 29

# *Release*

*Concord, New Hampshire*
*Friday, July 23, 2010*

A crowd of journalists was gathered before the entrance of the state prison. The door opened and a beaming Patricia Widsmith appeared. She turned and addressed someone standing behind her. She appeared to be coaxing a timid child. Then Eric Donovan appeared, taking his first steps toward freedom.

The cameras and microphones immediately turned toward Eric amid a confusion of rapid-fire questions. Terrified by the welcoming committee, he started to withdraw; then he saw Lauren and his parents and threw himself into their arms. After allowing the media to film the reunion, which would do much to sway public opinion, Patricia Widsmith began to speak, surrounded by the Donovans.

"Today, a family is finally reunited. After eleven years of struggle and suffering, Eric Donovan can go home. Though he is now a free man, Eric leaves behind, forever buried in this sordid prison, eleven years of his life. Eleven years stolen from an innocent man. An eleven-year nightmare of punishment and daily violence. Eleven years of hell. Eric Donovan was twenty-nine, with his whole life ahead of him, when he was ground up by our diseased legal system, which condemned an innocent man after a slipshod investigation and a hasty trial. At the time of his arrest, Eric was subjected to unbearable pressure by the police and the prosecutor's office, who forced him to plead guilty by threatening him with the death penalty if he dared to assert his innocence. Death, or life in prison—that was the choice Eric faced. And now the so-called overwhelming evidence against him has collapsed piece by piece: his sweater, found stained with the victim's blood near the scene of the crime, which a witness only recently confirmed was lent to a friend by Eric—as he had always claimed. Or his printer, which the investigators claimed had been used to print threatening messages. They asserted it had a *unique* defect, before they realized, only in the past few days, that it was part of a lot of two hundred printers with the same problem. In 1999 the police interpreted the evidence as they saw fit—they needed a culprit, and they created one. If you're shocked by my words, understand that Eric Donovan's case is, unfortunately, not unusual. Throughout the country, innocent men and women are spending their lives on death row. How many cases like Eric Donovan's will it take for the authorities to open their eyes? And while a global movement has, over the years, succeeded in abolishing the death penalty in many other countries, the US Supreme Court has since ruled it constitutional We can only suppose its reaffirmation was politically expedient, given that nearly 60 percent are in favor of it."

By addressing the media, Patricia was fulfilling her role as Eric's lawyer. But he wasn't yet officially exonerated. The prosecutor's office acknowledged that the weight of evidence warranted his release, but they did not feel the need to call for a new trial. It would all depend on the final results of the police investigation.

At around the same time, a few miles from the prison, another press conference was being held at state police headquarters. On a stage facing a crowd of journalists, Chief Lansdane announced the latest developments in the Alaska Sanders case. He broke the news about Walter Carrey's statement being forcibly obtained by a police officer who then committed suicide. Lansdane assured the crowd that they would spare no effort in resolving the case and that the incriminated officer would receive a posthumous dishonorable discharge and be stripped of his decorations. Lansdane was fulfilling his role as well, promoting the idea of an impartial police force, one that was above suspicion and had no hesitation about cleaning its own house. He wound things up by acknowledging the welcome cooperation of the Mount Pleasant police force and inviting Chief Mitchell, who was there for the occasion, to join him onstage for a well-rehearsed round of self-congratulation. Gahalowood and I were present for all this, watching from the back of the room. We listened to Lansdane with one ear, while following Patricia Widsmith's press conference on my mobile phone.

Patricia highlighted the failures of justice; Lansdane celebrated co-operation among the country's police forces for the ultimate triumph of Good over Evil. The truth lay somewhere in the middle. The day before, Gahalowood and I had gone to see Sally and George Carrey, then Robbie and Donna Sanders, to inform them of the situation and let them know what was about to be officially revealed. Robbie Sanders said to us, "I don't know if the hardest part of all this is having to relive our daughter's death all over again or the impression that we're never going to find out what happened." George Carrey replied, "So, our son was forced to admit to a crime he didn't commit before being murdered by the police." He demanded answers. I promised he would get them. Gahalowood simply said, "Justice will be served," a statement whose full context I wasn't aware of at the time. Leaving the Sanders and Carrey homes, I wondered how one overcame such grief. How does one repair a broken life? I still thought about my cousins, Woody and Hillel, and what had happened to them, and I concluded that we can't really fix life; we can only rebuild it by giving it meaning.

At the conclusion of the press conference, we ran into Chief Mitchell as he stepped down from the stage. "Thanks," he said to us.

"For what?" Gahalowood asked. "Putting you on television?"

Chief Mitchell was quick to change the subject. "Lauren isn't here, is she?"

"No, she's with her brother. You know, she's one helluva cop."

"I know, I'm the one who recruited her. I don't know if you've been told yet, Sergeant, but I'm retiring in a few months. I'm going to recommend that Lauren replace me."

"Your deputy isn't going to be happy," Gahalowood noted.

"I'm aware of that, and that's why I mentioned it. If you and Lansdane could send me a letter of recommendation about Lauren, I could add it to the file. She doesn't know yet."

Gahalowood agreed and we walked away. "Chief Mitchell's not as dumb as he looks," I said.

Gahalowood didn't respond and I realized he wasn't listening.

"What's up, Sergeant?"

"It's Eric. I led the questioning after his arrest. I can imagine it was a traumatic experience for him, and the fear of prison can push you to confess to anything to win clemency and sympathy from the investigators. That's old news. Except, Eric didn't admit anything: he just remained silent. At first, he claimed he was innocent; then, when the evidence seemed to pile up against him, he clammed up."

"You have nothing to blame yourself for, Sergeant."

"I'm not blaming myself: on the contrary. What I'm trying to say is that I shouldn't have questioned Eric. I was exhausted. Overcome by all sorts of emotions. I was a father for the second time, my partner had just been murdered—at least, that's what I believed. Lansdane wanted to send me home, but I refused. I should've let it go, given it to someone else. I was in no shape to question Eric. I did it in a rage of despair, but I didn't squeeze him too hard, not at all. So why did he remain silent? Something's not right here. When the prosecutor's office decided to jail him, I recall that I was worried about having to stand witness at his trial. The defense would have had no trouble tearing me to pieces—I should never have been in that interrogation room after everything I'd been through. But I didn't have to testify, because Eric pleaded guilty. But why?"

"Lauren told us—he was afraid of getting the death penalty."

Gahalowood didn't appear convinced. "I wonder if he was scared we might find out something else about him."

"Such as . . . ?"

"A case within a case. I keep thinking about that blue car Alaska mentioned. The one that suggests that Eric was the man in Eleanor's poem. In overturning the proof that pointed to Eric back then, we found another motive: he drove Eleanor to commit suicide, something Alaska discovered when she spoke with Eleanor's mother. She sends him anonymous messages; he finds out and confronts her. Then he tries to convince her he had no part in it, but he's still afraid she might warn Eleanor's mother. So he kills Alaska to preserve his secret."

"You're forgetting the note found in Alaska's pocket. It wasn't intended for Eric since he already knew she was the one delivering them."

"Eric told us he received two notes, right? We found one on him at the time. An oversight on his part, according to him. He thought he had gotten rid of it, but it was left at the back of a drawer. But what happened to the other one? He could have put it in Alaska's pocket after killing her to lead the police to believe that she was the victim of a blackmailer. As for the sweater, when he puts Alaska's groceries in the trunk of the car at the supermarket in Conway, he sees it. He then deliberately asks Alaska about it on the sidewalk so that people can overhear them: 'Where's the sweater I lent Walter?' As he expected, Alaska tells him to get lost and he returns to swipe it from the trunk, most likely at night, taking advantage of the fact that no-one locks their car in Mount Pleasant. It would've been the perfect crime. But Eric didn't realize that blackmailing Sally Carrey would backfire and Walter would point the finger at him to get revenge, making him the focus of our investigation."

"Sergeant, do you think we let out a guilty man?"

"I don't know, but I'm worried. And there's something else we never resolved: the debris from the broken taillight found in the woods. Was it from Walter Carrey's car? Is it a coincidence that his taillight just happened to break the night of the murder?"

"Let's suppose Carrey was at the National Anthem at the time of death, as the photo Lauren found shows. Someone could've grabbed the keys from his apartment and made their way to Grey Beach in his car. After Alaska is killed, the murderer breaks a taillight in their hurry to get away. When they return to Mount Pleasant, they park the car where they found it and return the keys. Meanwhile, Walter is still at the bar. And who would know he was there? Someone who was with him earlier . . ."

"Eric Donovan," Gahalowood said.

"Exactly."

"Damn. You know, it kind of makes sense."

A strange phenomenon was unfolding before us: the farther we advanced in the investigation, the more we were troubled by Eric Donovan. As Gahalowood put it, he was the "culprit who kept coming back." As the evidence against him was refuted, new and disturbing information came to light. It was as if everything were pointing in his direction. Had we moved too quickly in proclaiming his innocence? Had we undermined our investigation by assuming that the fact that Walter Carrey's statement was coerced necessarily invalidated Eric's guilt?

Either Eric was indeed Alaska's murderer or he was a marvelously well-framed dupe. "As long as we have the slightest doubt about Eric," Gahalowood warned, "we're going to be fixated on him and that's going to blind us to everything else." But now we had a way to definitively exonerate him: find out whether there was anything more to Kazinsky's accident. If we could determine that Kazinsky was run over deliberately and we could establish a connection between that and the Alaska Sanders case, we would then have real proof of Eric's innocence because he was in prison at the time.

So that same day, we drove to Barrington, New Hampshire, to question Nicholas Kazinsky's widow. It was strange to return to that house. Gahalowood had met Sienna Kazinsky only once before, at Vance's funeral. When she found us on her doorstep, she smiled. "Perry, what brings you here?"

"Hello, Sienna, I want to talk to you."

She stared at me, realized who I was, and immediately understood the reason for our visit. "You're here about the Sanders case, is that it?"

We sat in the same living room where her husband had revealed all that had happened in the interrogation room on that terrifying night of April 6, 1999.

"Nicholas often spoke about you when he was on the force," Sienna said to Gahalowood. "He liked you a lot. After the accident, he felt very alone. I'm sure a visit from you would have made him happy. It's a shame you only come now when he's dead."

From those words, we understood that Mrs. Kazinsky was unaware of our visit several hours before her husband killed himself. Maybe it was better that way.

"Why didn't you come to his funeral?" she asked.

Gahalowood shrugged. "I should have."

After a brief silence, Sienna said, without any prompting: "When I got back to the house that day, he wasn't in the living room or the kitchen. I called, but he didn't answer. I found him in his office; blood was everywhere. He'd shot himself with his revolver. I hated that gun. He said it was for our safety. He would say, 'Alarms are fine, but guns are better.' On his desk, I found a note."

> *My dear Sienna,*
> *It's finally all over.*
> *I love you and I'm waiting calmly for you in paradise.*
> *Nick*

Sienna rose and stood before the window. She turned her back to us, exactly as her husband had done. "Nick liked to sit here, watching the street. He could spend hours like that. In the weeks after his accident, I didn't think I could handle being a caregiver. Now that he's no longer around, I realize that it's living without him I can't bear."

"Sienna," Gahalowood asked, "why did Nicholas kill himself?"

"Why did Nick suddenly give up? I can't help wondering if there was something he didn't tell me. The day he died, he had visitors. I know because I found three cups and a plate of my cookies in the living room, which he always put out when he had people over. I don't know who came by that day, maybe some old pals from work. Too many memories, a moment of despair? I'll never know. But tell me, what brings you here? Because this isn't just a courtesy call."

"I don't want to beat around the bush, Sienna: I'm wondering about Nick's accident—if it was really an accident or if someone might have been trying to kill him."

"But who would want to kill him?"

"That's exactly what we want to find out. Maybe Nick had sensitive information about the Sanders case. Have you heard that Eric Donovan, who's been in prison for Alaska's murder for eleven years, was released this morning?"

"Yes, I saw it on the news. What's that got to do with Nicholas?"

"Nick told me his accident happened on January thirtieth, 2002."

"Yes, that's right."

"That's a few days after Eric Donovan was sent to prison for life for Alaska's murder."

"That's doesn't prove much," Sienna said. "And then, if someone had really wanted to kill my husband, why not finish the job after the accident?"

"Too risky," I said. "It would have looked suspicious. The police would have immediately concluded that it was a homicide. They would have begun following the trail, maybe all the way back to Alaska Sanders. The murderer had to leave it be."

"You were working on that case too, Perry," Sienna noted. "Why didn't anyone try to kill you?"

"Because, unlike Nick, I wasn't present for the so-called confession of the suspect we had arrested. But Alaska's murderer knew that his statement had been coerced. By eliminating Nicholas, they would be getting rid of the last person who could've revealed the truth."

"They talked about that on the television just a while ago," Sienna said. "They said that a policeman had gotten a confession by force . . ."

"That policeman was Matt Vance," Gahalowood revealed. "Vance forced the suspect to confess to a crime he hadn't committed."

Sienna Kazinsky was horrified. "Is Nick mixed up in all this? Is that why he committed suicide?"

"An investigation has been opened, Sienna. But I don't know what's going to happen."

"You should leave him in peace: he's dead! Do something, Perry!"

"I'm very sorry, Sienna."

She looked at us with suspicion. Then she cried out, "It was you! The cups I found the day he died: it was you who came here to fill his head with all that nonsense! I didn't realize it at first, but you said Nick told you his accident happened on January thirtieth, 2002. If you had been in touch with him recently, Nick would have told me. That means you were his last visitors!"

"Sienna . . ." Gahalowood implored.

She was trembling with rage. "Get out, both of you! Get the hell out of my house! His death is on your conscience."

Gahalowood wanted to explain, but Sienna Kazinsky was far too angry to listen to reason. I took the sergeant by the arm and we left, followed by Sienna's insults and recriminations, which drew unwanted attention. Her nosy neighbor must have called the cops, because by the time we got to the car, one came racing down the street. It was the same officer who had stopped me back in June when I was watching Kazinsky's house.

"You again?" he said.

"You're right on time," I replied. "We're heading to the station. Tell your chief we're on our way."

*

Gahalowood and I met with Captain Martin Grove, head of the Barrington police force. "What brings you here this time, Mr. Goldman?"

"Questions about Nicholas Kazinsky."

"About his suicide?"

"About his accident. We'd like to know who handled the investigation."

Because Chief Lansdane had personally come to get me at the station in June, I had a certain amount of credibility in Captain Grove's eyes. But he had no desire to make life difficult for himself with just a few hours to go until the weekend.

"It's Friday, you know. You couldn't come back Monday?"

"We're not going anywhere until you give us the information we need."

The case had been assigned to detective Paul Ricco of the local police. He was off that day, but the captain told him to come down to the station immediately. Half an hour later, Ricco arrived wearing shorts and sandals.

"As I recall, there wasn't much in the file," he said, as he accompanied Gahalowood and me to the basement, where the archives were kept. He located a thin folder. Gahalowood found a small table in the corner of the room and spread out the handful of documents.

For the most part, the report told us what we already knew: early one winter morning Kazinsky was out for his daily jog around the neighborhood. It was still dark and it was raining. He was bothered by the garbage bins on the sidewalk, so he decided to run in the street. Right before he reached the Campbell Street intersection, he was hit by a car coming down Norris Street.

"You see, it's pretty sparse," Ricco explained. "We didn't have much. The only witness was the driver of a school bus that had just left the depot."

According to the transcript of the interview, the bus driver had seen a fast-moving vehicle race past him.

It was 6:14. I was driving down Campbell Street. I was approaching the intersection when a car came racing down Norris Street at high speed. Without lights! It didn't slow down at the stop sign and went right through the intersection. Luckily, I drive slowly, especially with the road the way it was, all iced up. I had time to hit the brakes, but it was a close call. Good thing there were no kids on the bus. I was in shock, but I tried to get a look at the plate. Easier said than done, especially at that speed. You try to take it all in, so you can remember it later, and in the end, you don't catch anything. That happens a lot with witnesses, right? All I remember is that it was a Massachusetts plate. It was white and even though it was dark, I could clearly see "Massachusetts" on it. That struck me, I don't know why, I guess because I was expecting to see a New Hampshire plate. I didn't have time to read the numbers, the car was gone in a flash. And you couldn't see a damn thing.

"A Massachusetts plate," I said, raising my eyes from the document.
"Is this all you have?" Gahalowood asked.

"It's all there," Ricco confirmed. "We closed the case because we didn't have anything else to go on. We wanted to bring in the state police, but they would've laughed in our faces. Last year, there were more than 650,000 hit-and-run incidents in the United States; more than 100,000 people were injured and more than a thousand died."

"Nothing you can recall that you might not have put in the file?" Gahalowood insisted. "A small detail even. It could be important."

"Well, there were the calls from the Nut," Detective Ricco said.

"The Nut?"

"That's what we call one of Kazinsky's neighbors. She lives just opposite. She spends all her time looking out the window and calls the station for any little thing. A real pain in the ass."

"What did she want?"

"She said she'd seen a blue car parked for a long time in front of

Kazinsky's house before six in the morning on the day of the accident. The car finally left, and she decided not to call the police. Or, at least, not until she heard what had happened. You see what I mean about useless information."

"A blue car?" Gahalowood repeated. "You're sure?"

"It's what she told me. Ask her, she'll be happy to talk to you."

Captain Grove and Detective Ricco were delighted to see us walk out the door, and Kazinsky's neighbor was equally pleased when we stopped by to visit. She stared admiringly at Gahalowood's police badge when he pulled it out.

"Something's going on at the Kazinskys'," she observed, as she invited us in.

"Yes," Gahalowood said. "In fact, we wanted to ask about Nicholas Kazinsky's accident, when he was seriously injured. Detective Ricco tells us you saw something suspicious that day."

"Well, finally someone believes me! Those big lugs say I'm crazy because I call them all the time, but that's what they're there for, isn't it?"

"Absolutely," Gahalowood replied. "What did you see that day?"

"About six in the morning, a blue car was parked on my side of the street. It was there for at least twenty minutes. I know because I was up early and I like to see what's going on outside. There was someone in the car, that's for sure. But it was dark and I couldn't see them clearly. I could see a silhouette at the wheel. I would have gone outside to get a closer look, but it had started to rain and was very cold. So I went to make myself some tea and said to myself as I went back to the window, 'If the car is still there, I'm calling the cops.'"

"And you did?" I asked.

"No, because when I got back, it was gone."

"You said you couldn't see anything outside that morning, but you said the car was blue . . ." Gahalowood interjected.

"It was partly lit by a streetlight. That's how I could make out there was a person inside. It was a blue car, I'd swear to it."

According to the neighbor, the mysterious car had left at a little after six in the morning. That was about the time Kazinsky went out jogging. If this was the same car that hit Kazinsky, it had followed him for a while, waiting for the right moment. When Kazinsky left the sidewalk to avoid the garbage cans, the car hit him before driving away at breakneck speed. A blue car with Massachusetts plates.

"A blue car, like the one Eleanor Lowell's mother mentioned," I said when Gahalowood and I were back on the road. He nodded and took up the baton.

"The night of Alaska's murder, a witness saw a blue car with Massachusetts plates driving fast up Main Street in Mount Pleasant. Because the description matched Alaska's car, we always assumed it was her heading for Grey Beach right before she was murdered. But in reality, she was already dead. It was the murderer coming back from the beach! That same murderer also tried to eliminate Kazinsky. Because the one flaw in the perfect murder of Alaska Sanders was that Kazinsky knew that Walter's confession had been coerced."

We finally had proof of Eric Donovan's innocence: he had the perfect alibi—he was in prison at the time Kazinsky had been run down.

Who was this elusive shadow who sowed death from a blue car? Was there a connection with Eleanor Lowell? Because the file on Kazinsky's accident was basically empty and the evidence in the Alaska Sanders case had us going around in circles, we decided to look into the death of Eleanor Lowell.

What had happened to her the night of August 30, 1998? Did she commit suicide? Or had another perfect murder been orchestrated, with a trap set for Eric Donovan? It was looking more and more like it was all connected.

# 30

## *The Life and Death of Eleanor Lowell*

*Salem, Massachusetts*
*Saturday, July 24, 2010*

What was the definitive connection between Eleanor Lowell and the Alaska Sanders case? The answer had to be found in Salem, where Lauren, Gahalowood, and I headed the following morning to question Eleanor's parents.

Gahalowood and I were finishing our breakfast on the terrace of the hotel waiting for Lauren, when Patricia Widsmith arrived. She stood at our table, looking somewhat timid, something I had never seen before, and said with a shy smile: "Thank you, thank you both. You've given freedom to a man the world had abandoned. Yesterday, during the press conference, I was a bit harsh. I should have thanked you publicly. I didn't, and I regret it."

"Don't worry about it," Gahalowood reassured her. "Sergeant Vance should have been off the force by then. That's what happens when no-one takes responsibility."

"Well, you've certainly lived up to yours," Patricia said.

"Will you have some coffee?"

"Gladly." She pulled up a chair and sat down.

"What brings you to Mount Pleasant so early in the morning?" Gahalowood asked.

"I wanted to see Eric."

"How is he?"

"Like a man who's just spent the past eleven years behind bars and has to learn how to live again. He's not the same person he was before: he's going to have to accept that, his family too. The stress of reemerging into the world is likely to be harder than being jailed. Eric wants to go back to his job at his parents' store. He'll be exposed there, customers will see him, and I'm not sure that will be good for him."

"What are you afraid of?" I asked.

"The people of Mount Pleasant will think he's guilty as long as Alaska's murderer remains free. It's a recurring problem when a condemned man is later found innocent. With the evidence discredited, the whole investigation is suddenly worthless, and too much time has passed since the crime was committed for it to ever be solved. You can imagine the trauma for the families of the victims who find themselves without answers. For those proven innocent, it's the start of new worries—they have to find their place in a world where everyone looks at them with suspicion. Most people have confidence in the legal system, especially those who've never had anything to do with it. They can't help thinking that if someone really was innocent, they wouldn't have spent all that time in prison. Unfortunately, that's what it's going to be like for Eric as long as Alaska's murderer remains at large."

"About that, I have some good news," Gahalowood said.

"Good news?" a voice directly behind us echoed.

It was Lauren, her hair still wet from the shower. She had left my hotel room an hour earlier to return home and change. The night before, she had stopped by after dinner with her parents and brother. It was almost midnight. She saw the light on in my room and sent me a message:

—If you're awake, look out the window.

I put down my book and did as she asked. Lauren looked up at me and smiled.

—Can I come up?

—Of course.

She joined me in my room, and we spent the night together. At one point, she said, "I've gotten my brother back, thanks to you. I can breathe again. If I had known, two weeks ago when I stopped you for speeding, that you were going to change my life . . ." Once again, her declarations made me a little uncomfortable. I liked Lauren a great deal, but I sensed the depth of our feelings wasn't mutual.

At the breakfast table, Lauren sat between me and Patricia. She slipped her hand under the table and took mine, squeezing it hard.

"What's this good news?" she asked, grabbing a piece of bread.

"We made an important discovery yesterday," Gahalowood told her. "I think it's a turning point in the investigation. And it all hinges on Nicholas Kazinsky."

"One of the detectives who was working with you at the time," Patricia clarified.

"Precisely. He died last month. Suicide."

"How does that relate to the case?" Patricia asked.

"Nicholas Kazinsky was present in the interrogation room the night Walter Carrey died. He was the only person who knew that Carrey's confession was coerced and that his death was an accident. He also knew that if Walter had admitted to a crime he didn't commit, Eric was likely innocent too. At the end of January 2002, shortly after Eric was sentenced, Kazinsky was hit by a car. He survived with severe injuries. The evidence leads us to believe that it was no accident. Kazinsky was the victim of an attempted murder."

"Who would want to kill him?" Lauren asked.

"The only other person who knew that neither Walter nor Eric was guilty." Patricia now understood what we were getting at. "The actual murderer."

"Right," Gahalowood agreed. "By eliminating Kazinsky, the killer could ensure they would never be unmasked."

"Do you have anything concrete to link the Kazinsky incident with the murder of Alaska Sanders?" Lauren asked, suddenly doubtful.

"A blue car with Massachusetts plates," Gahalowood replied. "The car that ran Kazinsky over could be the one that crossed Mount Pleasant at high speed around the time of Alaska's murder. And it might be the one referenced in a poem written by Eleanor Lowell."

"We've already established a connection between Alaska and Eleanor Lowell," I explained. "Eleanor's death is the subject of the messages Alaska was delivering: 'I know what you did.' Something about it must have been troubling her. On March twenty-second, 1999, during the argument with Alaska, Eric told her he wasn't responsible for Eleanor's suicide. Alaska then realized that there was another man in Eleanor's life. We think that everything revolves around that lover. Alaska also had a lover, who was living in Salem, judging by the gifts he sent her. What if it was the same person? What if Alaska found out that he had been Eleanor's lover as well and she had proof that he was responsible for Eleanor's suicide? Alaska and Eleanor were friends; they both lived in Salem. They could easily have been seeing the same man."

"So that's why you want to go to Salem this morning?" Lauren said.

"Yes," Gahalowood replied, looking at his watch. "And it's time to go."

"Keep me posted," Patricia said. "When I see Eric, I'll try to get him to open up about his relationship with Eleanor. I'm sure he'll be more willing to confide in me."

\*       \*       \*

Stephen and Maria Lowell, Eleanor's parents, were waiting for us in their comfortable home in Salem. We had called ahead the previous afternoon. We had barely taken our seats in the living room when Maria asked us what was going on.

"As I explained on the phone," Gahalowood replied, "we'd like to ask you about your daughter."

"You also told me you were investigating the death of Alaska Sanders. What's the connection?"

"We're not sure yet, Mrs. Lowell. What can you tell us about Eleanor?"

Maria Lowell sighed. "Where do I begin? I can show you pictures and everything of hers I kept. She wrote a lot. She had an artistic side."

She brought out a set of photographs, taken the summer her daughter disappeared. Eleanor was an attractive blond with a thin face and long hair that fell over her shoulders. A cold beauty.

"She was very sensitive," Stephen told us. "Ever since she was small, she was always affected by other people's emotional ups and downs. She absorbed their sadness, their disappointments, and made them her own."

"She suffered from a deep sense of melancholy," Maria added. "We felt powerless to help her. She was twelve the first time she tried to kill herself. She tried again when she was sixteen. Both times she swallowed tranquilizers, then told us what she'd done. The doctors thought it was a cry for help. She had been to a so-called rest home twice. Psychiatric clinic might be a better word."

"Was she being monitored?"

"Yes, she saw several psychiatrists until she found a good one. Dr. Benjamin Bradburd was his name, a good doctor in spite of everything."

"Why 'in spite of everything'?"

"Because he wasn't able to stop her taking her own life. And at the same time, when someone decides to die . . . Here, I wrote down his number, he's waiting for your call. He's supposed to go on vacation today, but he put it off until tomorrow to talk to you. I also put together a list of Eleanor's friends."

"Did Eleanor try working as a model?" Gahalowood asked.

"Yes," Maria confirmed. "She had posed for magazines, and she often traveled to New York City. She was fairly successful. But I'm not sure it was good for her, that way of life. When she was in Manhattan, she spent her nights at so-called *chic* parties, but nothing very chic ever happened there, if you know what I mean."

"Drugs?"

"Yes, I think Eleanor was using cocaine. I tried to warn her several times about her lifestyle, but she got aggressive with me. She said her career spoke for itself and I would do better to mind my own business. Since she was an adult, I didn't know what I could do to intervene."

I picked up the thread of the conversation. "Excuse me, Mr. and Mrs. Lowell, but I have to go back to those painful days around August thirtieth, 1998. How was Eleanor at the time?"

"I'd say she was doing pretty well," Stephen replied. "She seemed to be in good spirits. But Dr. Bradburd has told us it's not unusual for someone who's suicidal to change their behavior right before they go through with it. Her friends may think she's doing better, but it's really the end of the road."

"All the same," Maria added, "Eleanor was very happy to have joined the Miss New England jury."

"That's the contest Alaska Sanders won in September 1998."

"Yes, that's right," Maria confirmed. "Eleanor had won it herself two years earlier. The organizers suggested she join the jury, and she enthusiastically accepted. It's an important competition, and it was good for her image and her career."

"When was she asked to join?" Gahalowood asked.

"Early August, if I remember correctly—in any case, a few weeks before August thirtieth. The night she died, Eleanor skipped dinner to exercise, as she often did. After her shower, she told me she was going out. I asked her where she was going and she told me she wanted to go for a swim. It was still light out, and very warm. I assumed she was going to meet friends at Devereux Beach in Marblehead, the neighboring town. She often went there. When I went to bed, around eleven, my husband was already asleep. I woke up around six thirty and found a message on my cell phone. It was from her: *I no longer have the strength to go on.* I called the police at once and they contacted Eleanor's friends. They said they'd spent the evening with her at Chandler Hovey Park. They'd all left around eleven thirty, except for Eleanor, who wanted to stay awhile longer. The police headed over and found her things by the lighthouse. Clothes, wallet, cell phone—it was all there. They searched the ocean nearby for several days, but they never found her body. The police concluded that she'd drowned herself."

"And you, what do you think?"

Maria Lowell's face expressed resignation. "After her first attempt, whenever I saw Eleanor standing before me, I told myself it was a miracle. I guess that should answer your question. You still haven't told me about the connection between Eleanor and Alaska, aside from the fact that they knew one another, obviously."

It was Lauren who filled her in. "In February 1999, you met up with Alaska in Mount Pleasant. You asked her about a relationship Eleanor may have had with an older man. Based on information in your daughter's diary, you suspected him of leading her to commit suicide."

"That's right. How do you know?"

"Alaska opened up to one of her friends," Lauren explained. "Did you ever find out who this man was?"

"Unfortunately, no. I talked to all Eleanor's girlfriends. I tried the police, as well; they didn't seem to care. They said information like that, from someone's diary, had no evidentiary value at all."

"Could we see the journal?" Lauren asked.

Maria rummaged through the box containing her daughter's things. She pulled out a notebook and read us the sections she'd shared with Alaska.

"I knew it was an older man because Eleanor told one of her friends. A few weeks after my visit to Alaska, I found something else." From the box she retrieved a school notebook, which she leafed through until she found the page she was looking for.

*He spoke about his divorce as if it were a release. He said to me,*
*"When I'm free, I'll be yours. We can be seen together in public." But*
*I think that even when he's divorced, he won't do it. He's ashamed.*
*Because of the age difference.*

Lauren summarized: "So Eleanor had a relationship with a man who was much older than her, was about to get divorced, and owned a blue car."

"Yes," Maria confirmed.

I had a question of my own. "We were wondering whether Alaska might had had a relationship with Eleanor's lover. At this point, it's just a possibility. You don't have any information at all about his identity?"

"None."

"Is there anything else you found out about your daughter we should know?" Gahalowood asked. "A small detail, even one that seems insignificant, could turn out to be important."

"Well, there's one thing that's always bothered me. The summer Eleanor died, as I was doing the laundry, I found a bus ticket in her jeans pocket. It was from Rockland, Maine, returning to Salem, dated July fifth, 1998. I always wondered what she could have been doing in Rockland."

"Wait a minute," Gahalowood said. "On the Fourth of July, Eleanor wrote in her diary that she was unhappy with her lover. And the next day she buys a bus ticket in Rockland to take her back to Salem. Did he live in Rockland?"

"I asked myself the same question. I asked her friends, but no-one could tell me. I even drove to Rockland and went around all the stores with a picture of my daughter, but nobody recognized her."

"Mrs. Lowell," Gahalowood asked, pointing to Eleanor's notebooks. "Could we take these with us? Obviously, we'll return them to you."

Following Maria Lowell's suggestion, we contacted Dr. Benjamin Bradburd, who asked that we stop by his office so he could consult his notes on Eleanor. Bradburd was well known in the area and was often consulted by the courts as a psychiatric expert. Not quite sixty, he was trim, elegant, and clearly took care of himself.

"Eleanor was a patient who left an impression on me. She was always dealing with these big metaphysical questions. She took on other people's suffering. But she was a complex personality, a little manipulative, manifesting a slight bipolar tendency that we could have taken care of with the appropriate medication. But Eleanor didn't always respect the dosages, and above all, I discovered that she used cocaine from time to time. I was afraid of the effect such a cocktail might have on her. When I learned of her death, I asked myself if it would have been better to have tried nonetheless. I've always had regrets."

"You say 'her death,' but her body was never found," Lauren remarked.

"I'm only repeating what the police said. Which seems logical, all things considered. I realize her body was never found, which is always terrible for the family and prevents them from grieving. I don't share the opinion of those who believe she's still alive somewhere."

"Could it be that she intentionally disappeared?" I asked.

Bradburd found the question amusing. "Eleanor didn't want to disappear. On the contrary, she dreamed of being famous."

"Yes, she had a career as a model," Gahalowood added.

"She wanted more," Bradburd replied. "She saw herself as a Hollywood star. Sometimes people recognized her on the street. They'd say, 'Aren't you the girl in the such-and-such ad?' That drove her crazy. She wanted to be more than just a face. She wanted to be someone; she wanted to be an actress. She tried to get on a few casting calls, but it didn't work out."

"Like Alaska," I said.

"Who?" Bradburd asked.

"Alaska Sanders," I said. "The girl we're inquiring about. She wanted to be an actress too. There are a lot of similarities between Eleanor and Alaska. I can't help but wonder whether they didn't have a relationship with the same man. Eleanor never spoke to you about Alaska?"

"Never. However, I do know that Maria Lowell was concerned about a man with whom Eleanor was said to be involved. She showed me what Eleanor had written about him. An older man, apparently divorced. But Eleanor never mentioned him during our sessions. I would have written it down, or in any case, I would have remembered something like that."

"It seems not even her girlfriends knew," Gahalowood added. "Could she have invented it all?"

"No, I doubt it. Fabrications like that are intended to be shared, to provoke a reaction in others. But Eleanor kept her diaries secret. I think she was ashamed of his hold over her. She was too intelligent not to be aware she was caught up in a toxic relationship."

"Did Eleanor ever mention the town of Rockland, Maine, to you?" Gahalowood asked.

"Rockland? No. I have no memory of that either. Sorry, I would have liked to have been of more help."

Dr. Bradburd's office wasn't far from where Alaska's parents lived, so we made an unannounced stop there after our visit. Robbie and Donna Sanders were both home. They greeted us with surprising warmth.

"You've come just in time," Robbie announced. "I was getting ready to go to Mount Pleasant."

"What for?" Lauren asked.

"To talk to you," he said.

"Me?"

"Yes. I have something for you. Like I said, I was getting ready to head out. Fifteen minutes later, I would have already left."

Robbie Sanders produced a rectangular box, which he held out for Lauren.

"What is it?" she asked.

"Open it."

Lauren did so. Inside was the gold watch.

"I'd like you to give it to your brother," Robbie said.

"But . . ." Lauren muttered, surprised. "I can't accept this! It's your watch. I didn't even know you got it back."

"Day before yesterday, Sergeant Gahalowood came over in the afternoon to tell us that your brother was going to be released. He explained the full circumstances. I didn't know Eric was your brother; I only found out when I saw you on television."

"Mr. Sanders, this watch belongs to you. It was stolen during the robbery."

"The police found it and returned it. It's mine to do with as I please. And I want to give it to your brother because it belongs to him. He bought it in good faith from my daughter. Lauren, eleven years ago, your brother's life was put on hold, but unlike my daughter, he can go on living. It's my way of trying to repair some of what happened as a result of my actions."

Donna Sanders then asked us, "Is there a specific reason for your visit?"

"Yes," Gahalowood answered. "We have a new lead and we wanted to ask you about it. Do you recall a young woman by the name of Eleanor Lowell?"

Donna lifted her head and looked at us cautiously. "Of course, I know Eleanor Lowell. She's the young woman who killed herself twelve years ago. That was shortly before the Miss New England competition if I recall correctly."

"That's right. What can you tell me about her?"

"Not much. She did some modeling, at a whole other level than Alaska. Eleanor's career had already begun. I remember Alaska showing me photos of her in magazines when she was only twenty. What's this got to do with the investigation into our daughter's death?"

"There could be a connection," Gahalowood replied. "Alaska and Eleanor were friends, right?"

Donna laughed. "Friends? You've got to be kidding. Alaska had nothing against Eleanor, but Eleanor detested her!"

"Oh? You're certain?"

"Absolutely. Eleanor was dying of jealousy. She wanted to break into film, but she never got anywhere. She saw that Alaska had what it takes to make the difference. Eleanor also knew that the Miss New England title would boost Alaska's acting career. The competition was known for that. When Eleanor was asked to join the jury, Alaska was very upset. She kept saying, 'She'll make sure I lose.' Eleanor was jealous. If you ask her girlfriends, they'll confirm what I'm saying."

"We do have a list of people we want to question," Gahalowood told her. "So Alaska was worried that Eleanor might sabotage her chances in the competition. What eventually happened?"

"Eleanor killed herself," Donna snapped, without realizing what she had just said. "Eleanor killed herself, and Alaska won the competition."

Donna and her husband looked at one another. Suddenly they seemed afraid. Lauren, Gahalowood, and I also exchanged glances, before Gahalowood continued with his questioning: "Besides whatever rivalry there may have been between Eleanor and Alaska, we believe there's a third person connecting them. Most likely a man, someone older, who was either divorced or about to be and drove a blue car with Massachusetts plates."

"Doesn't ring a bell," Donna said.

"Nor with me," Robbie admitted. "How was this man connected to Alaska?"

"They may have been lovers," Lauren replied.

"Are you saying there was someone else in her life when she was seeing Walter Carrey?" Donna said, sounding surprised.

"Yes."

Donna suddenly burst out laughing. "That's a lot of men for Alaska!"

"What's gotten into you, Donna?" her husband asked.

"Oh, Robbie, didn't you ever wonder why Alaska never brought any boyfriends to the house? As beautiful as she was, as desirable as she was, still she remained single . . ."

"I don't see what you're driving at," Robbie said to his wife.

"Do you know if your daughter liked women?" Lauren asked.

"I knew she was curious," Donna said, smiling. "But we never talked about it. I felt that she was still discovering what she wanted and what she desired, and I didn't want to interfere with that. I was going to wait until she was ready before discussing it."

"How did you find out?" Lauren asked.

"When she was about twenty, a former high-school girlfriend would always come to the house. A nice girl, kind, polite, discreet. Not especially pretty. One afternoon, I had made muffins and I took some up to Alaska's room. I opened the door; they didn't see or hear me. But I saw everything. My daughter had taken off her slacks and panties and was holding on to the headboard, and her friend had her face between her legs."

"Donna, really!" her husband shouted.

"Oh, my poor Robbie, you're so old-fashioned."

"And Walter?" I asked.

"Walter was just a passing thing. Maybe Alaska was still testing the waters. It wasn't anything serious. If it hadn't been for the incident with her bank account, which led to that damn robbery, she would never have gone off to live in Mount Pleasant."

*   *   *

That night, after returning to Mount Pleasant, Gahalowood and I had supper at the National Anthem. We sat in silence for a while, drinking our beers. On Saturday nights in the summer there was live music. The mood was mellow. Later that evening, Lauren and Patricia, who had dined at the Donovans', joined us for a drink.

"You should have come to my parents'," Lauren said with a faint note of reproach.

Gahalowood had rightly declined the invitation earlier. "The investigation isn't over," he said. "I wouldn't want to get too close to Eric right now; it could jeopardize the legitimacy of our work."

441

"I understand," Lauren said. "It's lucky your colleague Marcus isn't romantically involved with the sister of the former culprit."

Gahalowood burst out laughing. He rarely laughed, and it made me happy to see him relax for once. The musicians began playing an old funk tune, and Patricia took Gahalowood by the hand to lead him to the dance floor. I stayed with Lauren, who wrapped her arms around me. She kissed me, then her expression turned serious.

"How are you doing?" I asked her.

"Okay. It's strange having Eric back at my parents' place. No-one knows how to behave, me included. Patricia warned me it would be hard. I'd like to take Eric to the beach at Kennebunkport tomorrow. I think it would do him good."

"It's a good idea," I said, trying to sound encouraging.

She looked into my eyes. "Marcus, we're going to finish this case, and then what?"

*"And then what,* what?"

"And then what's going to happen to us? I've never had someone like you in my life, Marcus. I don't know how I'm going to keep you here and stop you going back to New York."

"Who told you I was returning to New York?"

"What would you do in Mount Pleasant?"

She was right.

Looking at Lauren, I thought of Emma, Helen, Aunt Anita, and how all these women were connected. I started to realize that they allowed me to idealize an imaginary way of life, being on an impossible quest for a calm, peaceful existence—the fantasy life of Uncle Saul and his family, the Baltimore Goldmans, whom I'd always considered to be spared life's torments and pitfalls. Beyond that illusion, someone was waiting for me. And it wasn't Lauren. Harry had reminded me of that the other night, after the opera. There was someone else, without whom my life was incomplete. And while Lauren spoke to me of our future, I was thinking about the ticket Harry had given me for the Alexandra Neville concert the following day. I was hesitant about going, torn between my desire to repair the past and the urge to accept the concrete future that Lauren was offering me. Did I have the right to make her suffer?

It was one in the morning when Gahalowood and I left the National Anthem to return to the hotel.

"Well, Sergeant, your little dance with the lawyer . . ."

"I'm going to stop you right there. There was nothing to it. She just wanted to get me away from Lauren."

"Away from Lauren? Why?"

"Patricia asked Eric about Eleanor Lowell. Apparently, he was very evasive. Strange. As if something wasn't right."

"Such as?" I asked.

"Patricia wasn't able to explain it in concrete terms. It was more of an intuition. When she asked him about his old blue car, he clammed up. He told her he'd sold it and there was no record of the sale. He said he was paid in cash."

"And what do you think?"

"I have doubts again, Writer. Always doubts."

# 31

# *Doubts*

Gahalowood and I set off for Salem, where we had arranged to question Eleanor Lowell's friends. We were silent, pensive, worried by what Patricia Widsmith had said. Even she was starting to question Eric's innocence.

Lauren hadn't come with us. She'd gone with Eric to Kennebunkport and the beach where they'd played as children. Patricia had agreed with Gahalowood that she would take advantage of their absence to discreetly question Janet and Mark Donovan about their son. As we crossed the Massachusetts border, Gahalowood asked me, "What are you thinking about?"

"Eric Donovan."

"Hmm . . . me too. He's the common thread that runs through this whole story. He seems to be involved in everything even though nothing really points to him."

"What is certain is that he didn't try to kill Kazinsky, since he was in prison. Someone else was at the wheel of that blue car. A car that connects Alaska, Eleanor, and Kazinsky."

It was clear that Eleanor Lowell's lover, the mature man on the verge of a divorce, was a key piece of the puzzle. We were hoping Eleanor's friends could provide us with information about him. "Who should we start with?" Gahalowood asked me.

I scanned the list of names that Eleanor's mother had prepared, which we hadn't yet properly examined. "We can follow the order Maria Lowell wrote them down in," I suggested. "First there's Melissa Williams, a childhood friend. They went to school together. Then, Tiffany Paulson, who met Eleanor at the psychiatric clinic when they were both sixteen. After that, Brooke Rizzo, also a model, and—"

Gahalowood interrupted me. "That name rings a bell. Who are the others?"

I continued. I recognized the names of three more of Alaska's friends, including the one who had alerted us to the existence of Eleanor Lowell nine days earlier.

"There's Andrea Brown, Stephanie Lahan, and Michelle Spitzer. Those are the same names that Donna Sanders gave us! And Brooke Rizzo, of course. We already questioned them, but about Alaska."

"The circle's getting smaller," Gahalowood exclaimed. "Same blue car, same group of friends. I'm really starting to wonder if Eleanor's disappearance isn't directly connected to Alaska's murder."

"You mean Eleanor didn't commit suicide?"

"They may have had the same lover; what if they also had the same killer? We can't rule it out."

We began our interviews with Michelle Spitzer, who had been the first person to tell us about Eleanor.

MICHELLE SPITZER: Of course, we were all friends, I already told you that. We met during the competitions and formed our own little group.
[. . .]
Were we jealous of each other? No, only Alaska and Eleanor made it their profession. For the rest of us, we took part when we were teenagers because it was fun. By 1998 it was already ancient history. Some of us were in college, some of us were working.

[. . .]

Eleanor was very moody and didn't confide in us much. You
had to accept her as she was. I knew she'd been involved with
an older guy for a while. She never talked about him: she was
very secretive. She mentioned a guy in his fifties. You should ask
Brooke, she loved that kind of thing. Me? I couldn't care less. In
fact, I thought it was sad.

BROOKE RIZZO: Why didn't I mention Eleanor Lowell? I
don't know. You didn't mention her either. You asked me about
Alaska, Walter, Mount Pleasant—I didn't make the connection
with Eleanor. How does Eleanor's suicide have anything to do
with Alaska's murder?
[. . .]
Yes, with the "older guy" it was endless . . . I never found out
who he was. Eleanor's mother tried to find him, but Eleanor was
careful to keep it a secret. One day I asked her why she never
talked about him, and she said, "I don't want to cause him
problems."
[. . .]
No, the "older guy" wasn't Eric Donovan. Eric wasn't old . . .
yeah, I knew Eric. We ran into him all the time when we went
out to bars. Eleanor never let on she was going out with him.
But one night she did tell me, when we were all together. Then
there was Walter, who was always making eyes at Alaska. I told
Eleanor that Walter was good-looking. And well built. She said
she preferred Eric and that they were sleeping together, but that it
had to remain a secret so the "older guy" wouldn't find out. As if
she was afraid of him. I asked her one day what she saw in him,
this older guy. She said she was in love, that's just the way it is.

ANDREA BROWN: Jealousy between Eleanor and Alaska? Sure, but that came later. For a long time, there were never any problems between them. And they were both trying to build their careers: Eleanor was doing modeling, Alaska wanted to be an actress. But that summer, Eleanor also got it into her head that she wanted to make it in Hollywood. I don't really know why. Alaska told us she had an agent in New York who believed in her, and I guess that really bothered Eleanor. But I don't think she wanted to hurt Alaska. At least, I never saw anything between them in public, any tension. There was one conversation, at lunch, just Eleanor and me. She had just been appointed to the Miss New England jury. I said to her, "You have to back Alaska, it would be great for her career if she won." She just stared at me and said, "Never! I don't want that bitch to succeed. She's starting to make me look bad." Did you ask Stephanie? Her mother and Alaska's were very close.

[. . .]

Yes, you could say Eleanor was kind of fearless. She liked to go swimming at Chandler Hovey Park. She'd stay late, sometimes alone. She said she wasn't afraid of prowlers: she kept a collapsible baton in her bag, just in case.

PERRY GAHALOWOOD: A metal baton?

ANDREA BROWN: Yes. Well, at night she always had it in her handbag. Why?

PERRY GAHALOWOOD: Because Alaska Sanders was killed with a similar weapon.

STEPHANIE LAHAN: Yes, I felt there was tension between Alaska and Eleanor over the Miss New England competition. Mrs. Sanders mentioned it to my mother. In that little world, everyone is jealous of everyone else.

[. . .]

Well, yeah, it was convenient for Alaska that Eleanor was no longer around. I don't know if Alaska would've won the competition with her on the jury. Apparently, Eleanor was determined to eliminate her.

[. . .]

No, I never met her boyfriend. But we talked about him a lot. Some old shmuck—she seemed to worship him. We never found out anything about him. Well, only once, in early August 1998. I remember because it was the last time I saw Eleanor. We grabbed a coffee together, and she had a small overnight bag. I asked her where she was going, but she didn't want to tell me. Her car was in the garage for repairs and she asked me to drop her off at the bus station. I dropped her off and then discreetly followed her. I figured she was going to meet her guy, and I really wanted to know what he looked like. But she just got on a bus to Rockland, Maine. She was by herself.

If Eleanor was with her lover in Rockland on July 4 and had returned there in August, it surely meant that our man lived there.

Leaving Stephanie Lahan's home, Gahalowood said to me: "A blue car, Massachusetts plates, a divorced older man, Rockland, Maine. Put it all together and you've won the jackpot!"

We had just gotten into my car when Gahalowood received a call on his cell phone. It was an officer working the reception desk at state police headquarters: "Sorry to bother you on a Sunday, Sergeant. The mother of Sergeant Vance is here and she's asking for you." We returned to New Hampshire at once. At the station, a small, frail woman was waiting for Gahalowood in his office.

"Mrs. Vance?"

"Perry!" With a spontaneous movement, she threw herself into his arms. They had met only once, at Vance's funeral.

"What are you doing here?" he asked.

"I had to talk to you. About what they said on television . . . about that Alaska Sanders case. It was Matt's last case, wasn't it?"

"Yes, it was."

"They said that a police officer forced a suspect to confess and then did something stupid. Was it Matt? If it was, tell me, please! I need to know. I have the right to know what's going on."

"Mrs. Vance," Gahalowood said. "I'm very sorry for what I'm about to tell you. But since you've come all this way for the truth, I owe you that much."

Gahalowood revealed to the mother of his former partner how events had unfolded on Tuesday, April 6, 1999, leading to the death of Walter Carrey and the suicide of Matt Vance. When he was done, the small woman stood in stunned silence. When she was able to speak once more, she said: "I recall one of the first cases Matt worked on, when he was a police officer in Bangor. A young girl, seventeen years old, had been killed returning home at night from a friend's house. Her name was Gaby. The poor thing was beaten to death and was so disfigured that her own parents couldn't identify her. They never found out who did it, and when his superior asked him to give up the case for lack of evidence, Matt was devastated. He said to me, 'It's not possible, Ma! We can't just give up. I promised that girl's parents that we'd find who did it.' Over the years, he told me that he thought about that girl every morning. He could see her face, damaged and broken. 'It was just mush,' he'd say. That case haunted him. Twice, thinking he had someone who could have been mixed up in it, he shoved his gun in their mouth to get them to confess. He told me about it. 'I could see Gaby's body in the ditch,' he said, 'and I pictured this guy punching her in the face, and I just lost it.' A colleague of Matt's informed on him, and his superiors asked him to look for work elsewhere, somewhere Gaby's ghost would leave him in peace.

"Unfortunately, as we might have expected, she followed him all the way to New Hampshire. Matt never wanted kids because of her. He said he didn't want to live through what her parents had lived through. I think he never really had a serious relationship because of that. He was too tormented. The last time I spoke to him was the weekend before his death. Over the phone, he told me he was working on a case, a young woman who had been found dead near a lake. I'll never forget her name because it was so unusual: Alaska. He said to me, 'Ma, I'm going to hang up now. I can't do this anymore. I'm going to solve this case, and when it's done, I'll forgive myself for not finding Gaby's murderer.' That was the last time we spoke."

Mrs. Vance stopped. There was a deep and terrible silence in the room.

"I'm very sorry for everything that happened," Gahalowood said.

"You have nothing to apologize for, Perry, you weren't there."

"Exactly."

She went on: "On the TV, they said my son will be posthumously demoted. Let them do it if they think that's what the public wants. Let them destroy his grave while they're at it. But I don't think it's going to change much—it won't bring that poor boy back to life, or Alaska. But you, Perry, you can fix all that by solving this case. I can still feel Matt's troubled soul in his coffin seeking redemption. Do this for him, Perry. And for that poor girl's parents. Find the murderer. During our last call, Matt said to me, 'All I want, Ma, is to go see Alaska's parents and tell them that justice—"

"—has been served," Gahalowood interrupted, finishing her sentence.

"How did you know?"

"Your son said the same thing to me."

On the way to Mount Pleasant, Gahalowood said: "I'm tired, Writer. It's time to settle this case. After that, I'm going to call it a day too."

"You want to quit the force, Sergeant?"

"At least take a break. You know what Helen's dream was? For the whole family to go sailing, take a trip around the world. That's what I'd like to do when I'm done here. Take off with my daughters."

"That's a fine plan."

"There might even be a place for you on board."

"Thanks, Sergeant, but I have a few things to settle before I come and ruin your cruise."

"Nah, you wouldn't ruin anything. Just the opposite."

\*     \*     \*

It was late afternoon and I was in my hotel room in Mount Pleasant toying with the ticket Harry had given me. Alexandra Neville's concert was that evening. It would soon be time. Would I go?

I couldn't decide. In one hand I held the photo of my cousins, Alexandra, and me, and in the other, the ticket. Finally, I decided to go. I left on the sly, not wanting to have to give anyone an explanation. In the neighboring room, Gahalowood was reading the notebooks that Eleanor's mother had given us. As I was getting into my car, I received a text message from Lauren:

—Are you coming over?
—No, I'm going to stay in my hotel room. I'm exhausted.

I left and drove to TD Garden in Boston, where basketball and hockey games and large concerts were held. If you followed music in the 2010s, you would have heard of Alexandra Neville, who was the artist of the moment.

When I arrived, I passed by the ticket counter and checked my seat number to see where I would be sitting.

I hadn't seen her behind me.

She had followed me as far as she could before being stopped at the entrance because she had no ticket.

She watched me disappear inside, shaken by my lie.

It was Lauren.

# 32

## *Vinalhaven*

*Monday, July 26, and Tuesday, July 27, 2010*

The day after the concert, Lauren asked to meet me at the Season for coffee. She was waiting at a table, her arms crossed, with a sullen look on her face. When I arrived, all she said was "Sit down."

Then she asked, "Did you have a good time?"

"Hmm, okay. And you?"

"Don't play games with me, Marcus! Who were you with at the concert?"

I didn't try to deny it. I simply asked her how she knew.

"I saw you leave your hotel yesterday. I had parked out front. You didn't see me. It looked like you were in a hurry, you got in your car, and that's when I texted you, 'Are you coming over?' It was a question. But you thought it was an invitation and told me you wanted to rest in your hotel room, when I was there watching you leave! Liar! I thought you were a decent guy, Marcus, someone different. But you're just like the rest of them. So tell me, is there someone in Boston? Did you take her to the concert?"

"Lauren, you won't believe me, but I went to the concert alone."

"Oh, really!"

"Harry gave me that ticket. I saw him last Saturday. He suggested I go to the concert."

"Why?"

"It's complicated, but he wanted to help me get in touch with someone. Someone who was important in my life."

"An ex?"

"Yes."

"Who is she?"

"The girl in the photo."

"What?"

"The girl in the photo with my cousins: Alexandra. That's her."

"And . . . ?"

"I stayed away, just watched. I was afraid to say or do anything."

"You didn't talk to her?"

"No."

"Are you in love with her?"

I hesitated, looking into Lauren's eyes. "I think so."

She grabbed her coffee cup as if she were going to throw it in my face. Just then my phone rang. It was Gahalowood. "Writer, where are you?"

"At the Season, with Lauren."

"Meet me at the hotel—both of you. I've found something."

*　　　*　　　*

Gahalowood, excited by his discovery, didn't notice the tension between Lauren and me. At a table in the hotel restaurant, he showed us one of Eleanor Lowell's notebooks.

"I read the whole thing, and look what I found." He pointed to a page covered in tiny handwriting.

*I'm going back to him. He says he'd be lost without me. Ever since that disappointing July 4, I promised myself I wouldn't go back there, but he needs me and I can't abandon him. He was even ready to come get me in his car, but I didn't want him to come all the way here, especially with that stupid parade blocking the town. I've never understood the appeal of giant lobsters.*

*I take the bus. As soon as I'm in my seat, my body is impatient. I want only one thing: to be with him again. So we can lock ourselves in our bubble, in our paradise.*

*When the foghorn blows, my heart skips a beat, I know he's not far. I meet him in his haven, where no-one can find us. Where no-one can bother us. It's a world apart.*

*In that gray house, surrounded by red maples, where I feel like a woman, we can be a couple. We're sheltered from the world.*

"Here, Eleanor mentions a bus ride after a disappointing Fourth of July. I assume she's writing about the trip to Rockland that Stephanie Lahan told us about. Eleanor mentions lobsters, and lobsters suggest Maine, which brings us back to Rockland again."

"I follow you so far, Sergeant," Lauren said.

Gahalowood continued. "Eleanor also mentions a parade. I went to check if there was anything like that with a lobster as mascot in August. And I found out that every year since 1947 there's been a Lobster Festival in downtown Rockland, and giant lobsters are a part of it."

"Eleanor goes to join her lover in Rockland, at a gray house surrounded by red maples," I summarized. "A foghorn blows, so there has to be a lighthouse nearby, which should help us narrow our search."

Gahalowood nodded, looking us both in the eye. "You know what we have to do . . ."

"Looks like we're off to Rockland," Lauren said.

*     *     *

It was a three-hour drive, and we would probably have to spend the night there, so we packed our things.

The municipality of Rockland was spread across an area of twenty-five square miles. Despite its proximity to a lighthouse, finding the gray house was no simple matter. To speed up our search, we took two cars: Gahalowood and me in one, Lauren in the other.

We got there late morning and set to work at once. Lauren would take the north part of town; Gahalowood, the south. I would walk around downtown, store by store, showing a photograph of Eleanor to shop owners, hoping to awaken some buried memory.

The day was nothing but a succession of false leads. We found several gray houses, some surrounded by maples, some not. We checked each of them down to the smallest detail, and each time something was missing. Some of the houses were built after 1998. Others had been a different color twelve years earlier and repainted since. The men who lived in some were either too young or too old to have been Eleanor's lover at the time. Seeking additional help, Gahalowood had contacted the Rockland police, who were very cooperative, but achieved little. As for my tour of the downtown stores with Eleanor's photograph, it was a waste of time.

By late afternoon we had turned up nothing. Lauren decided to go back to Mount Pleasant; Gahalowood and I continued until nightfall. When it was too dark to see, we stopped at a motel. In spite of our fatigue, we were too excited to sleep. We sat outside in plastic chairs, drinking beer.

"You okay?" Gahalowood asked. "You didn't look so good earlier. And you haven't said a word all day, which isn't like you. I missed your annoying chatter."

"It's Lauren."

"Oh, now that you mention it, I thought there was something strange between you two."

"I know. I did something stupid."

"Serious?"

"Yes and no. I lied to her, which is never a good thing. I'm fond of Lauren, but I've been asking myself a lot of questions."

"About?"

"An old story. I'll tell you about it one day."

"I'm here when you're ready."

"Sergeant, how did you know Helen was the one?"

Gahalowood shrugged. "You want an honest answer?"

"Yes."

"I've known ever since she's been gone. Of course, I loved her more than anything. I asked her to marry me because I could see myself sharing my life with her. We had our ups and downs, but I never once doubted my love for her. Do you know what it means when we say that someone's 'the one'? It means that when she dies, you realize you wanted to die with her. Your world falls apart. You can't live without her. I'm like a broken machine, Writer. When I lost Helen, I lost the ability to function."

"We'll fix you, Sergeant."

"I don't know if I can be fixed. And you know what—maybe it's better that way. Because it means our love was real. It hurts, it hurts a lot, but that's what gives meaning to the life we shared."

*   *   *

Early the following morning, Gahalowood and I continued our search for the mysterious gray house. We drove along the coast well beyond Rockland, inspecting all the houses we found near lighthouses. Always in vain.

By late morning, after several unsuccessful hours searching, we returned to Rockland, utterly discouraged. Not the shadow of a lead, and it felt like we were going in circles. We drank a coffee at the port. Nearby, a fisherman was unloading his lobster traps. We watched in silence. A ferry left the port, filled with tourists. I watched them enviously. I needed a vacation. When we finished our coffee, I asked Gahalowood, "What do we do now, Sergeant?"

"We go back to Mount Pleasant."

I nodded. At that moment, the ferry's horn sounded. Three long blasts. Three foghorn blasts. Gahalowood and I looked at one another, stupefied.

"Sergeant! Did you hear that?"

"Of course I heard it!"

He motioned to the fisherman. "Excuse me, where does that ferry go?"

"Vinalhaven," the man said.

"Vinalhaven?"

"The island of Vinalhaven. One hour by ferry. You don't know it?"

"No. Anyone live there?"

"About a thousand people. It's become very fashionable. Vacationers mostly."

Gahalowood took Eleanor's notebook from his pocket. He reread the passage where she mentioned a haven, a place where no-one could find them. An island was the perfect location. A fashionable vacation spot where a man of a certain age, about to be divorced, could find some peace and quiet.

Half an hour later we maneuvered Gahalowood's car onto the ferry. Once on the island, we set off again in search of a gray house surrounded by red maples. We spent the day examining the residences on Vinalhaven, one by one. Finally, we found a small house near the water that exactly matched the description: a structure of gray boards, surrounded by immense red maples. We left our car some distance away, so as not to draw attention, and approached the property. The place looked deserted. There was no vehicle anywhere to be seen. No name on the mailbox.

Gahalowood rang the bell. No answer. I started to walk around the house. Through the windows, I could see there was no-one inside. As I peered into the living room, I discovered something I hadn't expected.

"Sergeant, come look."

"What's up?"

"Look, in the living room, the back wall, behind the armchair . . ."

Gahalowood stuck his nose against the window. "Son of a gun, Writer!"

On the wall was a painting showing a sunset over the ocean—the one that appeared in the background of Alaska's video. It was here that she had recorded her final audition.

At that moment, we heard a motor. A car was arriving. Gahalowood, out of habit, led me into the bushes. It's then that we saw it—a blue car, at least ten years old, which parked in front of the house. The driver's side door opened and a man stepped out. Gahalowood and I remained stock-still, stunned by what we saw.

# 33

# A Gray House

*Vinalhaven, Maine*
*Wednesday, July 28, 2010*
Several state police cars and the Knox County sheriff boarded a Coast Guard patrol boat, which advanced slowly across the sea, escorted by a cloud of gulls.

On the bridge, Gahalowood and I watched Vinalhaven Island approaching. Lauren and Chief Lansdane were also present, as well as Chief Mitchell, whom Gahalowood had asked to join us.

It was noon, and we were headed for the gray house surrounded by red maples to apprehend Dr. Benjamin Bradburd. He was the older man, divorced, who drove a blue car (a Chrysler Sebring bought in March 1998, which he still owned) and had purchased this vacation home in the early nineties. We had also found out that his mother, Rosemary Bradburd, was a former beauty queen who had founded the Miss New England competition. He was a member of the organizing committee.

\* \* \*

The previous day, when we had learned that Bradburd was Eleanor Lowell's lover, the man we were desperately searching for, Gahalowood and I had been eager to question him. We would have liked to have detained him on the spot, but Gahalowood didn't have legal jurisdiction in Maine. So we discreetly moved away from the grounds of the gray house and, lacking a clear phone signal, returned to Vinalhaven, the small town that lent its name to the island, where the sergeant called Lansdane from a phone booth.

Lansdane wasn't too happy to hear of our latest endeavor. "You're on an island in Maine, outside your jurisdiction, and you entered private property without a warrant. Excellent! You know you could trash your entire investigation because you didn't follow procedure. Hurry up and get your ass back to New Hampshire! I'll be waiting in my office early tomorrow morning and you can tell me all about your suspicions concerning Bradburd. I'll alert the local authorities, and I want to be there in person when you cuff this guy."

We did as he told us. We took the last ferry off the island and returned to New Hampshire. Perry had suggested I sleep at his place, in Concord. I accepted. I wasn't sure I wanted to return to Mount Pleasant at all. I was glad to be back at the Gahalowoods' in "Marcus's bedroom" in the basement. I was already in bed when I got a call from Lauren.

"Perry just called," she said. "So you found Alaska's murderer . . ."

"We'll know tomorrow."

"Perry suggested I meet you at state police headquarters tomorrow morning. I hope that's okay with you."

"It's your investigation as much as mine. Why would it bother me?"

"Ever since the concert, I've had the impression that something's broken between us."

Lauren was right, but I didn't know what to say. We hung up.

\*     \*     \*

Twelve hours after that conversation, on the bridge of the Coast Guard boat, I stole a glance at Lauren, standing by my side. Her hair, blown by the wind, caressed my face.

We pulled into the port at Vinalhaven. The pleasure-boaters observed the arrival of the police with curiosity. It was something that had probably never been seen before on the island. Once everyone was on dry land, we set off. Ten minutes later, we arrived at Benjamin Bradburd's house. The police quickly deployed around the premises, blocking access to the surrounding fields and the ocean. The blue car was still there.

Gahalowood, Lansdane, Lauren, and I positioned ourselves by the front door. Bradburd, alerted by the noise, opened up before we even knocked. "What's going on?" he asked, very surprised.

"Benjamin Bradburd," Gahalowood said to him. "You're under arrest for the murder of Alaska Sanders."

*　　　*　　　*

"What?! You must be insane!" Bradburd shouted when we questioned him in the living room. "Who's Alaska Sanders? Why would I kill her?"

"That's for you to tell us," Gahalowood replied.

Lauren showed him a photo of Alaska. "Look at this face, you're sure you don't recognize it? Alaska was crowned Miss New England in 1998, a competition set up by your mother; you were a member of the organizing committee."

"Yes, yes, now that I see her face, I remember her."

"And yet," Lauren replied, "when we asked you about her the other day, in your office, you pretended the name meant nothing to you."

Bradburd gritted his teeth. You could see he was annoyed.

"Come on!" Gahalowood said, angrily. "Spit it out! Why did you lie about Alaska?"

"I didn't lie; at the time, it just didn't click. I don't keep the names of all the winners of the Miss New England crown in my head."

"You're lying!" Gahalowood screamed. "You're lying and it's obvious that you're lying. So, I'm going to ask you again: Why did you lie about Alaska?"

After hesitating for a moment, Bradburd lowered his eyes and said, "Because of Eleanor."

"You were having an affair with her," Lauren said.

"How did you find out?" Bradburd asked.

"From her diary," Gahalowood replied. "So you admit you were her lover?"

"Yes, okay, I admit it. It's true. I shouldn't have, I was her psychiatrist. But she was an adult: I didn't break the law."

"She killed herself because of you!" Gahalowood said, pointing an accusing finger at him. "You pushed her over the edge. She wrote in her diary about how you treated her. How could you? You were her doctor: you were supposed to help her, not drive her to suicide."

"Her illness made her kill herself," Bradburd pleaded. "She was fragile!"

"Right, and you knew she was fragile, yet you still spent the summer making her life miserable."

"It was a complicated time. My life was falling apart. I was getting a divorce, partly because of Eleanor, because my wife had discovered our affair. Eleanor was in love with me, and I didn't know how to get out of the situation."

"Because you weren't in love with her?"

"No. I couldn't even describe what we were, Eleanor and me. She was my last patient on a Tuesday. I ended the day with her. At that hour, my assistant had already left. One evening, in early 1998, I had a moment of weakness. For a while I had felt that Eleanor was attracted to me, and she, as you know, was very beautiful. I shouldn't have, but I cracked. It happened in my office, in the middle of our session. I promised myself never to do it again. But the following Tuesday, I just couldn't stop myself. And then every week, we'd end our session by making love on the couch in my office. It was sordid. When summer arrived, I hoped that being on Vinalhaven would allow me to end our affair, but she insisted on coming here several times. When I suggested we break it off, she threatened, maybe not in so many words, to report me for professional misconduct. She held my career in her hands. So I continued seeing her, hoping that my behavior might discourage her. Not only did it not, she wanted more. She even demanded to be placed on the jury for the Miss

461

New England competition. She said it would be good for her career. I spoke to my mother, who agreed. I thought after that, Eleanor would leave me in peace. But no, she insisted we become a 'real couple.' She wanted us to show the world we were an item. I tried to reason with her by telling her about my divorce proceedings, but I knew that excuse couldn't last forever. I didn't know how to get out of it."

"How did you feel when you found out about her suicide?" I asked.

"Relief. An immense sense of relief. And a great deal of guilt. Even now, a day doesn't go by that I don't think about it, that I don't wonder what would have happened if I hadn't given in to my stupid impulses. My life would be very different. I would still be married. Maybe I would have had children."

After a brief silence, Gahalowood resumed his questioning: "Alaska Sanders found out about your affair with Eleanor. She knew you had pushed Eleanor to commit suicide. You said it yourself: it would have been a terrible stain on your career. More than a stain, actually, because now you're looking at a prison term, Dr. Bradburd. You benefited from your control over Eleanor to seduce her and then get rid of her. Alaska discovered this: she knew you were responsible, so you murdered her to protect your little secret and your pathetic career."

"That's a baseless accusation!" Bradburd screamed. He rose so suddenly that two officers jumped on him to make him sit back down.

Gahalowood kept up the pressure. "How did Alaska make the connection? You were her lover too, right? You were the one she met on the evening of April second, 1999, for a so-called romantic dinner during which you killed her!"

"You're completely mistaken, Sergeant. You really should think about seeing a professional. You haven't a shred of evidence for what you're saying. Your version of events would be laughable if it weren't so pathetic. The joke has gone on long enough. I demand to speak to my lawyer. I'm not saying another word without him."

"You'll have a right to a lawyer down at the Maine State Police station, where we're taking you."

"You're not taking me anywhere!" Bradburd burst out. "You have nothing on me."

"Dr. Bradburd, you're going to prison. You drove one of your patients to commit suicide. You're going down no matter what. As for the rest, keep quiet if that's what you want. We have plenty of evidence against you. You're a very intelligent man, Bradburd, that's why it took us eleven years to find you."

From his armchair in the living room, Bradburd, now under guard, watched as the police searched the premises. When he saw Gahalowood reach for the painting showing the sunset over the ocean, he looked concerned.

"You're not going to empty my house, are you?"

"Don't worry, Doctor. Where you're going, you won't need any of this."

We found nothing else of note on the property.

While we were busy inside, the police inspected the surrounding grounds. It was they who found the well, partly covered with brush and tall weeds. They alerted us at once. It was an old stone affair, covered by a heavy wooden panel, most likely placed there to prevent accidents. Gahalowood asked that they bring Bradburd out.

"What's this?" he asked him.

"You can see for yourself, it's an old well. We never used it."

"Any other surprises on the property?"

"I don't know why you're so worked up, Sergeant."

Bradburd had an arrogant side to him that was infuriating. But the well was certainly of interest. The wooden panel was removed; the pit was deep. A quick sweep with a flashlight revealed there was something at the bottom. Gahalowood wanted to find out what was down there. He asked that a team be sent over with the necessary equipment to take a proper look.

The commotion around the well drew everyone's attention. Bradburd, who wasn't cuffed, took advantage of the confusion to make a run for it. He fled in the direction of the forest. All the police present took off in pursuit, but Bradburd was a surprisingly fast runner. In a few steps, he reached the edge of the forest and disappeared into terrain that was familiar to him, while the police found themselves on uncharted ground.

*    *    *

Two hours had gone by since Bradburd's escape, and he still hadn't been found. Teams from the Coast Guard and the Maine police maritime brigade inspected all the boats leaving Vinalhaven. Bradburd knew the island inside out, but he couldn't get very far.

During the search, the team sent to explore the well had arrived. A man attached to a rope line went down into the shaft.

"There's a body!" he yelled from the bottom of the well. "It's completely decomposed."

Once the man was brought up in the fresh air, he opened his fist to show us what he had found: a pendant on a gold chain on which a woman's name had been engraved: *Eleanor.*

# 34

## *The Reversal*

*Concord, New Hampshire*
*Monday, August 2, 2010*

Five days after the discovery on Vinalhaven, Gahalowood, Lauren, and I went to see Chief Lansdane to discuss our findings in the Alaska Sanders case.

The body found in the well was indeed that of Eleanor Lowell. She hadn't committed suicide, as everyone had thought for all those years. She died as a result of violent trauma to the head caused by a blunt object. Like Alaska.

Benjamin Bradburd was found dead in a shed near a house on Vinalhaven. He had killed himself with what was near at hand—he placed a plastic bag over his head and secured it to his neck with adhesive tape. He died from asphyxiation. Gahalowood told me it was a fairly common method. "You'd be surprised how efficient it is, Writer: once it's done, you can't go back. It's impossible to get the adhesive tape off to remove the bag, and in their panic they rarely think of puncturing the plastic itself."

In Lansdane's office, Gahalowood went over what we knew: "Eleanor and Alaska were killed with the same weapon. Eleanor was struck on the parietal bone; the medical examiner found a shard of metal from the baton used to kill Alaska."

"So, by Bradburd?" Lansdane remarked.

"That's our conclusion," Gahalowood replied. "Unfortunately, we have no formal proof. But we have a motive: Alaska thought that Bradburd had driven Eleanor to suicide. When she confronted him, he was afraid someone would find Eleanor's body. So he killed Alaska to shut her up."

"What was the connection between Alaska and Bradburd?" Lansdane asked.

"It seems they were lovers," Lauren replied. "Unfortunately, both Alaska and Bradburd are now dead, so we'll never know for sure. But it would explain everything."

Gahalowood resumed speaking: "We couldn't understand how Eric Donovan seemed to be in the middle of it all. Everything pointed to him. He had to have had some connection with the murderer. It's when we figured out that Bradburd was having an affair with Eleanor, who was also seeing Eric Donovan, that we began to unravel the real story."

I continued: "On the evening of August thirtieth, 1998, Eleanor was with her friends on the beach at Chandler Hovey Park. Around eleven thirty, they left, except for Eleanor, who wanted to stay a while longer. Bradburd must have met her on the beach. Their relationship was very strained by then. Bradburd wanted to break up with her, but she refused. They argued. Then they started fighting. Eleanor got scared and used her metal baton to defend herself. Bradburd wrestled it away and used it against her. He struck her and killed her. It probably wasn't premeditated. He sent a message to Maria Lowell from Eleanor's phone to imply that she had killed herself. Then he took the body to Vinalhaven and threw it into the well near the house."

"And then?" Lansdane asked.

Gahalowood picked up the story: "A month after Eleanor's death—and this is where the two cases intersect—Alaska discovered that her father was stealing money from her bank account. She left for Mount Pleasant. Her departure was temporary at first. After a few days, Alaska orchestrated the robbery to get back at her father and steal his watch. But things went south and a police officer who tried to intervene was badly injured. Fearing the consequences, she sought refuge in Mount Pleasant.

From there she continued a relationship with a man in Salem whom she had met during the Miss New England competition: Benjamin Bradburd. They were seeing one another in secret; he would send her gifts. A few months went by. After a visit from Eleanor's mother, Alaska came to believe that Eric Donovan, who she knew had been involved with Eleanor, had driven her to commit suicide. She told Bradburd about it. He may have tried to dissuade her from looking into it any further. But Alaska was stubborn. She delivered those two anonymous messages to Eric. When Eric found out that Alaska was behind them, he proved to her that he wasn't responsible for Eleanor's death. Alaska then realized not only that there was someone else in Eleanor's life, but that that person was Benjamin Bradburd."

"How?" Lansdane asked.

"In her diary, Eleanor mentioned a man who drove a blue car and lived in a gray house surrounded by red maples. Alaska was very familiar with that house because she had stayed there on more than one occasion and recorded a casting audition there in September 1998. It belonged to her lover, Benjamin Bradburd. She would pay for that discovery with her life. The evening of April second, 1999, Bradburd lured Alaska into a trap at Grey Beach. He killed her with the baton, the same way he had killed Eleanor. Bradburd was an intelligent man who considered all possibilities. He was an expert at manipulation. To throw the investigators off his trail, he gave them the perfect culprit, someone the police would later discover had been involved in a relationship with Eleanor and whom Alaska knew: Eric Donovan. Bradburd further confused the police by placing Eric Donovan's sweater near the scene of the crime, after staining it with Alaska's blood."

"How did Bradburd get his hands on the sweater, though?"

"Two weeks before Alaska's murder," Lauren said, "while Bradburd was probably planning his perfect crime, Walter Carrey left for a few days for a convention in Quebec. It was then that Bradburd found Eric's sweater, maybe at Alaska's place. He could've gone to see her on the sly while Walter was away and come across the sweater in the apartment. Remember that Eric had lent it to Walter during a fishing trip a few days earlier. Walter had left the sweater in the trunk of his car, but Alaska took it up to the apartment, maybe to wash it. Perhaps she complained to Bradburd about it because Eric kept asking for his sweater. In any case, Bradburd realized it was Eric's and stole it."

Lansdane again interrupted. "Why would Alaska still be seeing Bradburd if she thought he was responsible for Eleanor's death?"

"She was playing along. She didn't want to arouse suspicion. She was a week away from leaving Mount Pleasant and putting that part of her life behind her. After Alaska's murder, when Walter was arrested, and then Eric, Bradburd realized that he had pulled off the perfect crime. Yet there was one person who could gum up the works, and that was Kazinsky, who had been involved in Walter's interrogation. Bradburd knew that Walter had admitted to a crime he didn't commit and therefore that Kazinsky knew the confession was coerced. So he had to get rid of Kazinsky."

"And so Bradburd tried to kill Kazinsky by running him over," Lansdane said.

"Exactly," Lauren confirmed.

After our explanation, Lansdane clapped his hands noisily in a sign of approval. "Bravo! Case closed—for good this time."

Then Gahalowood said to him: "There is one detail. The remains of that broken taillight from the Ford Taurus found in the forest. I still don't understand what they were doing there."

"Coincidences happen, Perry."

"I don't believe in coincidences, Chief."

But Lansdane was ready to close the investigation. Mostly to please the governor, whose deadline had arrived. "You have to know when to let go, Perry," he said. "This case has dragged on for eleven years: it's time to turn the page."

*   *   *

That day Gahalowood, Lauren, and I went to see Robbie and Donna Sanders to tell them that the investigation into the murder of their daughter was over. Gahalowood filled them in on the recent train of events. When he had finished, he told them: "Justice has been served." Behind her parents was a portrait of Alaska. I had the impression she was smiling at us.

It was time to say our goodbyes.

We returned to Mount Pleasant. For me, this was the last time. I left the town with a sense of nostalgia. In spite of everything that had happened, I can honestly say I liked the place.

Gahalowood and I gathered our belongings from the hotel. We made one final visit to Main Street. First, we stopped by Carrey Hunting & Fishing to say hello. Then we visited Donovan's General Store, where we found Eric. He gave Gahalowood a warm handshake.

"Thanks, Sergeant."

Gahalowood nodded in recognition. Uncertain how best to reply, he simply said, "Good luck, Eric. I hope you can rebuild your life."

"Lauren told me you were angry with yourself, Sergeant, because of what happened. I can assure you I've never been angry with you. With Vance, yes, with Patricia as well. But you, you did your job. And this is proof—you're here now. You're a good guy, Sergeant Gahalowood. May Heaven protect you."

Leaving the Donovans' store, I ran into Lauren, who was waiting for me. Gahalowood moved away so we could be alone.

"Lauren, about the concert—"

She interrupted me. "Well, you did tell me that the girl in the picture was called Alexandra. But I didn't realize it was Alexandra Neville. Who would've guessed?"

"So how did you find out?"

She smiled sadly. "I'm a cop, Marcus."

Lauren was holding a celebrity magazine. She opened it and showed me an article on Alexandra Neville and her relationship with a hockey player with the Florida Panthers. Then she took her phone and showed me the photo she had sent me two weeks earlier—a screenshot of the photograph I had left at her place, showing my cousins and that same girl in Baltimore in 1995.

"I figured it out as I was flipping through the magazine. The girl in the photograph—that's Alexandra Neville. She was your great love when you were young."

I nodded in agreement.

"What happened between you?" she asked.

"There was a kind of family drama with the Baltimore Goldmans. Something that happened with Woody and Hillel."

"You feel like talking about it?"

"I don't think so."

She looked at me for a moment. The brilliance of her eyes revealed a mixture of regret and bitterness. "I don't know what happened with your cousins and Alexandra," she said, "but obviously it's still troubling you. It's keeping you from moving on with your life, from meeting someone. It's preventing you from being happy. I hope you fix all that someday, Marcus. You're a decent guy: you deserve to put your past behind you."

I offered nothing more than a clumsy goodbye. I wanted to take her in my arms, but I was afraid she would resent it. We both knew at that moment that we'd never see each other again.

"You heading back to New York?" she asked.

"Yes."

"I want to thank you. For everything. I also thought you should know that Chief Mitchell asked me to become the next chief of police in Mount Pleasant."

"I'm very proud of you," I said quietly.

As she turned to walk away, I noticed a tear on her cheek.

I went over to join Gahalowood, who was leaning against his car. "Okay?"

"Okay."

We stood there in silence for a moment. We too were getting ready to say goodbye, possibly for a long time. I was returning to New York, and Perry was going back to Concord. Finally, he said to me, "So, Writer, we've finished our investigation, are we both going back home?"

"Something tells me we'll see one another again soon, Sergeant."

"You know that there's a room for you at my place. Come whenever you like."

"Thanks, Sergeant. When do the girls get back from camp?"

"Next weekend. You have plans?"

"Not really. I'm supposed to go back to Burrows University at the end of August for a meeting to discuss the fall semester."

"Are you really going to teach there?"

"I don't know yet."


I drove nonstop to Manhattan and returned to my apartment. I felt alone. I flipped through my photo album, the one my mother hated. I stayed up late into the night, unable to sleep. Finally, I sat down at my desk and turned on my computer. I opened a new document and typed the title of my next book:

*The Alaska Sanders Affair*
By Marcus Goldman

# 35

## *Those Who Know*

*Burrows, Massachusetts*
*Monday, August 23, 2010*
After three weeks, I temporarily interrupted my book to go to Burrows University and assume my new role in the English department.

Upon my arrival, I was warmly welcomed by Pergal, who introduced me to my new colleagues. First came a long meeting about the program, and then we all sat down to lunch. Afterward, Pergal led me to Harry's old office. There was a plaque with my name on it by the door. Nearly twelve years after I had first met him here, I was walking in the footsteps of Harry Quebert. I entered the room, deeply moved. Nothing seemed to have changed since my last visit.

"If you need anything, don't hesitate," Pergal said, as he watched me from the doorway. "We have a small budget for new furniture if you like."

"Thanks, but this is perfect. Everything's perfect just the way it is."

I sat at the desk and looked around the room. Pergal left. I opened the drawer, the one in which I had discovered the small figurine of the gull the previous June. It was still there. And beneath it, the newspaper, which I hadn't paid much attention to before. I picked it up. It must have been at least twenty years old, if not more. I checked the date—and immediately understood.

Grabbing the paper, I ran out of the office. In the hallway, I ran into Pergal.

"Everything okay, Marcus?"

"Everything's fine. Don't worry, I'm coming back. I don't know when, but I'm coming back."

"You leaving?"

"I have an important meeting."

"With whom?"

I didn't answer, leaving him standing there, confused. He shouted after me in a somewhat amused tone of voice, "Well, student or teacher, we're never bored with you around, Marcus."

The paper I had found was the gazette for a small Canadian town called Lionsburg, on the border with the United States. The edition was dated August 30, 1975. It was a significant day in Harry's life because it was when Nola Kellergan had disappeared. The paper hadn't found its way there by accident: it was a sign that Harry had left for me months ago so I could find him. He had no doubt settled in that town.

After a few hours on the road, I reached Lionsburg. Now all I had to do was find Harry. I went to the nearest hotel, assuming I could easily question the locals. But right after I parked the car, I noticed a bookstore. The sign over the door read "Writers' World." I stood there with my mouth open.

I walked in, feeling a bit intimidated. I was met by a blond woman, who vaguely resembled Nola Kellergan, but a version of her in her forties.

"Can I help you?" she asked.

"Is Harry here?"

The woman turned toward the back room. "Darling, there's someone to see you."

Harry appeared suddenly. He was beaming. "Marcus, finally."

\*      \*      \*

I spent the next few days with Harry. It reminded me of my visits to Somerset, but for the fact that there was a woman in his life now. Harry and Nadya lived in a small, comfortable house in Lionsburg with a porch, not far from the ocean, just like Goose Cove but on a quiet street.

My first day there, I woke at five in the morning. I stepped out onto the porch, bathed in dawn light. It was already quite warm. As I looked out over the neighborhood, I heard Harry's voice behind me.

"I see you still get up with the dawn."

He was sitting in a wooden chair. I hadn't noticed him when I came out. He was holding a cup of coffee in his hands; a second, still steaming, was waiting for me on a side table. I took a seat next to him.

"How is it that you know me so well?" I asked after taking a sip of coffee.

"Because I'm your friend, Marcus. A friend is someone who knows you well and who loves you in spite of that."

I smiled.

"If you found your way here, it's because you found the newspaper in the drawer of my old desk. I assume you're going to teach that class at Burrows."

"Only for a semester. I committed to it: I don't want to renege on Pergal."

"Pergal wanted to throw you out of school when you were a student—remember?"

"I know, but that's the past. You have to put these things behind you."

"Is that right?" he asked, somewhat amused. "You know, Marcus, if I tried to dissuade you from going to Burrows, it was my clumsy way of trying to encourage you to live your own life. To put aside your loyalties and do what's best for you."

"I don't think I know what's best for me these days."

"I have a pretty good idea," Harry said. "And I'm here to help."

During those days with Harry, I rediscovered the profound connection I had formed with him over the years. We talked nonstop, as if to make up for lost time, on his porch, in his living room, in the restaurant near his house, where we spent hours, as we once had at Clark's in Somerset.

In the bookstore as well, where, one afternoon, he grabbed a copy of *The Truth About the Harry Quebert Affair* from the shelf.

"I don't know how many times I've read this book," he said. "I never told you how proud of you I am, Marcus. I realize I wasn't very subtle last July, when I saw you at that performance of *Madame Butterfly*. I didn't want to make a big mystery out of it, but I was nervous about getting in touch. I wasn't sure how to get back into your life after disappearing the way I did. At the time, I thought I was angry with you for having discovered my secret, before I understood that what I was most afraid of was losing you. I thought you hated me after you discovered the truth about *The Origin of Evil*."

"I was never angry with you, Harry. I desperately tried to find you."

"I admire you, Marcus. And I'm grateful to you. Thanks to you, and your investigation in 2008, I was finally able to turn the page on Nola. I don't need to wait for her anymore: I no longer live in the past. I was able to rebuild my life. And thanks to you, I finally understood that our demons never disappear. We get used to them, and they end up sharing our life without interfering in it. You fixed something in me, Marcus, and I wanted to do the same for you. That's why I sent you that ticket for the Alexandra Neville concert. To trigger something in you so you might find her again. She's the one, Marcus. It's not too late to fix it, despite what happened to your family in Baltimore. That ticket was meant to tell you that life goes on, that all you need is one small spark to ignite it again. After the concert you could have gone backstage, you could have let her know that you were there. You would have found her again. Why didn't you?"

"I don't know, Harry. It's too complicated."

"Nothing is too complicated, Marcus. I often think about the thirty-one rules for writing you included in your book about me—the ones you attribute to me. There's only one that matters."

"What's that?"

"Ask yourself why you write. Once you've answered that question, you'll know what makes you a writer. Do you know why you write, Marcus?"

I remained silent for a while. "I don't know, Harry. I don't know anymore."

"I can't answer for you, Marcus, but I'm going to tell you what I think. You write to fix things. *The Truth About the Harry Quebert Affair* was intended to fix me, and *The Alaska Sanders Affair*, which you said you've begun, will fix your friend Gahalowood. That's very generous of you—trying to fix everyone—but it might be time to think about yourself. Of course, you can spend your life crisscrossing the country like some magnificent literary vagabond, trying to resolve all the sordid murders that happen, but that won't fix you, Marcus. That won't fix what happened to your family in Baltimore. That won't bring back Alexandra or your cousins. It's time to forgive yourself, Marcus, and writing is the only way you can do that."

And that's how Harry Quebert, my rediscovered friend and mentor, pushed me to make a decision that would change the course of my life: to find a home fit for a writer.

"Your apartment in New York is nice enough, but you need a place where you can devote yourself to writing. A place that allows you to focus on yourself. Your very own Goose Cove."

"I like New England," I noted.

"Forget New England, Marcus! Your identity lies somewhere else. A place that defines you. Close your eyes and think of a city."

"Baltimore," I said without hesitation. "But I don't think I want to live in Baltimore."

"It may not be Baltimore, but we're making progress. When I hear 'Baltimore,' I obviously think about your family, your cousins. You've never written about them, Marcus. There has to be a place where you can do that. That's the place where Goldman can fix Marcus."

*

When I finally left Lionsburg, on Thursday, August 26, I felt at peace. Changed. A page in my life was being turned. Before getting in the car, I kissed Nadya on the cheek and embraced Harry. "See you soon," I said.

"Let me know what you're doing, Marcus. And come back whenever you like. You can make yourself at home here."

"You and Nadya are also welcome in New York, you know."

"Not New York," Harry replied with an amused smile. "I'll come to your writer's house when you've finally found it."

I drove off. As I left Lionsburg behind me, I listened to an opera. After crossing the border between Canada and New Hampshire, I got a call from Gahalowood.

"Writer," he said in a voice that sounded broken. "We got it wrong. Bradburd had an alibi for Alaska's murder. He's not our man. I don't know how it happened, but we've been conned."

# 36

# *Contempt*

*Salem, Massachusetts*
*Thursday, August 26, 2010*
In the days that followed the closing of the Alaska Sanders murder
case, Gahalowood's concern for the pieces of broken taillight that had
been found in the woods continued to grow. At first, he simply forced
himself to stop thinking about it. But it kept coming back, again and
again.

I met Gahalowood in Salem, in front of Bradburd's house.

"What's going on, Sergeant?"

"Trust me, I didn't disturb you for nothing . . . I've been wanting to
call for a while. Something didn't feel right."

"You can speak freely, Sergeant. What's bothering you?"

"Almost every part of our theory checked out: Bradburd stole Eric
Donovan's sweater and then left it where it would look like conclusive
proof. The same is true for the message in Alaska's pocket, which he
easily could have put there. But the broken taillight? Could that really
be a coincidence, as Lansdane said? I returned to Bradburd's office the
other day and looked through his records. He kept a pile of relics to his
glory. Clearly, the man was a narcissist. And look what I found."

Gahalowood held out an article from the *Canaan Standard*, a local
Connecticut newspaper, dated April 3, 1999.

On Friday, April 2, 1999, the Canaan Association of Physicians celebrated its twentieth anniversary. It was the occasion for a gala dinner at the Town Hall. The guest of honor was Dr. Benjamin Bradburd, a psychiatrist from Salem, Massachusetts, who gave a talk on the importance of psychotherapy in prison environments.

Gahalowood said to me: "The night Alaska was killed, Bradburd was giving a talk three hours away from Mount Pleasant. We were wrong: he can't be her murderer."

"So why did he kill himself, then?"

"To avoid prison for Eleanor's murder."

"But Alaska and Eleanor were killed with the same weapon. It doesn't make sense."

"I think we're still in for a few more surprises. Maybe we missed something. That's why I wanted to take a look at Bradburd's house with you."

We got to work, starting with Bradburd's home office.

"Looks like he collected a lot of cheap souvenirs," Gahalowood said.

We examined dozens of documents, none of which held much interest. Bradburd appeared to have kept everything. We were able to trace the contours of his life over twenty years, from bills and gym and video club membership cards to old photographs and airplane tickets. Some were even annotated. We didn't look closely at first because they just seemed like souvenirs. But then I found a wedding invitation.

THE MARRIAGE OF STEVEN HART & BELLA SWEDE
August 30, 1998
Plaza Hotel, Boston

"Sergeant, look at the date. Bradburd was invited to a wedding the night Eleanor Lowell was killed. Do you think he actually went?"

"We'll know soon enough."

Gahalowood found Steven Hart without much difficulty. Although it was late, he called him. Hart told us he had divorced Bella Swede three years earlier but confirmed that Benjamin Bradburd had been one of the guests at their wedding.

"Did he leave late?" Gahalowood asked.

"As I recall, he stayed overnight at the hotel. Is this in connection with the murder? That was a terrible business. Do we know anything more about why he did it?"

Gahalowood wasn't listening to Hart. He was looking at me with a mixture of incomprehension and determination. Ever since the start of the investigation, someone had succeeded in deceiving us.

After he ended his call to Hart, Gahalowood said: "Let's assume that both Bradburd and Eric Donovan were framed. The murderer is connected to Benjamin, Eric Donovan, Eleanor, and Alaska."

"And Kazinsky," I added.

While taking the invitation from the box of souvenirs, I had inadvertently grabbed the photograph beneath it. Gahalowood noticed it and took it from me. It was a wedding photograph: Benjamin Bradburd's.

"The bride!" Gahalowood cried. "The bride!"

I stared at the photograph, open-mouthed.

# 37

# *Endgame*

*Boston, Massachusetts*
*Friday, August 27, 2010*

The following afternoon, Gahalowood and I barged into Patricia Widsmith's office accompanied by a squad from the Boston police department, who arrested her. When she saw us, she understood at once why we were there.

She smiled sadly. "Ever since that July afternoon when the two of you came barreling into this office," she said, "I've been preparing myself for this. For eleven years, it all went well. Until you got involved."

She rose from her chair and stood by the window—as if to take advantage for one last time of the sun's generous light, which warmed Boston on this summer's afternoon. Gahalowood grabbed a pair of handcuffs.

"Don't take me in right away," Patricia requested. "I have no desire to tell you how it happened in some bleak interrogation room. I've seen too many of them already."

"Okay," Gahalowood replied. "I'll read you your rights and record your statement, which can be used against you."

"How did you find out?"

"We were missing a connection among the key people in this case: Eleanor Lowell, Alaska Sanders, Eric Donovan, and Benjamin Bradburd. When we found out that you're his ex-wife, that was the link we were looking for."

"I knew it would end like this."

Gahalowood turned on the recorder on his phone. "We're listening."

"My name is Patricia Widsmith. I briefly bore the name Bradburd during my short marriage. I killed Alaska Sanders in the early hours of April third, 1999."

She fell silent. Her face was frozen in a kind of rictus.

"Patricia," Gahalowood said, "I've been doing this job for a long time. But I have to say that I have no idea what could have led you to where you are now."

"What do you want to know?"

"Everything."

"Then we have to go back to 1998. I had been married to Benjamin for a year. He was something else. I was very much in love at the time. Benjamin was fifteen years older than me. I had always been attracted to older men, and he had a great deal of charisma—maybe that's what made me feel secure. We met at a seminar on the death penalty. He had been working in prisons for a long time and was fighting for a new approach to incarceration. We hit it off right away. When we started going out, I was a little afraid of how my family would react, because of his age. But they all liked him. He won over my friends, and my mother adored him. He was smart, kind, sociable, helpful. A gem. It all happened very quickly. I moved into his pretty house in Salem. He had a good job. And I was already working as a lawyer in Boston, just starting out. Not long after that, he asked me to marry him. I accepted. Without a shadow of a doubt."

\*       \*       \*

*January 1998*

Married a year and he was already cheating on her!

Patricia had just walked in on her husband with another woman. She left the building where he had his office and took refuge in her car. Her reaction surprised her: Why had she fled instead of confronting him? Why hadn't she caused a scene? On Tuesdays, Benjamin always stayed late at the office. He checked the billing, took care of some administrative details. And she also stayed on at work in Boston on those evenings. They would meet back at the house. But that night, she had left early to surprise him. She stopped at a Chinese restaurant they liked, ordered half the takeout menu, and headed to his office without letting him know. When she pushed the door open, even before she said hello, she could hear a woman whimpering and a low moaning. She walked quietly along the hallway. Through the partly open door to his office, she saw Benjamin, naked on the couch used by his patients, having sex with another woman.

Patricia stood there, horrified, watching them. Then she left, as silently as she had arrived, returned to her car, and cried. She hadn't disturbed a soul. She was as incredulous as she was powerless. She had always told herself that she would never tolerate adultery, that she would leave a man who was unfaithful to her at once. But now that it had happened, she was paralyzed. She went home and went to bed. She threw herself down onto the mattress, fearing his return, and when he came home, she pretended to be asleep. Benjamin undressed and went to bed. He shifted toward her and held her close to him. She remained motionless, frozen, disgusted.

The next day she wanted to tell someone but found she couldn't. She was ashamed. But shouldn't Benjamin be the one to feel shame? He seemed to be quite calm about it all. In a good mood as always. He didn't even notice the change in her.

A week went by. The following Tuesday evening, she returned to his office. Through the half-open door, she again observed their adultery. And once more, she did nothing. Paralyzed, just as before. And the following Tuesday evening they were there once more: Benjamin with the woman, and Patricia with them both. Sometimes she went upstairs and watched them have sex. Sometimes she stayed in her car, just sitting there, eating the Chinese takeout dishes she continued to order.

Their life as a couple gradually deteriorated. Silently. Benjamin seemed to be oblivious. Patricia waited for him to ask her what was wrong, waited for him to pay attention to her, but his mind was elsewhere. With the other one. Patricia didn't want him to touch her anymore, and the less he touched her, the more she imagined him with Her. Filthy images kept cycling through her head. She had the impression she was invisible. No-one seemed to notice her. He didn't even see her at the wheel of her car, parked on the other side of the street. He left the building with Her; they smiled at one another and politely said good night, satisfied with their perfect act.

That's how Patricia was able to put a face to the woman, whom she had only ever seen from behind. She was a petite blond, very young, with diaphanous skin and sad eyes. Soon she was able to put a name to the face: Eleanor, who, she discovered, was one of her husband's patients. Patricia's shame only continued to grow. If she were to reveal her husband's escapades, everyone would know that he was a predator who was sleeping with a patient young enough to be his daughter. She had no desire to be the wife of a man like that, the kind of woman people regard with pity. She didn't want to be the one to feel shame or remorse.

In Salem, Patricia got friendly with a young man, Eric Donovan. She found him charming, and they often went to the same places, and over time, they came to like one another.

In a moment of weakness, Patricia dreamed of sleeping with Eric, thinking it might free her. Though she gave up the idea at once, she still met him regularly at the Blue Lagoon, a fashionable bar. Eric sometimes brought along a childhood friend, Walter, a nice guy if a little uncouth, who tried too hard to draw attention to himself.

Patricia went to the Blue Lagoon for the last time one night in March. She passed a group of young women, among whom she recognized Eleanor. Seeing the girl, her stomach clenched. She felt nauseous. And to add to her misery, Eric pointed Eleanor out, saying, "I really like her; do you think you could talk to her for a bit and maybe introduce me?" Patricia, disgusted, took her drink from the bar and walked away, but as she turned, she brushed against another young woman. They both apologized, and the story could have ended there if, at the wheel of her car on the way home, Patricia hadn't seen that same young woman walking down an empty street. She was young and very beautiful, and Patricia didn't like to see her walking alone at such a late hour. She stopped alongside her and lowered her window.

"Are you walking?"

"Yes, I had a bit too much to drink so I don't want to drive. Everyone else left already and it's impossible to find a cab. A walk will do me good."

"Get in, I'll drop you off."

The young woman got into the car. Patricia was once again struck by her beauty—her face, her smile, her eyes, her hair. And that body. And who could forget her name: Alaska.

"Where do you live, Alaska?"

"In Mack Park."

As she drove, Patricia couldn't help glancing at her passenger. There was something magnetic about her beauty. She found her somehow sensual even though she had never thought of a woman in that way before. Alaska caught her looking.

"What's up?" she asked, a little annoyed.

"Nothing. I was just looking at you . . . you're very beautiful."

Alaska burst out laughing. Her voice was loud and warm. "Thanks. You're pretty good-looking, yourself."

"I didn't say it just so you'd compliment me back," Patricia explained.

"I know."

When Patricia dropped Alaska off in front of her parents' house, something electrifying passed between them. Patricia wanted to ask for her phone number, but she didn't dare. She was bothered by the fact that Alaska was a woman, and by the ten years that separated them, even though Benjamin was sleeping with a patient more than twenty years his junior.

Patricia returned home. Benjamin was already asleep. She showered and stayed under the water a long time. She felt an excitement she had never felt before. And she liked it.

Two weeks later, on a Tuesday evening, Alaska was going home on foot again. Walking down one of Salem's main streets, she saw Patricia eating in her car. Alaska thought this funny and tapped on the window. "What are you doing here?" she asked.

"Waiting," Patricia replied.

"Waiting for who?"

For the first time she could remember, Patricia felt the need to confide in someone. To tell that person what she was going through. She invited Alaska into the car and told her everything.

"So your husband is in his office banging his patient, and you're sitting downstairs in your car. But what are you waiting for?"

"For him to finish."

Patricia began to cry. She'd had enough. She was tired of being so passive. Alaska took her hand and kissed it. Patricia once more felt that pleasant sensation, multiplied tenfold. Then Alaska said to her, "Men are shit."

Patricia burst out laughing. Alaska brought her face close to hers. After a languorous kiss, Patricia asked, "What are you doing the next few days?"

"Nothing special, why?"

"We could go away for a bit, just you and me."

"What, just like that, now?"

Patricia said yes, nervously, not knowing how the girl would respond. She wanted to experience this adventure right away. To grab hold of the moment. Something was happening between them, and she wanted to follow her impulses wherever they led. She figured it wouldn't last very long. Their sudden attraction was probably a passing fancy. She was over thirty and had never thought about being with another woman. Why change now, so suddenly? She wanted that pure beauty, that was all.

"Okay," Alaska replied.

"Really?"

"Yes, you only live once, right? I'll get a few things from home and tell my parents that I'm sleeping at a friend's tonight and going to New York tomorrow for an audition." The mention of parents reminded Patricia of the girl's age. Suddenly, she felt a momentary hesitation. Alaska noticed this.

"I'm still living with my parents. I don't want to worry them, so that means I can't exactly tell them I'm leaving for two days to go heaven-knows-where with a woman I barely know."

Patricia burst out laughing. She dropped Alaska off at her parents', then went home. Finding the lights on in the house, she realized that Benjamin was in the bedroom. Probably taking a shower. She entered quietly, took the keys to the house on Vinalhaven, which were hanging in the entrance hall, and left as discreetly as she had come. She sent her husband a message telling him she was spending the night in Boston to attend to some last-minute work emergency. Then she went to pick up Alaska, who jumped in the car with her small bag.

"I took some clothes for you, like you asked," Alaska said. "You'll like them."

"Thanks."

They drove all the way to Rockland, Maine, arriving in the middle of the night. They found a motel room and fell into one another's arms, exhausted. The next morning, they took the ferry to Vinalhaven. On the ship's bridge, Patricia devoured Alaska with her eyes, her hair caught in the wind as she admired the landscape.

On the island, in the gray house surrounded by red maples, they spent two amazing days. Two days during which Patricia learned to make love to a woman. Two days of a pure and powerful happiness she had never known. On Vinalhaven, her life changed forever.

\*   \*   \*

"I'll never forget those two April days on Vinalhaven," Patricia told us. "It was amazing. Alaska electrified me; she gave me the strength I lacked to take control of my life. She told me, 'Leave that bastard. He doesn't deserve you! You're better off without him.' And I was, thanks to her. When I returned to Salem, I confronted Benjamin. I said to him, 'I know everything, you bastard! You've been sleeping with one of your patients. I even know her name. You see her every Tuesday night, in your office, while you're doing your so-called accounting.' Benjamin's reaction was completely unexpected. I wanted him to deny it, so we could have a real argument, but he simply shrugged and said, 'I'm not the first person to have an affair and I won't be the last. It happens.' And he went back to reading his paper.

"In confronting Benjamin after months of silence, I realized I'd allowed our marriage to stagnate. Maybe if I'd acted immediately, I would have had the will to salvage our life together. But now, it was truly over. He was a stranger to me. I was ready to call it quits. I'm always amazed at our ability to build relationships and then destroy them in the blink of an eye. A scorched-earth policy. I moved out and rented an apartment. I hadn't told anyone but Alaska about Benjamin's cheating, and I kept silent about it after our separation. I didn't want any drama, any commotion. I wanted to move on with my life. So I allowed my mother to reproach me, to tell me that I was giving up an extraordinary man. And Benjamin and my mother continued seeing one another even after our breakup."

"So you got a divorce," Gahalowood said.

"Not right away. Benjamin was cheap. We didn't have a prenup, and he had quite a bit of family money. I didn't care about that, but I did enjoy tormenting him. So I asked for half of his assets, as the law allows. That drove him crazy."

\*     \*     \*

*April 1998*

"You are seriously asking for half my assets for a single year of marriage!" Benjamin shouted, beside himself with anger.

"For better or worse, remember? Each of us stole from the other what mattered most: you took my pride, I'm taking your money."

"Your pride . . . stop exaggerating!"

"Am I? At any rate, Benjamin, I saw you screwing that blond!"

"You're so melodramatic, Patricia. That's what makes you a good lawyer. I hope you don't start telling stories about me to your friends."

"Oh don't worry, your secret's safe with me. And if your mother asks, I'll tell her we just don't get along anymore."

"Why would my mother ask you any questions?"

"She must be protective of the family's reputation, with her idiotic beauty competition."

"Don't talk about my mother like that: she's always respected you!"

The separation from Benjamin was a turning point in Patricia's life. Now she could devote herself fully to Alaska. Her passion hadn't waned. On the contrary, it blossomed. The apartment Patricia found was a cocoon for their secret love. She had never cared for anyone that way before. And Alaska's love was unconditional.

The weeks went by. Day by day, Patricia was surprised to find her love for Alaska growing. They dreamed of a future together. Alaska talked of moving to Manhattan. Or Los Angeles. Patricia found the idea appealing, but Alaska wanted to wait for the right opportunity.

"I don't want to vegetate, working as a waitress waiting for my starring role," she explained.

"I'll work for the both of us," Patricia replied. "You can concentrate on auditions."

"I don't want to be the struggling artist kept by her girlfriend either. I've saved up some money, but I don't want to touch it right now. We're

489

comfortable here in Salem. And I feel that things are going to start moving pretty soon."

Alaska was hoping that year would signal a new stage in her acting career. She had recently found an agent in New York who was sending her to a lot more casting calls. She rehearsed her lines with Patricia, and then filmed herself at her parents' place, in her bedroom, using her father's old camcorder.

"You can also come here to film yourself, if you want," Patricia offered.

"No, my mother watches my videos and helps me choose the best sequence, and I don't want her asking any questions."

"Questions about us?"

"Yes."

Patricia also wondered about their relationship. She now felt ready to embrace it fully. But this wasn't the case for Alaska, who feared how others would see her.

"People are idiots," Patricia said to her. "Who cares what they think?"

"Yes, but that's the way it is. I want to build a career, not change how people think. Do you know many famous actresses openly living with another woman?"

*       *       *

Patricia interrupted her story. She hadn't moved from the window until then. She took a few steps and opened a drawer. Gahalowood kept a close eye on her movements. She pulled out a photo and offered it to us. It was her posing with Alaska in New York, twelve years earlier. She said softly: "My sweet, beautiful darling. My angel. In early June 1998, she celebrated her twenty-second birthday. I took her to New York for the weekend. We imagined what it would be like to live there. I needed to dream. My divorce proceedings had gotten bogged down: I told Benjamin I was prepared to give up my claim on half his wealth in exchange for the house on Vinalhaven. I did that partly because it would drive him crazy—he loved that house—but also because I was thinking of spending my summers there with Alaska. It would have been our haven of peace. Benjamin obviously wanted me to drop my demands, but he had no leverage. He had hired a well-known lawyer, and I don't think he gave him any illusions about how things would pan out. I was determined to keep going.

"Early that summer, rumors began to circulate that Alaska wasn't interested in men. She had been seen with 'an older woman.' Alaska had just enrolled in the Miss New England competition, much to the delight of her agent, who felt it would help promote her career. One morning she called me at my office, frantic, and said, 'They're saying I like women.' I tried to calm her down and pointed out, somewhat amused, that it was the truth; but she replied, 'I'm not laughing. This is serious. I know the people on the Miss New England committee, and they're very old-fashioned.' That evening, Alaska went to the Blue Lagoon with her girlfriends and ran into Walter Carrey, who had been after her for quite some time. At the end of the evening, in the parking lot, she suddenly grabbed him by the collar and kissed him in front of everyone."

"So Alaska started seeing Walter Carrey just to change people's minds about her sexuality?" I asked.

"Yes," Patricia replied. "Walter was supposed to be around only until the competition was done. He was perfect for the part: good-looking, sporty, well built, a nice guy. Walter was easy, uncomplicated. He didn't give her a hard time, and crucially, he didn't live in Salem, so he was there only from time to time and never got in the way. Alaska told me they weren't sleeping together. I assume she said that to please or reassure me, but I understood that she was only twenty-two, her hormones were going wild, and she must have been questioning her sexuality. To be completely honest, Walter's presence in her life wasn't a problem for me. I didn't feel threatened. Paradoxically, it strengthened our relationship. Alaska could now more easily accept that we were seeing one another. She allowed herself new freedoms, like taking my hand discreetly under the table at a restaurant or throwing her arms around me on an empty street. Everything was going well. But it didn't last. Alaska had a rival: Eleanor Lowell. She was jealous of Alaska."

*     *     *

*June–July 1998*

Once she started officially going out with Walter, Alaska forced herself to talk about men whenever she could. When she was at the Blue Lagoon with her girlfriends, she commented whenever a young man passed by. Within the group, Eleanor Lowell was nurturing a growing sense of jealousy toward Alaska. She was the one who had quietly started the rumors about Alaska's sexuality. Eleanor's annoyance only grew when Alaska began to make a fuss over Eric Donovan, whom she said was good-looking, even going so far as to wonder whether she hadn't made a mistake in choosing Walter rather than his best friend. Alaska had lighted on Eric for no particular reason, and she had no idea that he and Eleanor had been sleeping together for a while. One evening, Eleanor took Alaska aside and gave her a warning: "Watch your step if you don't want any trouble. Stay away from Eric."

"Eric Donovan?"

"He's mine!"

"You're going out with Eric? *He's* your mystery man?"

"Stay away, got it? And not a word to anyone. We don't want anyone knowing about us."

When Alaska mentioned the episode, Patricia didn't tell her that Eleanor was also Benjamin's lover. She didn't see the point. But since she thought that Eleanor Lowell was a manipulative bitch, she knew she had to keep an eye on her.

*     *     *

Gahalowood and I listened to Patricia in religious silence. She had returned to her place by the window.

492

"When I learned, a few days later, that Eleanor was being mistreated by her lover, whom I knew to be Benjamin, I realized that he had been taking his frustration out on her that summer. The situation was getting out of hand. He dumped all the ill will caused by the divorce proceedings on her, shaming her, refusing to be seen with her in public, rightly fearing that I would use it against him in court.

"Then, in July, Alaska was selected to participate in the Miss New England competition. By the end of the month, she had learned that Eleanor had been appointed to the jury. In early August, Eleanor asked to meet Alaska in a coffee shop. There, she unleashed a torrent of lies and invective, concluding by informing her that she would never win the title and that she would do everything she could to make sure of it. She told Alaska, 'I'm sick of hearing about your shitty acting career. Be satisfied with your role as a lesbian slut—you're perfect for the part.' Alaska, ordinarily so strong, was devastated. She fell into a depression. I told her we'd go to New York no matter what, and she insisted that she wouldn't go just to be a waitress in a restaurant. I wanted to help her; I didn't care what it cost. And there *was* something I could do."

"Kill Eleanor Lowell," Gahalowood said.

"No!" Patricia protested. "Of course not. That idea never crossed my mind. I went to see Benjamin on Vinalhaven. I told him that if he made sure that Alaska won the Miss New England competition, I would sign the divorce papers without asking him for a cent."

"And he accepted?"

"Obviously. For him it was a gift! But I didn't say anything to Alaska. I wanted her victory to be a triumph, not the result of the pathetic negotiations of a failed couple. And then, there was that evening in August—August thirtieth, 1998. We were having dinner, me and Alaska, at a seafood restaurant near the ocean. She looked distraught. I asked her, 'What's the matter, angel? Is it that idiot Eleanor? Is she still bothering you?' 'Yes,' she told me. 'She's been talking about me behind my back. She's trying to push me out of the group. They all went swimming at

Chandler Hovey Park tonight, and no-one invited me.' I couldn't bear to see her suffer. She was so sweet, so kind. She didn't deserve it. I had to do something. I had to protect her from Eleanor. I was determined to put a stop to it."

After dinner, I left Alaska with the excuse of an early meeting in Boston so she wouldn't come over to stay with me. She went home and I headed for Chandler Hovey Park. I left my car at the far end of the parking lot, which was virtually empty. There were only three other cars, parked at the opposite end. It must've been about ten thirty. Hidden in the darkness, I observed the silhouettes of four young women by the light of the lampposts as they walked along the beach.

*     *     *

*August 30, 1998, eleven thirty p.m.*
The talking had died down a few minutes earlier. From afar, Patricia could see that the girls were busy gathering their belongings. She had been spying on them for the past hour. She was determined to confront Eleanor and demand that she leave Alaska alone, but she had no intention of making a scene in front of the others. Soon the shadows started heading toward her. Patricia noticed that one of the young women stayed behind. She was sitting on the sand smoking a cigarette. The other three reached the parking lot, which was far better lit: Eleanor wasn't among them. She must be the one who had stayed behind. The three young women climbed into two of the cars and drove off without noticing Patricia.

When they were gone, Patricia got out of her car, her heart pounding. She looked around. There were two houses nearby, but one was surrounded by a high wall, most likely to protect it from busybodies and unwanted noise. The other was completely dark.

Patricia walked silently in Eleanor's direction. She found her looking out at the ocean. She was in her bathing suit, sitting on a towel. Patricia made a noise; Eleanor jumped.

"Shit, you scared me," she said. "Hey, aren't you Benjamin's wife?"

"I'm surprised you recognize me," Patricia replied.

"I've seen photographs. Benjamin says you're a real bitch."

"I've heard the same about you."

"Yeah, well, why are you here? You have a problem with me? You jealous because I'm fucking your husband?"

"I mostly feel sorry for you. Thanks for taking him off my hands."

"Am I dreaming or is this not a coincidence? You here to pick a fight with me?"

"I'm not looking for trouble; I've come to ask you to leave Alaska alone. And not to wreck her chances in the competition."

"Oh my God, it's you!" Eleanor cried, smiling malevolently. "You're her girlfriend. You asked Benjamin to let her win. So that's why he's been hassling me about her for the past two weeks, telling me that she's his favorite contestant and that maybe I should support her, because that's what his mother wants. His mother, my ass. He made a deal with *you*. What did you promise him in return? Something to do with the divorce? Is that why he's been in such a good mood lately? You can forget it, lady. Go back to munching on Alaska's pussy and leave me the hell alone."

*     *     *

"The argument got heated," Patricia said. "Eleanor threatened to tell everyone we were a couple; I got angry and things got physical. At first it was almost comical. And then Eleanor pushed me hard. I fell back onto the sand. She ran over to her bag and pulled out a telescopic baton. She tried to hit me, but I ducked out of the way. Then I pushed her and we rolled around on the beach. I managed to snatch the baton from her hand, and with a sudden, almost reflexive gesture, I struck her in the face. She fell back onto the beach. Inert. I had killed her.

"My first reaction was panic. I started to cry. I hesitated over calling the police, imagining they'd show up anyway. But nothing happened. The night was perfectly still. Little by little, I calmed down. The tide was starting to come in. No-one had seen me, but I had to get rid of the body. The ocean would soon do its thing, erasing any traces of blood. I ran to my car and grabbed a blanket out of the trunk. I wrapped Eleanor's body in it, so I wouldn't leave any blood on the grass or the asphalt of the parking lot, which might tip off the police. With no sign of a struggle, everyone would assume she had drowned. I put Eleanor in the trunk of my car, then went back to the beach to grab the baton to get rid of it somewhere safe.

"As I was doing that, I heard Eleanor's phone. She had just gotten a message. I saw the illuminated screen among her things. That's when I got the idea to make her death look like a suicide. Alaska had told me that Eleanor had tried to kill herself twice before. I took her phone, checked her contacts, and sent a message to the number under 'Mom Cellphone': 'I no longer have the strength to go on.' I put the phone back and left. I pulled onto the road, not knowing where to go, where to get rid of the body. I needed to keep moving and avoid any routine police inspections; that's how they always get you. And suddenly I remembered the well near the house on Vinalhaven. I knew Benjamin was at a wedding in Boston that evening—Steven and Bella, who had been my friends initially but had chosen to invite him instead. I took the road to Rockland. I would arrive at dawn so it would only be a two-hour wait for the first ferry. That seemed manageable. Near Portland, I stopped at a gas station to get gas. I remember how hot it was. The night was steamy, and I was sweating. As I finished filling the tank, I heard a noise coming from my trunk. Something knocking against the metal. Then a groan. That's when I understood that Eleanor wasn't dead."

# 38

## *Confessions*

*Boston, Massachusetts*
*Friday, August 27, 2010*

Eleanor Lowell wasn't dead. The blow had simply knocked her out, and she was regaining consciousness. Patricia managed to contain her growing sense of panic. She was alone at the pumps, and no-one was around to hear anything. She went into the store to pay for the gas, trying to appear calm and relaxed.

"You could've ended it there," Gahalowood said to her.

"And go to prison for attempted murder? I was screwed. If I'd left her on the beach, that would've been one thing. But I'd put her in the trunk of my car to get rid of her. I risked being put away for thirty years."

"So what did you do?"

"I got back on the road and drove up and down the highway, hoping that all that time on the road would finish her off. Or at least that she would be unconscious again. At that point you're not really thinking. You're simply trying to save your skin. I arrived in Rockland just in time for the ferry to Vinalhaven. The crossing seemed interminable. Eleanor, who must have fainted at one point, suddenly started banging again. But the noise of the machinery and the ocean covered up her appeals for help.

"Finally, we reached Vinalhaven. I drove to the house. It was seven in the morning by then. The house was empty, as I expected. Eleanor had stopped making any noise. After hesitating several times, I opened the trunk. Her eyes were half-closed and I couldn't tell if she was alive or dead. I gathered my courage: once I got through this rough spot, it would all be over. I grabbed her and pulled her out of the trunk. At that moment, she took hold of my arms and opened her eyes wide. I was terrified. I dragged her to the well—I had already removed the cover. With one final effort I lifted her up. I was shivering and sick to my stomach. I positioned her on the rim of the well. She just kept staring at me. Finally, I pushed her hard, and over she went. She fell to the bottom with a dull thud. I guess she died from the fall. Maybe not. I put the cover back over the well, then returned to my car, but not before I threw up several times in the grass.

"Now all I had to do was get rid of the baton. Then I remembered the small adjoining garage, where Benjamin kept his Chrysler, so he wouldn't have to take it back and forth on the ferry. In high season, you had to reserve a spot twenty-four or forty-eight hours in advance, which made it harder to come on the spur of the moment. So Benjamin bought the Chrysler for the island and left his other car at the port in Rockland. When he reached Vinalhaven, he met a local who would give him a lift to the house. The lock on the garage door had a code that never changed, so I got it open without difficulty. The keys, as always, were in the ignition. I hid the baton under one of the floor mats. I figured that if by some unfortunate accident Eleanor's body was discovered and the police searched the premises, they would find the baton in the car and accuse Benjamin.

"After that, exhausted, I covered my tracks as best I could, then lay down in the grass and slept a few hours. It was almost noon when my phone woke me. It was Alaska, calling to tell me that Eleanor had disappeared, that she had sent her mother a message telling her she was ending it all, and that they had found her belongings on the beach at Chandler Hovey Park. The police believed she had drowned herself."

\*       \*       \*

*September 1998*

In spite of the absence of a body, the police had quickly concluded that Eleanor had committed suicide. Patricia, haunted by the events of August 30, did her best to convince herself that that was the truth.

On Saturday, September 19, Alaska was chosen as the new Miss New England. The next day, a director asked her to try out for an important role. If all went well, Patricia and she would soon be able to leave for New York. But Patricia was hesitant. She needed to get out of Salem so she could forget what had happened, but she was afraid a hasty departure would arouse suspicion.

Patricia kept her word with Benjamin about the divorce. The day after the competition she finalized the divorce papers, agreeing not to claim any financial compensation. All she asked for was forty-eight hours on Vinalhaven, a final pilgrimage to the house she had loved so dearly.

Benjamin agreed, and she left for Maine with the keys to the property. She took Alaska along to celebrate her Miss New England crown. But Patricia's primary reason for going there was to make sure that no odor was coming from the well and that her secret would remain safe forever. On the ferry she handed Alaska a gift: a digital video camera, the latest model. That afternoon in the living room of the house on Vinalhaven, in front of the painting showing a sunset over the ocean in the background, Alaska filmed her audition. The one that was supposed to open the door to fame. But it never did. Thanks to Walter Carrey.

On the weekend of September 26, a week after the competition, Walter drove to Salem. Alaska wanted to take advantage of his visit to break up with him. She asked him to meet her at a coffee shop, where he gave her a bouquet of flowers and some chocolates.

"I have a surprise," he said to Alaska before she had time to open her mouth. "To celebrate your win, I'm taking you to Mount Pleasant next weekend to meet my parents. I've been talking about you so long, now they'll finally get a chance to meet you."

"Walter," Alaska replied, embarrassed by what she was about to say, "I'm really sorry but . . ."

"What do you mean?"

"I'm breaking up with you. It's over between us."

"What? You can't do that to me!"

"I'm sorry. Really, I am. You're a nice guy but it's never going to work out between us. I want to live in New York, and your life is in Mount Pleasant."

Walter felt weak. He was almost in tears. "Alaska, you can't do this to me. I told everyone I was going out with Miss New England. If you don't come with me, no-one will believe me. I'll look like I'm just making it all up."

"Walter, I'm really sorry."

"You don't understand . . . four years ago, I had a problem with an ex-girlfriend. I went nuts: I went over to her house, she got scared and called the cops. And ever since I've been some kind of outcast back there. You're my redemption. If they see me with you, with the marvelous Alaska Sanders, Miss New England, even if you leave me after that, my reputation will shoot right up. I won't be some loser any more. Break up with me if you want, but come with me to Mount Pleasant next weekend. Just for two days. After that, I'll leave you alone. Promise."

*　　　*　　　*

"Alaska finally accepted," Patricia explained. "She accepted that damn invitation. I couldn't understand why. But that was Alaska—always putting others first. Much too nice. She explained, 'He begged me, I just couldn't say no. Besides, I owe it to him after the way I used him all summer. Two days won't kill me. It might even help change how people look at him in the town. He's a good guy.' She was determined to spend two days in Mount Pleasant, but on the Friday, right before she left, she discovered that her father had emptied her bank account to pay off his gambling debts. So she decided to stay in Mount Pleasant for several days, to show her parents how she felt and put some distance between them. But that imbecile Walter got it into his head to get back at her father by stealing his watch. I assume Alaska must have mentioned it, but I know it was Walter who suggested they rob the house. That week happened to be her parents' wedding anniversary—she knew they'd be out Thursday evening. So that's when they went, thinking it would be a piece of cake. Until Walter ran over the cop who jumped in front of the car."

*    *    *

*October 1998*

The day after the robbery, Walter and Alaska met Patricia at a small rest stop on Route 21, located right after the fork to Grey Beach. Walter had crossed paths with Patricia at the Blue Lagoon in Salem. Alaska had told him she was a very close friend and he could trust her completely.

"What the fuck have we done?" Alaska cried.

"Are we going to go to jail?" Walter asked Patricia.

"Calm down," Patricia said to them. "Everything will be alright. No-one is going to prison as long as you don't panic. I spoke to one of my contacts in the Salem police. They have no leads."

"I was careful to remove my plates," Walter told her.

"Great, you're a genius. It would've been better not to have put yourselves in that situation at all. What the hell were you thinking?"

Alaska was crying. "I'm sorry," she repeated. "I'm so sorry."

"Don't worry, no-one is going to trace it back to you. Walter, can you have your car repaired without attracting too much attention? You can't go to the dealership or a local repair shop."

"Yeah, I called my friend Dave. He can do it at home, in my parents' garage. I told him I hit a deer and didn't want to get a fine."

"Where's your car now?"

"In the garage, no-one can see it."

"Good. Alaska, it's best if you stay in Mount Pleasant for a while."

"What?"

"Let this die down. You don't want the cops finding out about your fight with your parents. Stay for a month or two, keep out of trouble. After that, you can go back to the way things were."

That morning, after their secret meeting with Patricia, Walter returned to his parents' store. Alaska went with him. She needed to start earning a living. But Sally and George Carrey told her they couldn't afford to hire anyone. She was distressed, anxious, so she went to the Season for a coffee and ran into Eric Donovan, who had returned to Mount Pleasant after Eleanor's death. She told him she was looking for work. Eric said his parents weren't hiring, but Lewis Jacob was looking for someone at the gas station.

A month went by.

Patricia visited Alaska regularly. To play it safe, they avoided Mount Pleasant, meeting at a coffee shop or motel in a neighboring town, usually Conway or Wolfeboro. It was a very difficult time for Alaska. She felt like a prisoner in Mount Pleasant, a place that gave her the impression she was simply going around in circles. Patricia tried to reassure her: "Don't worry about it. You're not going to be there all your life. Once the cops have closed the case for lack of evidence, you can return to Salem."

"And Walter? How can I be sure he'll keep it secret?"

"Why do you say that?" Patricia asked. "He has more to lose than you: he was the one driving the car."

A tear rolled down Alaska's cheek. She then told Patricia what had happened two days earlier. "Walter wanted to have sex," she said, "but I refused. I don't want to be with him."

"You know, Alaska, if you—"

"I don't love him!" Alaska cried. "I don't want anything to do with him. I'm trying to tell you that the other night he forced me to have sex with him. He said he'd reveal everything if I didn't."

"What are you saying?"

"He said, 'You didn't come all the way to Mount Pleasant just so I could watch you sleep.' He forced me to do all these disgusting things, saying that if I was nice to him, he'd be nice to me. He's not going to let me leave, Patricia; he's a pig. He asked about you too."

"Me? What did he say?"

"He asked me why I got you involved in this, what our connection was. He said that if I didn't do what he wanted, he'd turn me in to the cops for the robbery and say you knew about it and that they'd start asking questions about you as well. He said, 'You don't want everyone to get in trouble because of you, Alaska, do you?'"

Patricia closed her eyes. She had feared this moment might arrive. If the police started to investigate her, they might end up finding out about Eleanor as well. She couldn't take any risks. And she understood that it wasn't going to be so easy to get Alaska away from Mount Pleasant after all.

*     *     *

Patricia interrupted her narrative and stared at Gahalowood and me. She asked for some water and I passed her a bottle standing on a table. She took a sip, then lowered her eyes.

"At the beginning of 1999, Alaska had been in Mount Pleasant for three months. Walter kept putting more pressure on her. Her life was hell. Not only did he force her to have sex, he kept her prisoner and told her constantly that he would turn her in to the cops if she left him. But what could I do? Alaska was risking an awful lot and so was I. I was afraid that if he implicated me in the robbery, Walter would open a Pandora's box and put the police on Eleanor's trail. After all, I was the wife of her psychiatrist: they would have quickly made the connection, dug around a little, and maybe asked themselves whether she had really drowned herself. And if they started looking into Eleanor, I was screwed. I knew it. I didn't know how to help Alaska; I didn't see how we could escape Walter Carrey's grip. And if I was worried, Alaska must have been terrified.

"Unfortunately, I couldn't look after her the way I wanted. At the time, my professional life was very busy, very intense. The firm was involved in an important case for which I was the lead attorney—the trial of an oil tycoon that was supposed to start in March. The stakes were sky high for everyone involved. I spent Monday to Friday and all my weekends working on the case. I felt terribly guilty about not being able to spare more time for Alaska, for not taking better care of her. But what was I supposed to do? Abandon my career to vegetate by her side in Mount Pleasant? Still, she wasn't angry with me. As always, she showed just how kind she was. She said, 'Don't worry about it, I understand, it's your job, it's important. And besides, it's my fault that I'm stuck here. You can't compromise your career by wasting your time listening to me complain. Just promise me that when the case is over, you'll take me far away from here.' I promised.

"The case was due to end on April first. I told myself that between now and then, I'd find a way to neutralize Walter. It was clear that Alaska was wasting away. I didn't know how much longer she could hold up. And then, right after New Year's, Alaska told me she'd sold her father's watch to Eric Donovan. I was hysterical. I told her, 'If Eric tries to sell it to a jeweler, you're going to get arrested. That's how people get caught. The jeweler's going to figure out that the watch is stolen and contact the police. We're screwed.' She told me not to worry. Eric had promised not to sell the watch for at least a year, and by then she would have found a way to get it back. Eric had also assured her that he wouldn't mention it to Walter or anyone else. I couldn't understand why she had done such a thing, and when I kept asking, she ended up bursting into tears and telling me about Samantha. That she had found a girlfriend to make her miserable life a little more bearable. That she hadn't done anything wrong. She just needed to take her mind off things, laugh, forget. She hadn't told me because she was afraid I'd feel betrayed or cheated, although it was, as she repeated, 'just for fun.'

"Then she told me all about Samantha—their Sundays together, their flirting, the games with the video camera. And that it had all gone to hell when Ricky, Samantha's boyfriend, demanded ten thousand dollars from Lewis Jacob. I saw that the situation was going from bad to worse. I told Alaska that she couldn't stay in town any longer, that Mount Pleasant would kill her. But this time it was Alaska who reassured me. She said it would be okay. That I should focus on my work and we'd leave on April second as planned. 'And what are we going to do about Walter?' I asked. She said, 'Walter doesn't know I got rid of the watch. Without it, he's got nothing. But I want to make sure he's in a good mood for now and doesn't find out it's gone until we're far away. After that, he won't be able to touch us.'"

Patricia stopped, unable to go on. After a lengthy silence, Gahalowood asked her to continue. "What happened then?"

"At the time, I suggested to Alaska that I could reimburse Eric, but she refused. She wanted to take responsibility. She was like that. She had a big heart, but she was stubborn as a mule. I tried to spend more time with her, spoiling her to compensate for my absence. I gave her gifts, like those boots from a store in Salem that Walter noticed when she left him. Alaska had to hold on until April second. I had planned for us to go on a long vacation. If I won the case, my career would be secure. I wanted to take a few months off and travel around South America with her. That would give us time to reconnect and, crucially, to monitor Walter's behavior from a distance. Was he really going to contact the police? If it looked like there were going to be problems back in Salem, nothing was forcing us to return there, and we could settle in a country that had no extradition agreement with the United States. Being with Alaska was all that mattered. And if Walter had the sense to keep his mouth shut, Alaska and I could return after the summer and settle in New York. I could pass the bar there so I could continue to practice law, and she could finally fulfill her dreams of becoming an actress. April second was supposed to be the start of our new life. But unfortunately, eleven days before our departure, everything changed."

# 39

## The Decision

*Mount Pleasant, New Hampshire*
*Monday, March 22, 1999*

Walter was out of town for a few days, having left for Quebec for a fishing convention. Patricia took a break from work to surprise Alaska: she wanted to spend a night with her at a luxury hotel near Mount Pleasant.

Patricia had not yet been to Mount Pleasant. She hadn't gotten any closer than the rest area on Route 21, where she had met Alaska and Walter the day after the robbery in October 1998. Alaska had always told her not to risk it. "I could be a friend passing through; we could grab a coffee?" Patricia had suggested.

"That's not the problem," Alaska replied. "Walter will see us and I don't want him to start asking questions. He's going to ask me if there's a connection with the robbery; he's going to panic. It will just complicate things."

But that Monday, knowing that Walter was away, Patricia wanted to take advantage of his absence to see where Alaska had spent the previous five months of her life.

She began with the gas station on Route 21. Alaska wasn't there. The attendant, who she learned was Lewis Jacob, the owner, told her that she had taken the afternoon off. Patricia knew that Alaska and Walter were living above the Carrey family store. She drove down Main Street and had no difficulty finding the hunting and fishing store. But as she got there, Patricia saw Eric and Alaska on the sidewalk, looking like they might be arguing.

Patricia continued driving so Eric wouldn't see her. She then called Alaska and asked her to meet her at a coffee shop in Conway. A half hour later, Alaska arrived in Walter's black Ford Taurus.

"What happened to your car?" Patricia asked.

"An oil leak," Alaska replied, sounding frustrated.

"Everything okay, angel? You don't look well."

"No, I'm alright."

"What's wrong?"

"It's Eric . . . we had an argument."

"About what?"

"It's not important." Suddenly, Alaska burst into tears.

"What's going on?"

Alaska looked around. No-one was nearby: she could speak openly. "I did something stupid, Pat. I'm so angry with myself. I'm afraid that Eric's going to go to the cops. That he'll put them on to me. I'm afraid they'll trace it back to Walter and then to me."

"You spoke to Eric about the break-in?"

"No," she said, taking from her bag three identical pieces of paper. They all displayed the same message:

I KNOW WHAT YOU DID

"What's this about?" Patricia asked her.

"Anonymous notes. Meant for Eric. I put one in his mailbox a little while ago and he gave me the third degree. He knows I wrote them."

"And what did Eric do to make you give him threatening messages?"

"I think he killed Eleanor Lowell."

Hearing those words, Patricia thought she would collapse. She began to sweat. Her heart was pounding. She thought Eleanor had been forgotten. The case was closed. Seven months had gone by since that horrible night in August. Why had Alaska suddenly brought her back to life?

"What do you mean, *you think he killed Eleanor*?" Patricia stuttered, struggling to maintain her composure.

"Not in the literal sense," Alaska explained. "But he drove her to kill herself."

Alaska then told her of Maria Lowell's visit a few weeks earlier. Maria had asked her to look for a man with a blue car, who, she believed, was the reason Eleanor had ended her life. Eleanor had told Alaska that she and Eric were together. At the time, Eric drove a blue convertible. From that she'd deduced that he was the man Maria Lowell was looking for. She had sent the messages to put pressure on him, to scare him, because she didn't know how to confront him directly. But when he discovered she was behind them, she had no choice but to tell him everything.

"And . . . ?" Patricia asked, uneasy.

"And I realized it wasn't him. Eleanor mentioned spending July Fourth with the man, but she wasn't with Eric that night. I was wrong to accuse him; he was really angry. So now I'm afraid he'll tell someone about it or call the cops."

"I doubt that," Patricia reassured her. "Why would he? On the other hand, why did you print the same message so many times?" Patricia gestured at the three sheets of paper. Alaska smiled.

"It's that stupid printer, the one in Mr. Jacob's office. It prints out extra copies for no reason."

"Give me those," Patricia said, grabbing the sheets to put them in her bag. "I'm going to get rid of them."

Alaska wasn't finished though. "That means there was someone else in Eleanor's life. Someone who drove her to commit suicide. We have to find him."

"It's not your problem," Patricia remarked.

"Eleanor was a pain in the ass, true. But she was too young to die. I can't just forget about it."

Patricia tried to change the subject. Then they left the coffee shop and drove, each in her own car, to a charming hotel out in the countryside, where Patricia had reserved a room for a romantic evening. At least, that's what she had been hoping for.

That afternoon Patricia and Alaska took advantage of the luxurious comforts of the hotel. They had a massage and then relaxed in a very hot bath. As Alaska played with the faucet handle with her foot, she suddenly said, "Wasn't your ex-husband Eleanor's shrink?"

"It's possible."

"Yes, yes, it's coming back to me now, it was Dr. Bradburd. That's your ex-husband."

Patricia felt her stomach knot up. "Are you sure?" she said, in a voice that betrayed her discomfort.

"Yes. I remember now. Salem is a small town, you know."

With those words, Alaska stood up and got out of the water.

"Where are you going?" Patricia asked.

"There's something I just remembered."

"What's that?"

"Eleanor's mother read me excerpts from her daughter's diary. Eleanor mentioned a blue car and a gray house surrounded by red maples. But when I heard 'blue car,' I was so confused by Eric that I didn't really think about it. I barely listened to the part about the gray house: it just came back to me now. Did I hear correctly? I'm sure about the blue car. I need to call Mrs. Lowell to make sure."

"Why?" Patricia asked uneasily. She had now also left the bathtub and followed Alaska across the floor, dripping wet.

"A gray house surrounded by red maples! I have to check that with Mrs. Lowell—it's very important. Where'd my phone go?" Alaska rummaged in her bag hurriedly.

"Why's it so important?" Patricia asked. "Can you stop for a minute and tell me what's going on?"

"Your ex-husband's place on Vinalhaven. It's a gray house surrounded by red maples. And there's that blue car in the garage. In her diary, Eleanor says that he came to pick her up in his car. It must have been Benjamin coming to get her at the port on Vinalhaven when she went there to join him. He's the one who drove her to commit suicide. I have to . . ." Alaska trailed off suddenly.

"What? What is it now?" Patricia muttered, terrified.

"You're going to think I'm crazy," Alaska said.

"No, go ahead, tell me!"

"Could *he* have killed her? Eleanor was unbearable—he must've been at his wits' end. They go to the beach at Chandler Hovey Park. At that time of night, no-one's there. No witnesses. He kills her in a moment of uncontrollable rage and gets rid of the body on Vinalhaven. Oh my God, I have to call Mrs. Lowell immediately. Where's that damn phone?!"

Alaska found it in her bag, grabbed hold of it, and flipped through the contacts list to find Eleanor's mother. It was then that Patricia spoke, and her voice was dark: "Put down the phone."

"Wait, I just want to—"

"Put down the phone!" Patricia screamed.

Alaska froze. "What's up with you?" she asked.

Patricia burst into tears. She had to tell Alaska the truth—all of it. If she told Eleanor's mother about her suspicions regarding Bradburd, the police would reopen the investigation. They would search the house at Vinalhaven, find the body in the well, and detect traces of Patricia's DNA on it. She was desperate. She threw herself at Alaska's feet.

"Forgive me! Forgive me! I beg you, please, forgive me!"

# 40

## *The Night of the Murder*

*Mount Pleasant, New Hampshire*
*April 2, 1999*

It was the day they were to leave. The day Patricia would come to get Alaska. They would leave Mount Pleasant at last and go away, far from Walter. They would finally be free.

It was eight p.m. Leaving the gas station, Alaska didn't have to go very far to get to her romantic dinner. She drove to Grey Beach and parked her blue convertible in the parking lot. Seeing that there were no other cars, she began to worry: Where was Patricia? She wanted to call, but her phone wouldn't connect to the network. She got out of the car and walked around, trying to find a signal. No luck. She wondered whether Patricia was already on the beach and called out her name. Patricia called back. She was by the lake. Alaska hurried down the path to meet her.

When she reached the shore, Alaska stopped and marveled at what she saw. A tablecloth laid out on the ground with a bottle of champagne chilling in a bucket of ice and a dozen tall candles. Alaska ran to Patricia and kissed her.

"I've never seen anything so beautiful," she said, admiring the spread before her. "I was waiting in the parking lot. Where's your car?"

"On the road through the forest; it was easier to unload it there."

"You've learned all of Mount Pleasant's secrets," Alaska said, smiling. "I'm so glad you invited me here tonight."

"A page has turned in the life of this town," Patricia said.

"Yes."

"And Walter?" Patricia asked. "He doesn't suspect anything?"

"He surprised me a while ago," Alaska said. "I went back to the apartment around five to get some things. He was alone in the store. I didn't think he would, but he came upstairs. I didn't back down, though. I told him I was leaving him. He said that if I did, he would turn me in. I told him I wasn't afraid of him any longer and I had gotten rid of the watch. He was livid. He went to check where I had kept it hidden and came back, furious. He started shouting, 'Where's the watch, you bitch?' I told him it hadn't been there for a long time and left. He grabbed me by the door and pointed his finger at me, saying, 'I'm giving you forty-eight hours to come to your senses. If you're not back here by Sunday night, I'm calling the cops.'"

"But on Sunday night, we'll be safe and sound in Costa Rica," Patricia said, smiling.

Alaska smiled as well. They kissed.

The evening was as romantic as they could have hoped for. The night air was cool, but the two women were warm in each other's arms, wrapped in a thick blanket. They felt good. As they ate, they drank the first bottle of champagne, then opened another. They talked about the trip they were going to take. They would leave the following afternoon for Costa Rica. That night they would stay at a local hotel, and the next day they would drive to the Boston airport to take a plane to San José.

Around eleven thirty, Alaska stood up to walk along the shore. She stared out at the water. "It's even more beautiful at night." Those were her last words. A terrible blow landed suddenly on the back of her skull. She collapsed.

*       *       *

"Immediately after I struck her, I fell to the ground and cried," Patricia said. "I felt sick to my stomach. I didn't react the way I had with Eleanor. I couldn't think. All I wanted was to get away. I decided to leave the

512

body where it was. I got rid of the baton, which was covered with blood. I threw it as hard as I could into the lake."

Patricia suddenly went quiet. As if she'd said everything she had to say. "So that's how I killed her. Now you know everything."

"Wait," Gahalowood said. "That can't be all. What about Eric Donovan's sweater and the message in Alaska's pocket?"

Patricia smiled sadly. "I can tell you, but it wasn't my idea. It was Alaska's."

"Alaska's?"

She nodded. "I told you earlier about the night of March twenty-second, when I told Alaska that I had murdered Eleanor."

"Yes, but I don't—"

"You'll see . . ."

*       *       *

*March 22, 1999*

In the hotel room, Patricia had just told Alaska that she had killed Eleanor Lowell. Alaska was in shock, alternating between crying, screaming, and fits of rage. She kept asking, "Do you realize what you've done to me?"

"I did it *for* you . . ."

"Don't try to involve me," Alaska yelled. "I didn't ask for this. You threw her into that well while she was still alive! You're a monster!"

Patricia tried to hold Alaska against her to calm her down, but she slipped away. She told her that those hands had killed someone. Several times, she bent double as if she were about to throw up. She kept repeating the same thing over and over: "It's not true! It can't be true!"

Around one in the morning, as Alaska still hadn't calmed down, Patricia suggested she take a sleeping pill. Ever since the night she had killed Eleanor, she had always kept them with her: she couldn't sleep without them. Alaska, after some resistance, finally took a pill and immediately fell asleep. Next to her in the bed, Patricia stayed awake all night. She was terrified.

The following day, when Alaska finally woke up, she pressed herself against Patricia. She apologized for her behavior the night before. Kissing her again and again, she said, "Don't worry, we won't talk about it ever again. It's forgotten." They stayed in bed for a long time. Alaska was tender with her. She kept telling Patricia that she had forgotten everything already. But if she had, why did she keep talking about it? Patricia was consumed by anxiety. She bitterly regretted revealing her secret, but how else could she have dissuaded Alaska from calling Eleanor's mother?

Then, suddenly, Alaska had an idea. "Sweetheart," she said, "I know how we can get you out of this."

"What are you talking about?" Patricia asked, uneasy.

"You know how much I like crime novels. The last one I read was pretty good. It was the story of a perfect crime. A guy kills a woman and arranges it so the police arrest someone else entirely. The ending was kind of cruel, though: the husband escapes justice and a household employee is wrongly convicted. The husband then explains to the reader that a perfect murder isn't one where no culprit is ever found but one where the murderer manages to frame someone else."

"I don't see where you're going with this," Patricia said to her.

"We'll make it so Walter is convicted of Eleanor's murder. I can grab some item of clothing of his and throw it into the well with the corpse. And we can leave some other signs of his presence on Vinalhaven, something the investigators can trace back to his car."

"Such as?" Patricia asked.

"A broken taillight, for example. We can break it now, since I've got his car. We can drop the pieces in the parking area of the house on Vinalhaven. I can tell Walter that I had a small accident. He won't suspect a thing. When we leave on April second, we can swing by Salem. I'll pay Eleanor's mother a visit and share my suspicions about Walter. He was in Salem a lot the summer Eleanor died. Everything fits. During my visit, I'll pretend to go to the bathroom and hide one of the I-know-what-you-did messages in Eleanor's bedroom. Her mother told me she was trying to clear out her daughter's room: she's bound to find it. That'll worry her: she'll call the cops and mention Walter. The cops will trace it back to him. When leaving Walter's apartment, I'll make sure to hide the two other messages I printed. The cops will think Walter threatened Eleanor. All the proof will be there. Walter won't be able to do a thing about it. He'll be arrested for Eleanor's murder. We'll be rid of him once and for all, and you won't have anything else to worry about."

Patricia looked distraught, but said, "Thank you, darling. Thank you from the bottom of my heart. But it's better you stay out of this. Besides, what's Walter's connection with Vinalhaven? It doesn't work. My angel, I'd just like us to forget the whole thing, if that's alright."

"Of course, whatever you want. We won't talk about it again. We'll forget everything. I love you; I'd do anything for you."

With those words Alaska left the room to take a shower. When she heard the water running, Patricia froze. Alaska had awakened a vision of the night of August 30. Patricia saw herself dragging Eleanor's body to the car, tapping the farewell message on her phone, and sending it to "Mom Cellphone." She could still hear the dull banging from the trunk of the car at the gas station in Portland. She remembered Eleanor's terrified face when she finally opened it. The thud of the body when it fell into the well. For a while she had managed to put it all out of her mind. She wanted to forget it again. But she couldn't, not any longer. Not now that Alaska knew. Patricia was forever condemned to a life of uncertainty— her freedom depended on the silence of a twenty-two-year-old girl. How could she be sure that Alaska would keep her secret? And what would happen if they were to separate? If their love was just a passing phase?

*　　*　　*

Patricia wiped away a tear. She again looked at the photograph of Alaska and herself in New York. Then she continued speaking: "I knew better than most what to expect of prison. I realized that my fragile Alaska could condemn me to a life confined to a few square feet, a life of deprivation. That March twenty-third, 1999, I tried to make the best of it. We talked about leaving for Central America, we talked about our future together. I forced myself to make love to her. After lunch, Alaska insisted on taking me to a 'very special' place, the only place where she felt good in Mount Pleasant. She took me to Grey Beach. That's how I found out about it. We stayed there awhile. I was cold, so I went to my car to get another layer. Back in the parking area, seeing Walter's black Ford Taurus, I knew I had no choice but to kill her. My little Alaska. So gentle. So perfect. But too curious. I had finally found something stronger than my love for her: my need for freedom. I was going to kill her, following to the letter the steps she had outlined a few hours earlier.

"The Ford wasn't locked. I took advantage of my moment alone to rummage around, looking for something I could leave near the corpse that would lead the investigators back to Walter. And then, when I opened the trunk, I found the very thing Alaska had suggested: an item of clothing. A gray sweater with the initials *MU* on it. I took it and hid it in my car. Alaska reached the parking lot a few moments later. She was cold too and wanted to leave. I handed her two of the I-know-what-you-did notes. 'Here,' I said, 'hide these in the apartment. Make sure Walter doesn't find them, but they're somewhere the cops will look when they search the place.' Alaska smiled broadly. She asked, 'Are you going to follow my plan?' 'Yes,' I said to her. 'I'll keep the third sheet safe for when you go see Mrs. Lowell on April second.' Alaska was very proud. She kissed me and promised that if we followed her plan, I would be safe. Then, to get her to leave, I told her I had to return to Boston. 'See you in ten days,' she said to me as she drove off, taking the road back to Mount Pleasant."

"It was on that same day, March twenty-third," Gahalowood said, "when Alaska returned to Mount Pleasant, that Eric saw her park on the street and asked her to get his sweater from the trunk. Eric told us that after asking Alaska for his sweater the first time on March twenty-second, he phoned Walter, who told him where it was and said he was welcome to take it. On March twenty-third, seeing the Taurus, Eric followed Walter's advice, but the sweater wasn't there. Because you had it, Patricia. You thought it belonged to Walter."

Patricia nodded. "That was my first mistake. When Alaska left Grey Beach, I knew that's where I would end it. You know, I've been around a lot of criminals, and they all agree that for serious crimes, the first time is hard, but once you get over the hump, it gets easier. I'm not saying it was easy, just that the decision was easy to make. On March twenty-third, at Grey Beach, I knew it was where I would kill her. I wanted a beautiful spot and I wanted it to go smoothly. I didn't need a repeat of what had happened with Eleanor, whom I'd driven all the way to Vinalhaven. To be on the safe side, I pretended to leave Grey Beach only to return a short while later to explore the area. Following my little Alaska's recommendations, I applied the finishing touches to my plan for the perfect murder. I had already found the road through the woods leading to Route 21. That would be the perfect spot to leave the taillight fragments from Walter's car. There was also that abandoned trailer, where I could hide Walter's sweater. The police would find it easily enough without it appearing too obvious. And Alaska's I-know-what-you-did note, which I would slip into her pocket after killing her, would lead them to conclude that it was an act of revenge. Eric would surely tell the police about Alaska's watch, which would tie her and Walter to the break-in. And since Eric would report that Alaska had asked him not to mention it to Walter, everything should fall into place. Walter would be trapped like a rat.

"In the days that followed, it seemed that the stars were doing everything they could to align: Benjamin was at a conference in Canaan on the evening of April second. He couldn't help boasting about it. I knew there would be no-one at the house on Vinalhaven that weekend. That gave me the idea to use Benjamin's car so that my own wouldn't be seen in Mount Pleasant. There are always witnesses, no matter how many precautions you take. So on Thursday, April first, 1999, I set off from Salem to Vinalhaven Island. And on the ferry that brought me and the blue Chrysler back to the mainland, I started to feel nervous. In twenty-four hours I was going to murder my little Alaska."

# 41

## *The Perfect Murder*

*Mount Pleasant, New Hampshire*
*The night of April 2–3, 1999*

Patricia had struck Alaska hard with the metal baton. The young woman's body lay on the shore, blood flowing from a head wound. Patricia felt herself growing faint. But she had to keep going. She had to carry out her plan. Not knowing what else to do with the murder weapon, she hurled it into the lake. It would be stupid to keep it with her and risk being caught in the event of a routine highway stop.

Patricia had to erase any trace of their final date. She rolled up the picnic blanket and everything in it to take with her. She gathered up the champagne bucket and the candles and threw any small stones stained with wax into the water. After making sure that nothing of her presence remained, she hurried to collect the plastic bag she had hidden in the bushes. Inside was the gray sweater and the note. She slipped the note into Alaska's back pocket, where she found her cell phone. She put it with her things, planning to dispose of it later. She knew that it could lead the investigators to her.

Patricia then grabbed the gray sweater to rub it in Alaska's blood. She gazed at the young woman's head, beginning to feel nauseous again. She gathered her courage. *C'mon Patricia, just wipe the sweater against her face, then it will be over. After that, you'll be safe forever.*

But as she bent over the body, Patricia heard Alaska wheeze—she wasn't dead. Blood flowed freely from her skull, but she was conscious.

Her open eyes stared in Patricia's direction. They implored her. Patricia began to cry. She knelt by Alaska's side and stroked her hair. She whispered tender words: she told her that she loved her and she always would because their love could never be tainted. A few minutes passed. But death, though close, still hadn't come. Alaska continued to gaze at Patricia with a mixture of sadness and love.

Patricia didn't know what to do. She waited and waited. An hour passed, and Alaska still wasn't dead. It was unbearable. So she took the gray sweater, slipped her hands inside it, and squeezed Alaska's neck as hard as she could. And the harder she squeezed, the more she cried. Her tears bathed her lover's face. Finally, it was over.

Gathering her things, she disappeared into the woods. She tossed the gray sweater, now covered in Alaska's blood, into the old trailer and got into her car. There was one more thing she had to do to complete Alaska's plan. Somewhere along the forest road, she would leave a sign that Walter's black Ford Taurus had passed by.

It was 1:35 in the morning when the blue Chrysler appeared on Main Street in Mount Pleasant. Patricia drove slowly. Not just to make sure that no-one was around—no pedestrians, no police patrol—but also to look out for Walter's Taurus among the cars parked along the sidewalk. She caught sight of it a little before Carrey Hunting & Fishing. She stopped and got out of her car. With a heavy hammer she had brought with her, she struck the Taurus's rear bumper hard, then the right taillight, which shattered. She gathered the pieces, then jumped into the Chrysler and disappeared into the night. However, the noise of the breaking taillight drew the attention of someone living nearby. Cinzia Lockart, standing at her living room window, had just enough time to make out a blue car with Massachusetts plates driving away.

\*　　　\*　　　\*

Eleven years later, Patricia was nearing the end of her confession.

"I drove to the road through the woods and scattered the debris from the taillight at the foot of a tree, where it was clearly visible, then struck the trunk with the hammer to mark it with paint chips from the Ford."

"Two days later, Walter was arrested," Gahalowood said. "Everything pointed to him. Including the sweater, which wasn't his but Eric's, but showed traces of both men's DNA."

Patricia nodded. "For a reason I couldn't grasp at the time, when Walter confessed, he accused Eric Donovan of being involved in the murder. It was only through your investigation that I learned why: his confession was coerced, and he had recently discovered that Eric had blackmailed his mother. He got his revenge by taking Eric down with him."

Gahalowood thought about this and then said, "It was probably only when he saw the sweater in the interrogation room, by then a key piece of evidence, that Walter decided to accuse Eric."

"It's possible," Patricia said. "After his arrest, Eric asked his family to contact me to help him with the case. That's how I found out what was going on. I realized that my plan was working, in spite of everything. I wasted no time in informing Eric that I would represent him. This allowed me to follow the case from the inside and, crucially, to control it. During the questioning, I manipulated him expertly. He was panicking and he followed my advice as if it were gospel: I instructed him to say as little as possible. I made him believe that it would help him during the trial, although I knew very well that, in general, those who remain silent are guilty and that it would work against him. Then there was that business with the printer, which I obviously hadn't planned for and which came at just the right time. When he wasn't being questioned by the police, I put a great deal of pressure on Eric. I made him feel like he was guilty—in fact, I drove him crazy. He was finished, and I knew it. When Lauren wanted to launch her own little investigation to prove her brother's innocence, I got involved to make sure I kept abreast of any new developments and was in a position to introduce whatever fabricated evidence was required when the need arose. As long as Eric was in custody, I was safe.

"Then, my crowning stroke of genius: I told him that the only way to save himself was to plead guilty. And since he was prepared to do anything to escape the death penalty, he did. Then I knew I had achieved the perfect murder. Well, almost. There was one detail to take care of: Kazinsky. I knew Walter was innocent, so I suspected that his confession had been extracted by force. If Kazinsky were to reveal that fact, it could compromise everything. I had to get rid of him as well: I had no choice. So I spied on him and discovered that he went jogging every morning at dawn. One morning in January, I took advantage of the fact that Benjamin was on a ski trip in British Columbia to borrow the blue Chrysler and use it to eliminate Kazinsky. But I failed. He survived, in spite of the violence of the impact. Everyone believed it was an accident, and I couldn't try again without drawing attention. I had to resign myself to letting him live. I had time to get the Chrysler repaired and return it to the garage on Vinalhaven before Benjamin returned. The years passed and the case seemed to have been largely forgotten. I had pulled off the perfect crime. For eleven years, my plan worked flawlessly. Until you two showed up."

"And Benjamin Bradburd?" Gahalowood asked.

"Obviously, neither Lauren nor Eric knew Benjamin. All they knew was that I had been married. When Lauren told me you had followed the trail to a Dr. Benjamin Bradburd, I knew I risked being caught. But I stayed calm. Fortunately, he committed suicide. And it almost worked itself out, because the investigation was closed. To tell the truth, I wasn't surprised that Benjamin killed himself. I knew how important his reputation was to him, and the scandal surrounding Eleanor Lowell would have put an end to his medical career, ruined his mother's name, and cast a pall over the Miss New England competition. Benjamin had always said that life was all about power.

"Alaska and I came up with the perfect crime. The only snag was you two. Perry and Marcus. I have to say, you make a great team."

After Patricia Widsmith's confession, Gahalowood and I returned to Mount Pleasant. We stopped at Grey Beach and walked down to the water. Along the path I gathered some wildflowers.

Gahalowood took a few steps along the shore and looked out at the lake. "It was a little more than eleven years ago that I found myself here, with my partner Matt Vance. On these same pebbles we found the body of a young woman, unknown to us at the time, and a bear, a big one, that had been shot by the local police. That young woman was Alaska Sanders. I didn't know anything about her. Least of all how she would change my life."

I offered one of the flowers to Gahalowood. We threw them into the water and watched them float on its calm surface.

"To the memory of Alaska Sanders," I said.

Gahalowood nodded. "I'm glad I know how it all turned out. And I owe it to you, Writer."

After a silence, he went on: "It hurts me to say this, but I like spending time with you."

"Me too, Sergeant."

"You could come up to the house for a while if you want."

"That's very kind of you, but I have to stop living other people's lives and start to live my own."

"I'm glad to hear you say that."

We both laughed. And Gahalowood added, this time very seriously, "Thanks."

"For what?"

"You fixed my life. I hope one day I can help you fix yours."

# Epilogue

## *A Year After the Conclusion of the Alaska Sanders Case*

My novel, *The Alaska Sanders Affair*, was published in September 2011. The book marked an important step in my life. A turning point. It was the culmination of the years from 2006 to 2010, years that were both challenging and formative.

A few weeks after it came out, Sergeant Perry Gahalowood fulfilled his wife's dream: he set sail with his daughters on a boat named *Helen* for a trip around the world. I was with them at the dock in Portsmouth. Chief Lansdane was there too. We helped them with their final preparations. They would be away for a year, returning for Christmas 2012.

"I'll be waiting for you, Sergeant. Take care of yourself—and the girls."

"You can count on me, Writer."

I offered him a bag. "I brought you some books. Some good thrillers to keep you busy at night."

He looked at me with an ironic smile. "I brought you something to read as well."

He handed me an envelope, which I started to unseal. "No, not now," he said. "Wait until I'm gone."

I did as he asked, though the boat had barely left the dock when I opened the envelope. Inside was a file, not all that thick, with the stamp of the Bangor police force. On it, in felt-tip pen, were the words *Gaby Robinson*. It was the case file for the murder that had haunted Matt Vance for so long: a seventeen-year-old girl killed as she walked home one evening in the early nineties. A crime that had never been solved.

Gahalowood cried out from his boat, "I've got my own copy right here. We'll meet up in a year."

I cupped my hands and shouted, "You're completely nuts!"

"That's why we're friends."

I could not have imagined how busy the next year was going to be for me. In the days following Gahalowood's departure, the film rights for *The Alaska Sanders Affair* were sold—to the great delight of my editor Roy Barnaski. As I signed the contract, he asked me how I planned to use the money. "I'm going to buy a house," I said. "A writer's house."

And that's what I did.

In November 2011, I bought a place in Boca Raton, Florida, where I settled in early 2012. I drove down, leaving New York during a snowstorm, to find myself two days later in the tropical heat of Florida. On the way, I dialed the number of a friend I had lost and found. I was no longer alone.

"Writers' World bookstore," the voice of Harry Quebert responded.

"Harry, it's Marcus."

"Marcus! How are you?"

"I'm driving to Florida."

"So you decided to buy that house you were talking about?"

"Yes."

"I'm happy for you. You're finally on your way. You're finally going to write about them."

I smiled. I looked at the photograph sitting on the dashboard—the Baltimore Goldmans. Their expressions were kind as the four of them looked back at me.

"The time has come," Harry said.

"The time for what?"

"The time for healing."

JOËL DICKER was born in Geneva in 1985, where he studied Law. *The Truth About the Harry Quebert Affair* was nominated for the Prix Goncourt and won the Grand Prix du Roman de l'Académie Française and the Prix Goncourt des Lycéens. It was later adapted for television starring Patrick Dempsey. His subsequent novels, *The Baltimore Boys*, *The Disappearance of Stephanie Mailer*, *The Enigma of Room 622* and *The Alaska Sanders Affair* have all been phenomenal bestsellers in France and beyond.

ROBERT BONONNO has translated over two dozen full-length works of fiction and nonfiction, including René Crevel's *My Body and I* – a finalist for the 2005 French-American Foundation Prize – Hervé Guibert's *Ghost Image*, Henri Raczymow's *Swan's Way* and *The Enigma of Room 622* by Joël Dicker.